DOMESTIC ENEMIES

Author's Acknowledgements

I thank the following people for their technical assistance:

Murray White
Richard W. McDaniel

Cover graphics by: Danny Raustadt

Rigney Page Adventures

Chapter 1

May 1977
Gulf of Mexico

Enrico Mendoza lies belly down on the top of the scuba scooter; his hands manipulate the scooter controls. Although chilling darkness surrounds him, he breathes easily and comfortably through the scuba regulator. He glances at the luminescent compass on the gauge console of the custom made scuba scooter. Then he checks the depth gauge—twenty-six feet. Enrico checks his dive watch— 12:20 AM. He is on track and on time and should arrive at the offshore oilrig in ten minutes.

Maintaining a depth above thirty feet most of the time eliminates his concern for suffering the bends later. Riding the surface for most of the trip also eliminates his concern for exhausting his air tank supply before completing the eighteen-mile roundtrip journey. His cabin cruiser is anchored in a popular scuba diving location, nine miles from the offshore oilrig.

The three-hour trip from the cabin cruiser allows him time to reflect on his current career. Ten years ago, he was a young lieutenant in Che Guevara's National Liberation Army of Bolivia. After Che's execution, Enrico fled Bolivia in search of other Marxist revolutions to join. He discovered that his skills as a clever and brutal interrogator and as a ruthless killer were more in demand than his skills as a communist revolutionary. He spent several years working as a hit man for some of Central and South America's dictators.

Then, during a vacation in San Paulo several years ago, he met the American, Mr. Kendley. During their first meeting, The American contracted Enrico to execute an American politician in such a way that it appeared to be an accident. Enrico's success with that first contract led to steady work from Mr. Kendley. All contracts with the American are verbal and are always paid in cash, as is his current contract.

1

He met with Mr. Kendley two weeks ago in New Orleans, Louisiana to discuss the current mission. The American asked if Enrico could destroy specific Gulf of Mexico oilrigs during a specific period of time. Oilrigs were chosen for their closeness to shore and position within tides and currents. "The job must be done during the specified four day period," the American had insisted.

"Yes, I can do this," Enrico had told Mr. Kendley. "I have performed similar tasks in the past."

The American had reached into his pocket and pulled out an envelope that held the normal fifty-thousand dollars that Enrico had been paid for each of his previous jobs.

With a slightly protesting tone, Enrico had stated, "My experience knows the danger and expense to blow up oilrigs. My fee must be doubled for this one."

"Are you raising your fees permanently?" Mr. Kendley had asked.

"No, no!" Enrico had responded. "I know the market price for my services. Destroying an offshore oilrig carries many risks and dangers and expenses that my previous jobs did not have."

The American agreed to the increased fee but didn't have an additional fifty-thousand dollars with him. The American promised to deliver the other fifty-thousand dollars after the mission. Enrico is confident that Mr. Kendley will keep his word.

Enrico observes a pool of light ahead of him. He dives the scooter to one-hundred feet so that he avoids the range of underwater security cameras. He uses a low-power spotlight to accurately maneuver at the deeper depth under the oilrig.

Under the oilrig, he stops the forward motion of the scooter and hovers. He looks toward the surface and sees the pool of light above him. He slides off the scooter. Then he adjusts the air in his buoyancy compensator so that he becomes neutrally buoyant. Enrico tethers the scooter to his weight belt; then he swims ten feet to the oil supply pipe that comes up from the ocean floor.

He straps the explosive charge to the oil pipe. The charge is designed to open a hole in the pipe and ignite the oil, sending a path of flame up to the oilrig platform, resulting in explosion on the oilrig platform. Massive death and destruction are the objectives.

As Enrico drives the scuba scooter away from the vicinity of the oil rig, he wonders if all goes well with his compadres who are attaching the same type explosive devices to the oil pipes of two other offshore oilrigs. All three charges are timed to explode in unison.

When he is one-half mile from the oilrig, he surfaces the scuba scooter. He disengages the scooter's battery power source; then he starts up the scooter's gasoline engine. As the scooter makes headway on the surface, Enrico glances back toward the oilrig, verifying no vessels follow. He will stay on the surface for the remainder of the journey to the cabin cruiser.

Two hours later, Enrico pulls alongside the cabin cruiser. His compadre deckhand throws the line for the hand-crank crane. Enrico catches the line; then he connects the line to the lifting loops locate on the bow and stern of the scuba scooter. After they lift the scooter from the water and place it on the deck, they tie it down with nylon rope.

Enrico strips off his black wetsuit. He quickly towels down; then slips into a thick terrycloth robe. He climbs a ladder to the piloting deck. He sits in the pilot chair. He stares up toward the clear, starry night.

His compadre deckhand places a cup of steaming coffee on a flat surface near the piloting gauges. "Gracias, amigo," Enrico says to the deckhand. Enrico lifts the cup and sips the bold, thick Columbian blend.

Enrico glances at his watch—3:58 AM. He turns his focus to the northwest, his face expressing anticipation of a spectacular event. Then three flashes of light appear on the northeast horizon.

Enrico gives no thought to the twenty-eight lives extinguished during the moments of those flashes.

Chapter 2

July 1977
Isola di Santo Stefano
Maddalena Archipelago Sardinia

The *Isola di Santo Stefano* lies just a few miles across the water from the town of Palau on the northeast coast of Sardinia. *Isola di Santo Stefano* hosts only two enterprises. The U.S. Navy Submarine Maintenance Facility is located on the east side of the island; a small commercial resort is located on the west side of the island.

Today, the crew of the USS *Randal*, Fast Frigate 1046, stands in ranks in a small multi-purpose hall near the submarine pier and waits for the awards ceremony to begin. The awards presentation agenda includes delivering ten Letters of Commendation to *Randal* crew members who performed superiorly during a dangerous and classified mission. In addition, Commander Destroyer Squadron Twenty-Two will present to Commander Hampton, captain of the *Randal*, a Navy Meritorious Unit Medal which will allow every member of the crew to wear that medal.

A podium with microphone stands near the north end of the hall. The United States Flag and the U.S. Navy Flag hang on poles behind the podium. A dozen metal folding chairs for VIP officers and civilians stand to the side of the podium.

The USS *Randal* Senior Enlisted Advisor, Master Chief Machinist Mate Frederic Keller, formed the crew into ranks and he now stands in front of the formed ranks. The master chief's wiry, six-foot-and-four-inch-tall frame and short-cropped graying hair portrays the excellence of senior enlisted leadership. All U.S. Navy personnel wear the summer Full Dress White uniform.

The USS *Randal* commanding officer, Commander Gregory Hampton, comes to the podium and orders into the microphone, "Crew . . . atten'hut!"

The *Randal* crew snaps to attention.

Commander Hampton orders, "Crew . . . parade rest!" All in

4

ranks shift to *parade rest* stance.

Commander Hampton reads a Letter of Commendation that will be the same for all ten *Randal* sailors who will receive it. The letter does not list details and specifies only, "... awarded for classified actions during classified operations ..."

A code at the bottom of the letter matches classified files in the Office of the Chief of Naval Operations. Those files list the details of those classified operations for which the letter is awarded.

Commander Hampton calls the awarded sailors to the podium one at a time. When called, each sailor exits ranks and marches in ceremonial manner to the podium. Commander Hampton and each sailor exchange ceremonial salutes. The commander hands the award letter to each sailor; then each sailor returns to ranks.

Navy Captain "Commodore" Jerome Gallagher, Commander Destroyer Squadron Twenty-Two, takes the Podium and orders, "Commander Hampton, front and center!"

The *Randal's* commanding officer marches the few steps to the front of the podium, turns, faces the commodore, and snaps to attention. Commander Hampton epitomizes the manner and character of young officers who climbed quickly through the officer ranks. His five rows of ribbons tell of his achievements during wartime and peacetime.

During the next several minutes, the commodore speaks of his pride regarding the crew of the USS *Randal*. Then he reads the award for the Navy Meritorious Unit Medal. The award citation speaks of classified actions during classified operations. The code at the bottom of the written citation is the same as the code on the Letters of Commendation. The commodore explains that every member of the *Randal* crew may wear the medal with pride from this day forward.

The commodore moves away from the podium.

Commander Hampton moves behind the podium and orders, "Chief Page, front and center!"

Chief Page marches toward the podium, making several smartly executed ninety degree turns. He stops six feet in front of the podium and renders a salute. The salute is returned by Commander Hampton.

Chief Page, nicknamed 'The Tiger' by the *Randal* crew, stands ramrod straight in his Full Dress White uniform. His six-foot-and-one-inch-tall, broad- shouldered build, and rugged facial features present a powerful and intimidating image.

'The Tiger' nickname was respectfully given to Chief Page by the *Randal* crew after numerous crewmembers described Chief Page's manner as that of a prowling tiger who moved swiftly and stealthily and with agility throughout the ship, and who fearlessly and justly took a stand against those who violated navy regulations and against those who acted stupidly.

During recent months, Chief Page had engaged in hand-to-hand combat with America's enemies. All of his head wounds have healed. Only a one-inch jagged scar on his forehead marks the spot where he took a powerful punch from a Red Brigade leader. His trigger finger has healed. Thick reddish hair covers the bullet wound scar on his forearm. The scar on his forehead is the only visible evidence of his battle with evil.

Chief Page serves as an undercover field operative for the Office of Naval Intelligence. Among the *Randal* officers, only the captain and executive officer know the chief's function and purpose in the northern Sardinia area.

Commander Hampton says into the microphone, "Today, it is my honor to reenlist Chief Radioman Rigney Michael Page. An honor because Chief Page's strong leadership, strong moral courage, and superior technical expertise inspires those whom he leads. During his short time onboard, Chief Page earned the respect and admiration of his officers, peers, and subordinates. Chief Page is a credit to his ship, and he serves in highest traditions of the United States Navy."

Commander Hampton pauses while he is handed the reenlistment paperwork. Hampton raises his right hand and orders, "Chief Page, raise your right hand."

Chief Page raises his right hand.

Hampton directs, "Repeat after me."

"Captain," Chief Page interrupts, "I know the words. I do not need to repeat."

Hampton, expressing he is not surprised, says, "Go ahead, Chief."

"I, Rigney Michael Page, do solemnly swear that I will support and defend the Constitution of the United States against all enemies, foreign and domestic. That I will bear true faith and allegiance to the same, and that I will obey the orders of the President of the United States and the orders of the officers appointed over me, according to regulations and the Uniform Code of Military Justice."

Page lowers his hand. His misty eyes reflect the emotional commitment and deep sincerity he feels toward service to his country.

Commander Hampton directs the chief, "Come around to the podium and sign the paperwork."

Chief Page steps to the other side of the podium and signs his name to the reenlistment agreement.

After Hampton signs, he covers the microphone and asks the chief, "Would you like to say anything to your shipmates?"

"Yes, sir."

Hampton steps back from the podium.

Chief Page says into the microphone, "Crew of the USS *Randal* . . . atten'hut!"

All in ranks snaps to attention.

Chief Page says into the microphone, "Please accompany me in honoring the American Republic. Please follow me in reciting the Pledge of Allegiance."

All in the VIP section stand.

Rigney orders, "Hand Salute!"

Everyone in uniform snaps to salute stance. The VIP civilians place their right hand over their hearts.

Rigney turns smartly toward the flag and brings his hand to salute position. He begins, and all present recite: *"I pledge allegiance to the flag of the United States of America, and to the republic for which it stands, one nation under God, indivisible, with liberty and justice for all."*

Because all sailors in the hall are at attention, they remain quiet but are busting to applaud and cheer.

Rigney turns and faces the crew. He orders, *"Randal* crew . . . ready . . . two!"

All in uniform return their hands to their sides. They remain at attention stance.

Commander Hampton comes to the podium and announces, "That concludes today's ceremony. Dismissed!"

Cheers and applause resound throughout the hall.

Chapter 3

Several hours after his reenlistment ceremony, U.S. Navy Chief Radioman Rigney Page sits in the rear of the passenger compartment of the thirty-foot-long liberty boat. The sound of the boat's diesel engines blasts in his ears. The force of the engine vibrates through his body. The bouncing of the boat on choppy waves makes for an uncomfortable ride. He wears loose fitting civilian clothes to conceal his pistol and daggers.

The unusual July cold and rainy weather has all the sailors wearing coats or jackets. Diesel fumes gather inside the boat's enclosed passenger compartment. Those fumes and the bouncy ride have some sailors turning green and hoping the coxswain applies full power to make the trip as short as possible.

As the liberty boat rides *the chop* from *Isola di Santo Stefano* to Isola di Maddalena, Rig occupies his thoughts with the events of the day. Earlier, he and other members of the USS *Randal* crew received awards for their efforts in secret operations while on patrol in The Bonifacio Strait. Following the awards ceremony, Rig reenlisted in front of the entire crew. Then he led the crew in reciting the Pledge of Allegiance. The ceremony was full of comradery and emotional patriotism for the entire crew.

Chief Page reflects on the job offer he received some months ago from his friend and comrade-in-arms, John Smith. John had offered lucrative compensation if Rig left the navy and came to work in John's defense-contractor company that provides intelligence analysis and intelligence field operators to government agencies.

In reenlisting today, Rig confirms his patriotic commitment to serve is country where he believes he will be most valuable. Rig remembers a time ten year ago when all his goals were self-serving. When in high school and during his early years in the navy while attending submarine schools, all that motivated him was what he wanted in life, what pleasured him, and what would benefit him. Then, one day while he was still in submarine radioman school, he was recruited by Commander Bradley Watson to go on a mission for the Office of Naval Intelligence, ONI. During his second ONI mission in 1968, his goals in life changed. He discovered his calling to serve his country as an undercover agent for naval intelligence, and he turned away from self-serving goals.

The last ten years have been a continuous life of adventure, danger, and discovery. His mission during the past few months in the Maddalena area brought him close to death several times. During this Maddalena mission, his ONI training coupled with his skilled timing and agile physical prowess saved his life during several battles against America's enemies. With his reenlistment today, he committed to serve his country as a counterespionage undercover agent for at least another four years.

Senior Chief Yeoman Barbara Gaile stands near the shore end of the pier that serves as the U.S. Navy fleet landing for *Isola di Maddalena*. A light persistent rain falls from a fully overcast sky. The wind chill off the water has lowered the temperature to 63 degrees.

She wears a tan colored raincoat over an expensive Italian pants suit, and she holds a tan colored umbrella. Her tall, slim body and currently popular Italian hairstyle conveys European sophisticate to those around her.

The sounds of La Maddalena waterfront are typical for this time of day and for this weather. Seagulls caw overhead. Automobiles splash rain puddles on the street behind her. Impatient drivers incessantly honk their tinny sounding horns at the slowing traffic. Disappointed tourists with cameras around their necks moan and complain as they stand in doorways and under awnings. On La Maddalena's busiest street behind her, businesses are reopening after siesta. Water buses and water taxis blow their horns at . . . well, apparently for no reason at all.

Several navy dependent wives pace behind Barbara and impatiently check their watches. Some of the wives recognize Barbara as that fortyish attractive woman who has often been seen with that ruggedly sexy navy chief that some sailors call The Tiger.

Barbara waits for Chief Petty Officer Rigney "Rig" Page who told her this morning that he would be on the 1500 liberty boat, which would be the first liberty boat after his reenlistment ceremony. She decided to meet him with the car so he would not need to walk in the rain to their apartment. Rig was not on the 1500 liberty boat and now she waits for the 1600 liberty boat from *Isola di Santo Stefano,* some two miles distant from La Maddalena. Finally, the 1600 liberty boat, now fifteen minutes late, rounds the breakwater and docks smoothly at the end of the pier.

Rig is the third person to disembark the liberty boat. He lifts the collar of his jacket to protect his neck from the rain. He looks toward the shore end of the pier and sees Barbara waving at him. He waves back.

A tall, lanky man with shallow cheeks and sunken eyes walks past Barbara and proceeds down the pier toward the offloading liberty boat. She thinks it odd that a man with long stringy black hair and stringy beard and wearing a dirty knit cap, worn dirty jacket, and pants too short for his legs has reason to board the navy liberty boat destined for *Isola di Santo Stefano.* The man appears to be one of the many homeless that roams and begs in La Maddalena during the summer months. The homeless man stops twenty-yards down the pier. He steps to the side of the pier and leans against a lamppost. He stares toward the harbor. He shoves both his hands into the pockets of his jacket. Every five seconds or so, he glances sideways toward the liberty boat at the end of the pier, conveying he waits for someone or something to happen.

Alarms sound in Barbara's head as she considers: *A person out-of-place in an area normally occupied only by American sailors!* Training and instinct cause her to put her hand into her raincoat pocket and grip the .38 caliber automatic pistol.

Barbara looks toward Rig. He is ten yards from the homeless man.

The homeless man turns toward the approaching sailors from the liberty boat. He pulls a revolver from his jacket pocket but holds it at his side.

Rig notices the homeless man seven yards away near the lamppost. Then his eyes go wide in recognition—*Ensign Ryan!*

The navy deserter, Ensign Franklyn Ryan, raises the gun in Rig's direction and fires three shots.

Rig falls backward and lands on his back.

Sailors scatter in all directions to avoid the shooter.

Ryan runs toward Rig. He wants to fire three more bullets at close range into Page's head. *I must kill the person who ruined my life!* Ryan hears the sound of a person running toward him. He looks up the pier and sees a tall attractive brunette running toward Chief Page. Compelled not to be distracted, he dismisses the presence of the woman. He stops at Rig's side and points the revolver at Rig's head.

The sound of four thundering shots jolts everyone on the pier.

Ensign Ryan falls and lands close to Rig's side.

Sailors all over the pier stare astonished at the tall, slender attractive woman in a raincoat who holds an automatic pistol in two-hand firing position just ten feet from the man she just shot.

Barbara runs to Rig's side. She stoops and takes Ryan's gun. She notes that Ryan's eyes are open and lifeless.

She turns her attention to Rig. Blood flows from his head onto the pier surface. His eyes are open and his head sways back and forth. He says weakly over and over again, "I am the master of my fate. I am the captain of my soul. I am the master of my fate. I am the captain of my soul."

Bystanders, realizing the danger is over, move closer to the scene.

A chief petty officer in khaki uniform stoops on the other side of Rig and says, "I'm a hospital corpsman, ma'am. Please move back and let me treat him."

As Barbara stands, Rig stops speaking, his eyes close, his head flops to the side, and his body goes limp.

Chief Hospital Corpsman Randy "Doc" Stone from USS *Randal* checks Rig's vital signs.

Barbara's heart pounds heavily in her chest. Tears well in her eyes. Her lips quiver as she asks the chief corpsman. "Is he alive?"

From stooped position, Chief Stone looks up into the woman's eyes and replies, "I can't—"

"Drop those weapons, lady!"

Barbara looks to her right. Two U.S. Navy shore patrolman and an Italian policeman point pistols at her."

In a strong authoritarian tone, the senior shore patrolman orders, "Drop the weapons and put your hands behind your head."

Barbara drops both pistols. She raises her hands to the back of her head.

The Italian policeman steps toward Barbara. He stoops and retrieves both pistols.

The senior shore patrolman says in an authoritative tone, "Lady, we're going to handcuff you now. Do not resist."

Barbara nods compliance.

While she is being handcuffed, Barbara pleads with her eyes for a report from the corpsman regarding Rig's condition.

Navy shore patrolmen push the crowd back to make room for emergency vehicles.

Doc Stone checks Rig's pulse. He shakes his head and expresses resignation.

Barbara gasps. Tears flow down her face.

Approaching sirens sound in the distance.

Chapter 4

The harshly, over-illuminated, sparsely furnished interrogation room does not intimidate U.S. Navy Senior Chief Barbara Gaile. She has experienced worse. She sits alone in the room at the small wooden table. She sits in a straight-backed wooden chair designed to make her uncomfortable. The room, also designed for discomfort, has no windows and no air-conditioning. The only ventilation flows from a small fan installed high on the wall. Also for discomfort, a source of drinking water is absent.

She tugs at the cloth of her expensive, Italian made pants suit. Her clammy skin distracts her. The rain matted her hair. She knows her makeup runs. She wants to wash, but she will not ask her captors to allow it. She cannot relinquish any quarter. She must convey toughness and confidence.

She rests her forearms on the tabletop. Her wrists are still handcuffed. She stares into space. Sadness overcomes her and she weeps again. Her friend, lover, and comrade-in-arms, Rigney Page, was killed several hours before.

The door opens. A short, thin man with a receding hair line, sandy colored hair, drooping old-west-style mustache, and wearing a light brown summer weight suit enters and takes the chair across the table from Barbara. He opens a zippered leather binder that holds a letter size writing pad. He pulls a pen and poises it over the writing pad. He states, "I am Mr. Beltenmeyer. I am the U.S. Naval Investigative Service Special Agent in Charge for the Maddalena area." He does not offer his hand.

Barbara does not respond. She casts a blank stare at the NIS agent. Then she quickly glances at the open binder in front of him and observes that the top page of the paper pad is saturated with writing.

Beltenmeyer pulls a passport and military identification card from one of the binder pockets. He glances at the identification card. Then he opens the passport and studies the picture page. "Your passport and I.D. card say your name is Barbara Ann Gaile. Is that

14

your actual name and are you a senior chief petty officer in the United States Navy?"

"Yes," Barbara answers in a mild tone.

"Do you know where you are?"

"Yes."

Beltenmeyer exhibits impatience. He orders in a tight pitched tone, "Tell me where you think you are."

"I am in the shore patrol headquarters building located at U.S. Naval Support Activity La Maddalena."

Beltenmeyer casts an inquisitive expression at Barbara while he asks, "Do you know why you are here?"

"No."

"You are here because witnesses saw you shoot and kill Ensign Franklyn Ryan and because the U.S. Navy owns that pier where the shooting took place and because all involved in that shooting are U.S. Navy personnel. The Status of Forces Agreement between Italy and the United States grants jurisdiction to the United States in such situations. That's why you are here instead of an Italian jail."

Barbara expresses surprise that the man she shot was not a homeless Italian but was a navy officer.

Beltenmeyer observes Barbara's surprise. He questions, "What surprises you?"

"I didn't know he was a U.S. Navy officer. I thought he was a homeless man—an Italian."

"You didn't know Ensign Ryan?"

"No."

"Why did you shoot him?"

Barbara exhibits thoughtfulness for a few moments. She concludes its time for her to remain silent. She advises, "I should not answer any more questions until I contact my supervisors and talk with a navy lawyer."

"Senior Chief, it's in your best interest to be cooperative now and answer my questions."

Barbara shakes her head slightly, indicating she will not answer questions. She states, "I need to make a phone call. My superiors need to know where I am."

"No phone calls until you answer my questions."

Barbara asks Beltenmeyer, "May I have a piece of paper and a pen, please?"

The NIS agent rips away a sheet of paper, then pushes the sheet of paper and a pen toward Barbara.

Barbara writes three lines; then she pushes the paper back to Beltenmeyer.

The NIS agent stares at the paper. The top line is a La Maddalena telephone number. The other two lines are strings of code words.

Barbara requests calmly, "Please call that phone number and identify who you are. Then provide those code words." Barbara pauses and inhales deeply. She continues, "Do as I ask, and a sequence of events will be initiated that will result in all your questions being answered."

"I am not here to serve your demands. You would be wise to answer my questions."

Barbara attempts one more time to encourage the NIS agent to fulfill her request. "Sir, there is nothing you can do to intimidate me. Contacting the people at that telephone number will accelerate your investigation."

Barbara's confident tone and sincere manner causes Beltenmeyer to contemplate that he has entered a situation that includes sailors of a clandestine nature. He concludes that no damage will be done by discovering who is at the end of that telephone number. He stands, then walks to the door. As he opens the door, he advises, "We will talk more after I make this phone call."

Beltenmeyer walks along a short hallway and stops at the shore patrol shift supervisor's desk. He asks the supervisor, "Chief Collins, I need a phone with an outside line."

"Use any phone," the chief advises. "Just dial nine first, then wait for a dial tone."

The phone rings three times. Then a male voice with an American accent answers, "Duty officer."

Beltenmeyer considers that he has reached a U.S. military contact and wonders why the duty officer did not announce the command name as all other duty officers do. Beltenmeyer hesitates to respond while considering how to respond.

"Hello?" the voice queries.

Beltenmeyer responds, "This is Special Agent Charles Beltenmeyer with the United States Naval Investigative Service. To whom am I speaking?"

"Oh! Hello Agent Beltenmeyer. This is Sam Gallo. We met last week at the commodore's briefing?"

Beltenmeyer remembers meeting Gallo last week at the briefing. Gallo was introduced as the Officer-in-Charge of the local naval intelligence office.

After a long, awkward pause, the ONI duty officer inquires, "Do you have something to discuss with me?"

"Yes. I have a coded message for you."

"Okay. Go ahead, I'm ready to copy."

The NIS agent inhales deeply, then reads the message aloud, "*Pontus black alpha . . . Magnolia red delta.*"

Gallo responds quickly, "Where is the person who gave you that message?"

"I have her in custody at the shore patrol headquarters building."

"Are you there too?"

"Yes."

"What is she charged with?"

"Nothing yet," Beltenmeyer admits. "She shot a navy officer on the fleet landing pier. I was attempting to question her when she told me to call this number and provide the coded message."

Knowing he should not discuss the event any further over a non-encrypted telephone line, Gallo says, "Please give me thirty minutes to get there. I must stop by my office to verify those code meanings and call my superiors."

"Okay. I'll wait," the NIS agent promises.

Gallo starts to hang up but pauses and says, "Please treat her well and make her comfortable. You are not holding a criminal."

Beltenmeyer enters the interrogation room. Chief Collins, the shore patrol shift supervisor, follows the NIS agent into the room.

Barbara casts an optimistic expression at the NIS agent.

Beltenmeyer orders Chief Collins, "Remove her handcuffs."

Chief Collins unlocks the handcuffs. Then he stands aside and waits for another order.

Beltenmeyer informs Chief Collins, "I am waiting for Mr. Gallo to arrive. Do you know him?"

Chief Collins nods and affirms, "Yes, I know him."

Beltenmeyer asks, "Is there a more comfortable room to place Senior Chief Gaile—somewhere private?"

Collins stares curiously at Senior Chief Barbara Gaile, wondering about the attractive senior chief's relationship with the navy officer that she shot and killed and wonders how the navy chief that was shot and killed by the officer fits into the scenario. He wonders why she now warrants special treatment. He responds, "The master chief is on leave. His office is air-conditioned and there are some soft chairs and a couch."

The NIS agent advises Barbara, "You are still under arrest."

Barbara stands and asks, "May I visit the head, first, and may I have my purse?"

"I'll get your purse," Chief Collins advises. He exits the room.

Twenty minutes later, Barbara exits the head and walks along the short passageway; then she enters the cool and comfortable office. A small, four-foot high refrigerator stands in the corner. She opens the refrigerator door, then pulls out a bottle of chilled San Pellegrino mineral water. She removes the cap and takes a long drink. Then she sits on the leather couch, leans her head back, and closes her eyes. The events of the past few months flow through her mind.

Chapter 5

Sammy Gallo dials the combination of the vault-like door to the Maddalena ONI field office located on the U.S. Naval Support Activity compound. He steps into the four-room vault-like office space that is protected from electronic surveillance by a copper mesh grid in the ceiling, walls, and floor.

Sammy walks directly to the codes safe, enters the combination, and retrieves the applicable codebook. Then he carries the codebook to his desk. Thirty seconds later, he confirms his fears as to the meaning of the coded message from Magnolia.

He observes that the BUSY indicator on the crypto-covered AUTOSEVOCOM telephone unit is not lit. He picks up the telephone handset and pushes the immediate precedence button; then he enters the number for the Naval Intelligence Operations Center in Suitland, Maryland.

Sammy gives his report to the operations center duty officer. Then the duty officer connects Sammy to Captain Bradley Watson, Assistant Director Naval Intelligence for Counterespionage.

"Hello, Captain. Sammy Gallo here."

"Hey, Sammy, long time no hear. What's so important that requires immediate precedence?"

"Naval Investigative Service Agent in Charge for La Maddalena is holding one of our agents, codename Magnolia. She sent a coded message reporting that she is under arrest by NIS here in La Maddalena. In the coded message, she reports that Pontus is dead."

Captain Watson gasps loudly. He shakes his head slowly, expressing denial—considering the report is in error. "Have you confirmed the report?"

"Not yet. After I get off the phone, I will meet with NIS Agent Beltenmeyer and Magnolia to get more details. I thought it important to get the information to ONI headquarters."

"Have you told anyone else?"

"I told the ONI duty officer. He recorded my report. Then he suggested I talk with you."

Brad is silent for a few moments. Then he orders, "Go see Magnolia and get the details. How long will that take?"

"Probably two hours by the time I get back here to my office."

Brad directs, "Get absolute confirmation on Pontus. Call me back no more than three hours from now."

"Will do, Captain."

Brad hangs up. Then he calls the ONI Duty Officer in the operations center.

"Operations center, Lieutenant Mallory."

"Jeff, this is Captain Watson. I want you to put a lid on the report of Pontus's death. You know how fast scuttlebutt spreads. I want you to personally order anyone who has knowledge of the report to remain silent. Pass down my instructions to your relief and to the next watch section."

"Aye, aye, Captain."

"Sammy Gallo will call back in a few hours with more detail and, maybe, confirmation. After you record his report, forward him to me."

"Aye, aye, Captain."

Chapter 6

Sammy Gallo enters the U.S. Navy Shore Patrol building.

NIS Agent Beltenmeyer meets Sammy in the lobby.

After quick greetings, Sammy asks, "Where is she?"

Beltenmeyer leads them down the hall. He opens the door, and they step into the office.

Barbara rises from the couch. She expresses recognition when she sees Sammy Gallo. Sammy stares into the face of the attractive, fortyish woman, expressing that he recognizes her but cannot recall from where. They squint their eyes while staring at each other, attempting to remember when and where they previously crossed paths. Barbara is the first to remember. "Naples—Licola—ten years ago, Rig and me in the beach house."

Sammy nods. Then he states. "I heard that you joined field ops." He pauses, cocks his head to the side and queries, "Are you being treated well?"

Barbara nods.

Sammy directs, "Okay, tell me what happened."

All sit down around the desk. They face each other.

Barbara describes the shootings on the fleet landing pier.

Sammy asks Beltenmeyer, "Where did they take the bodies? I have orders to confirm that Chief Page is dead."

The NIS agent shakes his head as he replies, "I don't know. I'm still trying to locate them. My partner is tracking them down as we speak. Shore patrol reports that the ambulance boats went to Santo Stefano where the submarine tender USS *Howard W. Gilmore* is moored. The *Gilmore* is the closest medical facility that can quickly treat gunshot wounds."

Barbara sighs deeply and her eyes become misty. She pleads, "Rig's body must be treated with respect. He is an American hero. He was awarded medals of valor. He selflessly served his country."

Beltenmeyer assures, "We will ensure he is treated with respect. Don't worry about that."

Silence falls over the room. All reflect on the events of the past few hours.

Beltenmeyer wants to continue his interrogation of Senior Chief Gaile. NIS procedure requires the interrogation be held with no one else in the room other than him and the subject. Nevertheless, he is new to the area. He might need ONI's cooperation in the future. He decides not to ask Sammy to go. Beltenmeyer states, "Senior Chief, I fulfilled your request. Now, you must answer my questions."

Barbara casts an inquiring glance at Sammy.

Sammy advises, "Mr. Beltenmeyer, ask your questions. You should classify the information you gain as secret. For national security reasons, she cannot answer questions that would reveal top secret information."

Beltenmeyer poises a pen over his notebook. Then he asks, "Senior Chief, why were you carrying a firearm."

Barbara answers, "Standard operating procedure when in the mission operating area."

"Why did you shoot Ensign Ryan?"

"He was shooting Chief Page."

Beltenmeyer writes her answer in his notebook. Then he asks, "What was your mission in La Maddalena?"

"I can't answer that."

"How long have you been in La Maddalena?"

"About three months."

"Where are you living?"

"In an apartment on Via Gabbiani, near fleet landing."

"Do you live alone?"

"I lived with Chief Page."

"How long did Chief Page live there?"

Barbara expresses sadness and despair as she answers, "About four months, shortly after he reported aboard the USS *Randal*."

"Was Chief Page your partner on your mission?"

"Yes."

Beltenmeyer glances at Sammy Gallo. Then he lays his pen on the paper pad. He crosses his arms and expresses thoughtfulness. After a full minute, he asks Sammy, "Mr. Gallo, did you know that the she and Chief Page were on a mission here in Maddalena?"

"No," Sammy admits, "but it is not unusual for an undercover operation to be conducted without the knowledge of the local naval intelligence field office." Sammy has already concluded correctly that Barbara and Rig were involved in the attacks on the local Red Brigade cell during the past few months.

The expression of revelation on Beltenmeyer's face conveys that he concludes the same thing.

Barbara detects that both men have connected her and Rig to the attacks on the Red Brigade.

"Why did Ensign Ryan shoot Chief Page?"

"I don't know."

"Did Chief Page ever talk to you about Ensign Ryan?"

"No."

The NIS Agent pauses. The interrogation has no direction to go. Then he advises, "Senior Chief, I must demand that you stay in La Maddalena until the investigation is over." He slides a piece of paper to Barbara and orders, "Write down your address and a telephone number where you can be contacted."

Barbara flinches and blinks her eyes with surprise. "You're releasing me?"

"Yes," Beltenmeyer states. "But I emphasize you must not depart the area." Then he slides Barbara's purse and passport toward her.

"No problem. I have no orders to go elsewhere." Then Barbara writes her address and telephone number. She asks, "What about my weapon?"

"I must keep your weapon—evidence." Then Beltenmeyer casts a friendly smile and comments, "I'm sure that if you need another weapon, you have a resource."

Sammy Gallo stands and informs, "I must go to the submarine tender at Santo Stefano. I have orders to confirm Chief Page's death. I must see the body."

Barbara stands and states, "I'm going with you."

Chapter 7

One hour later, Senior Chief Barbara Gaile, Naval Intelligence agent Sammy Gallo, and Naval Investigative Service special agent Charles Beltenmeyer enter the medical clinic on the main deck of the USS *Howard W. Gilmore*. The waiting room is packed with sailors, officers and enlisted men; some sit and some stand. Some are in uniform and the others are in civilian clothes. Barbara hears several whispered comments, "She's the one who shot Ensign Ryan."

Chief Hospital Corpsman Randy Stone paces back-and-forth in the center of the waiting room. He expresses worry.

Barbara recognizes the chief who attempted to treat Rig on La Maddalena fleet landing pier. She rushes toward him and asks, "What happened to Rig's body?"

Doc Stone stops pacing, interrupted in thought. He stares into the eyes of the attractive brunette who looks late thirties and who wears civilian clothes; he attempts to understand the nature of her question. Then he recognizes her as the woman who was standing over Chief Page with a pistol in each hand. He glances at the two men in civilian clothes that stand behind her.

Barbara pleads, "Please tell me what happened to Rig!"

Doc Stone casts an understanding expression. He advises, "Rig is in surgery."

With wide-eyed astonishment, Barbara challenges, "He's not dead. I thought he died on the pier! The way you acted on the pier, I thought he was dead!"

Doc's expression turns compassionate as he says, "Sorry, ma'am. I was frustrated, I couldn't tell for sure. We revived him in the ambulance boat. I mean, he did not regain consciousness, but we got his heart pumping stronger and his breathing more regular. But he is in critical condition. He was shot in the head, shoulder, and chest—near the heart."

Tears again well in Barbara's eyes; she cries out, "Shot in the head!"

"Not the most serious wound ma'am. The bullet scraped the skull, did not penetrate the skull."

"What else do you know about his condition?" Sammy Gallo asks.

Doc Stone glances back and forth between the faces of the two men who accompanied the woman into the waiting room. He asks, "May I ask who you are?"

Sammy advises, "I am Agent Gallo—the OIC of the local naval intelligence office." Sammy nods toward Beltenmeyer.

Beltenmeyer states, "I am Special Agent in Charge Beltenmeyer. I am the OIC of the local Naval Investigative Service office."

Stone expresses understanding as to why the two men are present; he advises, "Just before Rig went into surgery, Doctor Bolten told me that Rig's condition is critical. Doctor Bolten said Rig might not survive surgery."

Doc Stone's comments are heard throughout the waiting room. Deep sighs and groans rise up in the room.

Beltenmeyer scans the room; the only person he recognizes is an officer who wears khaki uniform, Commander Gregory Hampton, Commanding Officer of USS *Randal*. Beltenmeyer asks Doc Stone, "Are all these sailors here in regard to Chief Page?"

"Yes," Doc Stone responds. "When they heard about Rig being shot, they all came in here offering to give blood and any spare organ that Chief Page would need to survive."

Beltenmeyer and Gallo express surprise.

Doc Stone expresses understanding. He casts an appreciative smile and states, "Chief Page is held in high regard by the crew of USS *Randal*. Many of them gave blood already."

Sammy Gallo asks Doc Stone, "What is your name and who are you exactly?"

"Oh, I am Chief Hospital Corpsman Randy Stone. Rig and I are shipmates on the *Randal*."

Sammy considers Doc's words; then he says, "We need to talk privately. Let's move out into the passageway."

A voice from behind Sammy offers, "We can use my stateroom

on the *Randal*."

Sammy turns his head toward the voice, sees Commander Hampton, and says, "Thank you, Commander."

Doc Stone turns toward a sailor who wears the dungaree uniform of a second class petty officer and orders, "Lynder, wait here until Doctor Bolten has information on Chief Page's condition. Then come to the captain's stateroom and provide a report."

Lynder nods acknowledgement of the order.

Fifteen minutes later; Barbara Gaile, Chief "Doc" Stone, Commander Hampton, Naval Intelligence Agent Sammy Gallo, and Naval Investigative Service Special Agent Charles Beltenmeyer have settled in Commander Hampton's stateroom.

Hampton says, "Except for Chief Stone and Mr. Beltenmeyer, I don't know all of you. Please tell me who you are and your association with Chief Page. We'll start with you ma'am."

With a serious tone and expression Barbara advises, "I am Senior Chief Yeoman Barbara Gaile. I am on vacation in La Maddalena and staying with Chief Page at his apartment."

Commander Hampton expresses anticipation that the Senior Chief will provide more information. When she does not, the commander smiles knowingly and queries, "And just what is it about your vacation in La Maddalena that causes you to carry a gun and shoot Ensign Ryan?"

Barbara glances at Sammy Gallo.

Gallo speaks up, "Commander, I am the OIC of the local naval intelligence office. What I am about to tell you is classified secret— no foreign dissemination. Senior Chief Gaile and Chief Page work undercover for naval intelligence. They were on a mission here in La Maddalena—a mission that was completed several months ago. I cannot provide more information."

Hampton nods and states, "Yes, I had concluded as much." He turns his attention toward NIS Agent Beltenmeyer and asks, "Charlie, I assume you are investigating the shootings of Chief Page and Ensign Ryan?"

"Yes, that's correct," the NIS agent confirms.

After a short pause, Sammy Gallo speaks. "Chief Stone, I have some questions."

Doc Stone focuses on Sammy Gallo and expresses he is ready to answer questions.

"Chief Stone, did you witness the shooting on the pier?"

"Yes."

"Tell us what you saw."

"I was behind Chief Page, about fifty feet. I saw what I thought was a homeless man step away from the pier rail and fire three shots at Chief Page. Page went down. The homeless man stepped purposely over to where Page lay. He aimed the pistol at Page, but then I heard rapid shots and the homeless man went down. That's when I noticed Senior Chief Gaile with a gun in her hand. I jogged to the scene. That is when I recognized Ensign Ryan. Senior Chief Gaile picked up Ensign Ryan's gun. That's when I started checking Page's vital signs. A few seconds later, the shore patrol had the Senior Chief in handcuffs. I thought I detected life within Page, but I wasn't sure. There was a lot of noise and vibrations on the pier. No doubt that Ensign Ryan was dead." Stone pauses as he remembers the sequence of events. "Then, what seemed a short time later, we loaded Chief Page into one ambulance boat and Ensign Ryan into another ambulance boat."

NIS Agent Beltenmeyer feels satisfied that Chief Stone's reported sequence of events is the same as what Barbara Gaile described.

Navy intelligence agent Sammy Gallo presses, "Chief Stone, you said that you revived Chief Page on the ambulance boat during the trip to Santo Stefano. How was he revived?"

"With medication and oxygen administered by the Italian medics. They had radio contact with a doctor who directed which meds and how much oxygen. It was the Italian doctor on the radio that approved bringing Rig to the *Gilmore*."

Gallo asks, "Did Chief Page say anything in the presence of

those Italian medics?"

"No. He never regained consciousness prior to going into surgery, but his vitals got better and better."

Gallo asks, "Were you present when Chief Page was stripped prior to surgery?"

"Oh! You want to know about the weapons we found on him."

Gallo nods.

"In pre-op, when we removed his clothes, we found a short-barrel automatic in an ankle holster and two daggers in his inside coat pocket."

Sammy asks, "Were there any foreign nationals in pre-op when the weapons were discovered?"

"No, just me, the navy nurse, and another corpsman."

"Where are the weapons now?"

"The nurse stored them in a patient personal property box, along with Page's clothes."

Sammy makes a mental note to debrief those in the pre-op room.

A knock on the stateroom door cause all to pause.

Doc Stone suggests, "Sir, that could be Lynder with an update on Chief Page."

"Enter!" Commander Hampton orders.

Hospital Corpsman Second Class Lynder enters the stateroom; he has a big smile on his face.

All stare at Lynder with hopeful expressions.

Lynder states, "Chief Page is in post-op recovery room. Doctor Bolten has upgraded Chief Page's condition from critical to serious."

All exhale a deep sigh of relief.

Chapter 8

The Director of Naval Intelligence—DNI, Rear Admiral Willcroft, enters the office of Captain Bradley Watson, the Assistant DNI for counterespionage. The admiral's tailor-made Summer White uniform accentuates his tall and trim broad shouldered frame. The gray haired, squared jaw officer always portrays a commanding presence.

Captain Watson stands and faces the admiral.

With a concerned tone, Admiral Willcroft inquires, "What's this report about Pontus being killed?"

Brad shakes his head and responds, "Not confirmed, Admiral. I attempted to put a lid on the report until I can get the report confirmed. Where did you hear about it, sir?"

"From my yeoman, Chief Browning."

"I need to go to the operation center and put a lid on this information leak."

"Tell me what you know," Willcroft orders.

Brad tells the Admiral the details of Sammy Gallo's report.

"Keep me informed," the admiral orders. Then he departs the office.

A few moments later, Captain Watson exits his office. He tells his yeoman, YNC Randson, "I will be in the operations center."

Randson stands and says, "Uh, Captain, I am collecting for flowers and sympathy cards for Chief Page's family. Do you wish to donate?"

Captain Watson halts; then turns toward YNC Randson. "Where and when did you hear about Chief Page?"

"Uh . . . about an hour ago in the coffee mess—couple of sailors were talking about it."

Brad turns abruptly and walks off in the direction of the operations center.

Chapter 9

July 1977
Central Connecticut

Diane Love exits the small private airplane and descends the four-step ladder to the tarmac. She wears a scarf over her head and wears sunglasses. Anyone watching through a window of the municipal airport terminal could not describe the facial features of the woman exiting the private airplane.

A shiny black Lincoln Town Car limousine comes to a stop twenty feet from the nose of the airplane. The limousine's trunk lid pops open. The sedan driver exits the driver's door, then opens the rear passenger door.

Diane's headscarf hides her flowing red hair, and her sunglasses disguise her facial features, especially her identifying sparkling green eyes. The limousine driver has no difficulty recognizing the tall, slim, attractive woman in black pantsuit.

"A pleasure to see you again, Miss Love," the driver says courteously and sincerely. He stares at her sunglasses as if peering into her bright green eyes.

Diane nods recognition toward the tall, solidly built, and physically powerful man with blond hair and Scandinavian features and Scandinavian accent who wears the traditional black suit and black tie of limo drivers. She knows him from previous visits. She notes the bulge under his coat that is made by his shoulder holster and pistol, which reminds her that he is also the bodyguard of her friend Edwin Kendley.

"Thank you, George. It's a pleasure to see you also. I hope Edwin will meet me at his estate when we arrive."

"Yes, Miss Love, Mr. Kendley is waiting for you."

Diane steps into the large backseat area of the limousine.

The driver closes the car door. Then he walks to the flight attendant who carries Diane's two suitcases. The driver takes the suitcases and places them into the trunk.

The heavy tint on the side and rear widows allow Diane to remove the scarf and sunglasses without her identity exposed to outside onlookers.

The limousine moves eastward on the interstate. The driver hugs the right-hand lane. He engages the speed control to the maximum speed limit of fifty-five miles per hour. Aggressive drivers pass the limo at twenty miles over the speed limit.

Diane sighs deeply and becomes irritable over the snails-pace advance of the limo. Then she surrenders her irritability knowing the driver cannot risk being stopped by the police and reveal her presence in Connecticut.

The limo exits the interstate, then moves along a two-lane paved country road. The woods are thick and lush on both sides of the road. Five minutes later, the limo turns onto a narrow private road that leads to the fifty-acre country Estate of Edwin Kendley. A sign warning *No Trespassing* marks the eastern boundary of the Kendley Estate. Although it is mid-afternoon, the driver must drive with lights on because the tall thick trees form a sunlight-blocking canopy over the road.

While Diane stares out the window at the familiar ground of the Kendley Estate, she recollects her relationship with Edwin Kendley. They first met during the 1968 Democrat Convention in Chicago. He and Diane were organizers of the Students for a Democratic Society—SDS. She was introduced to him the day before the protests started. Together, they organized students into protest groups and provided them with signs and locations to protest. On the streets outside the convention hall, Diane and Edwin led the protest chants and kept the protesters moving.

The, then, twenty-one-year-old Diane Love was immediately attracted to the, then, twenty-six-year-old Edwin Kendley who claimed to be a perpetual Harvard Law School student. She found his thin, flabby body with shoulder length black hair and long beard to be sexy.

Two nights after they first met, they slept together in Edwin's hotel room and every night after that. During their time in Chicago,

Diane learned that Edwin was orphaned two-years previous when his parents were killed in a boat fire on Long Island Sound. Upon his patents' death, Edwin inherited sixty-three-million dollars.

The Students for a Democratic Society dissolved in 1969 because its many factions could not come to agreement. Edwin formed a new group called The Longjumeau Alliance. Former moderate members of SDS joined Edwin's new group. The more violent members of SDS joined The Weather Underground.

Diane first visited the Kendley Estate in Connecticut during the summer of 1969—shortly after graduating from UCLA with a Bachelor of Political Science degree. She remembers her awe at the opulent and expansive fifty-acre estate. Her multi-million dollar trust fund appeared minor compared to the wealth of Edwin Kendley. He is executor of his parents' estate and his business savvy had grown his inheritance to nearly one-hundred-million dollars by 1969. Edwin had graduated from Harvard two years before with several business degrees. In 1969, he was still enrolled at Harvard Law School.

During that summer of 1969 when she visited the Kendley Estate for the first time, she met many former members of SDS and former members of the predecessor to SDS, the *Student League for Industrial Democracy,* SLID. She knew SDS had its roots in student organizations going back to the early 1900s. What she did not know before that summer was that members of the now dissolved SLID remained loyal to the revolution and donated money to the SDS and, now, donates to The Longjumeau Alliance. Some members of The Longjumeau Alliance were members of the SLID and, later, the SDS going back more than forty years. Some members of The Longjumeau Alliance are federal judges, Congressmen, federal government bureaucrats, state and local politicians, lobbyists, and educators who were once members of SLID, SDS, and the American Communist Party.

During her first visit in the summer of 1969, Diane arrived at the Kendley Estate a week earlier than the scheduled meeting of The Longjumeau Alliance leaders. She and Edwin slept in the same bed and made love for hours each night. Their daytime activities included lying around the Olympic sized swimming pool and horseback riding along dirt trails on the estate.

During that first visit to the estate, Edwin told Diane how he had formed The Longjumeau Alliance. Edwin's father, Reginald Kendley, had joined the SLID when he was in college during the 1930s. Reginald Kendley also became a registered member of the American Communist Party and was a lifelong member of the SLID. Edwin had discovered his father's affiliation with communist organizations shortly after his father's death, while going through his father's personal papers. Not only was Edwin's father a member of the SLID, he was the East Coast Director. When the SLID was reorganized into the SDS, Reginald lost his directorship to a member of SDS who was currently enrolled in college. The SDS leadership did not trust the old men who allowed the SLID to transform into an elitist old men's club.

"But your father was a capitalist," Diane stated. "How could he have believed in communism?"

"Dad was not a capitalist. He inherited millions from my grandpa. My father never did anything to increase grandpa's wealth. Managers grew the fortune. My father spent his time on populist causes. He went to an office most days, but it was just for show.

"Grandpa was the epitome of a greedy, robber baron capitalist. He was born poor in central Texas. He went to work in the oil fields when he was a boy. At age 20, he borrowed one-thousand dollars and became a wildcat oil driller and was successful with his first well. My grandpa's harsh business tactics earned him a fortune, but he treated his workers unfairly. He didn't care about them. He never understood that his employees were the foundation on which he built his wealth.

"My father always felt guilty about grandpa's treatment of employees. Grandpa squeezed every nickel possible out of his oil operation by oppressing his workers. When the unions threatened to organize grandpa's operation, he hired thugs to chase off union organizers."

Diane had declared, "Your grandfather could not do that today because now it is a crime to use force against union organizing."

"Agreed, but back in the 1920s, unions did not have federal government support, as they do now."

During that first week at the country estate, Edwin indoctrinated Diane in the philosophy and goals of The Longjumeau Alliance. During the second week when the directors of The Longjumeau Alliance met, Diane was sworn in and pledged allegiance to The Longjumeau Alliance; and she signed her loyalty oath. She swore to keep The Longjumeau Alliance a secret and swore to speak of The Longjumeau Alliance only in the presence of other members.

Diane experienced one chilling moment while attending orientation week. During security briefings, she sensed a threat that violation of security rules might result in physical harm to the violator. The threat was veiled behind obscure wording. However, her briefers were positive that Diane got the message.

Edwin Kendley has used Diane's tactical skills at developing and executing character assassination plans against popular rightwing politicians. Her ability to deceptively interpret words and manufacture false actions involving those politicians, and her talents to involve national media in deceptive collusion to convince the unwashed masses that her deceptions are true had earned her the nick name *The Assassin* among The Alliance Directorship.

Diane comes back to the present when the limo driver applies the brakes to stop at the gate house. She can see the eighteen-foot-high protective wall that surrounds the massive, fifty room Tutor style mansion. Large and lengthy manicured lawns lie between the mansion and the protective wall.

She recognizes the gate guard as one of those well paid estate employees who signed nondisclosure statements regarding events at the estate and signed a loyalty oath to The Longjumeau Alliance. Employees are forbidden to discuss topics other than estate business for which they are responsible. Activities of the Kendley family and of visitors are forbidden subjects of conversation.

Spoken in whispers far away from the estate, employees have

mentioned to each other about the maid who didn't come to work one day. Several weeks later, the police came to the estate as part of an investigation regarding the missing maid. The maid's family had filed a missing person report. Gate-guard records showed the maid exited the estate at 5:12 PM. the afternoon previous to the day when she did not show up for work.

During this week's meeting, Diane will become a member of the Board of Directors for The Alliance. She suspects she was nominated for the Board because she now works on the White House staff and not because of her devotion to The Alliance and not because of her past productive and effective efforts as a ground troop for the cause. She also wonders what the Board of Directors would do if they discovered she is an undercover agent for the Soviet KGB.

Her KGB controller, Jordan, had commanded her to never reveal her KGB affiliation to The Longjumeau Alliance. Jordan had explained, "Just because The Longjumeau Alliance and the Soviet Union have the same goals does not mean we are allies."

Jordan had demanded that Diane provide copies of all papers she receives from The Longjumeau Alliance. Jordan had expressed astonishment, then irritation when Diane informed, "I can provide copies of most documents, but The Alliance does not issue operating orders in writing to membership cells. All operating orders from the Board to membership cells are delivered verbally by messenger. The only record of operating orders is in a secret attachment to the minutes of director meetings and only the secretary and Edwin Kendley have access to those attachments."

Jordan had ordered, "You must obtain copies of those attachments. Until then, you must memorize all you see and hear."

Diane had nodded acceptance of the order.

The strategic timing of her appointment to the Board will allow her to vote on The Longjumeau Alliance's revised agenda and long-term plan. She anxiously awaits learning about some of The Alliance's secret operations, which only Board members and participating membership cells are aware.

Chapter 10

The murmur of voices penetrates the dark of his mind. The indistinguishable words nag him for clarity. Then the noise of shuffling feet and squeaking wheels drown the murmur of words. He floats on air—nothing is tangible. *Where is the light?*

He attempts to understand why he exists in this world of no images. The number of voices increases. *What is she saying?! What must I do to understand?!*

Now, he sees a pink world with dark shadows moving about. *What is that beeping noise?*

He opens his eyes. Then he squints against the bright lights. After a few moments, he opens his eyes wider.

He attempts to understand his surroundings. He realizes that he lies on his back in a bed and sheets cover him from his feet to mid-torso. A clear plastic tube strung from above him disappears under a bandage on his forearm. His eyes follow the clear tube as it curves upwards and connects to a clear plastic bag on a hook. Then he notices more clear tubes strung from oxygen bottles. The oxygen tubes disappear under his nose. He crinkles his nose and confirms that the tube runs along his upper lip. Feeling tightness at the top of his head, he presses his hand where he should feel hair but feels a bandage covering the top of his head.

Then a female voice persistently calls his name. "Chief Page . . . Chief Page . . . Chief Page."

Rigney Page focuses his attention on the source of the voice and sees a short, thin woman in a navy nurse's uniform. His eyes lock on her eyes and he nods, indicating he hears her. Then movement at the end of the bed causes him to focus on a man who wears a white medical coat and who has a stethoscope around his neck. Rig's eyes scan the room quickly. *I'm in a hospital room. Why?*

He tries to speak but feels a dry, harsh, and stinging sensation in his throat. In a fatigued soft voice, he requests, "Wa . . . wat . . . water . . . please."

The nurse lifts a blue colored plastic water pitcher with a clear sipping straw from a side table and brings it to the bedside. She pushes the straw to Rigney's lips.

Rig takes three large draws of ice water. The effort to suck in the water tires him, which makes him surprisingly aware of his exhausted condition. He expresses bewilderment at why he feels so weak. "Where am I?" he queries.

The nurse answers, "You're in the U.S. Naval Hospital, Naples, Italy."

Rig expresses surprise.

"What is the last thing you remember?" asks the man in white coat with stethoscope around his neck."

Rig expresses reflection for a few moments; then he responds, "I was walking on the navy pier in La Maddalena." Rig's eyes go wide and he inhales sharply. "Someone pointed a gun at me . . . Ensign Ryan!" Rig blinks his eyes several times as revelation comes to him. "I've been shot! Will I recover?!"

The man in the white coat advises, "You are recovering. With regaining consciousness, I think your recovery will be nearly one-hundred percent."

Rig stares at the man in the white coat. He asks, "You're a doctor?"

"I am Doctor Christianson. You are in my care while you are here."

Rig considers his condition; then he declares, "I don't feel any pain."

"You are on intravenous pain medication."

Rig sighs deeply. He prepares himself mentally for the big question. He inhales deeply; then, he asks, "What are my injuries?"

Doctor Christianson exhibits compassionate understanding. He advises, "You were shot three times. One bullet bounced along the outside of your skull, tearing away skin and hair, hard enough to give you a concussion. Caused a lot of scalp bleeding, but that was the least damaging wound. Another bullet entered your left triceps and lodged about an inch deep—muscle damage but less bleeding than the skull injury. The third bullet entered your thorax cavity, traveled through your left lung, and came to rest against the left atrium of your heart. The ballistics report states that your would-be killer used inferior, low-caliber, low-grade ammunition. His old thirty-two caliber revolver was loaded with old, damp, short-load bullets. Had he used dry, full-load ammunition, that bullet would have penetrated your heart. The quick actions of the medical staff in La Maddalena to increase your heartbeat rate and to control internal bleeding saved your life."

For a moment, Rig wonders if Chief Hospital Corpsman Randy "Doc" Stone was involved. Then he asks, "Where is Ensign Ryan . . . the officer who shot me?"

The doctor advises "I don't know. I only know about the ballistics report because NIS in La Maddalena info copied the hospital on the message. A Captain Watson and a female lieutenant commander are here from Washington, and they desperately want to talk with you. Maybe they can tell you more about the shooting."

"When will I see them?"

"This afternoon but not for more than a few minutes."

Later, during midafternoon, Rig stares out the window while attempting to find the location of the Solfatara volcano that emanates the sulfur gas that stinks up his hospital room. He had read somewhere that the U.S. Navy Activity Naples, Italy was built close to the Flegrean Fields—an area dense with inactive, ancient volcanos. At the sound of footsteps entering the room, he turns his head toward the doorway.

Captain Brad Watson and Lieutenant Commander Sally Macfurson enter Rig's hospital room. They wear Summer White uniforms with sharp military creases. The brass on their shoulder boards shines brightly.

Brad Watson's short-cropped blond hair is grayer at the temples and around his ears. Although, Brad is now ten years older than when Rig first met him, Brad still maintains a body builder shape on his medium-height frame.

38

Lieutenant Commander Sally Macfurson's flaming-red hair is pulled back into a fold to comply with female grooming regulations. Her five-foot-and-two-inch-high, petite body is still perfectly formed. Her green eyes are bright and wide as she smiles happily at seeing her friend and occasional lover after more than two years.

Both officers are shocked at the number of tubes penetrating his body and the number of bandages covering his wounds. The blanket only covers to his waist. Rig's thick reddish-brown body hair contrasts boldly with the white bandages around his chest, head, and left arm.

Although he is weak and pumped full of pain killer drugs, he thinks clearly and smiles enthusiastically at the two officers who have been a significant part of his life for the past eleven years. Rig greets them with his trademark clever wit. "Ah, so you were in the neighborhood, then?"

"Yeah," Lieutenant Commander Sally Macfurson responds. "But our car is parked at the curb and the motor is running."

Rig utters the best chuckle that he can muster, which isn't much.

Sally bends forward over his bed and plants an emotion-heavy kiss on Rig's lips.

Captain Brad Watson glances at the door to verify no one is watching the intimate kiss. He overlooks this breach of fraternization rules because he knows that Chief Page and Lieutenant Commander Sally Macfurson have had an on-off-on-again romance since before Sally joined the navy.

Sally pulls her lips away from Rig's lips. She returns to an upright standing position. She takes his hand in hers. Then, in an emotion-filled voice and with tears in her eyes, she says, "I was so worried about you. I nearly collapsed at the early reports of your death."

"My . . . my death?!" Rig stammers. Then he expresses concern and becomes worried that his family in Seal Beach believes he is dead.

Brad Watson advises, "Don't worry, Chief. Your parents never heard about reports of your death. Only a few people at ONI heard those early inaccurate reports. Your parents know nothing about you being shot. As soon as I return to Washington a few days from now, I will call your parents and advise them of your situation and medical condition."

Rig nods, expresses appreciation, and says, "Thank you, Captain."

Brad Watson gets down to business. "We are here to take some statements from you regarding events in La Maddalena. Your doctor said that starting tomorrow you can begin dictating to our stenographer all your memories of interactions with Ensign Ryan. Copies of your statement will be provided to the Naval Investigative Service, after we edit out all classified information."

"Where is Ensign Ryan?" Rig inquires.

Both Captain Watson and Lieutenant Commander Macfurson express surprise. Then the captain expresses understanding and comments, "Well, yes, of course you couldn't know what happened on the pier after you lost consciousness. Ensign Ryan is dead—shot to death by Barbara Gaile immediately after Ryan shot you."

Rig blinks several times and expresses astonishment. "What?!"

Captain Watson explains, "Ryan fired three bullets at you, and then you went down. Then Ryan ran to your side and was aiming his gun at your head. Before he pulled the trigger, Barbara shot him four times in the chest. Ryan died on the spot."

Emotion wells up in Rig. He sighs deeply and tears come to his eyes. He asks, "Where is Barbara, now?"

Sally expresses the same emotion. This is not the first time that Barbara saved Rig from being killed.

"She is still in La Maddalena helping NIS investigate the shooting."

"She is not in trouble over this?"

"No," Sally advises. "There were dozens of witnesses. Both the navy and the Italian authorities agree that Barbara shot Ryan in defense for you."

Rig remains silent for several moments; then he asks, "What happens next?"

Captain Watson responds, "Doctor Christianson says you will need long-term physical therapy. This hospital does not have such facilities. If you continue to improve at the current rate over the next two weeks, you will be strong enough for MEDEVAC to Bethesda Naval Hospital in Washington. I will depart a few days from now. Sally will stay here and collect your dictated statements. Then she will act as your escort for the MEDEVAC to D.C."

Rig is about to ask about what happens after physical therapy, but Doctor Christianson enters the room and advises, "Enough visiting for today. Chief Page must rest now."

"I'll be back tomorrow," Sally says in a compassionate tone.

Captain Watson and Lieutenant Commander Sally Macfurson turn and walk toward the doorway. Then Captain Watson turns and stares at Rig and comments, "I find it ironic, Rig, that over the past decade you have fought some of the toughest and most evil men ever born on this earth. You conquered them; but then a psychotic ensign with an inferiority complex and a faulty pistol brings you down."

Rigney nods his head, chuckles lightly, and responds, "Well, I forgot to eat my Wheaties that morning."

Sally casts a loving smile at Rig and says with respect, "You are one of a kind, Rigney Page. Please, never change."

Chapter 11

Edwin Kendley hands copies of The Longjumeau Alliance *Five Year Plan* to members of the Board of Directors. He announces, "We will resume our meeting at 4:00 PM. That will give each of you most of the day to review the *Five Year Plan*. When we resume, we will discuss the plan. Then we will discuss old business, followed by new business."

Edwin states in a serious tone, "Remember, you are not allowed to make copies. You must safeguard these documents at all times. You must immediately report unauthorized release of information in these documents."

Twenty minutes later, Diane sits at the desk in her room. She opens the *Five Year Plan*. She immediately pages to the section for her Directorate—U.S. Government, Executive Branch. Her eyes widen and she flinches with surprise when she sees the amount of her budget—six-million dollars. She turns the page and reads the mission statement of her Directorate. *"Exercise all power and influence to enact policies and processes within the U.S. Government Executive Branch that promote and forward the mission of The Longjumeau Alliance."*

Diane fingers to the beginning of the plan and reads the mission of The Longjumeau Alliance. *"By the year 2000, transform America into a single political party communist republic."*

At 4:00 PM, the Board of Directors reconvenes their semi-annual meeting. Each member has ten-minutes to ask and receive answers to questions. Forty-five minutes later, Diane's opportunity to ask questions arrives. She glances at the *Five Year Plan* and finds the first section that she underlined, which is *Protective Services*. Edwin is listed as the director who oversees operation and funding.

"What are Protective Services?" she asks.

Edwin answers, "That directorate provides security for The Alliance. When a threat arises that might expose us, Protective Services removes the threat."

Diane stares intently into Edwin's eyes as she attempts to understand what he means by *remove*. She opens her mouth to ask for clarification, but Edwin stops her. "We can talk about it outside this meeting."

She glances back down at line items and becomes curious about the line item titled *Strategic Operations*. She raises her eyes and finds Ronald Forbin—the director who oversees that line item. "What about Strategic Operations?"

Ronald responds, "Planning and execution of activities that sabotage rightwing campaigns and performs character assassinations on wealthy capitalists and rightwing politicians. I am the one who has funded and implemented all those plans you wrote over the years. It was my people who coordinated with you to put your plans into action. I am pleased that The Assassin is finally a member of the Board."

"The Assassin?" Diane questions while expressing curiosity.

"Yes," Ronald Forbin responds. "Your plans are so effective, so brutal, and so damaging to the target that we assigned you the nickname The Assassin."

Diane does not like that nickname, but she expresses appreciation anyway.

Diane turns the page and finds a line item with her name as managing director—Executive Branch Operations. "Regarding my Directorate, can you give me examples of what I will be doing?"

Edwin Kendley explains, "Whenever we need something from a political appointee or bureaucrat in the Executive Branch, you will use your White House influence to get it. From time-to-time we will use your position as one of Jimmy Carter's speech writers to insert words and phrases in his speeches. And, you will continue your character assassination planning."

"Okay, I understand my responsibilities, but I do not understand why I need a six-million-dollar budget to do it."

Edwin responds, "You will need that money to bribe officials within the Executive Branch to comply with your requests. When officials refuse to comply, you will hire investigators to dig up dirt on those officials and force them to comply. I will provide you with a list of private investigation companies."

Diane exhibits concern.

Edwin Kendley pronounces, "Diane, the justice, fairness, and benevolence of our mission justifies any means to achieve it."

"Oh, I understand that, Edwin, and I agree. But I am not experienced at pressuring others to provide that which they do not want to provide."

Edwin counsels, "It gets easier the more times you do it. I will help you through the first couple of times. Then I am confident you will do well on your own."

Diane commits, "I will do my best to succeed."

Edwin Kendley announces, "We will now move on to old business." No one objects; so Kendley shifts his attention to Professor Bartholomew Goldman, PhD who is The Longjumeau Alliance Director for Re-education and Propaganda, and in his professional life he is a tenured faculty lecturer at Georgetown University.

Kendley asks, "Professor, do you have an update on textbook revisions for K through twelve."

"Yes," Goldman responds. "We now have operatives in the writing and the editing divisions of the three major textbook publishers. All of them have signed their loyalty oaths to The Longjumeau Alliance and they have signed their compensation and bonus agreements that include specified goals of publishing revisions of history that support collectivism."

A chuckle from Ronald Forbin, Director of Protective Services, interrupts Goldman's briefing.

"What's so funny?" Kendley asks while expressing disapproval at Forbin's rude interruption.

Forbin says, "I think it ironic that we are using capitalistic motivations—merit based compensation incentives like bonuses—

to forward a communist cause."

Kendley shifts his eyes back to Goldman and directs, "Continue, Professor."

Bartholomew Goldman continues his briefing. "In our textbooks, the *Bill of Rights* will be declared obstacles to democracy. Textbooks will explain that the *Bill of Rights* provides protection to the wealthy and oppresses the working class and many examples will be manufactured and included in those textbooks. In America's classrooms, children will come to see the *Bill of Rights* as an old and now invalid philosophy. Our textbooks will convince children that individual liberty is the enemy of a fair society.

"We are also targeting the motivation of the American Revolution to convey that the Revolution was sponsored and directed by rich property owners for increased profit motives and not for increased freedom and liberty. The textbooks will emphasize exploitation against the Indians by White Europeans to include murdering Indians, confiscating Indian lands, and the forced westward migration of Indians.

"We are also targeting the American Civil War. All references will be removed that describe the Republican Party as the driving force behind freeing slaves and promoting civil rights legislation for Negroes. All references regarding the Democratic Party's agenda to oppress Negroes will be removed. The Democratic Party's actions to promote segregation will be removed.

"Textbooks will portray the Industrial Revolution as an evil movement by the rich to oppress the working class for increased profit. All references will be removed that claim the Industrial Revolution was a positive economic evolution that pulled millions of Americans out of poverty and generated wealth for those who were industrious and productive. Textbooks will also focus on forced child labor for profit and on sweatshops where the American poor were oppressed by low wages and tyrannical business owners.

"All references that suggest FDR's New Deal lengthened the Great Depression will be removed. The texts will be revised to state as fact that New Deal collectivism is the only successful process to turn around economic recessions and depressions.

"The massive redistribution of wealth brought on by LBJ's War on Poverty legislation will be promoted as the only fair and just process to achieve income equality.

"Throughout all the textbooks, collectivism will be advocated as the only valid process to move those in poverty to the middle class level and then up to the wealthy class. All references to the wealth-building process through liberty, self-reliance, and free-market capitalism will be eliminated. Dependence on government to achieve wealth or to achieve a comfortable life will be advocated throughout all textbooks.

"Some other changes to textbooks will be elimination of all references to Abraham Lincoln and Martin Luther King as Republicans. Also, all references that state Southern Democrats supported segregation and Jim Crow Laws will be removed.

"And most importantly is the destruction of the American family. Parenting rights to educate their children as they see fit must be eliminated. Children must no longer be seen as dependent on parents. Parents must be removed as the social and cultural educators of their children. Children must become products of the collective state. A direct link from government to child must be established so that all children become advocates of the collective state. All textbooks will promote the collective child as fair and just. The independent child will be declared evil and a social outcast."

Professor Goldman holds up several books and manuals. "These texts will govern our propaganda operators in the field and govern the Board's development of strategies. Included are *Rules for Radicals*, *The Communist Manifesto*, *Das Kapital*, the *Cloward-Piven Strategy*, and the writings of Vladimir Lenin."

Goldman pauses and takes a few deep breaths. Then he continues. "Above all else, when the time comes in the year 2000 for us to make our move to take control of federal and state governments, American citizens must be disarmed. We cannot sincerely declare our socialist revolution supports the common good while at the same time we are slaughtering dissenting gun owners who take up arms against us. We must exercise maximum effort through textbooks and other media to convince the American people that gun ownership is evil, racist, unethical, and un-American. Elimination of the Second Amendment must be a high priority." Goldman sits back in his chair and expresses that he is done.

Edwin Kendley says to the Board, "Last year, Professor Goldman and his team took on the task to set milestones, goals, and a detailed plan to move forward with all that he explained, and he tells me the task will be complete in time for our next meeting."

Kendley glances at the paper with the meeting agenda to see what is next. He shifts his attention to United States Senator Clay Porter and asks, "What is the status on the *Employee Fairness Act*?" Kendley refers to legislation that if it becomes law it would require all companies with ten or more permanent employees to hire union labor. The legislation establishes a Federal Business License Agency and that agency would verify employee union membership before issuing the Federal Business License. The legislation would make it illegal for any business with ten or more permanent employees to operate without the Federal Business License.

Senator Porter, who is the Director of Congressional Operations for The Alliance, replies, "As with all legislation that forces companies to unionize and would give the Executive Branch more power to prosecute anti-union capitalists, Republicans lead the filibuster against the legislation. We have sixty-one Democrats in the Senate, but six of those Democrats have joined the Republican filibuster. My unrelenting efforts to turn those six Democrats have not been successful. They cannot be bought with personal bribes or with millions in earmarks for their states."

Kendley asks, "What have you done to turn those senators?"

Senator Porter advises, "I'm having their backgrounds investigated to dig up dirt to use as blackmail to turn their vote. But after three months, no dirt of any value has been uncovered."

Kendley glances around the table; then he asks, "Any suggestions from the Board?"

Diane raises her hand.

Kendley points to Diane, indicating she has the floor to speak.

Diane suggests, "Hiring thugs to physically threaten those senators and their families should work."

"Always a last resort," declares Steven Stoner, Director, of Intelligence Operations for The Longjumeau Alliance and president of his own company—Grenadier Security. "However, I must report that I have been advising Billy Thayer, who is cell leader for Southern California, to use physical threats toward small business owners and their families as a method to force unionization. Thayer had some hired thugs rough up business owner family members and had to torch a few businesses to convince other business owners that the threats of violence are serious. It's working, where all other methods have failed."

Diane attempts not to appear startled to learn that her friend, United States Congressman Billy Thayer, is The Longjumeau Alliance's cell leader for Southern California. She has known for years that he is a member of The Alliance, but she did not know that he was a member of any of the operational cells.

Senator Porter says, "Violence is a last resort. I want time for nonviolent methods to work. We might manufacture dirt as we have before."

Kendley nods his head and says, "We will bring it up at the next Board meeting. Is everyone agreed on that?"

No one objects. Kendley moves on to the next old business item. "What is the progress of the *Fair Profits Tax Act*?"

Senator Porter answers, "Same status as the *Employee Fairness Act*, and I am employing the same methods to turn those Democrat senators who are against."

"What is their objection?" Diane Love asks.

Senator Porter answers, "They claim that government confiscating all company profits over five percent will destroy the economy."

Diane who graduated from UCLA with a Master's degree in Political Science and a minor in Economics responds, "Those dissenting senators are correct but is that not our objective—to destroy the economy so that the communist revolution can rise from the ashes."

Senator Porter responds, "Yes, that is the objective. Ironically, capitalists will be blamed for the economic crash; because several years leading up to the crash, corporations will be raising prices while at the same time they are laying-off workers or converting workers from full-time to part-time."

Kendley states, "If no one objects, we will hold discussion on the *Employee Fairness Act* until our next meeting. If no progress has been made by then, we will consider other actions."

No one objects; Kendley moves to the next item on the meeting agenda. "I open the floor to new business."

Professor Goldman raises his hand.

Edwin Kendley says, "Go ahead Professor. You have the floor."

Professor Goldman recommends, "We need to fund political campaign ads for radio and television—positive ads for the most socialistic of Democrats and negative ads against rightwing constitutionalists. Such ads are the most effective at swaying the American public."

Diane interjects, "We would need to form a political action committee, a PAC. It would be easy for The Alliance to route funds through fake companies, fake organizations, and fake people."

Goldman adds, "We can also use man-made disasters to fault capitalism for putting profit before the safety of the people. For months, major newspapers and magazines have been using those oilrig explosions and the distribution of those *poisoned aspirin bottles* to fuel growing anti-capitalism sentiment. But average Americans do not read newspapers and magazines. We need to air our ads during commercial times for the most popular television shows—like *The Love Boat* and *Fantasy Island*."

Homer Castle, Director of Logistics for The Longjumeau Alliance and a vice president for Charleston Bank, raises his hand."

Edwin Kendley says, "Go ahead, Homer."

"A political action committee sounds like an effective way to forward the revolution. I suggest we form a committee to determine the mechanics of establishing a PAC but keeping our involvement secret. I volunteer for such a committee."

Diane Love offers, "I have had some experience with forming PACs. I volunteer."

Edwin announces, "We have a motion to form a committee to research the mechanics of establishing a PAC to report at our next meeting, and Diane and Homer have volunteered to be that committee . . . all in favor?"

All directors respond with a "Yea."

Edwin glances at his watch; then he states, "Before we adjourn for the day, I want to emphasize that we need the Democratic Party to push our agenda. We have a Democrat Administration and an overwhelming Democrat controlled Congress. Democrats are on the increase in state governments. We must take advantage. Now is the time to push legislation that supports our cause. I fear that Jimmy Carter will be a one-term president and it could be twenty, maybe thirty years, before we have this advantage again. We must be aggressive in supporting socialist candidates, aggressive in socialist education, and aggressive in manufacturing situations that cause the average American to consider socialism as a just and fair society."

Chapter 12

Four gruff mannered men with mountain-man style beards and wearing denim trousers and plaid wool shirts sit quietly in the rear seats of the dark blue van parked near the entrance to the Reynolds City, Texas Athletic Center. The driver, a short-haired clean-shaven young man in his late twenties, glances at his watch. "He's late," the driver says over his shoulder to the four men in the back.

Five minutes later, Rory Chandler's limousine turns the corner one block from the four-thousand-seat Reynolds City Athletic Center. The Reynolds City campaign speech is his third this week. He runs his speech through his mind.

The recent, sudden death of U.S. Senator Lawrence Preston, Republican, Texas, has resulted in a special election. Rory Chandler is a self-made multimillionaire. He owns sixteen car dealerships across the state of Texas. Since his early twenties after making his first million, he has been active in Republican politics, holding positions in county and state Republican Committees. For twenty years, he acted as a behind-the-scenes political powerbroker and campaign contributor. On many occasions, Rory had publicly condemned the leftwing ideology that had spread across the nation during the past ten years—an ideology that allowed Jimmy Carter to be elected to the highest political office in the nation. Rory fears that Jimmy Carter and a Democrat controlled Congress will pass legislation to strangle commerce and decrease citizen liberties. President Carter's plans for a U.S. Department of Education and a U.S. Department of Energy fuel Rory's fears of destructive government intervention in free enterprise.

The Chairman of the Texas Republican Committee approached Rory several months ago and asked him to run for the open U.S. Senate seat. Rory accepted immediately. He faced weak competition in the primaries. Now, in the polls, he leads the Democrat candidate by fifteen points. The Texas Democrat machine failed in its efforts to cast Rory as a "robber baron" capitalist who was racist, fascist, antiunion, and who crusades to abolish Medicare and Social Security. Left-leaning media relentlessly misrepresents Rory's platform. Unfortunately, laws do not allow candidates to sue other candidates and the media for slander.

The limousine comes to a stop at a side entrance reserved for VIPs. Rory Chandler exits the limousine, glances at his watch, and then walks swiftly into a side door of the Athletic Center.

Several minutes later, the young driver in the parked van announces over his shoulder, "It's time gentlemen."

All four bearded men exit the van, carrying rolled-up banners. They walk past the news trucks for ABC, NBC, and CBS. They mix with hundreds of other sign-carrying attendees. Inside the 4000-seat arena, the four men position themselves at a strategic distance from the television cameras.

Ten minutes into Rory's speech, the four men unroll their banners. Their white Ku Klux Klan robes are wrapped inside the banners. They slip into their robes and coned shaped hoods. The *Burning Latin Cross* displays clearly on their robes.

Two men hold a banner sign declaring "KU KLUX KLAN SUPPORTS RORY'S ANTI-NIGGER POLICIES."

The other two men hold a banner sign stating, "KU KLUX KLAN VOTES FOR RORY."

Rory stops speaking and stares incredulously at the Klansmen.

The Klansmen parade all the aisles, ensuring all television cameras get lengthy close-up views.

Television commentators turn their attention to the activities of the Klansmen.

After three trips around the arena, the Klansmen proceed to the main doors and exit the Athletic Center. Reporters chase after the four men and shout questions.

The men in Ku Klux Klan robes move quickly toward the van. They shove reporters and cameramen out of the way. They lower their signs, toss the signs in the back of the van, and then take their seats. The van pulls away from the curb at a slow speed.

One hour later in his hotel room, the driver of the van that transported the fake Ku Klux Klansmen dials a memorized telephone number.

A voice on the other end answers, "Hello."

The van driver reports, "This is Jack. All went as planned."

"Excellent, Jack. You must affirm that you and your operatives wore their disguises at all times."

"Yes, we did."

"And you had a fake license plate on the vehicle you drove."

"Yes."

"Excellent! The remainder of your fee will be deposited in your account within the hour."

Four hours later, Diane Love answers the ringing phone in her Georgetown townhouse.

"Hello."

Edwin Kendley asks, "Did you see the evening network news?"

"Yes. Looks like we were successful."

"More than successful, Diane. ABC, NBC, and CBS together spent a total of thirty minutes on the Ku Klux Klan incident. Not once did any of the networks suggest that the incident might have been staged."

Diane states, "I estimate that Chandler will lose ten to fifteen points in the polls."

"Yes, he will. Thanks to you."

Diane responds, "By the way, I am nearly done with the plan for that governor's race in Nevada. I am just waiting for two of those lap dancers in Las Vegas to commit to their stories. I have an operative in Vegas ready to pay them when they provide written statements."

Chapter 13

After two months as an inpatient at Bethesda Naval Hospital, Rig has regained ninety percent of his strength and stamina. His doctor released him on the condition that Rig strictly follows a prescribed exercise program. Now, on this Friday afternoon, he stands outside the hospital's busy main door with a small suitcase at his feet and waits for Lieutenant Commander Sally Macfurson. All those who pass through the main door give him a quick glance and wonder about the purpose of the tall and rugged looking chief petty officer in Summer Khaki uniform. Rig, still somewhat gun shy, becomes cautious of anyone who passes too close to him.

Sally Macfurson stops her 1977, silver-colored Mercedes just yards from where Rig stands. She wears casual civilian clothes so as not to draw stares like she always does when she is in uniform. Today, her shining Mercedes draws the stares.

After placing his suitcase in the backseat and settling and buckling up in the front passenger seat, Sally presses the gas pedal and drives her car through the parking lot.

Fifteen minutes later, Sally drives onto the Washington Beltway, heading west toward Virginia. She advises Rig, "Brad directed that you live at one of ONI's safe houses. Actually, it's a small apartment house in Arlington. You have a small, one bedroom, third-floor apartment with outside entrance. All the apartments in the building have been equipped with anti-intruder doors and windows and grounded-wire-mesh grids in the walls and floors to prevent electronic surveillance of the interior from the outside."

"So I am going to be in D.C. for a while, then?"

"Yes. I have a number of operations that you will work."

"You're going to be my boss?"

"Yes, for your naval intelligence missions, but you will be officially assigned to the Test and Certification Division at Commander Naval Telecommunications Command."

Rig comments, "If I remember correctly, COMNAVTELCOM is located on Massachusetts Avenue North West near American

University."

"That's right," Sally confirms. "I talked with a lieutenant at COMNAVTELCOM who will be your immediate supervisor. He told me that your first project will be as Quality Assurance Testing Manager for the CUDIXS communications platform. Do you know what that is?"

"Yes—Common User Digital Information Exchange Subsystem. It's a shore based system with connectivity to the fleet via satellite."

"Oh, you're familiar with it, then."

"Well, I know what it does, but I have never seen one . . . read about it, though."

Sally asks, "Are you concerned that you will not be able to do your job?"

"Not at all," Rig responds confidently. "I will have it mastered in the first thirty days."

Sally chuckles and responds, "I have no doubt that you will."

"When must I report?"

"After you come back from leave. You're going to visit your parents and sisters in Southern California, right?"

"Yes, my flight is the day after tomorrow, Sunday."

During a few minutes of silence, Rig stares through the windshield and wonders if there is ever a time when the Beltway is not congested.

Sally breaks the silence and asks, "Did you make contact with Diane Love while you were in the hospital?"

"Yes, she came to see me at least once a week, and she called a few times. Twice, you and Diane missed each other by less than one hour during your visits with me."

"While you were away in Sardinia, we confirmed that she is controlled by the Soviet KGB."

Rig shakes his head and sighs deeply. He exhibits sadness and disappointment at the path that his high school girlfriend has taken. He says, "I had a feeling that she is up to something like that. She just asked too many questions about my work when I was here last winter. That is why a made a suspicious contact report with ONI before I departed for Sardinia."

Sally states contemptuously, "She works on the White House Staff. That makes her more dangerous to national security than most."

"So what will be my objective with Diane?"

"When you return from California, contact her and attempt to re-establish your romantic relationship. Then observe and report." Sally glances at Rig to see his response to her order.

Rig is grinning. He often compares the personalities and sexual talents of Diane Love and Sally Macfurson. The two women have similar physical features; both with flowing red hair and green eyes. Diane stands five inches taller than Sally. He has always considered Sally to be the better lover because of the emotional power she puts into their lovemaking. During the week he spent in D.C. last winter, he spent several long nights with Diane engaging in multiple sexual exercises, but Diane's sexual acts were mechanical and lacked emotion. Sally was in Hawaii during that week last winter.

Sally casts another glance at Rig, longer this time.

Rig is no longer grinning. He expresses thoughtfulness as he remembers times with the many women in his life. Nevertheless, he knows that Sally is the one he cherishes the most. He thinks back to when they first met in New London eleven years ago. He was attending submarine school. Sally had just earned her master's degree in European History and was working in the base library. They were immediately attracted to each other. At the time, Rig could not understand what the educated, wealthy, and attractive Sally Macfurson saw in him. Later that year during his first mission with naval intelligence, enemy agents abducted Sally. After naval intelligence agents slaughtered those enemy agents, Sally was freed. When Sally earned her PhD, she joined the navy reserve as an intelligence analyst. She became a university lecturer and a revered author of books on European History. During her required navy reserve drill time, she worked in the Office of Naval Intelligence. Her extraordinary knowledge of history and her ability to speak five languages made her an excellent intelligence analyst. Several years ago when she became frustrated with leftwing indoctrination in universities that required adapting her lectures to a leftwing slant, she fled academia and transferred from the naval reserves to regular active duty with the navy. Now, she directs intelligence operations projects and she is his boss.

He smiles appreciatively as he remembers that night nearly two years ago when Sally proposed to him. All he had to do was quit those dangerous missions and live a normal life and she and her wealth would take care of him. When he remembers all the women with whom he has had relationships, only the thought of Sally with other men causes a measure of jealousy to rise within him.

Sally interrupts Rig's thoughts. "We have you assigned to COMNAVTELCOM for a reason. You will become a member of the COMNAVTELCOM Inspector General Team. As a member of that team, you can travel the globe without anyone questioning why."

"Sounds interesting," Rig opines. "I am ready to get back into the game."

Thirty minutes later, Sally parks in front of a three story brick apartment building in an Arlington, Virginia residential neighborhood. They climb an outside stairway to a landing on the third floor. Sally retrieves a set of keys from her purse, then unlocks the front door to the apartment.

Rig follows Sally into the apartment. She walks a few feet to a wall mounted alarm system and enters a five numbered code.

Rig surveys the room, which is a combination kitchen, dining area, and living room. Five shipping boxes on the kitchen's tile floor catch his attention.

Sally informs, "Those boxes contain your personal items from your apartment in La Maddalena and from the chiefs' quarters on the USS *Randal*. Barbara Gaile took care of that several months ago."

Rig expresses appreciation; then he asks, "Is she still in La Maddalena?"

"No. Her ONI controller assigned her to a new mission. I do not know where . . . compartmented information."

Rig takes a quick tour of the small, furnished, one-bedroom apartment. Sally follows close behind. He opens the refrigerator and finds it fully stocked with his favorites. He also finds fully stocked kitchen cabinets with complete sets of glasses, dishes, silverware, and cooking pots and pans. The bottom shelf of one kitchen cabinet is stocked with his favorite scotch and brandy. He opens a narrow door next to the bathroom and finds the linen closet that contains sets of towels, sheets, and blankets. Then he enters the bathroom and finds a sink, toilet, and shower; but no bathtub. Fluffy, white-colored towels hang from a rail. In the single bedroom, he finds an inviting European queen sized bed made up with a navy-blue colored bedspread.

Sally points toward the closet and says, "There is a hidden closet on the other side of the back wall. I'll show you how to access it." Sally reaches into the closet and grasps a clothes hook and turns it counterclockwise. Then she pushes on the back wall and it opens like a door. The opening reveals a space equal in size to the normal bedroom closet. "To hide weapons, disguises, equipment, and anything else that could identify you as an undercover operative." She closes the secret door and turns the clothes hook to lock the secret door in place. Sally turns and faces Rig.

Rig comments, "Looks like I have all I will need. Who did all this?"

"I did."

"Thank you."

"You're welcome," Sally says while expressing a sensuous smile. She moves closer to him.

Rig takes her into his arms and bends at the waist to enable his lips to reach hers. Their kiss lingers; then their mouths open and their tongues dance. Rig's penis becomes hard. Sally can feel Rig's penis enlarge against her belly.

Sally pulls back from the kiss and places her face inches from his. She looks lovingly into his eyes and, says, "I have missed you

58

so much. We should not let years pass without seeing each other."

Rig responds, "You are the one person I long for when I am away."

"Well, Rigney Page, are you finally becoming a sensitive romantic?"

"When it comes to you, I could be."

Sally sighs deeply. Then, for a moment, she is distracted by the jagged one-inch scar near the center of his forehead. She says without much thought, "If I let you have your way with me, will you finally tell me how you got that scar."

While Rig begins to unbutton Sally's blouse, he says, "Sure I will tell you, if I am sexually satisfied."

Sally lowers her right hand to Rig's trouser zipper. She inserts her hand through the zipper and places her hand around his hard penis; she slowly pumps her hand. She promises, "I'll satisfy you, alright. I guarantee it."

Rig's heart beats faster and he pants as a result of Sally's light and sensuous pumping motion.

Sally whispers, "I can stay tonight and tomorrow night and take you to the airport on Sunday. I have an overnight bag in the trunk of my car."

With panting breath, Rig says, "I haven't had time to get any—"

"Already stocked in your nightstand."

They quickly remove their clothes; then slip under the covers of Rig's new bed. During fifteen minutes of foreplay, they rediscover the other's body. During the next six hours, they engage in their favorite sexual positions, including two sessions of extremely satisfying reciprocating oral sex, which has always been their favorite.

Chapter 14

Rig traveled on a military flight from Andrews Air Force Base, Maryland to Naval Air Station North Island, San Diego. He rented a car and drove to Seal Beach. When he arrived at the Page home in Seal Beach, he parked his rental car behind the garage—located across the backyard from the Page house.

Rig did not immediately enter his parents' home. He walked the property several times while remembering the carefree days of his youth.

The houses on Seal Way face the ocean. Seal Way is more like an alley than a street and runs behind the homes. House numbers are posted on the back of the houses or on the garage. The Page home on Seal Way faces the beach area of the Naval Weapons Station. A twenty-foot-wide cement walkway separates the front of the Page home from the chain link fence of the Naval Weapons Station. The town beach is a short walk southward on the cement walkway. The Page home is a small three-story structure. Including the attic family room, the house is only 1800 square feet, not counting the small one-car garage. The exterior is stucco. A small 150-square-foot courtyard outside the front door separates the house from the cement walkway that borders the beach. The interior of the house is a mismatch of furniture styles that Rig's parents purchased at auctions and yard sales. All the floors are polished hardwood. Area rugs of different colors cover most of the hardwood floors throughout the three-story house.

Rig's parents, James and Margaret Page, bought the house in 1949, when Seal Beach still had the remnants of a bad reputation. In the past, Seal Beach was called *Sin City*, and real estate prices were not outrageous at the time. Rig's parents borrowed the down payment from his father's brothers. During those early years, it took all of James's and Margaret's effort and income to make mortgage payments and maintain the house.

All family gatherings, celebrations, and all entertaining occur in the third floor family room. The family room is the most comfortable room in the house. The rug in the family room is thicker and softer than others in the house. Overstuffed chairs and sofas are strategically positioned throughout the room. The room has a wet bar, which is well stocked with scotch and bourbon. The Page's navy friends purchase the liquor at very low prices at the Naval Weapons Station beverage store. Two walls of the family room have custom installed bay windows, which provide a spectacular view of the Naval Weapons Station and the Pacific Ocean.

As a teenager, Rigney spent many hours at the bay windows with binoculars and scrutinized the ships and submarines that visited the Seal Beach Naval Weapons Station. Often, navy friends of his parents would stand at his side and describe the features of the vessels as Rig analyzed them through the binoculars. Rigney would ask those sailors many questions. Most of the time, those sailors answered; sometimes they would say, "Sorry, Rig, that's classified."

Rig's first night at home is a reunion with his parents and his two sisters—Kate and Teri. He easily quells their fears of his physical condition with acts of physical strength equal to what they knew he was capable during previous years. Eventually, the question about the scar on his forehead was asked by his sister Teri.

Before answering his sister's question about the scar, Rig remembers that hard punch he took five months ago to his forehead from that Red Brigade leader on the island of Maddalena. Ten stiches were required to close the wound. But that is not the story he tells his family. Instead, he provides the standard answer to the question about the scar. "I bumped into a low hanging pipe while running along the passageway on that ship."

During the following evening, Rig and his father are finally alone for a chat. "My business is expanding," James Page says in a happy tone. "After years of making a profit for others, I decided to strike out on my own, and I created Page Office Supply. You remember when you were home four years ago that I had established a home office in the third floor family room?"

"Yes, I remember. The family room was stocked with filing

cabinets and wholesale office supply catalogs."

"For two years I worked out of that home office and increased my customer base. Then the office supply orders were flooding in and I had to stock my own supply, so I could deliver rapidly. I took out a second and third mortgage on the house, rented a warehouse in Long Beach, and bought inventory. I now work out of a small office inside the warehouse.

"I am working eighteen-hour days. I'm selling directly out of that warehouse now. I have fifteen employees. And I bought two delivery vans. Six months ago, I was so financially stretched that I thought the whole business would collapse. Then potential customers discovered that my warehouse style selling provided higher quality office furniture at less cost than other suppliers. Now, office furniture orders and data-workstation orders are flooding in.

"After a lifetime of picking shit with the chickens, I am making profits. I took the risk, and now I am being rewarded. I can now make double mortgage payments on the house and buy your mother decent clothes. I am still working eighteen-hour days, seven days a week, and it is worth it. I bought that cabin cruiser I always wanted, and we are finally saving money for retirement."

"That's great, Dad. When can we go out on the cabin cruiser?"

"I am very busy for the rest of the week, but we can go out on Saturday."

Rig offers, "Is there anything I can do to lighten your load?"

"Well, now that you have offered, I must deliver and assemble some office furniture tomorrow morning. Do you want to give me a hand? Should take a few hours—are you up to it?"

"Sure. I can help. My body has healed."

Chapter 15

The next morning, Rig is up early. While waiting for his father, he sips coffee and watches one of the network morning T.V. shows. A report on the explosion of those three Gulf of Mexico offshore oilrigs last summer captures Rig's interest. The report advises that sabotage is known as the cause of the explosions in which 28 oilrig workers were killed. Automatic systems had shut oil pipe flow valves located on the ocean floor, but not before massive oil slicks formed and attacked the eco systems of the Gulf. Three separate American Oil companies are involved. The cleanup costs have already exceeded one-billion dollars. The lawsuits initiated by Gulf States and by business owners now total more than three-billion dollars. The news report includes video of members of Congress calling for the nationalization of America's oil companies. They claim that *"those oil companies place priority on profits and not lives, not safety, and not security of the American public."* The most outspoken supporters of nationalization are Representative Billy Thayer and Senator Clay Porter, both Democrats, who have submitted nationalization legislation in their respective houses of Congress. Each bill has more than thirty cosponsors, all Democrats. The outcry for nationalization also comes from several governors and several state legislatures, all Democrats. Republican leaders in Congress and most Democrat leaders in Congress oppose the call for nationalization. The news report ends by stating those responsible for the disaster have not yet been identified.

Rig and James Page depart the Page house at 8:30 AM. As James Page drives, they talk about hopes for the future.

When they pass a public apartment housing project, Rigney notices dozens of teenagers and a few young adults of mixed African-American, Caucasian, and Hispanic races milling around the common areas. He glances at his watch and notes the time— 8:47 AM. He wonders why on a Tuesday morning those teenagers are not in school and why those adults are not at work. He comments to his father, "I remember when the Crenshaw Housing Project was built ten years ago. It looked like a complex of modern efficiency. Now, it looks like a slum."

James Page comments, "That's the nature of welfare. Maintenance of those buildings is limited by government budgets. Only the most severe damage is repaired. Cosmetic appeal is left to the discretion of the residents."

"So they don't work, and they don't go to school?"

"Most of them are unskilled workers . . . quit high school."

"Is there no solution to their poverty?"

"Well, LBJ's Great Society was supposed to eliminate poverty; but as you can see more than ten years later, poverty still exists. There are dozens of those projects in Los Angeles County and Orange County."

Rigney shakes his head at what appears to be a problem with no solution. He thinks aloud, "I wonder what will happen to all those young people who live in those projects."

James Page responds, "Few will finish high school and learn a trade, and fewer will go to college. Those who learn a trade or earn a college degree will become responsible and contributing citizens. The rest will survive at the bottom of America's economic ladder and give birth to future project dwellers."

"I don't understand, Dad. If some can learn trades or earn college degrees, why can't all of them do it? Or, go into the military or government service, which does not require college degrees."

"Beats me, Son. Some people just have no pride, no ambition, and no dignity."

Rig appears thoughtful for a few moments; then he asks, "Dad, mom once told me that we lived in government housing when I was a baby. What did she mean by that?"

"When I came home from Europe in 1946, your mother and I got married, like so many vets did. There was not enough housing for the millions of new families. So the government refurbished old army barracks into housing units and charged low rent. We lived in that project for about a year. You were born while we lived there. Then your mother went to work. My sales increased, and we were making enough money to move into a decent apartment in Seal Beach. Shortly after that, we were doing well enough to buy our house on Seal Way."

After a few moments of thought, Rig asks, "You said you have fifteen employees. Are any of them minorities?"

"Yes. I have a Negro woman who does the paperwork and takes all the phone orders. Some of the warehouse workers are Negroes and Mexicans. One of the delivery men is a Jap."

"Dad, you need to read up on the current, culturally correct names for the races."

"I mean no disrespect, Son. That's what they've been called all my life. You're right though. I need to use the correct racial names."

Rig asks, "You hire foreigners—Mexicans and Japanese?"

"They are American citizens or have green cards."

"No problems, then?" Rig asks with a curious tone.

James Page responds, "Last year I fired one of those Negro guys in the warehouse for stealing my property and selling it out of the trunk of his car. Several days after I fired him, two gentlemen from the local NAACP showed up and demanded that I prove the Negro I fired was stealing. I told them to get out of my warehouse. They said that unless I could prove the man was stealing, they would organize and fund a boycott against my company, and they would organize and fund a unionization strike by my workers."

"What did you do?"

"I told them if they did not leave my property, I would call the police and have them arrested for trespassing. They left."

"Anything happen after that?"

"Several days later, I got a call from a union organizer who advised me that he was going to organize my workers. I told him to organize away. I also told him that federal and state laws protect my small business from unionization . . . heard nothing after that."

Rig nods and conveys understanding. He asks, "How do you know for sure that employee was stealing and selling out of the trunk of his car?"

"I hired a private detective. That detective caught him in the act of selling out of the trunk of his car."

"Did you explain that to the NAACP?"

"No. I have no obligation to explain my actions to anyone."

Rig expresses thoughtfulness for a few moments; then he asks, "Dad, do you remember Diane Love?"

"Sure, Son, she was that rich babe you dated in high school."

"She lives in D.C. now. She visited me while I was in the hospital. We're getting back together. She works on President Carter's White House staff."

"What! When did she become a Democrat? I remember her opinions were always conservative. I remember her saying she wanted to become a stockbroker."

"She became a liberal lefty in college. She claims that poor people are poor because rich people are greedy, except for her and her rich educated elite liberal friends."

James Page responds, "She suffers under a major misconception, ya know."

"Yes, Dad, I know. She believes that the world should be governed by the educated elite of the liberal mind. She says that those who are not of her educated and enlighten mind are not capable of governing themselves fairly and equally."

"Humph!" James Page utters. "She's not a believer of liberty and freedom, huh?"

"No, she's not. She believes in central government control of all commerce and of all cultural and social development."

"Sounds like she's a communist."

"I thought the same at first. But years ago when I listened to her and her friends discuss solutions to the world's problems, they sounded more like fascists than communists. They said that the American government needs a Department of Cultural Behavior, a Department of Commerce Equality, and a Department of Education. They believe in governmental central planning of our lives from cradle to grave in order to establish equality for all. They want

66

government to control what individuals buy, what individuals eat, and how much resources individuals consume."

Rig pauses for a moment while forming his thoughts; then he comments, "I would call Diane's philosophy a mixture of totalitarianism and communism."

"Nothing unusual about that, Son. Look at China, Soviet Union, and Cuba—all communist economies with totalitarian governments."

Rig nods agreement.

Chapter 16

At the Page Office Supply warehouse, James and Rig spend twenty minutes loading furniture components into a panel van with the words PAGE OFFICE SUPPLY displayed on both sides.

The drive to the delivery location takes fifteen minutes. James Page drives his panel van through the gate of the Harris Shipping Company complex. A dozen tractor-trailers are backed against loading docks. One minute later, they enter a small parking lot with fifty parking spaces. A recently completed, unoccupied single-story building stands on one side of the parking lot, and a building under construction stands on the other side of the parking lot. James Page brings his panel van to a stop in front of the completed building.

James explains, "This is the new administrative building for Harris Shipping. They bought all their new office furniture and data equipment from me. I've been here the last few days assembling desks, bookcases, and filing cabinets."

"By yourself?" Rig inquires.

"No. My warehouse employees double as installers. But they are on a higher priority installation today."

James and Rig exit the panel van; then proceed to the van's rear door. Rig notices five construction workers across the parking lot near the building under construction. They wear work clothes, hardhats, and tool belts; they cast menacing stares at Rig and his father. Rig glances around the parking lot and notes several trucks with *Dover Construction* signs painted on the cab doors.

"Dad, what's with the mean stares from those men?"

James Page glances over his shoulder; then he advises, "Union labor . . . they harassed me the first day for not using union labor."

"What did you say to them?"

"I told them to fuck off and that I will conduct my business as I want."

"How did they respond to that?"

"They walked off."

Thirty minutes later, James and Rig have completed the

unloading of the van. They begin to assemble an executive desk.

Five minutes later, three men who wear denim coveralls with *Dover Construction* logos, hardhats, and tool belts enter the office space where James and Rig work. All three men appear to be in their late twenties—Rig's age. All three have long greasy hair to their shoulders and bushy beards. Each stands taller than Rig and each outweigh Rig by twenty pounds. Each has solid muscle tone. Each worker has their palm resting on a hammer or short crowbar that hangs from their tool belts. They appear identical, except for the color of their hair—one black hair, one brown hair, and one blond hair.

James and Rig furtively watch and evaluate the manner of the three construction workers. James and Rig know these three construction workers are ready to start trouble.

The worker with black hair and beard stares at Rig and questions in a menacing tone, "What union da ya belong ta?"

Rig casts a blank stare into the man's eyes and does not answer.

After a few moments, the black-haired worker says in a raised and sarcastic tone while pointing his finger in Rig's face, "Hey, pal! I asked ya a question!"

Rig hopes that answering the question will avoid violence. "I am in the navy. No unions in the navy."

All three workers express bewilderment, wondering why a sailor is working on the construction site.

"Why ya here, squid?!" demands the blond-haired, bearded worker.

Rig focuses on the blond-haired worker. The use of the word "squid" is most often used by soldiers and marines when referring to sailors.

"Army Rangers—three years," the blond-haired worker advises. He pulls his hammer halfway out of its loop on the tool belt, making it obvious that he plans on using the hammer to persuade Rig to answer the question.

Rig nods toward James Page and says, "I'm helping my father assemble this furniture."

Rig's answer appears to anger the three workers.

The black-haired worker turns his attention to James Page and warns, "I tol' ya da utter day dat dis a union site . . . that scabs enter dis site at der own risk."

"Are you threatening me?" James Page asks fearlessly.

The blond-haired, bearded, ex-army ranger steps forward and says, "No, Mr. Page, but we cannot control what other union members might do. You must leave and not comeback unless you hire union labor to do this job."

"Fuck you union punks!" James Page blurts angrily. "It's my business, and I will conduct my business as I want!"

All three union thugs flinch and express surprise at James Page's obvious lack of fear and willingness to fight. The union punks then reflect anger and take one step toward James Page. "You are on dangerous ground!" the blond-haired ex-army ranger says in a raised voice and menacing manner.

Rig believes there will be a fight. He considers his father's ability. James Page is six-feet and four-inches tall with powerful broad shoulders and rock solid muscled arms but has a soft, protruding belly. James Page was a vicious street fighter in his youth and taught hand-to-hand combat in the army during World War II. James Page is now fifty-three years old, and Rig worries about his father's ability to fight these punks. Rig is confident in his own fighting ability but knows his dad must occupy one of the punks for Rig to beat the other two.

The blond-haired ex-army ranger walks toward Rig; then stops three feet away. He stares at the desk that Rig had just assembled and decides to drop his hammer on the desktop. He calculates that this action will cost James Page money.

Rig watches the blond-haired ex-army ranger union thug draw his hammer. Rig does not know the union thug's intentions, so he assumes the thug will attack. As the thug raises the hammer over the desktop, Rigney springs forward and with blurring speed rips the hammer from the thug's hand.

The claw of the hammer tears through the thug's palm, cutting a deep gash. The violent and overwhelming force of the hammer being snatched from his hand causes the tough, hardened ex-army ranger to step back with alarm and fear. He stares at the blood flowing from his hand. He had not considered that the squid was a physical threat.

The other two workers move toward James Page with the intention of punching him. When they get within arm's length of James, James smashes his right fist into the face of the black-haired thug, breaking the man's nose and knocking him backwards.

The black-haired worker falls on his back, moaning in pain as blood floods from his nose and mouth.

James turns to fight the second worker—the one with brown hair and beard, but the worker backs off.

All three workers back toward the door. The ex-army ranger wraps a red handkerchief around his bleeding hand. The black-haired worker continues to moan and holds a handkerchief to his bloody nose.

Rig points the business end of the hammer toward the three thugs and threatens in an angry tone, "If any harm comes to my father, my family, or my father's business; I will assume you three caused it, and I will come after you! I will not face you! I will come at you in the dark, from behind, fully armed! When I am done with you, you will regret the day you walked in here!"

The three workers hurry through the doorway.

James Page smiles at his son and says, "Rig, I have never seen such speed and power as in the way you disarmed that punk. If that was an example of your ability, I can easily see how you overpowered those terrorists in Scotland."

Rig stares angrily at the doorway. His entire body is flexed with muscles bulging. His face is flushed, and he breathes rapidly—his image being of one who stands defiant before the gates of hell and has no fear to fight the devil. Then in an angry, determined tone he proclaims, "I hate fuckin' bullies! Thinking they can violently force their will on others! I'll fuckin' kill them before I allow them to harm my family!"

James queries, "If something happens to our family or my business, will you fulfill your threat to kill them?"

"Yes! But they will never get the chance to harm you!" He continues to cast a menacing stare at the door.

James has no doubt that Rig will fulfill the threat.

After Rig calms, he says, "They will try to accuse us of assault," Rig announces confidently.

James shakes his head and states, "Those accusations will not stand." He turns his eyes toward the corner of the room and points his finger in the same direction.

Rig focuses on the direction that his father points. Then Rig smiles as he sees the security camera mounted in the corner near the ceiling.

"One of the first systems installed. Those assholes probably don't know it."

Rig nods and expresses agreement.

"Back to work," James orders casually.

Rig comments, "Dad, you're acting as if nothing significant just happened. They could come back with a more men. Aren't you alarmed by what just happened?" He curses himself for not carrying his gun today. From this day forward, he will be armed at all times.

James Page chuckles; then informs, "Son, I have been battling union thugs all my working life. They have no concept of the risk and reward of owning your own business. They only understand the power of numbers. They believe wages should be based on the wants of workers and not the value of their work. They have no understanding of the economic force that drives this nation. Their indoctrinated minds have them believing they are victims of rich, undeserving capitalists."

Rig responds, "But it is capitalists that employ them—give them jobs. Don't they understand that?"

James answers, "Their indoctrinated minds are too small to connect the dots."

"But not all union workers are like them, right?"

"No, but the big problem is that federal and state elected

politicians are making laws that force companies to unionize. Because of the small size of my company, the laws do not apply to me and I can hire who I want. In some companies, people are forced to join unions if they want a job, which is true for most everyone in the trades. Most union members are ordinary people leading normal lives—like your Uncle Brad and cousin Bob. When union toughs do show up, they are following some union boss's orders."

Rig asks, "Why are elected politicians making laws to force unionization?"

"To get union votes," James answers.

"Oh."

James and Rig go back to work.

Forty minutes later, a medium height, slight of build, balding gentleman in coat and tie enters the office where James and Rig assemble furniture.

James Page says to the gentleman, "Hey, Cal, what's up."

Cal responds, "Jim, we cannot risk union trouble. Would you please hire union workers to install and assemble these offices?"

James asks, "Has the union threatened to strike against your company?"

"No, that would do them no good because they are employees of the Dover Construction company that we hired to construct these two buildings. The union leaders know if they strike, we will never again enter into a contract with Dover Construction and that we might hire an out-of-town non-union construction company. More likely they will destroy property or beat up on people, like they have before. Union vandalism is a cost of doing business. We even have an accounting code for it."

James Page expresses understanding and nods; he informs, "My price quotes to you for this job did not consider union wages, benefits, and working hours. If it had, my price would have been thirty percent higher. Then you would not have accepted my bid, right? If I hire union workers, I lose money on this job."

Cal stands in thought.

"Cal, I want to introduce my son. Rig, this is Cal Seward. He is the purchasing agent for Harris Shipping."

Rig and Cal shake hands. Cal comments, "Rig, your father is always boasting about you. He showed me the newspaper articles about you. He is a proud father."

"And I am a proud son," Rig responds while beaming an appreciative smile toward his father.

Cal turns to James and offers, "How about if you just deliver everything to the front of this building? I will hire the workers to offload your vans, uncrate everything, and assemble it all."

"Okay with me," James Page responds. I have contract amendment forms in the truck. I'll get one."

Twenty minutes later, Rig and James Page are on the highway and driving toward Seal Beach.

Rig is curious and he asks, "What did you and Cal amend in the contract?"

"That Page Office Supply would not offload delivery vehicles, not assemble furniture, not assemble data workstations, and not make the data workstations operational."

"Will problems with the unions cause Harris Shipping to never again buy your stuff?"

"Oh, they will still buy from me because of my discount prices. Cal asked that future bids include union labor costs and that I use union labor in the future."

"Did you agree to that?"

"Sure, if they want to be pussies about union threats, then they must pay the price. I will price the products separate from the labor, so that they understand the high cost of union labor."

Rig concludes aloud, "Sounds like it all worked out okay, then."

"Uh, not yet. Harris Shipping will not find any union workers who know how to setup and make operational those data workstation and data disk equipment."

"How will that problem be resolved?"

"They will call me and ask me to do it."

"Has that happened in the past?"

"Yes, but not all because of union hassles. Some companies attempt to save costs by thinking they can assemble and make that data equipment operational themselves. When they discover they do not have the knowledge or skills, they give me a call."

Rig asks, "You know how to setup and operate computer equipment?"

"No. I hire a college student who studies computers at U.S.C."

Rig expresses thoughtfulness; then asks, "What stops your customers from directly hiring the college student?"

"Nothing."

After several minutes of silence, James comments, "You exposed your strength and ability to that ex-army punk. You made him fear you, and that makes him even more dangerous. He won't announce himself the next time he comes after you."

Rig comments, "I am more concerned about organized and targeted retaliation from their union on you and mom."

"Me too, Rig. I will need to deal with them eventually, just like I have in the past."

During the next few days, Rig tails each of the three union thugs. He discovers their places of residence. He steals their mail, allowing him to become knowledgeable of their names and some information on their lifestyles. He tails them to the local union hall, and he obtains the name of the local union boss. He tails the local union boss and obtains all the same information on him.

One night Rig follows Max Robertson—the blond-haired ex-army ranger. Rig notices the thick white gauze bandage on Robertson's right hand. After dark, Robertson departs his apartment, driving his red-colored crew-cab pickup truck. He picks up Horace Lombardi—the black-haired and bearded worker who James Page punched in the nose. Lombardi has a large bandage over his nose. Robertson then picks up Allen Villanueva—the brown-haired and bearded construction worker.

Robertson's next stop is James Page's warehouse. At the warehouse, all three construction workers exit the truck and walk around the warehouse several times, testing door and window locks. Then Robertson drives to the Page residence in Seal Beach. Robertson parks behind the Pages' garage for more than thirty minutes.

Rig becomes alarmed and decides he needs to disable these evil men—physically and permanently.

Chapter 17

Rig sits in the small office in his father's warehouse. He waits for James Page to arrive so they can go to lunch. While waiting, he thumbs through the installation and operating manuals of the data terminals, workstations, and data disk drives that his father sells.

Several minutes later, James enters the office. He asks the young black woman named Rose who tends to the office, "Any messages?"

Rose hands James a stack of messages. He pulls one from the stack, studies it for a moment, then he goes to his desk, picks up the phone and dials a number.

James says into the phone, "Hi, Cal, returning your call." James listens for several minutes. "That training is done by CDC in San Francisco, takes five days, and costs fifteen-hundred dollars." James listens. "Hold on, let me check." James pulls a pamphlet from a desk drawer. He scans the pamphlet. Then he says into the phone, "Next training not scheduled until next month. . . . uh, huh . . . yes . . . okay I'll have them there tomorrow morning." James hangs up the phone, glances at Rig, and says, "Ready for lunch?"

After James and Rig have seated themselves in the closest Bob's Big Boy restaurant, James tells Rig, "That was Cal Seward that I called just before we left the warehouse. He said the union workers put all the data equipment in place, but do not know how to connect it all and make it all operational. He said the union demanded to be trained in setup and operation as the union contract requires. So Cal asked me about the training. I told him my contract with CDC does not allow me to conduct training. Anyway, to make a long story short, I promised to have my computer experts there tomorrow morning."

"What about the training requirement in the union contract?"

"That union contract is between Dover Construction and its employees, doesn't obligate Harris Shipping, and in no way obligates Page Office Supply." James pauses, then he says, "The cost of union labor is raising prices everywhere. A union carpenter's hourly wage is two times more than competitive market hourly wage. Don't know if you noticed, but a lot of companies are moving their manufacturing plants to Mexico where wages are much lower. It's getting to the point where America's manufacturers cannot compete on the world markets because American union labor costs are too high."

Rig chuckles as he comments, "This is one of those times I appreciate the simplicity of military structure. Do as you're told and don't complain about it and the military machine continues to move."

"Good point, Son, but business is more complicated. Contracts control everything. For example, I agreed to a deadline of the end of the week to have all the equipment operational. I need another computer expert, and they are difficult to find for these UNIX based systems."

"Doesn't Harris Shipping have a system administrator for their computer systems?"

"Yes, but he works in Harris's Chicago office. When something needs done on the local system here, he connects over the telephone lines through something called a MODEM. Any physical work like installing equipment must be done by people in the local office."

"I could help," Rig offers.

"You know about these UNIX systems?"

"A little, we have some UNIX based systems in navy communications. I was reading those manuals in your office for that equipment; they provide all the connectivity instructions and all the UNIX commands for making the terminals and data disk operational." Rig evaluates the situation for a moment; then he asks, "Have all the signal cables been run from the mainframe to the data terminal locations?"

"Yes."

"I could do it by myself within eight hours."

"Are you sure, Rig? My college student computer expert usually takes three days to do the work for a job like this."

"Dad, that college kid is probably milking the job to earn max payment. He is taking advantage of his rare knowledge and skills."

Rigney pauses; then advises, "If I run into a computer problem, I'll call Harris's expert in Chicago."

"Cal says he will have guards posted inside the door, but I worry about the safety of my computer expert. I think I will keep him away from this job. I know unions. They will continue with their violence and property destruction until they get their way. What will you do if they come after you?"

"I'll kill them," Rigney responds without emotion.

James Page flinches and sits back. He expresses astonished apprehension.

"Dad, what would you expect me to do—allow them to beat the crap out of me and maybe kill me in the process?"

"I know you're tough, Son, but three or more of those guys . . . they're not pussies."

"Don't worry, Dad, I have my ways." Rigney thinks about the snub-nose Beretta automatic that he carries in his inside jacket pocket. "Make arrangements for Harris Shipping to open those doors at 6:30 tomorrow morning. I'll arrive before the union workers get there. I'll drive my rental car."

James nods; then he states, "I'll take care of it."

The waitress delivers their cheeseburgers and coffee.

Chapter 18

Rig telephones the Harris Shipping UNIX system administrator at the Harris Shipping corporate headquarters in Chicago. He tells the administrator that all terminals and disk storage units are powered up and connected to the local mainframe. The system administrator asks Rig to stay on the phone.

Several minutes later, the system administrator comes back on the phone and says, "I polled all workstation terminals and all disk drives. All responded. All looks good. Who'd you say you are again?"

Rig responds, "My name is Rig. I am the installer hired by Page Office Supply."

"Well, Rig, you are certainly more competent than those union clowns that called me last week. Do we have your resume on file? We are expanding our computer network to all our locations worldwide. We could use someone like you."

"Thanks for the offer," Rig responds sincerely, "But I am happy with what I am doing now."

"Okay, Rig, but if you ever change your mind, please contact me."

"Will do," Rig responds.

"Okay, thanks again." The system administrator hangs up.

As Rig hangs up, he looks out the window and notices the dark of night. He glances at his watch—7:15 PM. He retrieves his jacket; then walks toward the front door.

As he approaches the door, the two armed and uniformed security guards glance at their watches.

"I'm done," Rig advises.

One of the guards turns to unlock the door.

Rig asks the other guard, "Anyone try to get in here today?"

"Yeah, four construction workers wanted to come in about two hours ago. Said they had to finish a job. Following our orders, we would not let them in."

Rig stands in thought for a moment. Then he says, "I need to go to the head. Give me a few minutes, okay?"

"Okay," says the guard with the keys as he relocks the door.

After entering the men's room, Rig unzips the inside pocket of his jacket. He pulls out the snub-nose Beretta automatic and a four-inch-long suppressor. He screws on the suppressor; then he slips the weapon back into his inside pocket.

Back at the front door, Rig asks the guards, "Would you two escort me to my car?"

"Of course," one of the guards replies.

As they step outside, Rigney observes Max Robertson's red crew-cab pickup truck in the parking lot. Although the parking lot is dark, Rig sees the outline of men wearing hardhats sitting in the cab. Burning ends of cigarettes randomly flare.

Rigney says to the lead guard, "Please record the license number and description of that truck."

"Will do," the lead guard says. He pulls a pen and small notepad from his breast pocket.

Rigney drives out the main gate of Harris Shipping, turns right, and drives in the direction of Seal Beach. Max Robertson's pickup truck follows.

Thirty minutes later, Rig approaches a stop sign at a dark intersection in a Seal Beach residential area. He pulls the Beretta from his inside jacket pocket and lays it on the seat beside him.

Rigney brakes to a stop at the stop sign.

Max Robertson's pickup truck speeds up, passes Rig, then comes to a screeching stop in front of Rig's car, blocking his forward path. Rig considers speeding in reverse to get away; then he dismisses that idea because he knows they will follow. He concludes that he must prevent them from following.

Three of the four union thugs exit the pickup. They wear work clothes, hardhats, and safety glasses. Each carries a crowbar or baseball bat. Max Robertson remains in the vehicle in the driver's seat.

Rig grabs his suppressor equipped Beretta, opens the door as wide as it will go and steps out of his car. He uses the door as a shield between him and the union thugs. He raises the Beretta and points it at the chest of the lead thug. Rigney recognizes the lead thug as one he investigated, Horace Lombardi; the grammar-impaired union punk who James Page punched in the nose in that Harris Shipping building.

At the sight of the gun, each thug freezes his movement.

In a growling, threatening tone, Rig orders "Back in the truck or I shoot you where you stand!"

All three thugs back toward the truck.

Rig fires a round into the passenger-side rear tire.

The union toughs turn and run for the truck.

Rig fires a round into the front tire.

As the thugs enter the pickup, Rig walks to the front of the pickup and fires two rounds into the radiator.

As Rig steps backward toward his car, he keeps the weapon aimed at Horace Lombardi's head, which is visible through the open passenger-side window. Horace focuses his eyes on Rigney's eyes and warns, "Yo a dead scab!"

Rigney stops his backward movement. He cocks the hammer and takes careful aim at the Horace's head.

Horace closes his eyes and tightens his body in preparation of being shot in the head. After several moments, the bullet does not come. Horace opens his eyes in time to see Rig driving off.

After arriving at his parents' home on Seal Way, Rig worries about the smell of burnt gunpowder in the car and on his clothes. He spreads deodorizer powder over the driver's seat and driver side floor. Then he brushes the powder into the fabric.

Inside the house, he strips down and places his clothes and sneakers into the washer. After starting the washer, he takes a shower.

Chapter 19

The next morning, Rig sits at the kitchen table. He yawns; then he takes a sip of coffee and glances at the headlines of the local newspaper. He forewent his normal run around Seal Beach this morning. He is too tired because he had sat in the living room all night with his weapon close—protecting his parents and their home should those thugs show up. The night passed without incident and several times he nodded off to sleep.

He glances at his watch—9:30 AM. Both his parents departed for work more than an hour ago. He considers changing his clothes because they are severely wrinkled from a night spent in a living room chair. He goes to his suitcase and selects Levi's and a lightweight navy-blue sweatshirt with the words *U.S. Navy La Maddalena* across the chest.

The front doorbell rings.

Before opening the door, Rigney looks through the window at the side of door. He opens the door and faces two men of his height but heavier through the midsection. Both men are dressed in the khaki uniform of the Orange County Sheriff's Department. Their large .357 magnum revolvers are strapped into their black-leather holsters. The deputy standing closest to the door wears officer rank bars on his collar. The other deputy has sergeant stripes on his sleeve.

Rig opens the door and looks into the face of the deputy with officer bars.

The deputy with the officer bars asks, "Are you the son of James Page—the same James Page that owns Page Office Supply?"

"Yes," Rig answers.

"Mr. Page, I am Lieutenant Mitchell from the Orange County Sheriff's Department and this is Deputy Sergeant Davis. May we come in?"

"Yes, come in."

As the deputies enter, Rig offers, "Shall we sit in the living room?"

The deputies nod.

Rig sits in his favorite overstuffed chair. The deputies sit on the couch.

Lieutenant Mitchell casts a glance at Sergeant Davis.

Davis asks, "For the record, Mr. Page, what is your full name?"

"Rigney Michael Page."

Lieutenant Mitchell states, "We are investigating a shooting incident that happened last evening here in Seal Beach."

Rigney responds, "I didn't hear or see any shootings."

Sergeant Davis records Rig's words on a pad of paper.

Mitchell asks, "Where were you last evening at 8:00 PM?"

"I was just arriving here."

"From where?"

"I did a job for my father?"

"Where?"

"At Harris Shipping in Long Beach."

"What time did you depart Harris Shipping?"

"Around 7:15."

"Do you work full-time for your father?"

"No. I'm a chief petty officer in the navy. I am on leave from my command in Washington D.C."

Lieutenant Mitchell stares at Rig for a few moments; then he asks, "Mr. Page, do you own a handgun?"

"No." Rig tells the truth because the Beretta automatic currently hidden under a floorboard in his upstairs bedroom belongs to the U.S. Government.

Mitchell states, "Mr. Page, four citizens have sworn complaints against you for assaulting them with a deadly weapon last night at approximately 8:00 PM at the intersection of Central Avenue and Eleventh Street."

Rig shakes his head and states, "Wasn't me."

The sound of Sergeant Davis writing furiously on the notepad causes Rig to stare at him.

Lieutenant Mitchell asks, "Do you know anyone who owns a red 1976 crew-cab pickup?"

"I don't know the name—only know that some union thugs in a red pickup truck followed me home from Harris Shipping last night. Those same thugs attacked me and my father last week at Harris Shipping. And someone who drives a red crew-cab pickup has been stalking my father's warehouse and has been watching this house."

For a few moments, Mitchell casts a curious stare at Rig; then he asks, "Can you prove any of that?"

"Yes. Harris Shipping will have security tapes of the attack in the Harris office building. My father has warehouse security tapes of those thugs arriving in a crew-cab pickup truck and walking the perimeter of the Page Office Supply warehouse several times—late at night. And I have personally observed those thugs watching this house at night. And the security guards at Harris will confirm the same pickup truck followed me out of the Harris Parking lot last night around 7:15."

Mitchell expresses thoughtfulness.

Rig suggests, "Maybe you should check and see if any of those in the pickup last night owns a gun."

Mitchell express doubt as he says, "You're saying they shot up their own vehicle to frame you?"

"They've got something against me. They have been stalking me and my father since that night in the Harris office building."

"What happened in the Harris office building?"

"Some union construction workers entered the building where my father and I were assembling furniture. They called us scabs. Then they attacked us."

"What happened?" Mitchell's tone turns curious.

"My father and I stopped them."

"Stopped them? How?"

"My father and I defended ourselves. That surprised them, and they backed out of the building. The security video will reveal all that happened."

Lieutenant Mitchell nods. Then he says, "What were the exact dates and times that were recorded by security cameras? So that I can get subpoenas for them."

Rigney provides the information and Sergeant Davis records it.

"Thank you for your cooperation, Mr. Page. We will probably have more questions after we watch the security tapes."

Lieutenant Mitchell was the first out the door.

Deputy Sergeant Davis delays his exit by a few seconds. He turns to Rig and says, "Chief, what's your rating?"

"Radioman."

"I was a yeoman for three years on the USS *America*. I really miss the navy sometimes."

Rig nods and expresses understanding.

Davis crosses the doorway and pulls the door shut behind him.

When Mitchell and Davis are clear of the Page property, Mitchell asks Davis, "Did you write down Rigney Page's physical description?"

"Yes."

"Did you include short, reddish-brown hair and that distinctive scar in the center of his forehead?"

"Yes."

Chapter 20

The Construction and Laborer Workers' Union of America—CLWUA—Southern California District Sergeant-at-Arms, Melvin Spartan, sits at his office desk in the district headquarters located in an industrial area of Long Beach.

Ben Jolly, shop steward for Dover Construction, explains the incidents between the Pages and employees of Dover Construction who are also union bullies for the CLWUA.

"Max Robertson and three of his coworkers attacked those scabs twice but were beaten each time. The first time was on the Harris Shipping worksite. They tried to scare James Page and his son off the worksite. The Pages fought back, and our workers backed off. The second time was last night in Seal Beach about a block from the Page home. Robertson and his friends were going to smash up the son's car and rough him up, but the son pulled a gun and shot the tires and radiator of Max Robertson's pickup. After the son departed, Max's truck was disabled and blocking the intersection. Eventually the police showed up to clear the intersection. Our workers had no choice but to claim they were innocent victims of a rightwing, anti-union lunatic."

The CLWUA Sergeant-at-Arms shakes his head with disbelief and asks, "Do any of our workers live in Seal Beach."

"No."

"Then how did Max and the boys explain why they and Mr. Page crossed paths at an intersection close to Page's home when both Dover Construction and Harris Shipping are located more than seven miles away in Long Beach?"

The Dover Construction shop steward flinches and blinks his eyes; then he answers, "Uh, well, I don't know. We didn't talk about it. The cops must have asked that question, though. In my haste to inform you, I did not get all the details on their statements to the police."

The CLWUA Sergeant-at-Arms shakes his head and displays frustrated disapproval. "As shop steward, you need more control over your workers."

Ben Jolly responds, "They never said anything to me. They were on their own. The damage is done. What can we do now?"

Melvin Spartan asks, "Does anyone else know about the shooting last night? I mean anyone other than the police."

Ben's face flushes red. He hands a copy of the morning paper to the Sergeant-at-Arms. Ben says, "Bottom right-hand side of the first page."

Spartan's eyes widen and he expresses concern as he reads the news article:

SHOOTING IN SEAL BEACH NEIGHBORHOOD.
By Weston Pyth, City Desk
At 8:30 last evening, Orange County sheriff deputies were called to a Seal Beach neighborhood to investigate a large pickup truck blocking an intersection. Statements from the four occupants of the pickup truck—four constructions workers on their way to a bar for after work drinks—reported that they were shot at by a deranged rightwing, anti-union extremist with whom they had a previous argument over union labor rights.

The pickup truck was disabled under the hail of bullets. Sheriff's deputies recovered high caliber shell casings at the scene. The shooter's weapon was equipped with a silencer, leaving no doubt as to the rightwing extremist's intentions.

This reporter concludes that the physical evidence collected so far substantiates the account of the incident as told by union workers. The Sheriff's department is withholding the names of all four victims and the name of the perpetrator until completion of the investigation.

This reporter will aggressively investigate this incident of attempted murder and will reveal the identity of the deranged rightwing extremist who targets members of worker unions.

Spartan lays down the newspaper. He shakes his head and says in a questioning tone, "Deranged rightwing, union-hating extremist?" He shakes his head; then comments, "Those must be the words of the reporter. I cannot see our four dummies using that vocabulary."

Ben Jolly nods his agreement.

"And this 'hail of bullets' report. Didn't you say that Page shot at the tires and radiator?"

"That's what Max Robertson told me."

"So our dummies weren't shot at?"

Ben Jolly sits in thought for a few moments; then he states, "I'm not sure. At the time Max told me about it, I wasn't thinking about clarification on whom or what was shot at."

The CLWUA Sergeant-at-Arms advises, "I must take this to the district president. If this story busts wide open, he must be knowledgeable of what happened."

Ben Jolly asks, "What do you want me to do?"

"Go back to Dover Construction. Talk with Robertson and the others. Get more details on that shooting and report back to me. And control those idiots. No more actions against James Page and his son until I say so."

Chapter 21

Weston Pyth, reporter for the *Long Beach Times*, sits alone in the thirty-desk newsroom at 8:30 PM. The acrid smoke from the smoldering cigarette in his desk ashtray irritates his eyes and nostrils. He pounds the lit end of the cigarette into the ashtray several times before it is extinguished.

He pushes the bangs of his brown shoulder-length hair back from his forehead. He tugs on his beard. Then he repositions the round-rim glasses on his nose. He rereads for the fourth time his article that appeared in the morning edition.

He rolls up his shirtsleeves as he calculates the number of hours it will take to update the story about the shooting in Seal Beach. The story includes details that Weston had pumped from his contact in the Orange County Sheriff's Office, Deputy Sergeant Ogden Davis. He knows that Davis did not provide all the details. The construction workers in the pickup did not call the shooter a deranged rightwing, anti-union extremist. Weston came up with that characterization after he analyzed the situation as a conflict between union workers and a union hater. Weston omitted the details that the shooter fired shots at the vehicle and not at the occupants, and he omitted that only four shell casings were found at the scene. By omitting those details, Weston misrepresented the intentions of the shooter. He does not want his readers to know that four shots were carefully directed toward the pickup, which would mean that the shooter did not intend to harm the union workers in the pickup.

I must have more information!

Weston crusades to discredit the American rightwing. He misleads his readers by labeling the rightwing as fascists. He calculates that he can vilify America's rightwing with a series of articles that connects rightwing leaders to anti-union actions, resulting with him becoming recognized by the national news services for his journalistic talents.

I must go after the shooter! I must know who he is, and I must know the names of the victims!

Weston checks his rolodex and finds the card for Deputy Sergeant Davis. He dials Davis's home telephone number.

"Hello, Ogden, this is Weston. I need your help. My editor is really applying the pressure for the names of those involved in that shooting last night and the details of the conflict between the shooter and those construction workers."

"I'm sorry, Weston. Like I told ya last night, I cannot give ya any additional details."

"I beg you, Ogden. My job is on the line here. I must prove to my editor that I have a reliable source in the sheriff's department."

"I will get into trouble if I am caught releasing information to the press. It's just too risky."

"Ogden, I read that police report of the arrest you and your partner made last month. The one where you exchanged gunfire with some illegal immigrants, they finally gave up, and you and your partner confiscated two-hundred-and-eighty-thousand dollars in drugs and guns."

"Yes, what about it?"

"That arrest got no press."

"That's a common arrest these days," Ogden advises in and dismissive tone.

Weston queries, "You're up for promotion to detective next year, right? A highly competitive promotion, right?"

"Yes." Ogden becomes cautious.

"It would help if some of your cases got exposure in the press, especially if I enhance your heroic competence."

"No way! If I give you confidential information about the Seal Beach shooting—information that only a sheriff's department employee could reveal—then articles about me start appearing in the *Long Beach Times* . . . well . . . well, it would be a dead giveaway that I provided that confidential information."

Weston offers, "Look, you give me the confidential information and I don't report it for five days. If someone from the sheriff's office demands to know where I got the information, I claim investigative journalism. My editor will back me up. Then, five months from now, various reporters start writing articles about you and your heroics. We'll write articles about other detective candidates, but only you get the royal treatment."

After a short pause, Ogden advises, "Okay, I'll need to go to my office and copy the case file. I'll meet you at the usual place two hours from now." Ogden hangs up.

Chapter 22

Rig and his mother and his father and his two sisters sit at the dining room table in the Page home. Both James Page and Margaret Page scheduled this special family dinner for the night before Rig returns to Washington D.C. Rig appreciates that his two sisters, who no longer live at the Page home, traveled a long distance to be at this dinner. Kate is a teacher and lives in San Diego. Teri works as a model and actress and resides in a small apartment in Hollywood. Margaret Page came home early from work to prepare the family favorite dinner—roast pork, mash potatoes, and sauerkraut.

The conversation has been casual and mostly about catching up on their lives and what is happening with relatives. No mention is made regarding the incidents with the CLWUA. When the family finishes their meal, Rig's mother and his sisters clear the table and take all the dishes to the kitchen.

James Page says to Rig, "Let's go up to the family room and enjoy some brandy."

After James and Rig are seated in the family room with brandy glasses in hand, James Page tells Rig about what happened earlier in the day. "I had another encounter with those union punks this afternoon. I delivered some office furniture to a new shopping center being built in Lakewood. I took along a couple of my warehouse workers to offload and assemble the furniture. We had offloaded half the truck when two union thugs blocked the door and told me scab labor is banned from the construction site. They were two of the same assholes that we forced out of the new Harris Shipping office. I told them to move aside, or I would call the police and have them arrested for blocking the progress of commerce."

"That's a law?" Rig inquires.

"Yeah, I learned about it last week at the Chamber of Commerce monthly meeting. Anyone who attempts to block, slow, or impede the legal practice of business is committing a crime."

Rig questions, "So, then, union strikers can be arrested and charged with a crime?"

"Only if the strikers block or hinder the progress of commerce, and the business involved files a complaint with the police."

Rig asks, "How did those union thugs react to your warning?"

"They backed off."

"So they know they're breaking the law, then?"

"They must. According to the Chamber of Commerce, there is a surge in union attacks on small businesses in Southern California."

Thinking about the shooting several nights ago, Rigney asks, "Did they threaten you?"

"Yes, and they said you and I will pay for the shooting the other night." James casts a speculating stare at Rig and questions. "That was you the other night that shot up that pickup truck, right?"

Rig nods affirmative.

"They followed you from Harris Shipping, right?"

Again, Rig nods affirmative. "I'm sorry, Dad. I have placed our family and your business in danger."

"What happened?"

"They blocked me off at the intersection. Three of them jumped from the truck with crowbars and clubs and came toward me. I showed them my gun, and they backed off. I disabled the truck by shooting out tires and the radiator. Then I came home."

"The paper said you shot at the union workers because you are a rightwing union hater."

"I didn't shoot at them. I only shot at the truck."

James Page shakes his head in disgust at newspapers that don't bother to get the facts straight. James asks, "You carry a gun often?"

"Yes."

James casts a knowing smile at Rig and opines, "Kind of unusual for a navy radio operator to carry a gun."

Rig sighs and expresses resignation. "Dad, I'm sure you have figured out by now that I am more than a navy radio operator."

"Yes, I have. You're some sort of spy."

"No, not a spy, I am a counterespionage field operative. I'm more like a hunter of spies and other enemies of the American people."

"You hunt foreign enemy agents?!"

"Yes . . . and a few American traitors."

"Like whom?!"

"Sorry, Dad, no details."

James Page sits in thought. He takes several sips from his brandy glass.

Rig stares at his father. He worries about his family's safety. He says, "Dad, I must return to Washington tomorrow. I worry about that union coming after you."

"Son, nothing has happened that would not have happened otherwise had you not been involved, uh . . . except for shooting up that truck. I would have stood up to those union bullies whether you were here or not. I will not allow anyone to push me around. You know my past. I'm a fighter. Don't worry about us. The Chamber of Commerce has agreed to help any business that comes under attack from unions. After that encounter this afternoon, I called the local Chamber of Commerce. They are posting armed security guards outside my warehouse at night. And I have several guns of my own here in the house."

Rig nods, then he offers, "If you need help, call me right away. I'll fly back here immediately and help out."

James Page casts a questioning stare at his son; he asks, "How do you get your guns through airport security?"

"I am a registered military courier. Federal law allows me to carry a concealed weapon at all times. But to avoid attention, I fly on military aircraft with waivers on any search of me or my luggage."

"So your flight out of San Diego tomorrow is a military aircraft?"

"Yes, out of Naval Air Station North Island."

"Is it like a reservation type of thing?"

"Yes, I have Priority One status."

James Page appears impressed and appreciative as he comments, "I am proud of what you are doing for your country."

"Thanks, Dad."

Chapter 23

Horace Lombardi sits in his parked car away from the streetlights. He arrived one hour ago, and he waits for the dead of night before he performs his evil deed. He is parked on Electric Avenue. The U. S. Naval Weapons station lies to his left. Seal Way lies to his right and he can see the Page home. Revenge for being punched in the face and his nose broken by that union hater James Page and being shot at by that scumbag scab Rigney Page fires his motivation.

Mixed orders from his union leaders confuse and frustrate him. At one building site, union officials ordered him to damage property and beat up scabs. While at another building site he is told not to take any actions against the greedy capitalist owners. That confusion and frustration motivated him to join Max Robertson and others in an unauthorized attack against Page Office Supply on the Harris Shipping building site several weeks ago. This morning, union officials scolded him for taking those unauthorized attacks against Page Office Supply. But then he was issued an attack order against Page Office Supply. The order is clear, and he is anxious to payback James Page.

Horace exits his vehicle; then opens the trunk. He pulls a full, five gallon gasoline can from the trunk, along with two flares. He turns and looks for any activity along the darkened Seal Way. He can see the Page Office Supply panel van parked behind the Pages' garage. All of the houses on Seal Way face the beach. Seal Way runs behind the houses. Street numbers are posted on the back of the houses or garages.

At six-foot-and-four-inches, two-hundred-twenty pounds, broad-shoulders, barrel chest, jet-black-colored hair and beard; Horace casts a menacing shadow as he walks along Seal Way. The rubber soles of his athletic shoes muffle his footsteps. No one else moves about in the chilly night. Horace approaches the Pages' garage. He has been ordered by his union to torch the Page Office Supply panel van.

Rig sits in the passenger seat of his father's panel van. Through the side rearview mirror, he watches Horace approach.

Sounds of rattling trashcans cause Horace to dash to the side of the garage and outside Rig's view.

Believing that Horace moves toward the Page house with the purpose of setting it on fire, Rigney exits the panel van. He tightens his grip around a five-foot length of iron pipe.

The sound of an opening and closing car door causes Horace to move past the garage and into the backyard. He senses someone near but does not know in which direction. He thinks he sees movement on the back porch. Fearing that either James Page or his son might be on the back porch with a gun causes Horace to place the gas can on the ground and pull a .38 caliber revolver from a holster on his belt.

A cat jumps from the porch toward Horace.

Startled, Horace utters a soft yelp and steps back. Immediately after stepping back, he senses someone behind him. His military training instinctively initiates—*always turn in the direction of your hand holding the gun, so you can quickly aim at your target.* He whirls around to his right. He glimpses a figure in black clothes and black ski mask swing something in a downward motion.

Rig uses all his power to slam the pipe into Horace's forearm. A loud cracking noise sounds as Horace's right forearm radius bone breaks and punches through is skin. The force of the blow knocks the gun out of Horace's hand.

Horace exhales a scream, but only for a second, because Rigney's next blow at quarter-strength connects with the back of Horace's head just above the brain stem. Horace, now unconscious, falls facedown to the ground.

Rig slips his right foot under Horace's hip and kicks forward. Horace rolls onto his back—still unconscious. Rig pulls a small flashlight from his pocket and shines it at the man's face. Rig recognizes the man on the ground as Horace Lombardi—one of the union thugs that attacked Rig and his father in that Harris Shipping office and who Rig investigated during the days following the attack.

Rig smash the pipe into Horace's right kneecap—twice.

Horace is unconscious and does not feel the pain of his broken kneecap.

Rig reasons that if Horace regains consciousness Horace will not be able to stand and pose a threat.

Rig rolls up the ski mask and uncovers his face. Now the ski mask appears to be the common ordinary knit wool cap worn by many during cold weather. Rigney points the flashlight toward the house's kitchen window and flashes it twice. A few seconds later, the back door opens; then James Page steps into the backyard.

James stares at the body on the ground. "Is he dead?"

"No," Rigney responds.

James Page states, "I'll call the police and an ambulance." James turns to go back into the house.

"Dad."

James turns around and faces Rig.

Rig states, "There is an alternative action."

"Alternative to what?"

Rig explains, "If you call the police, there will be a lot of press and notoriety about this. Eventually the unions' war on the Page family and on Page Office Supply will become public knowledge. Your friends and customers will see you as someone who attracts danger. You will lose friends and business. The alternative is that he disappears. No police—no press—and he does not have a second chance to do us harm."

James Page expresses horror as he says to his son, "Rig, we can't kill him."

Rig counters, "He's an enemy . . . not only to us . . . to all freedom loving Americans. He is a useful idiot of an evil organization. He is a drone warrior for the devil's cause." Rig pauses and sighs deeply. Then he says, "We let this enemy go, and he will be back with help. They will never let it go until they destroy us."

James argues, "Killing him will not change that threat. They'll just send someone else. I don't want anyone to die in this conflict. I cannot agree with you on this one."

"Dad, eventually someone dies. We need to show these bastards that the Page family is not afraid to get brutal."

"But if we kill him, we must dispose of the body where it will never be found."

Rig explains in a cold and callous tone, "We can take him to your boat, go out a couple of miles, wrap an anchor around his feet, and drop him into the sea."

James Page reacts with an astonished and fearful tone, "The union sent him here. They will know we killed him, and they will come after us."

"Dad, they will come after us anyway."

"I'm going inside and calling the police."

Rig states, "We need to get our stories straight. The police cannot know that I saw his car from my bedroom more than an hour ago and did not call the police. The police cannot know that we conspired to wait and attack him . . . that I sat guard in the van, and you stood guard with a gun in the kitchen."

"Okay, what's our story?"

"Hold on a minute. I need to do a few things." Rig pulls his nine-millimeter Beretta automatic from his jacket pocket. His Beretta is wrapped in a white oily rag. He rubs the rag over all the gun's surfaces. He is not concerned about his fingerprints being on the bullet casings or the magazine. His counterespionage training taught him to always load the magazine with his hands covered with gloves or a cloth.

Keeping his fingers covered with the cloth, he holds the barrel of the Beretta between thumb and index finger. He puts the Beretta in Horace's right hand, pressing Horace's fingers onto the gun's surfaces. Then Rig removes the gun from Horace's hand and slips it into Horace's left jacket pocket.

Rig pulls the suppressor from his other jacket pocket, wipes it down with the oil cloth. He wraps Horace's right hand around the suppressor; then Rig slips the suppressor into Horace's inside jacket pocket.

Rig advises his father, "When the police questioned me about the shooting at the intersection, I suggested to the police that those union punks shot up their own car to make me look like the villain."

James Page stares at his son with wonderment in his eyes. He now understands the cold, calculating skill and proficiency that his son must use in his role as a counterespionage field operative.

Rig Explains, "Here is our story. We were in our beds. We heard a noise outside like someone knocking over trashcans. We got up, dressed quickly, and arrived in the kitchen at the same time. We agreed that I would go outside and investigate. I took a flashlight to signal you if I found anything. You couldn't see anything from the kitchen window. All you saw was shifting shadows. After I signaled you with the flashlight, you came out and we decided to call the police immediately."

"Okay, Son, that's our story."

Rig hands his father the oily rag and says, "Before you call the police, store your gun where you normally keep it and put this rag with it."

James enters the house.

Rig remains in the backyard.

Seven minutes later, sirens fill the dark, chilly night.

About thirty seconds apart, three Orange County Sheriff vehicles with sirens blasting brake to tire skidding stops on Seal Way behind the garage. Each vehicle's driver silences the siren but keeps the vehicle's emergency lights flashing.

In the Page house master bedroom, Margaret Page awakes, turns on the light, and dashes to the window facing the backyard.

In houses for one-block distant, people awaken in response to the nearby sirens and skidding tires. They turn on their inside and outside lights, then dash to windows that face Seal Way.

Light fills the backyard as deputies cautiously enter the backyard with a pistol in one hand and a high-power flashlight in the other. Within seconds, the beams from those flashlights focus on Rig and the body at his feet. From behind the lights a voice shouts, "Down on the ground—hands behind your back!"

Rig complies.

Five deputies move about the backyard. One deputy stoops to take Horace's vital signs. One of the deputies handcuffs Rig; then two deputies pull Rig to his feet and keep hold on his arms. Another deputy who wears sergeant stripes searches Rig for weapons and identification; he finds none, then asks, "What is your name?"

"Chief Petty Officer Rigney Page United States Navy. This is my parent's home. I am on leave and staying with them. That's my father, James Page, looking out the kitchen window."

"I know James Page," says one of the deputies. "He delivers office supplies to our substation. That's him in the window."

The deputy checking Horace's vitals says, "This man is alive. He's unconscious. There are wet blood stains on his right sleeve."

The sergeant asks Rig, "Who is he?"

"He's a union thug that has been threatening to harm me and my parents." Then Rig lies, "I don't know his name."

The sergeant asks, "This have anything to do with that shooting the other night a few blocks from here?"

Rig responds, "I don't know."

A not too distant siren tells of the approaching ambulance.

The sergeant observes Horace's revolver, the two flares, and the gasoline can on the ground. While pointing at the gun, the sergeant asks Rig, "Is that your gun?"

"No."

"Do you know who that gun belongs to?"

"I don't know. I knocked it out of his hand when I hit him with that pipe. I knocked the gas can out of his hand at the same time." Rig nods toward the iron pipe several feet from the gun.

The sergeant expresses doubt, he asks, "You faced a gunman with a pipe?"

"I didn't know he had a gun in his hand. I surprised him."

"Where did you get the pipe?"

"From the back porch. There's a stack of pipes for work my parents are having done inside the house."

The sergeant points his flashlight at the gas can and questions,

"Are you saying that he carried that gas can into this yard?"

"Yes," Rig answers.

"Bring that gas can to me," the sergeant orders one of the deputies.

The deputy hands the gas can to the sergeant.

The sergeant inspects the can with the beam of his flashlight. The name "Lombardi" is scratched into the side.

A deputy who searched Horace's clothing stands up straight and says to the sergeant, "Found this in his right jacket pocket. It's a nine-millimeter automatic."

The sergeant remembers that the report of the shooting at the nearby intersection specified that the shooter used a nine-millimeter automatic.

The sergeant turns to the deputy who said he knew James Page and orders, "Bring Mr. Page out here to identify his son."

Less than a minute later, James Page stands with the group of deputies that are questioning his son. "That's my son, Rigney Page. He's a chief in the navy."

The sergeant considers all that he has heard and all that he has observed, including the presence of the Page Office Supply van on the other side of the garage. He concludes that James Page and Rigney Page are who they say they are. He orders, "Remove the handcuffs."

The ambulance parks as close to the scene as it can. The ambulance siren becomes silent. The ambulance's emergency lights add to the red and blue colors flashing over the scene.

Neighbors begin to gather around the perimeter of the Page residence.

James Page and Rig Page stand and wait while the deputies work with the paramedics to remove Horace from the scene.

One minute later, the crime scene investigators arrive.

The sergeant asks James Page, "May we go inside and take your statements."

"Yes, sure." James Page responds.

James, Rig, the police sergeant, and two other policemen enter the house and sit at the kitchen table.

Margaret Page goes about ensuring all have a continuing supply of hot coffee.

One hour later, all the police have departed. Rig sits at the kitchen table and drinks coffee with his parents. Rig evaluates those violent events with union thugs during the past few weeks. He casts a perplexed expression.

Margaret Page inquires, "What bothers you, Rigney?"

"I wonder what personal conflict motivates these union thugs to attack you and dad and his business. It makes no sense to me."

Margaret Page responds, "It's easy to understand. Union members consider themselves victims of a compassionless capitalist system. To them, your father is a victimizer because he refuses to hire union workers."

"I don't understand such a mentality. Dad owns his business. He has the right to hire anyone he pleases at any wage he pleases."

"Unions don't see it that way," Margaret explains. "Unions believe that workers should be paid based on their needs on not on their skill value."

Rig shakes his head and expresses dismissal of such reasoning; he comments, "If they want a more prosperous life, why don't they do what is necessary to earn that prosperity. I mean, look at dad. He began life in poverty. When he went out into the world, dirt was all that he had in his pockets. He took advantage of America's opportunities and prospered, the same opportunities that are available to every American. I think it un-American that union workers believe they are entitled to more than what their labor is worth in a free and open marketplace."

James Page states, "Rig, not all union workers believe they are entitled to a bigger unearned slice of someone else's pie. Many are forced to join unions in order to get employment. For others, union membership is just a way of life. Others undergo indoctrination that convinces them that violence is a justifiable process to force businesses into complying with union demands, and these days state and federal government takes the side of unions." James expresses concern. Then he adds, "It's like government is biased toward union growth, regardless of methods."

Rigney asks, "Dad, what guides you to set wages for your people?"

There are business magazines and the Chamber of Commerce that publish the current competitive wages by skill level. I comply with those."

"How do the wages you pay compare to union wages for the same work?"

"The wages I pay are about 20 percent to 35 percent lower than union wages."

Rig states, "Makes me wonder why any company would want to employ union workers."

"Protection," James Page declares.

Rig raises he eyebrows. "Protection?"

"Yeah, like paying protection to the mob. That's basically what union wages are. Companies willingly pay it to keep their property from being vandalized or destroyed."

Rig nods, conveying understanding; then he comments, "But higher unmerited union wages will cause companies to charge more for their product."

With a sarcastic grin and tone, James states, "The irony is that union wages are pricing American-made products out of competition on the world market. In other words, unions are working toward their own elimination."

Rig nods and expresses that he understands.

James adds, "It's already happening. Did you notice that all those office machines at that Harris Shipping office were foreign made?"

"Yes," Rig responds.

James informs, "When I first bid that job, I provided two separate bids on the office equipment because Harris said they wanted IBM, XEROX, NCR machines. The bid for those American made machines were forty percent higher than the bid that I worked up on foreign made machines. The Harris purchasing agent went directly to those American manufactures but could not get more than five percent less than my bid. And that furniture we assembled—all made in Mexico by American companies. Yesterday, I read that several American companies are closing their American plants and moving manufacturing to Central America. Unions that have contracts with those companies are protesting the U.S. Department of Labor and have filed suit with the U.S. Labor Relations Board to stop those companies from moving their operations to foreign countries."

Margaret Page steps into the conversation with concern in her tone, "James, right now, I am more interested in what will happen to us. What do you think that union will do next?"

James Page responds, "I don't know. I must stay on my guard."

Rig comments, "But now the police know the union is attacking you. Won't the union back off for fear of prosecution?"

"They will be more cautious next time. Whatever they do, they will be careful not to reveal themselves."

Rig expresses thoughtfulness for a few moments; then advises, "I'm going to ask for an extension of my leave. I must be here to protect you."

"Son, your mother and I have been battling unions our entire working life. We can take care of ourselves. You should go back to D.C. and resume your valuable contribution to your country."

"But, Dad, like you said, unions have recently intensified their efforts to intimidate and manipulate the independent small businessman. Union strikes and union violence are all over the news this year."

James states, "As they have before, and we survived. I think the unions have become embolden to increase their violent tactics because liberal Democrats presently rule the nation and rule California. I think the unions believe they will not be prosecuted. When Republicans regain control of the national government and state government, unions will retreat."

James beams a confident smile. "Son, go back to the navy. I will call you if we need you." James Page knows he will not call. He is confident that he can handle anything the unions throw at him. And his son's work is important and should not be interrupted.

Rig Responds, "Okay. I should get moving to catch that flight out of San Diego."

Chapter 24

At 7:35 AM, Enrico Mendoza stands on a hilltop overlooking the small town of Elias, Idaho—population 3606. Binoculars hang from his neck on a leather strap. The crisp, cool morning with a cloudless sky allows a clear, detailed view of the valley and town below. A pile of cigarette butts lies at his feet.

He uses his binoculars to check the railroad tracks to the west. Then he focuses the binoculars on the center of town where the railroad tracks cross Main Street. He checks his watch.

Earlier, while it was still dark, he parked his pickup truck next to the tracks one block from the center of town. Around the tracks, he laid out a mix of rotted railroad ties, rusted and broken rail spikes, and rusted and broken rail connector bolts. Then he buried the explosive device under a rail joint.

Motion to the west catches his attention. A seventy-car train moves toward the town. Ten of the train cars are gasoline tankers.

During the dark hours of early morning, One of Enrico's operatives jumped aboard the train when it slowed to a safe three miles per hour to maneuver a sharp curve. The operative placed explosive devices on the underside of each tank. Then he jumped off the train—total time onboard was twenty-two minutes.

Enrico places his right hand on the shoe-box-sized remote multi-detonator that sits on the hood of the pickup truck. He extends the antenna.

When the train is one-half mile from the town, Enrico flips the two arming switches. One switch activates a pulsating radio frequency that arms explosive devices that his operative placed on the underside of each tanker car. The other switch initiated a different pulsating radio frequency that arms the explosive device that Enrico buried under the rail joint located one block from the center of town.

When the third tanker car arrives at the location where Enrico planted the device, he flips the denoting switch. He does not hear the small explosion over the sound of the moving train and its warning whistle. Several tanker cars lean sideways and run off the railway elevation to the left.

When the third tanker car slides against the ground, Enrico flips the detonator switch for the explosives attached to tanker cars.

This time the explosion is deafening. A fireball shoots two-hundred feet into the air. The explosion spreads burning fluid over homes and business buildings for three blocks in all directions. Thirty-seven adults and twenty-three children are incinerated in their beds.

Enrico drives to the east away from the town. Over the next few minutes, he hears three more explosions.

Thirty minutes later, Enrico drives into a truck stop. He exits his vehicle and goes directly to a phone booth. An answering service responds, "J. R. Kelly's office."

"Please tell Mr. Kelly that the package has been delivered."

Twenty minutes later, U.S. Senator Clay Porter sits in his office in the Capitol Building. In a chair facing Porter is a senator from a western state with whom Porter has been discussing the *Fair Profits Tax Act* and the *Employee Fairness Act*.

The senator's Chief of Staff enters the office and states, "Edwin Kendley called and insisted that I give you this message immediately: 'The package has been delivered.'" The coded message advises Senator Porter that the railroad bombing occurred on time and as planned.

"Okay, thanks," Porter responds. Then Porter returns to the conversation with his colleague.

Chapter 25

Harold Oatman, Director of the Southern California Region of the Construction and Labor Workers Union of America, CLWUA, sits at his office desk in the district headquarters, located in an industrial area of Long Beach. Oatman's large fat butt just fits his desk chair. The cheap brown suit that fit him ten years ago is now four sizes too small. Attempting to button his suit coat over his belly defies the laws of physics. His fat pudgy face is flushed red. The last two inches of a cheap cigar smolders from the corner of his lips.

On the other side of Oatman's desk, Melvin Spartan, the union's district sergeant-at-arms informs Oatman of the early morning incident at the Page residence two days ago.

Oatman, who authorized the torching of James Page's business vehicle, shakes his head and expresses disbelief at the incompetence of Horace Lombardi, who had never before failed to secretly destroy property of business owners.

Spartan continues. "Horace is now in the police ward at the county hospital. He has regained consciousness and has been informed that he has lost most of the muscle in his right forearm and that for the rest of his life he will not be able to walk without assistance of crutches or at best a cane or walker. He will never be able to work as a carpenter again. Dover Construction has fired him, and neither the Dover Construction's insurance company nor our union health insurance company will pay his medical bills because he was injured in the perpetration of a crime. He is physically and financially ruined.

"But that's not the worst of it. The Orange County District Attorney has charged Horace with assault, attempted arson, illegally discharging a firearm, and making fraudulent written statements to the police. Charges are also being prepared against Max Robertson and Allen Villanueva for assault and conspiracy to commit several crimes. They too have been fired from Dover Construction."

"What did they do to warrant all those charges?"

"A few weeks back, they attacked Page and his son at Harris

Shipping's new office building. The police have surveillance video of the incident. The police also have surveillance video of them walking around the Page Office Supply warehouse late at night looking for ways to enter. And the gun used to shoot up Max's truck was found by the police on Horace's person at the Page residence."

Oatman shakes his head and expresses disgust. "Horace's failure puts us right in the middle of it. Our image will suffer irreparable damage. We need to distance ourselves from this."

"I don't think we can," the Sergeant-at-Arms states. "Horace demands we provide him with a free union lawyer and pay his medical bills and provide him with a disability pension or he tells the press and the police about his previous union sponsored vandalism and violence. Max and Allen are also demanding free union lawyers and threatening the same revelations of past union sponsored violence and sabotage."

Oatman releases a big sigh; then comments, "If we provide lawyers, we expose ourselves as advocating those attacks on James Page and his son. If we provide lawyers, we must do all in our power to make James Page and his son look like the bad guys."

Spartan appears bewildered as he queries, "But they are the bad guys, right?"

"Of course they are!" Oatman declares. He advises, "Tell those three pecker heads that I am taking their threatening requests to national headquarters. We should have an answer in a few days."

The sergeant-at-arms asks Oatman, "Did you see Weston Pyth's article in *The Times* this morning?"

Oatman shakes his head.

Spartan hands Oatman a copy of the *Long Beach Times*. "Bottom half of front page."

Oatman reads the article.

SEAL BEACH SHOOTER IDENTIFIED:
By Weston Pyth, LBT Investigative Reporter:
Competent and reliable sources reveal that the rightwing anti-union extremist who attacked union workers last week at a Seal

Beach intersection and shot up union workers vehicle is U.S. Navy Chief Petty Officer Rigney Page and son of James Page who is the owner of Page Office Supply with offices and warehouses in Long Beach.

Reports from those same competent and reliable sources state that Rigney Page stalked those workers, then attacked them during that Seal Beach shooting spree. Obviously, Page was angered by a confrontational incident that occurred several weeks ago when those construction workers successfully fought off James Page and his son.

This reporter challenged the Orange County Sheriff's Department as to why Rigney Page who presents an extreme danger to the public safety has not yet been arrested. The sheriff's department declared no comment to my repeated inquiries.

This reporter is compelled to ask questions: Could it be that uniform wearing sheriff's officers are favoring another uniform wearing comrade—a navy chief petty officer? Is this a conspiracy by uniformed fascists to give a fellow fascist a pass?

This reporter promises to demand justice for the violent attack against honest, union working men and their families.

Oatman lays the newspaper on his desk. He comments, "No mention of the arrest of Horace Lombardi at the Page residence. I wonder why Pyth did not report it."

Melvin shakes his head, indicating he does not know.

Oatman asks, "What else do we know that the public and, obviously, the press don't know?"

A gas can with Horace's fingerprints and name were found next to Horace in the Pages' backyard. Horace told the police that the gas can, and guns were planted on him."

"Guns . . . more than one?"

Melvin answers, "Two guns were found in the Page backyard. A revolver with Horace's prints was found by the deputies a few feet from Horace when he was lying unconscious. An automatic pistol with Horace's prints was found in Horace's coat pocket."

"Anything else?" Oatman asks.

"Yes, one of the sheriff's department investigators said something about those guns that are thought provoking. He said that the Smith and Wesson thirty-eight caliber revolver is a common weapon and can be purchased at any gun store, but the nine-millimeter Beretta automatic found in Horace's coat pocket is a foreign gun with the serial number filed off. So the investigator wonders why Horace would take two guns, one easily traceable and the other untraceable.

"And one final detail. Horace claims he exited a bar in Long Beach, and someone hit him from behind. Next thing he remembers is that he woke up in the hospital."

Oatman chuckles, "Horace tells a creative story. He is not an intelligent man. Someone has coached him."

Spartan casts a knowing expression and advises, "That bar where Horace says he was in before being knocked unconscious—well, the sheriff's investigator discovered Horace was talking with Weston Pyth of the *Long Beach Times* in that bar five hours before Horace was found unconscious in the Page backyard."

Oatman flinches and blinks his eyes. The implication that Weston Pyth is involved invites unlimited conspiratorial speculations. "Okay, that is more justification to get union lawyers involved. We need a lot of evidence legally suppressed, and I doubt that a lawyer that Horace and his buddies can afford will be smart enough."

Spartan stands; then he advises, "I will contact Weston Pyth and see what I can find out." He turns and starts for the door.

"Mel, wait," Oatman orders.

Spartan turns around and faces Oatman.

"How were you able to get all that information regarding the sheriff's investigation?"

"Your predecessor was a campaign fund raiser for the sheriff's last election campaign. The union gave generously. The sheriff is appreciative and wants to show his gratitude."

Oatman nods and expresses understanding.

Chapter 26

Jack opens the door to the garage located at the Office of Naval Intelligence motor pool located on the Suitland, Maryland Federal Complex. Then he leads Rig to a tarp covered vehicle. Jack and Rigney pull the tarp off the vehicle and uncover a two door, gray colored with black trim Jeep Cherokee. The paint is faded, scratched, and chipped with some rust marks appearing in scratched surfaces.

Jack says, "This baby is a powerhouse, with a four-hundred-cubic-inch engine with a four-barrel carburetor and its all-wheel drive. This baby will climb trees."

"So why do I need to drive this? I already have suitable transportation."

"Didn't Captain Watson tell you about this vehicle?"

"No. He just sent me a note to come here, see you, and check out a vehicle."

"I don't know the reasons for issuing this vehicle to you. Anyway, this is an armored vehicle, armor plating in the roof, sides, and engine. The windows are bulletproof. The tires are combination on-road off-road and the tires are solid rubber, a composition that provides the same ride and utility as air-filled tires. The suspension is reinforced with special metal alloy materials. The extra-large gas tank is armor plated."

Rig interrupts, "No hidden machine guns or ejections seats?" He chuckles.

Jack expresses bewilderment and shakes his head, conveying he does not follow.

Rig clarifies, "Like James Bond's Aston Martin."

Jack expresses disapproval of Rig's attempt to be funny. He shakes his head while he responds, "Uh, no, nothing like that."

Rig turns serious and asks, "Is the underside armored?"

"Yes."

Jack opens the passenger-side front door. He points to the dash, "Mobile HAM radio mounted there, with ONI frequencies preprogrammed with that auxiliary pushbutton select assembly. Jack hands Rigney an index card that lists four frequencies with associated pushbutton number. "Memorize those within 24 hours; then destroy the card. Headquarters will provide you with applicable call signs."

Rig nods acceptance of the information. Then he stares at the eight-foot-high whip antenna attached to the rear bumper. He states, "That antenna makes my communications capability obvious."

Jack nods and responds, "Yes, but not unusual for off-road vehicles like this and not unusual for sailors whose specialty is radio communications."

Rig nods and expresses agreement. He scans the interior of the garage; then he asks, "Okay, anything else?"

"Yes," Jack responds as he opens the rear cargo area door. "Look here."

Rigney walks to Jack's side and views the Jeep's cargo area.

Jack slides open a side panel on the left and slides open a side panel on the right, exposing a row of five small electrical switches on the left and a row of five identical electrical switches on the right. All switches are in the center position. Jack points to the switches and directs, "Change the position of all those switches. Choose whatever order you want."

Rigney observes the row of five small switches on the right and the row of five small switches on the left. Then he flips the switches to up or down in no particular order.

"Now, lift up on the floor panel handle."

Rigney wraps a few fingers under the handle and lifts. The floor panel does not budge.

Jack flips switches on both panels. The soft sound of a small motor reveals that the floor panel is now unlocked. "Okay, now memorize the sequence of the switches."

Rig spends a few seconds staring at the two panels of switches. Then he wraps a few fingers under the lift handle.

Jack places his hand of Rigney's hand and says, "Wait. Did you memorize the position of the switches?"

"Yes."

Jack expresses doubt and argues, "But you only looked at the switches for a few seconds. I need to test you. Stand back a few feet."

Rigney takes a few steps backward.

Jack uses his body to block Rig's view of the switches. He rearranges the switch positions. The small locking motor locks the floor panel. "Okay, Chief, now enter the correct switch sequence."

Rigney steps forward and rapidly sets each switch up or down according to his memory. The motor engages the locking lever.

Jack stares at Rigney with a curious smile. "How did you memorize so quickly?"

"Charlie Foxtrot," Rigney responds, "Baudot code Charlie Foxtrot—characters C and F."

Jack shakes his head as he expresses lack of understanding. "Baudot what?"

"Baudot code," Rigney explains. "It's the five level binary code used in teletype communications. The up and down of those switches represent the high-low binary sequence of C and F in the Baudot code. That's the way I memorize most sequences and combinations."

Jack nods understanding. Then he says, "Okay, take out the floor panel."

Rig pulls up on the handle; then he pulls the floor panel out of the cargo area. The padded cargo bin contains three strapped-down, hard-plastic cases. Rigney loosens the straps that hold down the largest case. He opens the case and exposes a modular automatic rifle with scope and suppressor. He recognizes the same model Chinese sniper rifle he used in the Philippines several years ago. Then he opens the other two cases and finds four handguns: One snub-nose .357 magnum revolver; one long-barrel .357 magnum revolver; one short-barrel nine-millimeter Beretta; one long-barrel nine-millimeter Beretta. The barrel of each weapon is modified to fit a suppressor and the suppressor for each weapon is included with its associated weapon. Each case contains a box of 100 rounds of ammunition.

"Any questions," Jack asks.

"No."

Jack directs, "Stow the gun cases and re-install the floorboard. Then I will show you all the security safeguards."

Forty minutes later, Rig drives the Jeep Cherokee out of the motor pool compound.

Chapter 27

During the past six weeks, Rig was Diane's escort to several dinner and cocktail parties hosted by work associates and VIPs in the Carter Administration. Twenty or more people attended those parties and included members of Congress, White House staffers, and other VIPs. His mission at those events was to gather information and report back to his ONI Controller, Sally Macfurson. His naval intelligence task at those events was made easier by attendees not asking him a lot of questions. He always wore his Full Dress Blue uniform. Those party guests were aware that he is the Hero of Thurso and that he is that navy chief who was shot by a navy officer in Sardinia last year. But all that was old news and few people engaged him in conversation. The main topics of conversation among the guests were The Panama Canal Treaty and President Carter's plans to establish a U.S. Department of Education and to establish the Environmental Protection Agency. He became aware of the liberal, radical mindsets of those party guests. Rig came away from each of those parties bewildered as to how people who were raised in America became so willing to surrender America's most strategic asset in the Western Hemisphere—the Panama Canal—and to surrender more liberty to large federal government through establishment of a U.S. Department of Education and to an Environmental Protection Agency. Although most of the guests advocated socialist government; they criticized the Soviets, the Chinese, and the Cubans for inept and brutal totalitarian government that resulted in a negative view of socialism. The most pleasing part of those party evenings were that Rig would spend the night at Diane's Georgetown townhouse and they spent hours involved in sexual activity.

Tonight Rig sits with Diane and five of her friends at the dining room table in Diane's Georgetown townhouse. U.S. Congressman Billy Thayer, Democrat, Southern California, is the only guest at Diane's party who was also a guest at all those parties that Rig had previously attended with Diane.

On the invitations, Diane listed the dinner party as *casual with tie*. Rig wears his Winter Blue uniform that includes matching black shirt, trousers, tie, anchor collar devices, and ribbons, but no jacket. The other men wear slacks, causal jacket, and tie. Women wear tasteful pant suits.

When Diane advised Rig that her UCLA college friends would be guests at her dinner party, Rig readily accepted her invitation to attend. His mission to discover the width and depth of Diane's political and social circle requires him to find ways to mix within that circle.

Because she is the hostess, Diane sits at the head of the table. To Diane's right, sits Diane's coworker, Peter Mandrake and his wife, Sandra. Georgetown University Professor, Bartholomew Goldman PhD and his wife, Amanda, sit to Diane's left. Rig and Congressman Billy Thayer sit at the opposite end of the table from Diane.

Professor Goldman asks, "Rig . . . uh, may I call you Rig?"

For a few moments before answering, Rig studies the forty-year-old Georgetown University Professor who conveys the ultimate academic with shoulder-length hair and a short trimmed beard and wearing tweed coat with elbow patches, wool slacks, and dark cotton tie. Goldman was one of the older postgraduate students at UCLA when Diane was an undergraduate. Rig responds, "Sure. May I call you Bartholomew or Bart?"

Goldman straightens his back, raises his nose and advises, "I prefer being addressed as doctor or professor."

Rig responds, "Okay, Professor, in that case, I prefer being addressed as Chief."

Unaccustomed to the uneducated, unwashed masses acting boldly and irreverently toward him, Professor Goldman's face flushes red and he exhibits irritation. An awkward period of silence follows, and the diners focus on their salads.

Several minutes later and with a haughty tone, Professor Goldman asks Rig, "Uh, Chief, I am interested in how navy personnel are handling President Carter's unconditional pardon of Vietnam War draft evaders. What are you hearing?"

Rig directs his eyes toward Professor Goldman and says, "Before I answer that question, Professor. Would you please share with me what you teach at Georgetown University?"

"I lecture on the subject of international relations."

Rig responds, "Then I assume you're a PhD of International Relations and Affairs. Is my assumption correct?"

"Yes, Chief. You are correct."

Rig answers the professor's question. "I have not heard or read any official navy response to President Carter's pardoning draft dodgers. I have had conversations with military personal on the subject. Most I spoke with believe President Carter's pardon is an egregious abuse of Constitutional power. They believe that President Carter disrespects all those military people who obeyed America's laws and went to Vietnam, whether they wanted to or not."

In a tone challenging Rig to be truthful, Professor Goldman inquires, "Do you feel the same way?"

"Yes," Rig replies confidently.

"So you supported the Vietnam War, then?"

"I didn't say that," Rig responds calmly.

"Are you saying you did not support the Vietnam War?"

"Professor, whether I supported the Vietnam War is irrelevant to the illegal act of draft evasion. Those draft evaders broke the law. Opposition to the war is not a legal defense against prosecution for draft evasion."

Goldman states, "But, Chief, I am interested in whether or not you supported the Vietnam War."

Rig declares, "No comment on that."

Congressman Thayer appears perplexed by Rig's response. He advises, "Chief, Vietnam is no longer a political issue. Your government allows you to reveal which side of the issue that you advocated."

Rig expresses annoyance as he contemplates his response. He promised Diane that he would not talk politics and that he would not become defiant and silent if he were probed with political questions.

He responds, "I advocate that the men and women who served in Vietnam be forever respected and honored by the American people. I also advocate that those who came back from Vietnam with physical and mental disabilities receive lifetime care. They earned that care and America is obligated to provide that lifetime care." Rig pauses as he considers the inflammatory nature of his next comment. "Vietnam will be forever a political issue. President Carter made it such when he pardoned one hundred thousand draft dodgers. Those who served, voluntarily or involuntarily, will always consider that pardon an irreverent political act."

"Not all," Amanda Goldman chirps. "I know some Vietnam veterans who supported the pardoning actions of both President Ford and President Carter."

Rig studies Amanda Goldman's manner. The tall, pudgy, black-haired woman casts a pleasing personality. Rig nods acceptance of Amanda's comment and responds, "Yes, I am aware that there are some vets who feel that way, although I have never met any."

Congressman Thayer queries, "Chief, did you serve in Vietnam?"

Rig stares into the face of the athletic, clean-shaven young Congressman who attended UCLA during the same years as Diane. Thayer wears his brown hair short enough to convey he is more conservative than the long-haired radicals, but long enough to convey he is aware of modern fashion. Both Diane and Thayer earned their master's degrees in 1970. Unknown to Rig, Thayer and Diane had a short romance during their junior year at UCLA.

"No. I did not serve in Vietnam," Rig lies. His official navy record shows no time spent in Vietnam, although he spent several months there during 1974 on a mission for naval intelligence.

"How did you avoid it?" asks Peter Mandrake, Diane's coworker and college friend from UCLA.

While answering, Rig studies Peter Mandrake's manner. He is curious about Mandrake's clean-cut, blond crew-cut hair style, and overall 1950s collegiate appearance. "I didn't avoid Vietnam duty. I just never got orders to go."

Congressman Thayer offers, "Maybe the navy thought you were doing too good of a job killing Soviet-funded terrorists in Europe."

Rig casts a cold, calculating stare at Congressman Thayer. He wonders how much Thayer knows. The fact that those Scottish terrorists were backed by the Soviets is classified information and was never released to the public. *Does Thayer know about my mission against the Red Brigade in Maddalena?*

Thayer casts back an inquisitive stare, followed with an inquisitive, "What?"

Rig holds his cold calculating stare on Congressman Thayer. He reasons that Thayer's inquisitive "what" must mean that Thayer does not know he revealed classified information. *Congressman Thayer must think its public information, but how did he learn that information?*

Diane queries, "Rig, were those Scottish terrorists funded by the Soviets?"

Rig shrugs and shakes his head, conveying he cannot confirm the Congressman's statement.

Diane and her friends turn their eyes toward Congressman Thayer.

With a questioning tone, Peter Mandrake comments, "The press that I read on that group was that they were Scottish separatists acting to bring attention to their cause. I read nothing about them being Soviet funded."

"I never read that," Professor Goldman states. "Billy, what do you know that we don't?"

Congressman Billy Thayer exhibits befuddlement; then he responds, "I don't remember where I gained that information. I just know it." Thayer expresses thoughtfulness, conveying he attempts to remember when he first gained that information.

Professor Goldman explains, "If Scottish separatists are backed by the Soviets, then the purpose of the Scottish separatist movement needs redefined, and the U.K. government needs to redesign its battle plan against those separatists."

After a short pause, Peter Mandrake asks Rig, "Do you have any details not known by the public that you can share?"

"No," Rig reports calmly.

Professor Goldman casts an evaluating stare at Rig as he queries, "Chief, did you really stab one of those terrorists in the testicles to make him talk?"

Rig shakes his head and expresses his annoyance with this subject of conversation. He responds, "Some of my shipmates acted bravely that night. Master Chief Hilton went searching for terrorists in the antenna field and engaged terrorists in a shootout. He was seriously wounded in the leg. He must now walk with a cane for the rest of his life." Rig pauses and takes a breath; then advises, "I am embarrassed by all the attention focused on me. May we please change the subject?"

Amanda Goldman comments, "Rig, you certainly live an exciting life. You have traveled all over the world, and you actively participated in international events. Diane tells us that you are an explorer, always anxious to discover the other side of the mountain. Diane told us about your three years on an international military NATO staff in Belgium and about how during those three years you traveled extensively throughout Europe, discovering the European culture. Then you served in the Western Pacific and spent your leisure time sailing a small boat in search of deserted island to camp and scuba dive. Most of my students are military people and we talk a lot, and according to them, military life is boring and a burden."

Rig nods; then responds, "Military people live and work in dangerous places and are exposed to life-threatening situations. Nevertheless, there are times during military life when one can take advantage of the locations in which they find themselves and involve themselves in exciting activity. Life is what you make it. If some believe military life is boring and a burden, then they are not doing what is necessary to make it otherwise. I am honored to serve my country in the military, and I am pleased that the military also provides a path to experience adventure and discover the world."

Sandra Mandrake waited anxiously while Rig talked; now, she is bursting to ask a question. "A year after you killed terrorists in

Scotland, you are shot by a navy officer in Sardinia, a shooting that was reported in the press around the world. Is it true that the navy officer who shot you was your boss?"

Sandra Mandrake's short pageboy style hair, clothes, and perky manner reminds Rig of a 1950s cheerleader—well the way the movies and T.V. portray 1950s high school cheerleaders. Again, he wonders about the 1950s high school manner of the Mandrake's. He remembers Diane explaining that the Mandrakes graduated from high school in 1959 but neither began college until 1965. Between high school and college, Peter and Sandra traveled the world first-class for five years—funded by Peter's wealthy trust fund. They toured in limousines and associated with the white-bowtie and evening-gown society. Concerts, plays, and five-star hotels were their touring grounds. Diane said they went to college to experience it, not to learn. Nevertheless, they maintained high grades while actively participating in the 1960s protest movement.

In a flat and unemotional manner, Rig replies, "He wasn't my boss at the time he shot me. He was declared a navy deserter months before." Rig pauses. Then, with a contemptuous tone he comments, "The press never mentioned that Ensign Ryan was a deserter at the time he shot me. The press stoked the flames of sensationalism by claiming there was a feud between Ensign Ryan and me."

Sandra Mandrake inquires, "So why did he shoot you?"

"I don't know." Rig's tone conveys slight annoyance.

Amanda Goldman queries, "Who was the woman that shot your division officer and saved your life? The press called her a *mystery woman*. The press reported she was whisked away by the navy minutes after the shooting, and the navy would not reveal her location or her identity."

"I cannot comment on that," Rig replies with a slightly defiant tone. Then he attempts to change the subject. "I feel uncomfortable that the entire dinner conversation so far has focused on me." His gaze darts around the table as he says, "You are friends of Diane that I never met before. I was hoping to learn about your lives. I hope that friends of Diane will become my friends."

Diane's friends exhibit expressions that broadcast they do not usually make friends with military enlisted men, and that they have not yet decided if they want to claim Rig as an acquaintance. Currently, Rig is a person of interest because of his *Hero of Thurso* status; he may not be a person of interest tomorrow.

Rig focuses on Congressman Thayer and asks, "Congressman, maybe you can tell us something interesting about Congress or maybe some interesting stories about Diane that we might not know."

An amused expression crosses Thayer's face as he asks, "Did Diane tell you about the time she was shoved into the Trevi Fountain by an angry Italian woman?"

"No," Rig responds. He chuckles, then queries, "When did that happen?"

Thayer glances at the ceiling while recollecting the time frame. "That would be the summer of 1970, after we all earned our masters degrees. We traveled through Europe." Thayer again stares at the ceiling while expressing thoughtfulness. Then he informs, "I believe that was August of 1970 when we were in Rome."

"We?" Rig inquires, "Did all of you travel together during that time in Europe?"

"We all did!" Thayer reveals. "We traveled together—a great time! So this Italian woman and Diane got into an argument about the arrogance of Americans. The Italian lady started yelling at Diane. Then she pushed Diane into the fountain's pool."

Rig presses for more information by inquiring, "So all of you toured Europe for two years?"

Professor Goldman states, "No. Amanda and I came home in December of 1970. I needed to finish my doctorate program."

Billy Thayer responds to Goldman's comments. "I came home several months before the Goldmans."

Peter Mandrake adds, "Yes, Amanda and I came home around the same time as Billy."

Rig shifts his attention to Diane and inquires, "So you stayed in Europe for another year after your friends came home? What was your interest?"

Sandra Mandrake blurts, "Diane found an Italian boyfriend." Sandra stares at the ceiling, attempting to remember the boyfriend's name; then she remembers. "Oh, I remember—Marco." Sandra shifts her focus toward Diane and queries, "What ever happened to him?"

Diane blushes. She glances at Rig; then she looks at Sandra as she answers. "I don't know. One day he went out and never returned. I never saw him again."

Diane's Italian boyfriend, Marco, was the person who introduced Diane to a KGB recruiter. Shortly after Marco disappeared from Rome, the KGB recruiter convinced Diane to become an agent for the KGB. Shortly thereafter, she traveled to East Germany using a passport and visa with a cover name. She spent nearly a year going through KGB training. No one at the table, except for Rig knows that Diane is a KGB agent. When asked about her two years in Europe, she says she traveled everywhere and learned much about the Western European culture.

A long pause occurs while Diane and Sandra replace salad plates with dinner plates. Then they place plates of veal and bowls of vegetables on the table. A caterer had prepared the food in Diane's kitchen, then departed. Diane did not want any strangers in the house while her powerful and influential friends interrogated Rig.

Rig is the first to break the pause, "Congressman, what committees are you on?"

"Oh, uh . . . well . . . the Foreign Relations Committee and the Armed Services Committee and the Intelligence Committee." Congressman Thayer pauses as he considers what to add. Then he mentions, "Oh, and several sub-committees."

"Sounds interesting," Rig states. "Anything going on in the Intelligence Committee?"

Thayer responds, "I am prohibited from discussing committee business but believe me, Chief, not interesting at all. We gather facts, evaluate those facts, and decide if we need to construct legislation or allocate more money. Actually, somewhat boring."

Rig turns his attention to Diane's coworker at the White House, Peter Mandrake. "What about you, Peter, anything interesting going on in the White House political analysis office?"

Mandrake answers, "Diane and I are coworkers. We basically do the same thing. I'm sure Diane has told you that about her work."

"Yes, she has." Rig responds. Then he focuses on Professor Goldman and asks, "Professor, what interesting subjects are you teaching this year?"

With his elitist nose in the air, Goldman responds, "Teach is not the correct word, Chief. I lecture on the subject of international relations, I answer questions, I specify reading assignments, and I administer tests."

Rig decides he does not like these people. He decides to cease attempts to drive the conversation.

Amanda Goldman queries, "Chief, what was the most interesting sea life you saw when you were scuba diving in the Philippines?"

Rig expends ten minutes telling the group about his scuba diving and island camping trips in the Philippines. When he is asked questions relating to his work in the Philippines, he states, "My work is classified. I am not permitted to talk about it."

After dinner, they move to the living room for after-dinner cordials. Diane and her friends reminisce their college days. Ten minutes into the conversation, Amanda Goldman asks Rig if he graduated from college.

"Associate degrees only," Rig responds.

"More than one?" Amanda asks.

"Yes, two degrees. One in *Electronic Engineering* and one in *General Studies*."

Congressman Thayer rolls his eyes, expressing condescension.

Professor Goldman expresses bewilderment as he declares, "Chief, you come across more intelligent and knowledgeable than the degrees you hold."

Rig chuckles; then he comments, "After watching many well-educated people act stupidly, I conclude that the level and quality of one's education in no way reflects one's level of intelligence or knowledge."

Professor Goldman smiles and nods, "Yes, Chief, I believe that is true."

The conversation turns to politics. Diane and her friends believe in redistribution-of-wealth by government, and they all believe America is the problem in the world and not the solution. They consider the profit motive to succeed as being evil. Corporations and the rich never pay their fair share in taxes and all industries should be nationalized. They believe that the government should make all citizens equal instead of every citizen having the equal opportunity to succeed. They declare the U.S. Constitution to be an irrelevant and dead document. They support a socialist America controlled by totalitarian central planners. Illogically, they describe those who want America governed per the Constitution to be fascists.

They endorse a central planning federal government that decides what should be produced and how products should be distributed. Government control is the fairest and prevents citizens from being victimized.

Rig opines, "That doesn't work well in the socialist nations of the world. The people of the USSR and Soviet Bloc suffer from lack of necessities. Government central planning is inefficient. Only private enterprise can efficiently provide what the people need and want."

Professor Goldman declares, "That's because the leaders of those countries are more concerned with advancing communism than concerned with the needs of their people. Socialism works when educated, compassionate, and enlightened leaders are in control."

Diane and the others announce their agreement with Professor Goldman, which further validates Rig opinion that the most common trait of leftwing ideologues is their inability to grasp fact, logic, and reality.

Rig stands and announces, "I must get back to my quarters and get some rest. I have duty tomorrow. It was a pleasure meeting all of you, and I hope to gather with you again."

Amanda Goldman asks, "Chief, what do you do when you have the duty and where do you have duty? Uh, if you are permitted to reveal that information."

"I stand duty in the COMNAVTELCOM duty office. An officer and a junior enlisted man stand duty with me. There are approximately thirty Naval Communications Stations and Naval Radio Stations around the world that come under the direct command of COMNAVTELCOM. After working hours and during the weekend, the duty officer reads messages that are action to COMNAVTELCOM to determine if immediate action is required. If it is, then we contact the applicable on-call department representative, usually an officer. We also take phone calls of an emergency nature and, then inform the applicable on-call department representative."

Sandra Mandrake advises, "All these government and military abbreviations confuse me. What is COMNAVTELCOM?"

Rig answers, "Commander Naval Telecommunications Command."

"Do you get a lot of immediate action messages or emergency calls?" Amanda Goldman asks.

"Rarely do we get emergency calls. Those Naval Communications Stations under COMNAVTELCOM control are commanded by navy captains or navy commanders who are more than capable to handle emergencies affecting their bases. We usually handle ten-to-twenty immediate action situations on a Sunday duty day."

Sandra Mandrake raises her hand to announce she has a question. "Chief, what do you do specifically, if you are permitted to reveal that information?"

"I serve as technical advisor to the duty officer."

Professor Goldman expresses bewilderment as he inquires, "Are not those duty officers more knowledgeable than you regarding navy communications?"

"Not usually," Rig responds.

Professor Goldman shakes his head, indicating non-comprehension of the concept and conveying that in his mind Rig speaks illogically. He raises his voice over the others and challenges, "How can officers be your superiors if they do not know more than enlisted men? How do officers teach in your radio schools if they do not know more than enlisted men?"

Realizing that this conversation might become lengthy, Rig returns to his seat; then he responds to the professor's questions. "Officers function as managers and leaders and depend on chiefs to advise them on the technical aspects of communications systems. Officers do not teach in naval communications schools. Chiefs and first class petty officers teach the classes."

With a confused expression and confused tone, Professor Goldman states, "But they do not have teaching credentials, correct? They do not have college degrees, correct? Only officers have the college degrees necessary to obtain teaching credentials." Goldman pauses and shakes his head. He declares. "You are not making sense, Chief."

"Teaching credentials based on a bachelor degree is not required to teach navy courses. Navy courses are taught by experts in their fields. Like for radioman schools, chiefs and first class are experts in the subject they teach."

"But that's not enough," Goldman objects. "Without knowledge of teaching methods that mold and motivate students, learning objectives cannot be met."

Rig advises, "Graduation rates are ninety-nine percent. Rarely is a student dropped for academic reasons."

Goldman shakes his head and expresses disbelief that teaching can be successful without at least four-year college degree and teaching credentials.

Sandra Goldman, who teaches literature at a local junior college, queries, "Chief, what is the education level of these navy teachers?"

"They are not called teachers. They are called instructors. They attend an eight-week course to learn how to write curriculum and how to manage the classroom."

"An eight-week course!" Professor Goldman declares. "Impossible to successfully teach any subject with so little education!"

Rig shakes his head and expresses dismissal of the professor's logic; he advises, "Successfully done every day in hundreds of navy schools . . . actually hundreds more when you include schools of all the military services. Instructors are already experts in the subject they teach. They usually have eight or more years' experience in their fields when they become instructors."

"But knowledge of the subject matter is not enough," Amanda Goldman argues. "Just because a person knows the subject does not mean that person will be a good teacher."

Rig counters, "I don't know what you mean by a *good teacher*. Like I said, graduations rates are ninety-nine percent."

Professor Goldman asks, "What teaching style do these instructors use? Do they all use the same style?"

"They lecture on the subject, specify reading assignments, grade lab work, answer questions, and administer tests."

Diane chuckles at Rig's clever association with what Professor Goldman said earlier.

Professor Goldman's face flushes red.

An awkward pause causes Rig to stand and announce, "I must really go now. I hope we all dine again."

Diane follows Rig to the door.

After a short, non-passionate kiss on the lips, Diane says, "Call me tomorrow. I'll be home after five."

"Will do," Rig responds as he walks out the door.

Chapter 28

Fifteen minutes later, Diane's remaining guests have made trips to the bathroom, have refilled their brandy glasses, and have resettled into their seats on the couch and overstuffed chairs in Diane's living room. Congressman Billy Thayer opens the conversations. "Diane, your navy friend is an unusual and interesting person."

"He is that," Peter Mandrake confirms. Then Peter asks Diane, "If you and Chief Page had not been high school friends, do you think you would have become attracted to him had you first met him now, here in Washington?"

"Like you said," Diane responds. "Rig is an interesting man."

Professor Goldman points a finger at Diane and suggests, "You should be dating military officers. That would get you into senior officer circles."

"I do date military officers," Diane informs.

Sandra Mandrake chuckles and expresses devilishness as she opines, "Yeah you date the officers, but it is the chief who shares your bed. Your Chief Page is a ruggedly handsome man."

Diane smiles knowingly.

Sandra Mandrake adds, "But that ugly scar on his forehead is distracting. How did he get it?"

"Last year in Sardinia," Diane states. "He ran into a low hanging pipe on his ship."

Professor Goldman declares, "Well, I am not impressed with the *Hero of Thurso*. The military's education process is extremely flawed. No wonder as to why the military is so inept."

Congressman Thayer expresses doubt at Goldman's word; he comments, "I dunno, Bart. I sense something different about Chief Page. We need to be careful about what we say around him. I am not so sure it was wise to express our political beliefs in his presence."

"What?!" Sandra Mandrake challenges. "No secret that we are progressives, the same as our President. Washington finally has enlightened and educated people in charge."

Thayer retorts, "Chief Page leaves no doubt that he is a rightwing extremist."

Diane advises, "Rig is rightwing, but he's no extremist. He is just a patriotic American man who wants to serve his country. He is not a threat to us."

"All rightwing fascists are threats," Amanda Goldman states. "Anyone who is against achieving social justice through nationalization of industry and redistribution of wealth is a threat to the revolution."

Diane explains, "Having him in our circle is advantageous to our cause—to the revolution. Makes us look different from what we are."

Professor Goldman stares skeptically at Diane and warns, "You and Peter work on Jimmy Carter's White House staff. Sandra is a lobbyist for several labor unions. Billy exposed his progressive agenda during his campaign. No one will believe we are conservative right-wingers. We can't let your Chief Page get too close to us. We might make a mistake, and he will discover The Alliance."

Diane argues, "But isn't that true about any of our friends who are not members of The Alliance?"

Congressman Billy Thayer challenges, "But none of our other friends are rightwing extremists."

Diane ignores the extremist comment and counters, "With Rig in our circle, we will appear less radical. Remember The Alliance's strategy for revolution. We must hide who we are and hide what we are doing until more than half of the voting populace is willing to accept our doctrine. Then we step forward, reveal ourselves, we get voted into power, and implement our doctrine. Rig will be our camouflage. He will not gain knowledge of The Longjumeau Alliance unless one of us tells him. The Alliance is secret, and I have no plan to tell him about it."

As Rig drives along the damp, dark streets of Georgetown

toward the Francis Scott Key Bridge, he recollects conversations that he and Diane had about her friends during the weeks leading to the dinner party. Diane, the Mandrakes, the Goldman's, and Congressman Thayer come from wealthy families. Comfort and privilege were handed to them. They were all handed trust funds with tens of millions of dollars when they turned twenty-one. Tens of millions of dollars not earned by them but earned by fathers or grandfathers or great grandfathers.

Rig shakes his head and expresses bewilderment about people like them—people that he refers to as Marxist millionaires. They lead luxurious lives while crusading for redistribution of their own wealth. *Bewildering! Could be guilt or shame about unearned wealth, maybe.*

Chapter 29

As Rig drives his Jeep through the main gate of the navy installation at Cheltenham, Maryland, he recollects the history of the base. The base was once named U.S. Navy Communications Station Washington D.C. and was once a key component in the worldwide navy communications high frequency radio teletype network. With the arrival of computerized message processing systems and satellite radio paths, the need for numerous naval communications stations around the world with large antenna fields became redundant. The navy downsized its worldwide communications assets and realigned the mission of the Cheltenham base. Along with the realignment came a name change to U.S. Navy Communications Unit Cheltenham, Maryland. The land of the Cheltenham base is now home to a number of navy commands. The Office of Naval Intelligence has maintained a secret presence on the base since the early 1950s.

Captain Watson, ONI Assistant Director for Counterespionage, ordered that all of Rig's briefings with his naval intelligence superiors take place in the secret building on the Cheltenham base. Rig's current mission is in the D.C. area and Captain Watson does not want any tails to observe Rig entering the ONI headquarters building located on the Suitland, Maryland federal complex. Entrance to the Cheltenham base requires a NAVCOMMU CHELTENHAM sticker on a vehicle's windshield and a DOD or military I.D. card shown to the main gate guards.

The area of the base that contains the ONI secret building and other secret operations is separately fenced and guarded by gate sentries. Entry requires specified decals on vehicles and a separate I.D. card for individuals.

Also aiding in Rig's cover is that the navy's CUDIXS Testing Center is located on the Cheltenham base. His cover assignment to Commander Naval Telecommunications Command Test and Certification Division requires frequent visits to the CUDIXS Test Center.

Rig parks his Jeep Cherokee in the small parking lot next to the ONI building. At the ONI building front door Rig does not attempt to enter the combination to the cipher lock that must have been changed several times during the past year. He pushes the talk button of an intercom device. "Chief Page to see Commander Macfurson."

A male voice responds, "Okay, Chief, hold on a minute."

Several minutes later, a petite female YN2 wearing Winter Blue uniform opens the door and invites the chief to enter. Her voice wavers because she is physically affected by the presence of the tall, ruggedly handsome chief in Dress Blue uniform.

Two minutes later, Chief Page sits at a conference table with Captain Brad Watson, Lieutenant Commander Sally Macfurson, and civilian Senior Intelligence Analyst Bob Mater. Bob Mater, a portly and graying man with long hair and a beard in his late fifties, has been a naval intelligence analyst since 1943—first, as a navy officer for three years; then as a civilian since 1946. Bob is ONI's most senior analyst.

Bob Mater begins the briefing. "While you were vacationing in Sardinia, we followed your friend, Diane Love. She has been involved is some mysterious activities. Of course, it was your suspicions that motivated us to tail her.

"Shortly after you departed for Sardinia, we tailed her to rendezvous around the D.C. area with a KGB agent who poses as a member of the Soviet Embassy's Office of Cultural Affairs. Those two meet several times a month.

"Then we discovered that every couple of months she boards a private airplane at National Airport. We traced the airplane and flight plans. The airplane belongs to Tollison Management, Inc., which is a subsidiary management company of Kendley International, Inc. During the last couple of months, Miss Love has been making more frequent trips on that airplane to the Kendley Estate in Connecticut."

Rig interrupts in a quizzical tone, "Kendley International?"

"An oil company," Bob Mater informs. "That airplane always

delivers Miss Love to a small municipal airport in central Connecticut. A limousine owned by Kendley International meets the airplane on the tarmac and takes her to the country Estate of Edwin Kendley.

"When Miss Love visits the Kendley Estate, there are always the same visitors at the same time. All the visitors stay for a few days, normally over a weekend. Those visitors include prominent businesspeople, President Carter Administration personnel, and two U.S. Congressmen.

"During the past five years, two people who worked at the Kendley Estate have mysteriously disappeared. The most recent was eight months ago.

"After the visitors have gone, Edwin Kendley delivers a large yellow envelope to a dark skinned, mustached man name Enrico Mendoza. We believe that he is of Central or South American origin. Kendley and Mendoza never meet in the same place twice. One time it was the Boston Train Station and another time it was at a hotel in Buffalo, New York. Another time it was a truck stop on Interstate 95 in Connecticut. The last time was at Kennedy Airport.

"Mendoza lives in a large sprawling hacienda located on the outskirts of Panama City, Panama. We put a surveillance team on Mendoza's hacienda. Visitors to that hacienda include members of the American Embassy staff and military officers from various commands around the Canal Zone. Some spend the night there. Those military officers always wear civilian clothes when they visit Mendoza's hacienda, but their short hair, American style clothes, and manner betray their identity. The most frequent U.S. military visitor is Lieutenant Commander Roberto Pantero. He is the executive officer at the U.S. Naval Communications Station at Fort Amador in the Canal Zone. We continue to have tails on everyone who visits Mendoza's hacienda."

After a few moments of thought, Chief Page comments, "Tailing all those people must be stretching ONI resources."

Bob Mater responds, "This is a joint ONI and CIA effort. CIA provides most of the surveillance personnel."

"Okay, what's my mission?"

Lieutenant Commander Sally Macfurson advises, "Your first priority is to find out what that Panama hacienda is all about. You must penetrate the security and get inside. Best case is that you find out the content of information Edwin Kendley is passing to Mendoza.

"Second, discover Commander Pantero's involvement with Mendoza. We are building a dossier on Pantero and you will get separate, detailed briefings."

Chief Page asks, "Do you have any information on his background?"

Sally Macfurson answers, "He's a submariner. Normally when submarine officers rise to lieutenant commander, they are assigned as executive officer of a submarine or assigned to a submarine staff, but for some reason that we have yet to uncover, he is assigned as executive officer of U.S. Naval Communications Station Panama."

Rig asks, "When do I go to Panama?"

Sally advises, "Your cover trip to Panama must be open, announced, and officially unclassified. Tell your friend Diane Love, and when the opportunity presents itself, tell her friends that you are making a trip to Panama."

"Won't that put them on guard?"

"Good chance that Diane Love and her friends and associates who meet at the Kendley Estate don't know about the connection between Edwin Kendley and Enrico Mendoza. If Kendley is up to no good, compartmentalization is in effect."

Chief Page responds, "I saw a memo yesterday announcing that the COMNAVTELCOM I.G. Team travels to Panama three weeks from now to inspect the Naval Communications Station. Since I am assigned to COMNAVTELCOM, no one should think it unusual that I be on the I.G. Team."

Captain Watson expresses agreement and says, "I will contact Captain Blakely and ask her to put you on the I.G. Team for Panama."

Chapter 30

Lieutenant Angela Ramos had seen the chief's picture in newspapers and magazines. She was not expecting to be immediately intimidated by his mere presence. His posture conveys powerful self-confidence. His eyes communicate his unconquerable spirit. His overall manner conveys that of a prowling tiger.

"Sit there Chief," the medium height, slim, black female lieutenant says while pointing to the armchair in front of her desk.

The impeccable condition of the lieutenant's uniform and the neatness of her office reflect her dedication to order and discipline.

Rig unbuttons the jacket of his Dress Blue uniform, then sits.

"Chief, I serve as the I.G. Personnel Officer and Equal Opportunity Officer. We inspect a command's equal opportunity program. Therefore, we must ensure that all members of the I.G. Team support the Navy's Equal Opportunity Program." The Lieutenant stares directly into Chief Page's eyes and asks, "Do you support the Navy's Equal Opportunity Program?"

"Ma'am, I support equal opportunity for all sailors."

The lieutenant nods acceptance of Chief Page's response but notes that page did not answer the question. She asks, "How does the navy provide equal opportunity to every sailor?"

"I don't know, ma'am. Those processes take place outside my area of knowledge and influence."

Lieutenant Ramos asks, "Specifically, what is outside your area of knowledge and influence regarding the navy's Equal Opportunity Program?"

Rig answers, "Recruiting, advancement boards, school assignments, duty assignments."

Ramos finds Chief Page's short, direct answers irritating. *Obviously, the chief is not a conversationalist.*

"What is your support level of the navy's affirmative action program?"

"I don't know the details of the navy's affirmative action program, other than that the navy promotes and assigns some sailors based on their race, gender, or ethnicity. I assume that the navy knows what it is doing."

"That falls short of open support," Ramos opines. "Please expand on what you accept."

"Navy leadership believes it is the right thing to do. So I do not speak or act against it."

"But you do not believe it is the right thing to do, correct?"

"Ma'am, my considerations have no impact on the navy's programs. I see no value in revealing my considerations."

"Chief, COMNAVTELCOM is committed to supporting the navy's equal opportunity programs. As a member of the I.G. Team, you will inspect a command's equal opportunity culture. The I.G. Team loses credibility if any team member is not openly supportive of all navy programs. Now, reveal to me your support or non-support regarding the navy affirmative action program."

Chief Page stares intently at Lieutenant Ramos for a few moments, "Then he asks, "Ma'am, you are a woman with dark skin and with a Spanish sounding name. Were you promoted and assigned to the I.G. Team, which is a career enhancing assignment because you are a minority that filled a quota?"

Ramos expresses irritation and declares, "Chief, you are out of line! Your question is totally inappropriate!"

"Ma'am, I am attempting to explain my opinion of affirmative action. I am asking that question to help you understand my opinion. Please allow me some freedom here."

After a few moments, she responds, "I don't know if my current position is a result of affirmative action."

"Why don't you know, ma'am?"

Ramos expresses annoyance as she explains, "Advancement boards and assignment detailers do not explain why someone is selected or not selected."

Page asks, "So you could have been selected on your merits or because of need to fill a quota."

"Yes, Chief, that's true."

"Well, ma'am, I don't care why you were selected. I couldn't care less whether your rank and position has been achieved as a result of merit or a matter of filling a quota. It makes no difference to me. The navy decided you are worthy of your rank and position, and it is not my place to judge the navy's action in such matters. So I accept the navy's action."

Ramos casts a disapproving stare. Then she asks, "Tell me how you ensure everyone in your charge is provided equal opportunity."

"When making decisions regarding my sailors, I do not consider their race, ethnicity, or gender."

"What actions have you taken in the past when you observed equal opportunity violations?"

Chief Page stares quizzically at Lieutenant Ramos. He is not sure he understands her question. He answers, "I have never observed race, ethnic, or gender discrimination by any sailor."

Lieutenant Ramos flinches and expresses surprise. She considers the chief's words; then she states, "That is unique, Chief. I must say that I find it hard to believe that during your twelve years in the navy you have never observed any discrimination."

Chief Page is silent and waits for a question to answer.

The lieutenant casts a calculating stare at Chief Page. Then she asks, "Chief, I have reviewed hundreds of reports of discrimination while in this position—many from Naval Communications Stations around the world. I am amazed that during the past twelve years you never heard an accusation of discrimination."

"I guess I wasn't clear ma'am. I am aware of some discrimination accusations over the years. What I said was that I never observed acts of discrimination."

"I am not following you, Chief."

"I am aware of discrimination accusations but not aware of any acts of discrimination."

"You're saying that those accusations were false?"

"False or lack of evidence."

Lieutenant Ramos studies Chief Page for a few moments. Then she flips through a few pages of his service record and studies his last evaluation. Then she asks, "Were you ever accused of discrimination?"

Because there is no record of the times he was falsely accused and because he does not want to go deeper into this subject, he lies. "No ma'am."

Lieutenant Ramos casts an inquisitive stare at Chief Page.

Rig stares back. He believes that the lieutenant is the first black person he has seen that has bright-blue eyes.

"Chief, as an Inspector, you might be accused of discrimination when you file a negative inspection report. I need to know that you will be cooperative in any investigation into your conduct."

"I must be clear, ma'am. I will never respond to accusations of misconduct. I will not engage in wasteful and pointless efforts to appease. I will not participate in investigations into innuendo or hearsay. If my accusers have relevant facts, then charge me under the provisions of the UCMJ. Otherwise, stay out of my space with theatrics. I will always demand court-martial in such situations. My reasoning is simple—lay out the relevant facts or shut up."

"Okay, Chief, I understand your position. We must move on to other questions." She glances down at the chief's last evaluation, which was a transfer evaluation from USS *Randal*. Then she asks, "Chief, where do you see yourself as a valuable asset to the I.G. Team?"

"Ma'am, I was told my role on the I.G. Team would be as a technical inspector of communications center operations, security, maintenance, and documentation. All my performance evaluations report that I am expert in those areas."

A doubting expression appears on the lieutenant's face while she sits in thought. After nearly one minute, she comments, "If you are selected for the I.G. Team, you will travel a lot. Do you have a problem with that?"

"No ma'am."

Ramos hands Chief Page a sheet of paper. "You are scheduled for interviews with the technical inspectors. They will test your level of communications expertise. You are dismissed."

Chapter 31

"Enter," Master Chief Andrew Crowe orders.

Rig enters the small conference room and finds one master chief, tall and thin with peppered black hair, and with the name tag *RMCM Crowe*; and one senior chief with brown hair, glasses, a pot belly, and with the name tag *RMCS Graves*. Rig immediately recognizes RMCS Graves who Rig knows from NAVCOMMSTA Philippines.

After introductions and greetings, the three chiefs sit. Crowe and Graves sit on one side of the table, and Rig sits on the other side of the table. Five, three-ring binders are stacked on the end of the table to Rig's right. Crowe and Graves have pens in their right hands poised over writing pads.

Master Chief Crowe begins. "Chief Page, Senior Chief Graves has briefed me on your performance at NAVCOMMSTA Philippines. He tells me that you initiated actions that turned the communications center around. He says that he replaced you in the communications center after you were sent back to the States. He told me that he benefitted from your implementations—in that you made his job easier for the six months that he was in your previous position."

Rig expresses appreciation for the accolade.

Senior Chief Graves comments, "You've experienced a lot since departing the Philippines. How are you feeling?"

"I am fully recovered and ready to get back into the game."

"The game?" Master Chief Crowe questions with a slight challenging tone.

"Back to work," Rig clarifies.

Master Chief Crowe states, "Chief, the purpose of our meeting today is to evaluate the level of your technical knowledge. Technical knowledge is important because we don't want our team members discredited in the field. We don't expect you to be an expert in all aspects of communications, but you need to be expert in the areas in which you inspect." Crowe pauses to gauge Page's response.

Rig is silent and stares at Crowe.

Crowe casts back a quizzical gaze and asks, "Do you have any questions before we get started?"

Rig offers, "I think that my advancement to chief is proof of my technical expertise. I think Senior Chief Graves can attest to that."

Master Chief Crowe states, "Don't take it personal, Chief. If this were ten years ago, I would agree that advancing to chief proves your expertise, but the navy's priority for advancement has changed and many with marginal technical expertise and no sea duty are being advanced to chief."

Rig nods and conveys understanding.

Crowe opens a three-ring binder. He fingers through a few pages; then he directs, "Define the security areas commonly found at a Naval Communications Station."

Rig sighs deeply and consciously suppresses an attitude of annoyance: he responds, "Security areas include Exclusion Areas, Controlled Areas, Limited Areas and Restricted Areas. An Exclusion Area is defined by physical barriers and subject to access control, where mere presence in the area would result in access to classified matter. A Controlled Area is defined ..."

After an hour of questioning, discussions, and a few challenges to Rig's answers; Senior Chief Graves asks the final set of questions, "What document specifies procedures for torn-tape relay procedures?"

Chief Page responds, "ACP 127, U.S. Supplements."

"What if the tape relay includes AUTODIN terminals?"

"JANAP 128," Rig replies; then he sighs deeply. He glances at his watch.

Master Chief Crowe chastises, "This exercise boring you, Chief?"

"Yes," Rig responds in a soft, even tone.

Master Chief Crowe comments, "We are done with our questions. You did very well. However, I must say that you became confrontational and arrogant when I told you that you answered incorrectly. If you act that way in the field when your inspection reports are challenged, you will tarnish the image of the I.G. Team."

Crowe glances at Graves; then he returns his attention to Chief Page. Crowe states, "Senior Chief Graves warned me that you respond defiantly and arrogantly to challenges of your actions."

Because he is being scolded by a senior and not being asked a question, Rig does not respond.

After a long, awkward silence, Master Chief Crowe asks, "Chief, what is your response?"

"Response to what?"

"To my concerns that you will act confrontationally and arrogantly."

Rig declares, "That's not my manner. You misperceived my response. I will not act that way."

"You declared boldly that you are right, and we are wrong; that is arrogance."

"That's not what I said, Master Chief. I declared my answers are correct. I did not declare your answers are wrong."

Crowe expresses understanding. He speculates, "So you're saying that your answers and the checklist answers are both correct."

Rig responds, "I don't know if your answers are correct or incorrect. I only know that my answers are correct."

Crowe asks, "Can you prove your answers correct?"

"Absolutely," Rig responses with confidence and raised eyebrows. "I need access to a Registered Publications Library."

Senior Chief Graves advises, "The Documentation Branch has an RPS Library. You're welcome to use it."

Master Chief Crowe advises, "One more thing, Chief. Your technical expertise is of primary importance, but so is the way you present yourself. I detect that you are one of those disrespectful and confrontational chiefs who relies on some past accomplishment to carry him." Crowe pauses and collects his thoughts. "Your *Hero of Thurso* reputation will only carry you so far. During the past year, I have heard many stories about you." Crowe pauses as he casts a curious stare at Rig. Then he asks, "Is it true that you get into bar fights?"

Rig responds, "I have never voluntarily engaged in a bar fight. I have fought back after being attacked."

Crowe Responds, "Senior Chief Graves told me about the fight in *Blow Heaven Bar* in Subic City. He told me about you being placed on report for assault and battery and dereliction of duty. But instead of accepting Article Fifteen punishment, you demanded court-martial."

Rig shakes his head slightly and wonders how the *Blow Heaven* incident is relevant to serving on the I.G. Team.

Master Chief Crowe inquires, "Why did you do that?"

Rig appears bewildered by the master chief's question. "Why did I do what?"

"Why did you get into that fight in *Blow Heaven* and why did you demand court-martial?"

Rig exhibits calm as he responds. "I don't answer *why* questions about my behavior. *Why* is not relevant."

"Your past conduct indicates how you might act in the future. We can't have you punching out people when we're traveling on I.G. Team business. So as part of my consideration to approve you for the I.G. Team the *why* you did those things is relevant."

Rig glances back and forth between Crowe and Graves a few times. Then he comments, "No section in an evaluation form requires *the why* of a sailor's behavior be explained. *Why* is irrelevant."

Senior Chief Graves expresses disapproval and comments, "So you are not going to tell us *why*."

"Correct." Rig responds with confidence.

Master Chief Crowe asks, "Do you have any concern about being on the I.G. Team negatively affecting your primary duty as CUDIXS Testing Manager?"

"No." Rig answers confidently.

The master chief advises, "Okay, our session is over. You can return to your duties."

After Rig departs the room, Senior Chief Graves tells Master Chief Crowe, "I think Page will prove he is correct on those technical questions. In the P.I. he proved he knew the books."

Crowe responds, "That does not concern me. We are always updating our references on inspection checklists. I am concerned about his military manner. He is stubborn, arrogant, and intimidating. He draws trouble and controversy like a magnet."

Senior Chief Graves comments, "Having the *Hero of Thurso* on the I.G. Team will improve our image in front of the commands we inspect. The first few days of the inspection, members of the local command are usually distant and cautious."

Master Chief Crowe nods and expresses agreement.

Chapter 32

Chief Radioman Rigney Page sits across the desk from Master Chief Yeoman Eileen Crammer. The master chief wears her Service Dress Blue Uniform. She reviews Rig's interview checklist.

While the master chief reviews Rig's interview checklist, Rig occupies his time by counting the seven gold service stripes on the master chief's uniform, which convey 28 years naval service.

She looks up from the interview checklist and stares at Rig's face.

Rig shifts his attention from her service stripes to her slack jawed face. Because of her seven service stripes, Rig knows that the master chief must be at least forty-six years of age, and she looks every bit that age. Her hair is evenly streaked with brown and gray. She wears black rimmed navy issue glasses. Rig estimates she is thirty pounds overweight, most of it in her hips and belly. What he might look like at age forty-six flashes through his mind.

"Chief, my role on the I.G. Team is inspector of command admin and personnel offices. As a collateral duty, all reports from enlisted inspectors are routed through me for editing and rewrite, if necessary. The purpose of this interview is to evaluate your writing skills. Part of your job as an inspector is to write daily reports to Captain Blakely and to write final inspection reports.

"All reports are submitted to me. My job is to edit the technical inspectors' reports so that they make sense. These reports are read by senior officers both at the local commands we inspect and by COMNAVTELCOM himself. In the past, I spent way too much time editing and rewriting reports from the technical inspectors.

"With the objective to shorten the time it takes to finalize reports, Captain Blakely has given me the authority to reject inspector candidates for poor writing skills. We must reduce the time-wasting effort to fix incomplete sentences and dangling participles." Crammer pauses to judge Page's reaction.

Rig is silent.

After several moments of silence, she asks, "Chief do you know what they are?"

Rig expresses curiosity. "Know what are?"

With an impatient gesture, she questions, "An incomplete sentence and dangling participles. Do you know what they are?"

"Yes, I do. My performance evaluations show the highest marks for writing skills."

"No shit, Chief. All chiefs get superior marks in writing skills. I need to know if you really have superior writing skills." Crammer lifts a sheet of paper from her desk and hands it to Chief Page. She directs, "Circle the incorrect grammar, incorrect spellings, and incorrect punctuation in those three paragraphs."

Rig takes the paper and chuckles.

"What's funny, Chief?"

"I am reminded of an amusing incident several years back."

Rig spends five minutes identifying and circling errors. Then he hands the paper back to the master chief.

Crammer quickly scans the paragraphs for the most common errors that test takers miss. Rig did not miss them. She slides the paper across the desk, face up, toward him; she asks, "In the second sentence of the first paragraph you circled the word *lay*. What is the error?"

The *lay* error is one of her deceptive tests. All previous test takers who circled *lay* as an error explained the difference in usage between *lie* and *lay*, but that is not the error.

Rig reads the sentence; then he answers correctly, "In the sentence, *lay* is a transitive verb. It must be followed by an object, but isn't."

In a surprised tone, Master Chief Crammer queries, "Do you know the difference between transitive and intransitive verbs?"

Rig responds, "Well, I know the basic differences . . . doubt that I could give an expert's explanation."

Crammer nods. She pulls the sheet back across the desk and studies the chief's circles. She notes that he circled the word *affect*. That is not one of the errors she inserted into the test. She slides the paper across the desk again and asks, "Third paragraph—you circled *affect*. Why?"

Rig responds, "As the object of a preposition, *effect* is the correct word, not *affect*."

"Why?" she demands.

"The general rule is that *affect* is a verb or complements a verb and *effect* is a noun. That's my understanding, and, again, not an expert's explanation."

Master Chief Crammer does not know if Page is correct. She makes a note to research it.

Rig gauges the validity and relevance of this English test as a qualification to be an inspector.

Master Chief Crammer orders, "Explain the difference between a phrase and a clause."

Rig knows the difference but remains silent and expresses thoughtfulness.

After thirty seconds, the master chief challenges, "It's essential that you know the difference."

Rig casts an amused smile and inquires, "Essential to what?"

"Essential to you getting my recommendation for assignment to the I.G. inspection team."

"Oh, well, in that case, a clause has a verb and subject, and a phrase does not."

Master Chief Crammer is impressed. She holds a B.A. in English from Old Dominion University, and she considers herself an expert in English grammar. She asks, "I'm curious. How did a chief radioman gain excellent writing skills?"

Rig chuckles at the master chief's stereotype of radiomen. He answers in a calm, serious tone, "Lucky, I guess. I missed the knuckle-dragging Neanderthal indoctrination that most radioman go through."

Crammer's face flushes red with embarrassment as she realizes how elitist she must sound. "Excuse me, Chief. I incorrectly formed my question. What I meant is that most of the enlisted inspectors have poor writing skills. So I wonder why you are the exception."

"I apply what I learned in high school and college English

classes."

"How many college English classes have you taken?"

"Six, including the three correspondence courses."

In a haughty tone, Crammer challenges, "Correspondence courses? From where?"

Rig expresses amusement as he answers. "University of Maryland, European Division."

The master chief notes Chief Page's amusement. Again, her face flushes red.

Chief Page asks, "Are we done, Master Chief?"

"Yes, Chief. You will get a positive recommendation from me to be added to the I.G. Team."

"Great!" Rig responds. Then he stands, turns, and exits the master chief's office.

Master Chief Crammer casts a bewildered expression toward the closed door of her office. She cannot shake the feeling that she, and not Chief Page, was the person being evaluated. Then she retrieves her college English text on grammar. She begins her research on the correct usage of *affect* and *effect*.

Chapter 33

The next morning, the COMNAVTELCOM I.G. Team meets to discuss the upcoming inspection at NAVCOMMSTA Panama Canal Zone. The Inspector General, Captain Mary Blakely, explains the travel schedule, and she explains the inspection schedule. After the meeting adjourns, Captain Blakely tells Lieutenant Ramos to stay.

The captain directs, "Tell me about your interview with Chief Page."

Ramos advises, "I interviewed Chief Page yesterday. I do not believe he has the interpersonal skills to be an effective member of our team. He is intimidating and arrogant."

Captain Blakely smiles knowingly, then questions, "You found him blunt and direct, correct?"

"Yes, Captain."

Captain Blakely casts a knowing smile and comments, "I have known Chief Page for ten years, since he was a second class petty officer. He does not consciously intimidate others. He is not arrogant, and he is not domineering. People feel intimidated by his physically powerful and confident presence. He does not push himself on others. He lives, breathes, and works in *literal-ville* and has little tolerance for those who do not operate within the realm of reality. 'Touchy-feely' subjects, as he calls them, are not worthy of his time. His attitude is talk facts and reality or don't talk at all. He finds opinion irrelevant and rarely accommodates those who opinionate. He will not provide his opinion unless asked."

Ramos responds, "Ma'am, with all due respect, you just described someone who thinks he knows it all and is above it all."

Captain Blakely counters, "Believe me. That is not Chief Page's manner. I think that you misinterpret his behavior, just like I did when I first met him."

Ramos shakes her head slightly and casts her eyes downward—an action to convey her polite disagreement. She opines, "Captain, I believe that on inspection trips, he will become confrontational with anyone who challenges his inspection techniques and his inspection reports."

"No, Lieutenant, he will not become confrontational. He will remain calm and resolute. It's not his nature to become confrontational with other sailors. If anything, other sailors become confrontational with him. He will not respond to challenges of his inspections, unless he is proved wrong. Then his response will be an apology, and he will amend his inspection report."

Ramos expresses doubt. "I just don't read him that way. Master Chief Crowe interviewed Chief Page yesterday afternoon. The master chief came to the same conclusions about Chief Page as I did. Master Chief Crowe objects to such a junior chief being on the I.G. Team. We have always had seasoned senior chiefs and master chiefs with more than twenty years' experience . . . to maintain an image of credibility."

Mary Blakely understands Ramos's doubt. Comprehending Rigney Page's personality is not an easy task—even for those who have known him for a long time and who know his ONI affiliation.

Blakely tells Ramos, "Chief Page is a walking encyclopedia of communications operating procedures, technical manuals, 3-M System, security manuals, and safety manuals."

"So are the other chiefs," Ramos declares.

Blakely nods agreement; then says, "Not to the same degree as Chief Page. Let the interviews run their course, then assign him to the I.G. Team. I want him on the Panama trip."

With a doubting tone edged with disagreement, Ramos responds, "Aye, aye, Captain."

Chapter 34

U.S. Naval Communications Station Panama
Fort Amador, Canal Zone

Chief Page presses the doorbell at the message center door. Several seconds later, a window in the top half of the door opens; immediately the sound of teletypes and the smell of dirty ashtrays flow over his senses. Rig looks through the bars of the open window and into the face of a young navy woman who has a smile on her face and cheerful air about her.

She asks, "May I help you, Chief."

Rig hands the young female sailor his I.D. card through the bars; he advises, "I am Chief Page with the COMNAVTELCOM Inspector General Team. You should find my name on your Temporary Unescorted Access List."

The seaman studies Chief Page's I.D. card. Then she looks at him and studies his face.

Unescorted Access Lists are posted next to the door. She steps to the right and studies those access lists and does not find Chief Page's name. Then she returns to the barred window and advises, "Sorry, Chief, your name is not on any of the access lists."

Rig queries, "Do you have an access list for the COMNAVTELCOM Inspector General Team?"

"No, Chief."

Rig nods and exhibits impatience; then he requests, "Would you please get your division officer or division chief?"

"Okay, Chief. I will show them your I.D. card." The seaman closes the window panel.

Several minutes later, the window panel opens, and Rig looks into the face of Chief Radiomen Martin Elliot. Rig and Chief Elliot served together at the Naval Radio Station Thurso, Scotland.

"I'll sign you in," Martin says through the barred window.

The door opens.

Rig steps into the copy and distribution room. He stretches out his hand to Martin and states, "A pleasure to see you again."

Martin shakes Rig's hand and responds, "Likewise, Rig." Then he leads Rig to the message distribution worktable.

Rig appraises the difference in Chief Elliot's appearance. Elliot, who is the same height as Rig, is now fifteen pounds lighter and has gained more muscle tone. Elliot now wears a regulation trimmed beard, which Rig believes improves Elliot's physical persona.

Chief Elliot pushes the Guest Logbook toward Rig.

Rig opens the Guest Logbook and fills in his information. He writes "RMC Elliot" in the ESCORT column. He advises, "I will need unescorted access for the next ten days and so will others on the I.G. Team."

"I'll look into it."

Martin's words befuddle Rig. While quizzically staring into Martin's eyes, Rig comments, "Look into it? The I.G. Team's pre-arrival package requires unescorted access for all I.G. Team members. Names, social security numbers, and security clearance levels were provided."

"Yes, I know. I prepared the access list three weeks ago and sent it to the communications officer for signature. Never got it back, which is what happens to all paperwork that enters The Pit."

"The Pit?"

Chief Elliot glances at the two seamen working the copy room; he says, "I'll tell ya about it later. Let's go to my office." Martin guides Rig across the communications center.

As they cross the Communication Center operations floor, Rig quickly recognizes two DSTE AUTODIN terminals that stand in the center of the room and occupy twenty-five percent of the floor space. He sees several radiomen walking Baudot code paper tape from the DSTE equipment to teletype equipment along the far wall. He assumes that area is the fleet center where USNAVCOMMSTA Panama communicates with ships at sea via radio teletype circuits.

In another area of the Communications Center, three radiomen sit at desks and process messages; one radioman sits at a teletype machine and prepares outgoing messages on Baudot code paper tape. Rig identifies that area as the message center.

They cross a carpeted area with half a dozen desks where several second class petty officers have message files open in front of them. "This is the Statistics and Traffic Checking section," Martin informs.

They enter an unoccupied office with two desks. Martin sits behind one, and he offers a chair against the wall to Rig. "I share this office with the technical control chief."

Rig inquires, "Where is technical control?"

Martin points forward and advises, "On the other side of that wall."

Rig opens his mouth to ask about the communications division organization, but Chief Elliot says first, "Tricia and I were saddened when we read about you being shot in La Maddalena. You look okay now. Are you?"

"Yes, I am fully recovered."

Martin comments, "I often think about that night in Thurso when you just happened to be carrying a gun when those terrorists stormed the chiefs club." Martin shakes his head slightly and exhibits incredulity; he states in a challenging tone, "I can't think of another chief that walks around with concealed weapons. Are you carrying a weapon now?"

"Only the one hanging between my legs," Rig answers with a grin and a chuckle.

With an expression of remembrance on his face, Martin chuckles.

From the doorway, a scolding toned voice declares, "We do not appreciate crude comments like that around here, Chief."

Chief Page and Chief Elliot turn their heads toward the doorway. A lieutenant (junior grade) of medium height and slender build with black hair stands in the doorway. The officer wears meticulously pressed khakis with sharp shirt pleats and sharp trouser creases. The officer's black leather shoes reflect a perfect shine.

Chief Page stands up.

Chief Elliot remains seated.

The officer enters the office.

Martin performs the introduction. "Chief Page, please meet my division officer, Lieutenant Van Thorton."

The officer steps toward Rig; then stops four feet away. The lieutenant advises, "We have a mixed group of men and women here, and sexual and sexist comments are not tolerated. Do you understand, Chief?"

Rig responds with a nod and replies, "Yes, sir, I understand."

Starting with Rig's shoes, the officer slowly moves his eyes up Rig's frame, obviously performing a uniform and grooming inspection. He frowns several times as he lingers on several areas of Rig's khaki uniform.

Rig is not concerned. He knows his military appearance exceeds minimum standards.

The officer asks in a challenging tone, "Who are you, Chief, and what is your purpose here?"

"Chief Page, sir. I am with the COMNAVTELCOM I.G. Team. My task is to inspect the communications center."

Van Thorton glances at the calendar; then shoots an inquiring glance at Chief Elliot."

Chief Elliot informs, "We knew it would be sometime over the next three weeks, but we never received a detailed schedule."

The lieutenant stares at Chief Page, waiting for an explanation.

"Sir, I mailed the detailed schedule myself. The package included copies of checklists that I will use during the inspection."

"More paperwork lost in The Pit," Chief Elliot opines.

Van Thorton orders, "Stow the negativity, Chief!"

Elliot looks away from the officer—a disgusted expression on his face.

Van Thorton asks Chief Page, "What is your inspection schedule?"

"I will conduct the inspection over the next two weeks."

With a challenging tone, Van Thorton questions, "Two weeks. Why so long?"

Rig responds, "The inspection itself will only take about twenty-four man-hours. I'll be coming in here at random times, day-and-night."

"Without notifying me first?!"

"I am notifying you now, sir. Uh, the schedule had me briefing communications center officers and chiefs during this first day—today."

Van Thorton exhibits thoughtfulness. He examines Rig's face and calculates Rig's age. Then he glances at Rig's collar devices. "How long have you been a chief?"

"Three years sir."

The officer appears perplexed.

Rig waits patiently for the officer to speak.

With a condescending tone, the officer declares, "I am not impressed by your manner, Chief. Your crude remark and less than impressive military appearance alarm me. And not confirming with me first that you were to begin your inspection today leads me to doubt your reliability and your competence. And your inexperience causes me to doubt the validity of your inspector credentials. I don't want my sailors exposed to you. I will repeat my concerns to your immediate superior. Who would that be?"

"That would be Master Chief Crowe."

"Where can I find him?"

"I believe he is inspecting the Farfan Receiver Site."

"Who is the master chief's immediate supervisor?"

"That would the Inspector General, Captain Blakely."

"Okay, Chief, where can I find him?"

"Captain Blakely is a woman. I believe she is topside in your commanding officer's office."

Van Thorton orders, "You and Chief Elliot wait here until I come back." The lieutenant about-faces and marches smartly out of the office.

Rig lowers himself into the chair. He casts a contemplative expression toward the open doorway, attempting to understand what just happened. He glances at Martin.

"So what do you think of my division officer?"

Rig shakes his head slightly and queries, "Is he always quick to judge and judge incorrectly?"

"All the time!" Martin replies in a sharp tone. "But that's not all he was doing."

Rig casts a curious stare at Martin.

Martin informs, "He was marking his territory and establishing the pecking order in the room."

Rig frowns, then expresses doubt.

"Believe me, Rig. Everyone in the room knowing that he is the senior man present is very important to him."

"But wouldn't that be obvious to everyone in the room."

"Yes, but not only does he want all in the room to know it, he wants all in the room to acknowledge it."

"I don't get it," Rig admits.

"Me neither, but that's his reputation and manner."

"Do his seniors know his manner?"

"I don't know."

Rig exhales a weak sigh. He asks, "What's the lieutenant's background?"

"He was a radioman aboard a destroyer for his first three years. Then he reenlisted for that two year associates degree program. He spent two years at a community college in San Diego. Remember that program?"

Rig nods.

"When he was in that college, he advanced to first class on his first try. Then he went to recruiting duty for four years in Wyoming or Idaho or someplace like that. He should have gone to sea after recruiting duty, but the navy offered him recruit company commander duty. So he pushed boots for three years. Then he applied for Limited Duty Officer and was selected first time before the selection board. Then he came here."

"What's his LDO specialty?"

"Navy Communicator."

Rig shakes his head slightly and expresses bewilderment. He queries for clarification, "He hadn't worked in navy communications for nine years and he was selected first time up for Navy Communicator LDO?"

"Yeah! Go figure!" Martin responds sharply, expressing sarcasm.

"Was he a chief when he was selected for LDO?"

"No. He was a first class."

Rig, again, looks contemplative for a few moments; then he inquires, "So what kind of officer is he?"

"A spit and polish empty suit—arrogant—condescending."

"That's unusual for an LDO," Rig declares.

"Sure is," Martin agrees.

"How's his navy communications knowledge?"

"Not very good—his knowledge hasn't advanced much past his RM2 days back in the 1960s aboard a destroyer. He constantly orders me to implement the dumbest policies and procedures. When I first got here, I was constantly arguing communications technology and procedure with him."

"How long you been here?"

"Six weeks."

"Six weeks?" Rig expresses confusion.

"After Thurso, I spent a year aboard a Military Sealift Command freighter. You know, a USNS, Military Sealift command."

Rig nods and expresses understanding. Then he asks, "What do you mean by when you first got here you argued procedures?"

Martin explains, "This Communications Center has some problems that need fixed. At first, I started making changes on my own initiative. Van Thorton found out and he ordered me to stop. He said it took him six months to get the Communications Center operating the way he wants. He told me not to make any changes or suggest any changes. He said that if he wants something changed, he will direct me to change it.

"And not only that!" Martin slams his fist on the desk. "He ordered me not to correct sailors who violate regulations and procedures. He said I am harsh and demeaning. He said that I am a chief of the *old guard* that disrespects and insults juniors."

Rig shakes his head and expresses negativity, conveying his disagreement with the lieutenant's behavior.

Martin responds to Rig's expression, "Yeah. I know. The man is a nut-job."

Rig looks around the office. He queries, "You got a coffee mess?"

"Yeah—in the break room." Martin stands. "I'll get us some. Wadda ya take in it?"

"Just a dash of cream."

Several minutes later, Rig sips coffee from a dark brown porcelain mug. Then he raises the cup slightly in the manner of a toast and comments, "Umm, that's great coffee."

"It's a local Panamanian brand."

Rig smiles while exhibiting appreciation. He is about to ask the brand name when the phone rings.

Martin picks of the phone handset and recites, "Naval Communications Station Panama Fort Amador Canal Zone—Communications Center Office—this is Chief Elliot—this is a non-secure line—how may I help you sir or ma'am?"

Rig chuckles.

Martin listens for a few moments; then he says, "Yes Captain. He is sitting here with me. I'll tell him." He cradles the handset.

Rig stares curiously at Martin.

"Captain Blakely wants to see you in the conference room. Do you know where that is?"

Rig shakes his head.

"Upper deck of this building. That's where the administrative offices are, including C.O. and X.O."

Rig stands and says, "Okay, Martin, I'll see ya later."

"I must escort you out," Martin advises. "You're not on the access list, yet."

Chapter 35

Rig enters the conference room.

Seated randomly around the rectangle shaped conference table are Captain Blakely, Lieutenant Ramos, Lieutenant Van Thorton, a commander that Rig assumes is the USNAVCOMMSTA Commanding officer, and Senior Chief Graves. All stare at Rig with serious, disapproving expressions. Rig focuses on Captain Blakely's face, snaps to attention, and declares, "Chief Page reporting as ordered ma'am!"

Blakely orders, "Stand easy, Chief."

Captain Blakely directs, "Lieutenant Van Thorton, return to your duties. You will be informed of my decision."

Without looking at Chief Page, Lieutenant Van Thorton stands, turns, and departs the room.

The USNAVCOMMSTA Commanding Officer stands, faces Captain Blakely and states, "I have some business that I must attend to. I support whatever you decide regarding Chief Page."

Captain Blakely nods acceptance of the commander's words.

The USNAVCOMMSTA Commanding Officer walks to Chief Page and extends his hand. Rig shakes the commander's hand. The commander says, "Chief Page, I am Commander Perkins, Commanding Officer of USNAVCOMMSTA Panama. It's a pleasure to meet a true American hero. Your service to our nation is greatly appreciated. I hope the outcome of this meeting allows you to continue your duties with the I.G. Team."

Rig blushes and feels uneasy at the unexpected compliment from a senior officer. Rig responds, "Thank you, Commander."

After Commander Perkins departs, Captain Blakely directs, "Take a seat, Chief."

Rig takes a chair between Senior Chief Graves and Lieutenant Ramos.

Captain Blakely advises, "Tell us what happened between you and Lieutenant Van Thorton."

"Chief Elliot and I were talking in the Communications Center

161

Office. We didn't know that Lieutenant Van Thorton was listening. I made a comment that the lieutenant declared crude and inappropriate. Then he criticized my military behavior and my military appearance, followed by challenging my competence and my credibility."

Lieutenant Ramos asks, "What did you do to cause Lieutenant Van Thorton to accuse you of all that?"

"I don't know."

Senior Chief Graves challenges, "C'mon, Chief, you must have done something."

"I do not know why Lieutenant Van Thorton acted the way he did."

Senior Chief Graves shakes his head, expressing disbelief.

Captain Blakely inquires, "What was the crude remark that you made?"

"I didn't make a crude remark."

Captain Blakely smiles and casts a knowing expression as she remembers Chief Page's style of reasoning. She rephrases. "Okay, what did you say that Lieutenant Van Thorton interpreted as crude?"

"Ma'am, restating the comment here, out of context, will not convey the humor that it did between Chief Elliot and me. What I said relates to an action I took that night when Scottish separatists attacked the base in Thurso. Chief Elliot was there. My comment only has a humorous meaning to those few who observed my actions that night."

Lieutenant Ramos scolds in a raised, irritated tone, "Chief, you must always be aware of what you say and who might hear you—to avoid offending anyone!"

Captain Blakely, Senior Chief Graves, and Chief Page stare at Lieutenant Ramos; each of them wondering where the hell that outburst came from.

Chief Page turns his attention to Captain Blakely and requests, "Captain, may I speak with you privately?"

Senior Chief Graves rolls his eyes at Rig's bold, improper but typical for Chief Page request.

Lieutenant Ramos feels outrage that Chief Page directly requested a private meeting with a senior that does not include her. She considers herself to be the I.G. Team's appropriate behavior and military protocol policeman. She blurts, "Chief, you must submit such requests through the chain-of-command."

An awkward silence falls over the room while all wait for Captain Blakely's response.

Captain Blakely responds with a question to Rig. "Chief, is the subject of your request the incident between you and Lieutenant Van Thorton?"

"Yes, ma'am."

The captain responds quickly, "Okay. Granted. Lieutenant Ramos and Senior Chief Graves, please give Chief Page and me about five minutes."

The Lieutenant and the senior chief depart the conference room.

"Captain, what is going on? Are you considering removing me from the I.G. Team?"

"No, Chief, I am going through the motions of investigating a complaint from an officer who declares a member of my team is not qualified to inspect said officer's work center."

"Going through the motions?"

The captain responds, "If you were not qualified, I would not have allowed you on the team, regardless of what the Director of Naval Intelligence requests or demands. Removing you from the team never entered my mind. Lieutenant Van Thorton is not the first officer to challenge the competence and credentials of one of my team. However, this is the first time it happened within the first hour after the team arrived onboard, and the first time the challenge included a complaint of crude language."

Rig responds, "Crude is Lieutenant Van Thorton's perception."

Captain Blakely declares, "Lieutenant Van Thorton fears that you will discover something negative about him during your inspection. That is why he complained to his C.O. about you. As soon as you discover what he hides, let me know immediately."

"Might be that he is just an asshole."

"Chief! Respect for the uniform!"

Rig and Mary Blakely shared a still-classified, top secret experience from their days at USNAVCOMMSTA Nea Makri, Greece ten years previous. She was the executive officer, and he was assigned to the communications department. She unknowingly entered a situation that Rig was working undercover and she came to know about his naval intelligence affiliation. Because of her knowledge of Rig's undercover work, several times during the last ten years the Office of Naval Intelligence employed Mary Blakely to deliver secret messages to Rigney Page.

Because of their classified and personal association, Captain Mary Blakely allows Chief Page some latitude that she does not allow with other chief petty officers, such as personal conversations and unchecked boldness and unchecked disrespect for those who deserve disrespect.

Their relationship never became romantic or sexual. When they first met ten years ago at NAVCOMMSTA Greece, they both fantasized about each other for a short period of time but then dismissed such an inappropriate relationship. Rig often considers how well the forty-one-year-old Mary Blakely, who was a college swimmer, retains her youthful, shapely, sexual appeal.

Rig suggests, "Could be that Van Thorton has nothing to hide but is insecure about his leadership ability."

"Could be, Chief. We administer the Command Climate Survey during the first week. If he has a leadership problem, it will show up in the survey."

Rig exhibits satisfaction, then says, "Well, I guess that's all I wanted to discuss." He stands; then comments, "With your permission, I'll return to my inspection duties." Rig exhibits that he just remembered something; he advises, "They don't have access lists for the team in the communications center."

Mary informs, "I've received the same report from our inspectors at the Farfan Receiver Site and the Summit Transmitter Site."

Rig waits for the captain to dismiss him.

She directs, "So that I believe I made the correct judgment to exonerate you, I must know what you said. You must tell me the context of the alleged crude remark."

Rig does not object. He knows he owes it to Mary Blakely. "Chief Elliot and I were discussing reports of my actions in the international press. He commented that it is unusual for a chief petty officer to carry concealed weapons. He asked me if I am carrying a concealed weapon right now. I told him only the one hanging between my legs."

Mary jerks slightly, expressing disapproval. She queries, "And it was that last part that Lieutenant Van Thorton found crude?"

"I assume so."

Captain Blakely opines, "I can understand why between two men who are bonding that it might be funny, but some would find the comment crude and offensive."

Rig casts an amused smile at Mary and asks, "Captain, have you heard my philosophy regarding reality versus perception?"

Mary returns an amused smile and says, "Uh, maybe. Refresh my memory."

With a pontificating tone, Rig state. "Reality is what exists or does not exist; perception is in the mind of the beholder."

Mary shrugs and expresses dismissal as she responds, "Well, yes, I have heard you say that, but how does that apply to this situation?"

Rig shoves his right hand into the right front pocket of his loose-fitting khaki trousers. His hand moves through the hole in the bottom of the pocket and down his thigh.

Mary flinches, blinks her eyes rapidly several times, and exhibits curiosity as she watches the moving bulge made by Chief Page's hand under the cloth of his khaki trousers.

Then, slowly, Rig pulls his hand up, through the pocket, and reveals that he holds a thin-blade, thin-handled dagger.

Mary chuckles and rolls her eyes. She is not surprised that he is armed because she knows he is on a naval intelligence mission in Panama, although she does not know his mission. She states, "Okay,

Chief, point made."

Rig waits for the captain to dismiss him.

Mary advises, "There is something I have always wanted to ask you."

He raises his brow in anticipation.

"When you look at me, do you see a frail, frightened, naked woman tied to a bed frame about to be raped and murdered or do you see a successful naval officer who has advanced ahead of her peers?"

Rig recalls that day ten years ago in Nea Makri, Greece when he saved Mary Blakely from being raped and murdered by international thugs. At the time, Mary was the executive officer of the nearby U.S. Naval Communications Station. He was a radioman second class assigned undercover to the base to investigate possible espionage by a navy master chief. He wonders why the captain believes his opinion of her is important or relevant.

He responds, "I see you as a navy captain who will probably be the next COMNAVTELCOM. Occasionally, I recall visions of you and me in that bedroom while I fought for our lives against those two thugs." Rig appears reflective, then reveals, "What nags my thoughts about that day is had my timing been half a second off, you and I would be dead."

Mary suppresses appearing astonished by Rig's revelation. She remembers those few moments when the thug appeared to have the upper hand in the fight against Rigney Page. She needs to convey she no longer fears those memories.

After a few moment of silence, Rig asks, "Should I go back to the communications center now?"

"Yes."

Rig exits the conference room. He smiles at Lieutenant Ramos and Senior Chief Graves who pace impatiently.

When Ramos and Graves see Rig, they dart for the conference room doorway.

Ten minutes later, Rig is back in Chief Elliot's office. After he sits and is handed another cup of coffee, Rig asks, "What is *The Pit* that you mentioned earlier?"

"That's the operations officer's office. It's a paperwork hoarder's paradise. We call it The Pit because most paperwork that enters that office never again sees the light of day. For example, I suspect that all the I.G. paperwork that you sent from Washington to prepare us for your inspection is gathering dust in that office. Leave requests enter his office but are seldom signed by him and sent to the personnel office. The operations officer is incompetent and has been passed over twice for Lieutenant Commander. Everyone knows it. Yet, the C.O. keeps him in place. Morale is low because of him."

Rig responds, "All that you said should show up in the Command Climate Survey. Your C.O. might take action after that."

Elliot declares, "Oh, it will show up, alright. I have twenty-five people in my division who have talked of nothing else since they were told a Command Climate Survey will be administered by the I.G. Team."

Chapter 36

As Chief Page walks up to the Communications Center door, he glances at the twenty-four-hour clock on the foyer wall. He writes the time 2355 on the inspection checklist. Then he rings the doorbell.

In the Communications Center copy room, RMSN Geraldo Gonzales hears the doorbell. He glances at the clock on the wall and expresses irritation that someone would be picking up messages at this time on a Friday night—the busiest time of the week in military communications. Gonzales has a fifty message backlog to copy and distribute to the appropriate command slot box.

Gonzales glances at his assistant—an RMSA only three weeks graduated from RM "A" School who works busily at the copy machine. Gonzales decides to answer the door.

Gonzales opens the top-half of the service door. He sees a tall and rugged looking chief in Summer Khaki uniform that he does not recognize. The chief carries a clipboard and a briefcase. "Can I help ya, Chief?"

"I am Chief Page with the COMNAVTELCOM Inspection Team. You should have me on your access list for unescorted access."

"Just a moment, Chief." Gonzales removes the access lists clipboard from a hook located next to the door; he flips through the first several pages.

Chief Page stares patiently at the short, thin, and wiry seaman with black hair and black regulation-trimmed mustache.

Gonzales advises, "Chief, I need to see your I.D. card."

Rig hands his I.D. card to Gonzales.

Gonzales checks the access list and finds Chief Page's name. A note by the chief's name orders that when Chief Page enters the Communications Center, he is to be taken directly to the Communications Center Watch Supervisor. Gonzales opens the door and allows Chief Page to enter.

When Chief Page enters the copy room, he hears the familiar

sounds of a communications center—air conditioning fans, equipment cooling fans, and the clacking of teletype machines off in a distant area not within his view. The same stale ashtray smell irritates his nostrils. He lays his briefcase on the first flat surface he finds. Then he quickly surveys the copy room and notes the location of two industrial size copying machines, message distribution slots, and a full wall of shelves with binders for message center files.

Gonzales hands the I.D. card back to the chief. Then he turns and shuts the door. When he turns back around, he sees Chief Page looking behind one of the copy machines.

Chief Page reaches down behind the copy machine and pulls out six full, stapled-closed burn bags and sets them on the floor—clear of any equipment. He reaches down and places the palm of his hand against the copy machine power supply housing which is too hot to keep his hand there. Then, he grabs a handful of paper dust off the floor between the copy machine and the wall. He dumps the handful of paper dust into an open burn bag. He makes notes on his inspection sheet that burn bags are stored between the copy machine and wall and those burn bags blocked the power supply blower fan exhaust vents.

Gonzales advises, "Uh, Chief, you are supposed to report to the Communications Center Watch Supervisor as soon as you enter Communications Center spaces."

"You can tell the supervisor that I am here. I will begin my inspection in this copy room."

"Aye, Chief." Gonzales steps quickly out of the copy room.

Ninety seconds later while Chief Page pulls full, stapled-closed burn bags from behind the other copy machine; Gonzales leads a first class petty officer into the copy room.

"Chief Page, I am RM1 Lang—the Communications Center Watch Supervisor. I need to assign someone to accompany you so that we can record the discrepancies you find."

Chief Page dumps another handful of paper dust into an open burn bag. Then, he responds to Lang, "Not necessary. I will provide a copy of discrepancies to your division officer. Your division will have time to correct those discrepancies. I will inspect again after your division officer reports the discrepancies are cleared."

Lang responds, "I will assign someone anyway."

Chief Page nods acceptance.

"What have you found so far?" Lang asks.

"Storing those burn bags between equipment and walls is a safety hazard. In this case, burn bags are blocking power supply ventilation screens. Find another place to store those burn bags."

"Aye, Chief."

Chief Page asks, "How often is the area between the copy machines and wall cleaned?"

"Sunday eve watch," Lang answers.

Chief Page expresses surprise. "There is three inches of paper dust back there. Are you sure it's once per week?"

"Cleaning Bill says Sunday eve watch. I know my section complies with the Cleaning Bill. I can't speak for other sections."

Chief Page says, "You should have someone clean back there, now, and make sure they clean those copy machine power supply cooling vents."

"Aye, Chief, will do." Lang pauses; then advises, "I must notify Chief Elliot and Lieutenant Van Thorton that you are here." Lang turns; then exits the copy room.

Chief Page turns toward Gonzales's assistant and notes the name stencil on her dungaree shirt is *Davis*. Her youthful, innocent, angelic face and manner remind him of a child at her first communion. He asks her, "Davis, how long will it take you to power down one of those copiers; then power it up to operational condition?"

"I don't know, Chief. I have never done it." The young seaman apprentice's voice quavers as she looks up into the intimidating face of the tall and physically powerful chief.

Chief Page, understanding that the young seaman apprentice is intimidated, softens his tone as he says, "Let me see your Personnel Qualification Standard checklist for Copy Operator."

She trembles slightly as she answers, "I don't know what that is,

Chief."

"How long have you been aboard, Davis?"

"Almost three weeks."

Chief Page directs, "Return to your duties." Then he turns toward Gonzales and asks, "How long to power down a copier, then power it up to operational condition?"

"Ten minutes."

Chief Page orders, "Power down one of the copiers; then de-energize the power to the copier at the circuit breaker."

Gonzales comments, "Ya know, Chief. We have a big backlog of messages. I don't think—"

"Do you have a backlog of high precedence messages?"

"No, Chief."

"Power down one of those copiers."

"Aye, Chief."

Gonzales walks to the copier that Davis is not using and flips the power switch to the off position.

The sound of a power supply cooling fan slowing down is noticeable.

Gonzales reports, "Chief, I don't know where the breaker switch is located."

Chief Page writes a note on the inspection sheet that the copy operator does not know the location of breaker switches. Then he asks Gonzales, "Do you have a Personnel Qualification Standard check sheet for Copy Operator?"

"I don't know what that is."

"When was the last time you were involved in a fire drill on one of those copiers?"

"Never, Chief."

Rig asks, "How long have you been working in the copy room?"

"Three months, Chief."

Chief Page orders, "Go find the circuit breaker."

"I'll ask RM1 Lang," Gonzales advises. He turns and exits the copy room.

The chief opens his briefcase and removes a screwdriver and

small multi-meter with red and black six-foot leads. He carries the screwdriver and multi-meter to the rear of the powered-down copier. He notes that the power cable runs in pipe conduit from the back of the copier to an electrical junction box on the wall. He measures the resistance from the copier chassis to a ground plug in a wall outlet. If the copier chassis is grounded as it should be, the meter will read zero. But the meter reads infinity, indicating the chassis is not grounded, Chief Page takes another reading from elsewhere on the chassis. The meter still reads infinity. To prove that the power outlet ground contact is actually grounded, he takes a reading from that power outlet ground to another power outlet ground. The meter reads zero resistance—proving the power outlets are properly grounded. All the resistance readings prove that the copier chassis is not grounded, which is a safety violation. He checks "copier not grounded" on his inspection sheet.

Gonzales and RM1 Lang enter the copy room. Gonzales reports, "We cannot find the power breaker for the copiers. Labels are missing from some of the breaker panels."

"Show me the panel," Chief Page directs.

RM1 Lang leads the way onto the operations floor; through the message center; then into the fleet center. Lang points to a power breaker panel.

Chief Page is relieved that access to the breaker panel is wide and open. He inspects the panel. He writes on his inspection checklist that half of the breaker switches have no labels.

The chief turns around and faces RM1 Lang and Seaman Gonzales. "You can power up the copier."

Lang says to Gonzales, "Go power up the copier and get back to work."

Gonzalez turns and walks toward the copy room.

Lang advises, "I called Lieutenant Van Thorton and Chief Elliot. The lieutenant ordered me to follow you around until he gets here."

The chief nods acceptance of the information. Then he asks, "Did Chief Elliot say he was coming in?"

"He didn't say."

Chief Page looks at his clipboard and flips through the checklist pages. He says, "I will inspect the fleet center next. I will need a copy of the S.O.P. for the fleet center."

Ten minutes later, Lieutenant Van Thorn storms onto the Communications Center operations deck. He expresses anger as he searches for Chief Page.

Chief Page stands next to the ship-to-shore operator who processes messages to and from ships at sea. The chief is writing a negative comment regarding use of incorrect procedures by the ship-to-shore operator when he senses someone standing behind him. He turns and sees an angered, red-faced Lieutenant Van Thorton.

In a tight and brusque tone, Van Thorton challenges, "Chief, I left orders that you are not to inspect without someone from my division accompanying you."

Rig responds, "Sir, my orders for inspecting the Communications Center come from Captain Blakely and do not require that I be accompanied by anyone."

Van Thorton torts back, "I told RM1 Lang to accompany you! Where is he?!"

"I don't know, sir. He was here with me several minutes ago. I didn't notice until now that he walked off."

Irritation replaces Van Thorton's anger. In a more civil tone, he asks, "May I see your inspection sheets?"

Rig hands his clipboard to the lieutenant.

Van Thorton begins to tremble as he reads the volumes of *noncompliance* checkmarks and detailed remarks. He looks up from the clipboard and challenges angrily, "Chief, is it your intention to fail the communications center?!"

Page comments calmly, "Sir, I only record what I find. The Inspector General decides pass or fail."

Van Thorton expresses thoughtfulness for a few moments; then he challenges, "You marked a lot of items in non-compliance. How can I trust that you know what is compliant and what isn't?"

Chief Page responds, "Sir, I have no control or influence over what you trust. What you trust belongs to you and has nothing to do with me." Rig casts a grin at the lieutenant. He advises, "The references for each inspection item are listed on the inspection checklist. If you doubt the marks I assign, I recommend you review the referenced documentation."

Van Thorton retorts sarcastically, "It would have helped if we had copies of these inspection sheets before the I.G. got here."

"Sir, checklists were included in the pre-arrival package mailed to this command more than a month ago."

"We never got them."

The chief informs, "This command got them, sir. The pre-arrival package was sent via Armed Forces Courier Service, signature receipt required."

Van Thorton expresses frustration as he turns and walks away.

The chief returns to observing ship-to-shore operations.

Forty minutes later, Chief Elliot comes to stand beside Chief Page. "How's it going, Rig. I heard you are giving us a beating."

"Yeah, it's looking bad," Rig responds. "Are you aware that those copiers are not grounded and that the power breaker panels are missing half the labels?"

Chief Elliot appears concerned as he answers. "I did not know about the grounding problem on the copiers. We rent those copiers and all installation and maintenance is performed by a company in Panama City. Yes, I do know about labels missing on the breaker panels."

Rig asks, "Do you have a plan to label those breaker panels?"

"No."

Rig flinches with surprise. He knows that Martin Elliot is more competent than what he currently represents.

Noting Rig's surprise, Chief Elliot explains, "Remember, I told you that orders from Lieutenant Van Thorton prohibit me from making changes or improvements without his approval. I told him about the labels. He said he would take care of it, but that was three weeks ago, and nothing has been done."

Rig shakes his head, expressing his disapproval of Martin's reasoning. Rig states, "Martin, you must fix that problem, regardless of Van Thorton's orders or non-action."

Martin sighs deeply and nods agreement. He responds, "Yeah, you're right. I was hoping that Van Thorton's incompetence would eventually cause himself embarrassment in front of his superiors. I will place a work order with Public Works first thing in the morning for labeling those panels and for grounding those copiers."

"Good!" Rig states emphatically. "I must continue with my inspection, now." Rig turns and walks toward the technical control area.

Chapter 37

Enrico Mendoza's sprawling twenty-thousand square foot hacienda stands on the top of a hill two miles east of Panama City. The hacienda faces the coast and has an expansive and spectacular view of the Gulf of Panama and most of Panama City. For security purposes, Mendoza had the jungle cut back and cleared one-hundred-fifty feet on all sides. Surveillance monitors scan the cleared area. A narrow and private paved road leading off Corridor Sur provides access to the hacienda. But first, a visitor must be verified at a security stop on Mendoza's property line.

On this warm and humid evening, Rig and his Panama contact, U.S. Naval Intelligence Field Agent Frederico Murphy, do not travel any roads. Using a handheld satellite geo-positioning device and night-vision goggles, they trek through the jungle toward a predetermined location that is fifty yards from the hacienda's south clearing. Both wear combat jungle camouflage, combat boots, and an army green web belt equipped with pistols, ammo pouches, sheathed machete, and combat knife. Each carries a jungle camouflage backpack filled with binoculars, telescopic lens cameras, and one-day food rations and water canteens. Their boots are muddy from the soggy ground that took a pounding from a rainstorm several hours earlier. At periodic intervals, they apply bug spray to their clothing and exposed skin.

The occasional loss of the satellite geo-positioning signal, caused by jungle foliage forming a canopy over their head, does not concern them. Frederico has traveled this course many times during the past year, and he marked the way. Frederico leads and every few minutes he places his hand on a machete cut he made on a tree trunk the last time he made this journey.

When they arrive at the predetermined location, Frederico advises, "This clearing has served as our basecamp before. Prior to departing the area, we must be meticulous in removing all evidence of our visit here."

Rig adjusts his night-vision goggles; then he checks his geo-positioning device. He looks to the north. He can see the outside lights of the hacienda through the trees. He proceeds in the direction of the hacienda.

Frederico follows.

When they reach the edge of the jungle, they put away their night-vision goggles and pull binoculars from their backpacks. The illumination around the hacienda provides adequate light for the binoculars.

They quickly scan the south-side of the hacienda which includes the front of the hacienda and the horseshoe-shaped driveway. Rig comments, "A lot of cars up there tonight. Intel said nothing about a gathering."

A black Lincoln Town Car turns off the road and enters the horseshoe-shaped driveway.

Rig focuses his binoculars on the Lincoln.

A telescopic lens camera hangs around Frederico's neck. He lifts the camera to his eyes and targets the Lincoln.

The Lincoln stops near the hacienda's front door.

The Lincoln's rear door is darkly tinted, and the passenger is not visible. A young man with Latino features and wearing dark slacks and a white guayabera exits the driver's seat. He opens the rear door of the Lincoln; then the passenger steps out.

"Well, wadda ya know!" Rig whispers in a surprised tone.

Frederico focuses the camera on the medium-height Lincoln passenger who wears dress slacks and open colored white shirt. Frederico snaps six pictures.

"Do you know him?" Frederico queries.

Rig advises, "Yes, I know him personally—Congressman Billy Thayer."

"That name is familiar to me," Frederico states while still taking pictures.

"His name has been mentioned in the intel reports for Operation Shark."

Enrico Mendoza exits the front door of the hacienda and approaches Thayer. The thin and wiry South American and the young Congressman shake hands, and they express exuberant smiles as they exchange enthusiastic greetings.

Rig asks, "You're photographing them, right?"

"Oh yeah."

Enrico Mendoza and Billy Thayer enter the hacienda.

Several minutes later, a late model, red-colored with white-trim, high-riding Ford Bronco enters the driveway; then stops at the end of the row of eleven vehicles. United States Navy Lieutenant, junior grade, Christian Van Thorton exits the Bronco. He wears light colored slacks and a red-colored, long-sleeved, formal guayabera. As he steps quickly toward the hacienda's front door, he glances at his watch.

"He must be late," Federico states as he snaps pictures.

"Yes, but for what?" Rig responds.

Five minutes later, a large four-door Chrysler sedan stops near the front door. Lieutenant Commander Roberto Pantero, Executive Officer of United States Naval Communications Station Panama, exits the driver's seat and hurries into the hacienda without ringing the doorbell or knocking on the door.

Federico advises, "That naval officer makes a visit at least once each week—sometimes twice per week."

Rig responds, "Yes, I read about that in intel reports. My goal tonight is to discover Lieutenant Van Thorton's and Commander Pantero's connection with Señor Mendoza."

"What about that congressman?"

"Guess that's a plus—solidifies the evidence that the U.S. Congress and The Longjumeau Alliance are associated with a known terrorist."

Frederico comments, "When all this is made public, the American government will be torn apart."

"If it's made public," Rig responds.

Rig and Frederico remain quiet for several minutes as they continue their surveillance of the hacienda. They note that guards with automatic rifles are posted on the southeast and southwest corners of the hacienda.

The sound of movement in the jungle behind them causes Rig and Frederico to look over their shoulders toward the basecamp clearing.

Frederico glances at his watch, "That must be the rest of the team with the rest of our equipment. I'll go greet them."

At 2:00 AM, the joint ONI and CIA team is ready to penetrate Mendoza's hacienda. All of Mendoza's guests departed hours ago. Rig estimates only four people remain at the hacienda: Enrico Mendoza, one security guard who sits inside at a security camera console, and two outside roving armed security guards.

All U.S. intelligence team members wear backpack air-tanks with a breathing regulator built into the full-face mask. They wear vented lightweight cotton gloves so that they leave no fingerprints in the hacienda.

The six field operatives are divided into three sub-teams. The two CIA field operatives are assigned to maintain security and safety for all the U.S. operatives. Rig and Frederico will crack all safes and filing cabinets and will photograph all contents; then they will throw all papers to the floor to make it look like the paperwork is discarded and has no value. The other two ONI operatives will ransack the place and remove as many valuables as they can during the ninety minutes that the air tanks allow—the objective being that the intrusion be later judged by Mendoza as a robbery and not a U.S. intelligence raid.

The two CIA operatives will operate the compressed-air mortar launcher. The cellulous covered mortar warheads are designed to arm at one-hundred feet above the ground and on the descent burst at fifty feet above the ground and release sleeping gas in all directions. Anyone already asleep will notice nothing. Anyone awake will be knocked out within thirty seconds. The CIA operatives will bombard the hacienda with sleeping gas every twenty minutes.

At the edge of the jungle, one of the CIA operatives sets the final angle-of-fire on the mortar launcher. Then they fire four rounds. Each round bursts evenly spaced over the roof of the hacienda. The gas spreads one-hundred feet in all directions. Ventilation systems and air conditioning systems suck sleeping gas into the hacienda. One minute later, the two outside guards are lying on the ground, asleep.

The two CIA operatives step out of the jungle and move toward the hacienda. When they are within eighty feet of the hacienda; the density of insects, birds, and bats falling from the sky increases.

The two CIA operatives separate; one goes to the sleeping guard on the east end of the building and the other goes to the sleeping guard on the west end of the building. They test each guard's depth of sleep by slapping the guard in the face. Each guard remains asleep. Both CIA operatives signal an okay sign with their fingers back toward the jungle.

The four ONI operatives come out of the jungle and move quickly toward the hacienda.

Then the two CIA operatives return to the mortar launcher.

During the next hour, Rig and Frederico forcibly open every safe and every filing cabinet in Mendoza's hacienda. After photographing the contents, they throw the documents around the room, leaving the impression that the robbers found nothing of value in those documents. The robber team takes expensive guns, antique weapons, and expensive paintings. The safe located in Mendoza's bedroom contains the most valuable bounty of jewelry and hundreds of thousands of dollars. The robber team fills five duffle-bags with valuable items from the hacienda.

Before Rig departs Mendoza's bedroom, he points his pistol at Mendoza's head and considers how easy it would be to kill him. Killing Mendoza was strictly prohibited by the mission planners.

Chapter 38

USNAVCOMMSTA Panama
Fort Amador

A command's administration of the navy's Maintenance and Material Management (3-M) System is always audited by the COMNAVTELCOM I.G. Team. Because USNAVCOMMSTA Panama has three locations spread miles apart, a separate I.G. auditor is assigned to each location. In the case of USNAVCOMMSTA Panama, Master Chief Crowe audits the Farfan Receiver Site, Senior Chief Graves audits the Summit Transmitter Site, and Chief Page audits the Fort Amador Headquarters Site. The headquarters location includes several work centers and the command 3-M Manager's office. The command 3-M Manager is Lieutenant Van Thorton.

During the 3-M audit's final phase, all three auditors meet and compare records for any inconsistences. The USNAVCOMMSTA Panama conference room serves as the I.G. Team office. Today, Captain Blakely, Master Chief Crowe, Senior Chief Graves, and Chief Page sit at the conference table in a closed meeting. Maintenance schedules and file folders from each site and files from the 3-M manager's office lie spread from one end of the conference table to another.

"No doubt about it," Master Chief Crowe states while looking at Captain Blakely. "The Command 3-M Manager files include a maintenance work-center for the Summit Transmitter Site that does not exist. Records and maintenance schedules at the Summit transmitter site prove it."

Captain Blakely expresses curiosity and asks, "You're sure it's not a work-center that has been deactivated and it's just a paperwork glitch."

Master Chief Crowe responds, "The 3-M Manger's file is active on that Summit work-center. Chief Page has gone through the 3-M Managers files for that work-center." Crowe shifts his gaze to Chief

Page and asks, "What did you find Chief?"

Chief Page answers, "Lots of 2-Kilo forms reporting parts replacement—more than other work-centers. All the 2-Kilos have the same three signatures—the Executive Officer, Van Thorton, and a First Class Storekeeper in the NAVCOMMSTA supply department. Another strange thing about that nonexistent work-center is that the equipment assigned to that work-center does not exist. Senior Chief Graves and I checked the inventory twice."

Captain Blakely expresses thoughtfulness for several moments; then she asks, "So what does it mean, Master Chief."

Master Chief Crowe responds, "The only time in the past twenty-eight years that I saw a situation similar to this was when several members of the command, including the 3-M Manager, were faking parts replacements and were selling those parts on the black market."

Captain Blakely expresses surprise, then queries, "So you think that Lieutenant Van Thorton and Commander Pantero are involved in black marketing?"

Master Chief Crowe replies, "There needs to be a full investigation. Someone is not playing by the rules."

The captain queries, "How many people know about this?"

"Just the four of us in this room," Master Chief Crowe informs.

Captain Blakely orders, "I don't want anyone else to know about this. We will not put this in our inspection report. We will prepare a separate report and send it to the Naval Investigative Service."

Chapter 39

Rig sits in his office at the Massachusetts Avenue NW location of Commander Naval Telecommunications Command. He works on his final report regarding the I.G. Team inspection of USNAVCOMMSTA Panama.

The phone on his desk rings. He picks it up on the fourth ring.

"Good Morning. This is Chief Page, Commander Naval Telecommunications Command. This is a non-secure line. How may I help you sir or ma'am?"

A chuckle comes across the line, followed by, "Wow, Rig. That greeting is a mouthful."

Rig recognizes his sister's voice. "Hello, Kate, nice to hear from you. Oh, that greeting is required by the military." Rig pauses and waits for Kate to speak. She doesn't. Rig asks, "What's up?"

"Three nights ago, someone set fire to dad's warehouse. The night watchman died from smoke inhalation. Mom and dad have been getting threats over the telephone. Last night, I got one. Teri called me, and she got one last night too."

Anger fires Rig's quest for justice. He asks calmly, "What are the police doing about it?"

"They're investigating. There have been many fires at non-union companies in Los Angeles County and Orange County during the past two weeks. Police have not arrested anyone."

"What are the threatening calls about?"

"That if dad's business does not become a union shop, harm will come to all of us."

"What do the police say about the phone calls?"

"Dad talked to the police. They came to the house, and dad gave them recordings of some of those threats. The voices were disguised. The police said there was little they can do. They have put a tap on dad's home phone."

"Who was the security guard who died in the fire?"

"His name was Larry something. He was a Vietnam vet, married with two small girls. The irony is that the security guard rental

183

company he worked for was a union shop—the same union of those union bullies you and dad fought."

Rig sighs deeply and considers the stupid criminality of union violence. Then he asks, "What is the damage at the warehouse?"

"Over fifty percent destroyed. It's all covered by insurance. Dad has moved his office back into the house. Three of his employees quit for fear of being harmed. It will take months for dad to get the business back on a profit basis."

"What about dad's other employees?"

"He gave them two weeks' pay and laid them off. He promised to call them back to work in several months."

Rig's anger is fueled by outrage. At this moment, he wants to kill those responsible. Then he calms. He says into the phone, "Who are these union criminals that believe they can force their will on others through violence?"

Kate responds, "Dad thinks they are from the same union as those who attacked you and dad in that office building."

"Why didn't dad call me?"

"I don't know. I do know that he does not want you coming home. He believes he and the police can handle this without your help."

"I have my doubts," Rig comments.

Kate informs, "The Chamber of Commerce is paying for night guards at what's left of the warehouse, and they paid for a security system installed at the house. That asshole reporter at the *Long Beach Times* discovered what the Chamber of Commerce is doing for dad and accused them of funding anti-union scabs. That reporter wrote several articles that ask why the police are not investigating James Page and Rigney Page for setting fire to their own warehouse to frame the union. That reporter asks why the police did not investigate the possibility that the union guy who you beat up in at the house was abducted by you and taken to the house to frame him."

Rig says under his breath, more his thoughts than a comment directed at Kate, "Domestic enemies."

"What was that, Rig?"

"Nothing."

Kate says, "You shouldn't come home, Rig. I don't think there is anything you can do. Dad has had trouble with violent unions before. He knows how to handle them. I thought you should know about it."

"Okay, Kate. Thanks. Uh, how's the teaching going."

"Same routine . . . each year basically the same thing." Kate pauses; then she asks, "How is it going with the navy?"

Rig chuckles and states, "Actually, something different most of the time."

"Are you doing something dangerous there in Washington?"

"No,"

"I worry about you, Rig. Danger seems to find you."

"Don't worry about me, Kate."

"Okay, Rig. Take care and we are looking forward to your next visit home. Goodbye, now."

"Goodbye, Kate."

After hanging up, Rig considers vengeful actions against those union thugs and CLWUA officials. He formulates a plan. He reaches for his rolodex; he finds the number and dials it.

After three rings, a voice answers, "Extension 4289."

Rig says, "I need to meet with you."

John Smith recognizes Rig's voice. He asks, "When?"

"As soon as possible!" Rig's tone conveys urgency.

"How about lunch today at that place we had lunch the last time?" John refers to an Irish Pub on the Virginia side of the Potomac located halfway between the Chain Bridge and the CIA complex at Langley, Virginia.

Rig asks, "Noon?"

"Yes," John confirms; then he hangs up.

Rig fingers through the rolodex, finds the number he wants and dials it.

After three rings, a voice on the other end answers, "Air Operations, Department Echo. This is a non-secure line."

Rig says into the phone, "Priority Alpha Alpha One One—I.D. Pontus."

The air force master sergeant remains silent while he retrieves the appropriate file from his computer system. Then he challenges, "Authenticate *ford pickup*."

Rig responds, "Authentication is *surfboard*."

"Departure date and destination?"

"Tonight—destination Lima Tango." The coded destination decodes to San Diego."

"Wait."

Rig studies the calendar on his desk. Today is Friday. If all goes as planned, he can be back in the office by Monday morning. Rig anticipates that he will be assigned to a military flight departing Andrews Air Force Base tonight nonstop to San Diego.

Rig's travel priority and classified profile tell the flight-booking sergeant that Rig's travel request is classified and is of such importance that once the flight and seat are assigned to Pontus no one of any rank or position can cancel it.

The air force sergeant informs, "Confirmation sequence is Foxtrot One Seven, report at twenty-one-fifteen hours."

"I need to know the arrival time at my destination."

"Twenty-three-hundred hours."

Rig states, "Acknowledged."

The air force sergeant hangs up.

Rig glances at his watch. He has just enough time to meet the rendezvous time with John Smith.

Danny's Irish Pub is a popular lunch spot for those who work at Langley. The décor epitomizes the rich dark wood paneling of the real thing in Ireland. Irish symbols and icons hang on the walls. The wood-plank floors are covered with small, loose woodchips. All the pub's employees wear green colored bib aprons and green bowties.

Rig drinks from a glass of unsweetened, lemon flavored iced tea. He stares across the table at his longtime associate in the intelligence community, John Smith, who currently works at a defense contractor's office on the Langley CIA compound. John was Rig's mentor and protector when Rig first went to work for naval intelligence.

John takes a bite of the corn beef and rye sandwich. As he chews the tasty morsel, he casts a knowing stare at his old friend and protégé. They have been friends and comrades in arms since Rig's first mission with naval intelligence more than ten years ago. Last year when Rig was considering leaving the navy, John offered Rig a job as a civilian intelligence operative. He knows that Rig is about to ask a favor. John will grant that favor if it is within his power to do so.

Rig sees himself in John's persona. Their appearance is so similar that they are often thought to be brothers, although John is ten years older. Rig reaches into his breast pocket of his Dress Blue uniform, pulls out a slip of paper, and slides it across the table toward John. Rig advises, "I need those items delivered to that location at twenty-three hundred Pacific time tonight."

John scans the slip of paper.

"Rig emphasizes, "All that equipment and all those weapons must be untraceable. I might not be able to return any of it."

John looks up from the paper and comments in a quizzical tone, "Nondescript car—untraceable?"

Rig chuckles, "Well, I'll do my best to return that."

"That's not what I mean, Rig. You're obviously going on an unofficial mission. I can have all this delivered to you, but I cannot afford to eat the cost. You must pay for what you do not return."

"Deal," Rig assures.

John asks, "Will you share with me what you're going to do?"

"I can't."

"If you get into trouble, don't hesitate to call me. I have friends out there in San Diego. I can call in some favors."

"Thanks, John. I'll keep that in mind."

Chapter 40

At the Andrews Air Force Base Department Echo departure counter, the master sergeant stares curiously at the man walking toward the counter. The man has reddish-brown shoulder length hair, full trimmed beard, and wears a black leisure suit, a black silk shirt, and a black Panama hat with white band. The man carries a small suitcase and a black trench coat.

Rig feels conspicuous. All other personnel in the departure area wear uniforms. His civilian disguise draws stares. Of the three disguises he normally has locked in a chest located in a secret closet in his apartment, this disguise best aligns with his purpose, which is to travel to and from Southern California unrecognized.

This particular departure area is reserved for those departing on classified missions. Those who stare at Rig know he is not what he appears to be, and Rig knows that those who stare at him are not what they appear to be either.

Rig focuses his attention on the slim, fortyish, and balding master sergeant standing behind the counter. He attempts to judge the master sergeant's manner.

"I have a reservation," Rig announces as he reaches the counter.

The master sergeant opens a drawer to his right under the counter. "Confirmation number?" he asks.

"Foxtrot One Seven," Rig answers.

The master sergeant pulls an envelope from the drawer, opens the envelope, and pulls out a small card. He studies the card for a few moments; then he challenges, "Authenticate *football.*"

"*Undesirable,*" Rig replies.

The master sergeant pulls a red colored rectangle shaped card from the envelope and hands it to Rig. "Here is your boarding pass. Your flight will board in twenty minutes."

Rig queries, "May I ask about the type of aircraft and flight time?"

"It's a jet cargo plane. Flight time to San Diego is four hours. You and the army lieutenant over there are the only passengers."

Rig glances toward the army lieutenant with supply corps insignia. Rig doubts that the solidly built, crew cut, rugged looking individual is a lieutenant in the army supply corps.

"Thanks," Rig says. Then he takes a seat near the departure door.

Twenty minutes later, the master sergeant taps Rig and the army lieutenant on the shoulder and directs them to the boarding door. "Hand me your boarding passes," the master sergeant directs. "Go through that door. A petty officer from the aircraft crew will direct you to the plane."

Several minutes later, Rig and the army lieutenant are strapped into their seats and their luggage is stowed. They exchange a few words regarding the rough condition of the passenger area and regarding the boredom of flying.

The lieutenant spends a few moments scrutinizing Rig's head and face. He attempts to determine if Rig wears a disguise. He cannot detect details of a disguise.

Rig smiles and challenges in a friendly tone, "And you are a lieutenant in the army supply corps, right?"

The lieutenant casts a knowing smile and remains silent. Then he sits back and turns on his reading light. He pulls a paperback novel from his briefcase and turns to the dog-eared page. The lieutenant is not being rude. They both understand they cannot carry on a conversation.

For the next ten minutes, crewmen scurry fore and aft as they prepare the plane for takeoff. None of the crew appears curious about the long-haired, bearded civilian wearing a leisure suit. Rig assumes that he is not an unusual appearing passenger to this experienced aircrew.

Rig opens a copy of the best seller, *Roots*, a book of faction by retired U.S. Coast Guard Chief Petty Officer Alex Haley. Within moments, he is absorbed in reading about the life and times of Kunta Kinte.

Four hours later, Rig walks into the passenger terminal at Naval Air Station North Island, San Diego. Rig, still in civilian disguise, draws stares from the people in the terminal. All in the terminal wear navy uniforms. He was given his luggage prior to departing the aircraft; so he proceeds toward the main entrance at a fast pace. He has a rendezvous with John Smith's contact just outside the main gate at midnight—forty minutes from now.

He exits the terminal and steps outside into the chilly February night air. He slips into the lined trench coat and buttons it up. Then he begins his walk toward the main gate. He carries his small suitcase in his left hand.

Several blocks from the air terminal, a navy security sedan passes Rig. Then the sedan stops at the curb thirty feet ahead.

Rig stops and sets his suitcase on the sidewalk. A navy security patrolman wearing the khaki uniform typical of law enforcement exits the passenger side of the vehicle. The patrolman carries an energized flashlight and wears a black leather utility belt that includes a large caliber revolver and a nightstick. He stops four feet from Rig and runs the beam of the flashlight quickly up and down Rig's frame. Then he demands in an official tone, "Show me some identification."

Rig reaches into his back pocket and retrieves a wallet. He pulls an I.D. card from the wallet and hands it to the patrolman.

The patrolman points the flashlight beam at the I.D. card and studies it. The I.D. card informs that Rig is one Mr. Adam Davies, a GS-11 civilian employee of the U.S. Navy. The patrolman asks, "Do you have additional I.D.?"

Rig pulls a driver's license and an American Express Card from his wallet.

The patrolman examines the addition I.D. items. Then he asks, "Where do you work Mr. Davies?"

Rig replies politely, "Naval Electronics Systems Command in Washington D.C."

"And what purpose has you walking the streets of this base at this time of night?"

"I'm on my way to Pearl Harbor to provide technical assistance on some electronic equipment aboard a submarine. I just arrived on a military transport plane and was bumped by a higher priority passenger. I called a friend I know here in San Diego. I'll spend the night at his place. Then I'll catch a commercial flight out tomorrow afternoon."

"Where are you going now?" the patrolman asks.

"I am on my way to the main gate. I will meet me friend there."

The patrolman expresses thoughtfulness for a moment; then he offers, "We'll give you a ride to the main gate. Climb in back."

Several minutes later, the security sedan arrives at the main gate. Rig thanks the two patrolmen. He walks quickly past the main gate guard shack and exits the base.

The patrolman who offered Rig the ride opens his logbook. He pulls a pen from his shirt pocket; then logs the event regarding Mr. Adam Davies who works at Naval Electronics Systems Command in Washington D.C.

Rig scans the parking lot outside the main gate. He sees only one person standing in the parking lot, and that person watches him. He walks toward the man. When he is within ten feet he asks, "Did John Smith send you?"

The middle-aged, pudgy man with thinning black hair nods affirmative.

Rig observes that the man leans against a 1975 two-tone gold and dark brown colored Mercury Cougar XR-7. He comments, "I asked for a nondescript car. This one will draw attention."

"Sorry," the man apologizes. "It's all we have on such short notice. All our other untraceable cars are in use on other missions."

Rig nods, expressing his understanding; then he asks, "Did you bring all the equipment and weapons I requested?"

"Yes, I have everything on the list—all in the trunk."

"I'll put my suitcase in the trunk."

After placing his suitcase in the trunk, the man hands Rig the keys to the car.

Rig asks, "Can I drop you somewhere?"

"Not necessary. Taxicabs come through here often, or I can call one from those payphones near the gate."

"Okay, thanks." Rig enters the car, starts it, and drives off.

With the national maximum speed limit at fifty-five miles per hour, the drive to Long Beach along Interstate 5 takes two-and-a-half hours. Shortly after crossing the Long Beach city limits, Rig finds a cheap motel on Pacific Coast Highway. He registers as Mr. Adam Davies and pays cash for a two night stay.

He backs the car into a parking space in front of his room door. He opens the door to the room. Then he hauls his suitcase and the canvas weapons bag into his room. He hangs the Do Not Disturb sign on the outside door knob.

He glances at his watch—3:35 AM, but his body is still on Eastern Time, which is 6:35 AM. He decides to get six hours sleep. Then he will go out and hunt his prey. He removes the long hair wig and peels off the fake beard. He undresses; then takes a shower. He falls asleep two minutes after his head hits the pillow.

Chapter 41

Rig stands naked before the bathroom mirror in his motel room. He carefully applies the glue that holds the fake beard to his face. While looking in the mirror, he presses the fake beard to his face. The process takes about 60 seconds. He is satisfied with the results. The mustache fits perfectly to his upper lip, and the beard looks natural. The color of the beard perfectly matches the reddish-brown body hair that covers him from his neck to his ankles.

Next, he dons the wig of the same color as the beard. The wig flows over his ears and touches his shoulders. Then he dresses in worn, loose-fitting denim jeans, denim shirt, and thigh-length denim coat. He tops off his denim ensemble with a blue colored ball cap with a *CAT* construction equipment logo on the front. While inspecting his image in the mirror, he expresses approval of his credible long-haired, bearded construction worker appearance.

A few minutes later, Rig sits on the bed and digs through his suitcase. He finds the pocket-sized notebook in which he has logged everything he has learned about the Construction and Labor Workers Union of America—CLWUA—and about the union thugs that the CLWUA sent after him and his father.

Biographies of those thugs were provided by John Smith some weeks ago as a favor to Rig. All of those thugs were born and raised in Southern California, and all of them served in combat roles in Vietnam, which means they are qualified in hand-to-hand combat skills. Rig knows that when he attacks them he must have the advantage.

Union goon, Max Robertson, served as an Army Ranger in Vietnam; so Robertson will be the most dangerous. Rig estimates that Robertson's right hand should be healed from the damage Rig inflicted with that hammer claw in the Harris Shipping building four months ago.

Union goon, Allen Villanueva, served as an infantryman in Vietnam. After being discharged from the Army, Villanueva served two years in prison for robbery. He learned his electrician skills while in prison.

Horace Lombardi is no longer a threat. The beating that Rig inflicted on Lombardi that night in his parents' backyard resulted in permanent damage to Horace's arms and legs. Rig concludes that justice has been served upon Lombardi, and Rig will take no further action toward him.

There is a fourth union thug who is the unidentified construction worker who joined the other three that night in the attempted attack on Rig at the Seal Beach intersection. Rig has no information on him.

His data on Weston Pyth, reporter for the *Long Beach Times*, is a photo from the article clippings that his sister Kate had sent him.

While studying the data in his notebook, he decides on his targets and where to start looking for them. He slips the notebook into his breast pocket. Rig had decided early to yield to his father's plea not to kill anyone in this war with the CLWUA, although those criminals deserve to die for killing the night watchman at the Page warehouse. He commits to maiming those union criminals for life.

Rig empties the contents of the canvas weapons bag and lays out the contents on the floor. He identifies those weapons that he will need. He straps a dagger with wrist sheath to each forearm. Both edges of the dagger blades are serrated. Then he stares at the nine-millimeter Beretta, attempting to decide if he should carry it. He knows that he must always be proportionally armed and ready to respond to danger. He remembers how he was caught off guard by Ensign Ryan in La Maddalena. And he remembers how being armed with a gun saved him from a beating and possible death that night at the Seal Beach intersection.

He slips the nine-millimeter snub-nose automatic into his right-hand jacket pocket and slips the suppressor into his left-hand jacket pocket.

A thirty-six-inch, telescoping steel baton normally used by police and martial arts experts lies on the bed in its leather holster. He removes the baton from the holster. The baton is in its collapsed state of twelve-inches long. He grips the textured steel base of the baton in his right hand; then he flips his wrist like a fly fisherman casting a fishing line. The telescoping baton extends to its full length of thirty-six inches. The sound of sliding steel smacking steel stop-rings is too loud. Rig knows that when he approaches his targets from behind, the baton must already be extended—out of the hearing range of the target. Or, he must be so close to his target when he pulls the baton that the sound of the baton extending to its limit will not matter. He collapses the baton to minimum length of twelve inches. Then he pulls on the knobbed end and extends the baton to its maximum length, which results in a nearly silent deployment. He collapses the baton to its minimum twelve-inch size, slips it into its holster, and attaches the baton holster to his belt near his right hip. His thigh-length denim coat hides the weapon.

Five minutes later, he loads the canvas weapons bag and his suitcase into the trunk of the Cougar. Although he paid for the room for two nights, he takes his suitcase with him in the event that he must quickly turn and flee towards San Diego.

He drives to his father's warehouse to assess the damage. The warehouse looks totally destroyed. He wonders how his father recovered any goods from that burned out shell. His father worked long and hard to build his business from scratch, risking all his money and property. Rig feels deep sadness for the security guard, father of two girls, who died in the fire. His emotions turn to revenge against those who crusade to violently impose their redistributionist and collectivist agenda on others.

Rig drives away from the warehouse in search of his targets. His first stop will be their homes. He strikes pay dirt on his first stop. Allen Villanueva's pickup truck sits in front of his small house in an old section of east Long Beach. Two little girls, about age seven, play in the front yard; they giggle and laugh as they play tag.

He drives another block and parks the Mercury Cougar at the curb. He has a good view of Villanueva's house and pickup truck. He worries about his sports-luxury Mercury Cougar drawing attention in this dilapidated neighborhood of rundown ten-year-old vehicles.

Rig slips on sunglasses; then exits his vehicle. He opens the trunk and removes a cigarette-pack-sized radio beacon transmitter from the weapons bag.

As he walks toward Villanueva's house, he passes several people who pay him no attention. He feels confident that his manual laborer's disguise of denim clothing and long hair and beard does its job.

As he comes abreast of Villanueva's pickup truck, he scratches his nose and forces his sunglasses to fall to the ground. Rig stoops. While wrapping his left hand around the sunglasses, he uses his right hand to attach the magnetized case of the beacon transmitter to the underside of the rear bumper. He walks away in a casual manner. He circles the block and returns to his vehicle. He energizes the beacon receiver. The beacon emits a strong signal. He starts the car and drives four blocks away and parks in a strip mall parking lot where his 1975 Cougar XR-7 is less conspicuous.

As he waits for Villanueva to make a move, Rig wonders about the mindset of workers who know their earnings are not based on their value to a company, but based on the fear of business owners who surrender to threats of union violence and vandalism. *Do such workers have any self-respect?* Like his father said, "Allowing unions to invade your business is the same as paying protection money to the mob."

After four hours, Rig is ready to give up on Villanueva. He considers beginning a search for union goon and former U.S. Army Ranger, Max Robertson. The sun is low on the horizon and Rig worries he wastes the short time he has to complete his tasks.

Just as he puts his hands on the keys to start the engine, the beacon receiver beeps rapidly, indicating the beacon transmitter is on the move toward Rig's location. Thirty seconds later, Villanueva's pickup truck comes into view and Villanueva is driving. Rig waits for one minute before he drives into traffic. He follows the beacon signal. Twenty minutes later, the beacon leads him to the same large country and western themed dancehall that he discovered when he followed Max Robertson four months ago.

As Rig drives into the Wagon Wheel Dancehall parking lot, he spots Max Robertson's pickup truck, now repaired from the damage done by Rig's handgun. Rig is pleased that two of his targets are at the same location. He is also pleased that many late model sports-luxury cars are parked in the lot and his vehicle will not be conspicuous. He remains inside the Cougar and waits for the dark of night.

When he enters the dancehall through saloon style swinging doors, his attention is immediately drawn to the song *Margaritaville* coming over the sound system. He quickly scans the expansive interior that includes a long bar with five bartenders, a large dance floor, hundreds of tables, and a railed area with twenty pool-tables. Being early Saturday evening, only sixty-some people occupy the place. Rig easily blends with the denim wearing crowd.

Robertson and Villanueva sit together at the far end of the bar.

Rig walks to the bar; then he sits on a stool that provides him a distant but clear view of the two union goons. He orders a beer. For an hour he sips the same bottle of beer and observes every action within the dancehall. Another twenty people enter during that hour.

Finally, Villanueva stands and walks toward the bathrooms.

Rig slips off his stool and walks thirty feet behind Villanueva.

Villanueva turns left into a corridor, disappearing from Rig's sight.

Rig increases his pace. He enters the corridor and turns left. The door to the men's bathroom is ten feet ahead. Again, he quickens his pace. As he opens the men's door, he looks to the right and sees Villanueva standing at one of the six urinals. Villanueva's back is toward Rig, and the six-foot-and-five-inch tall, broad-shouldered construction worker would appear undefeatable to anyone, except "The Unconquerable" Rigney Page.

Rig presses the doorknob lock to the locked position. As he moves toward Villanueva, Rig passes three toilet stalls. The door to each stall is open and Rig confirms all stalls are empty. Rig and

Villanueva are alone in the bathroom.

He is five feet from Villanueva; Rig reaches for the baton. Villanueva turns. He had heard steps behind him; so he is not surprised to see someone approaching the urinal bank. Villanueva's manner is not to acknowledge strangers with a smile and a greeting; so he does not look the stranger in the face. From the corner of his eye; he notes the man wears denim clothes, has long hair and a beard, and wears a blue colored ball cap. Villanueva jerks to a stop when he notices a short metal rod in the man's right hand. The metal rod is familiar to him, but its purpose momentarily escapes him. He raises his eyes to look at the face of the man, but the man's hand movement forces him to look back at the metal rod.

Rig flips his wrist and the baton expands to its full length.

Villanueva jerks backwards as he recognizes the weapon. His eyes again move toward the attacker's face, but the rapid movement of the attacker causes Villanueva to look back at the baton, which is now pointed at the floor. His army hand-to-hand combat training instinctively causes him to go on the offensive. He steps forward with both hands reaching for the arm holding the weapon. He anticipates the attacker will raise the weapon, then swing down.

Rig gauges Villanueva's forward movement. At the most advantageous distance for the weapon's length, Rig swings the baton in an underhand upward arc. The end of the baton slams into Villanueva's testicles.

Villanueva bends over, grabs his crotch, and yelps in pain.

Taking advantage, Rig swings his left fist in a full-strength uppercut and connects with the underside of Villanueva's nose.

Villanueva falls backward. The back of his head hits the edge of a urinal bowl. He is unconscious before he hits the floor. Broken teeth fall from his open mouth. Blood flows from his broken nose and cut lips.

The bathroom doorknob rattles, followed by a knock on the door.

Rig glances at the door.

"Hey, what's going on in there!" a male voice says loudly from the other side of the door.

Rig returns his attention to the unconscious Allen Villanueva. Without further hesitation, Rig repeatedly slams the baton against union thug's right kneecap. Blood seeps through the thug's pants. Blood stains appear on the baton.

Villanueva regains consciousness and sits up. He begins screaming in pain. From his disadvantaged position on the floor, he uses his arms in a futile attempt to fight off his attacker.

Using all his strength, Rig throws a left-handed, downward punch at the thugs face. The full-force punch knocks Villanueva unconscious again.

Then Rig repeatedly slams the baton across the back of Villanueva's right hand. After ten slams of the baton, every bone in Villanueva's right hand is broken. Where there was once a functioning and strong hand; now, only a bloody mass of flesh and broken bones exists.

Pounding on the door tells Rig that he only has moments to finish the job.

He stoops and lays the baton on the floor. Using his right hand, he reaches under his left coat sleeve and pulls the serrated dagger from the sheath strapped to his left forearm. Using the serrated dagger, Rig slices through the leather of the Allen's right boot, just above the heel. Blood pours through the cut in the boot. Rig does not stop the slicing motion until he is sure he has severed the Achilles tendon.

Villanueva becomes conscious again. He screams in pain as he comes to a sitting position.

Rig delivers a kick to the side of Villanueva's head. The force of the kick causes Villanueva's head to crash into the side of a urinal. Once again, the union criminal lies unconscious on the bathroom floor.

The pounding on the door becomes more forceful and more frequent.

Rig slips the bloody dagger into its sheath on his left forearm. He retrieves the baton and collapses it to its shortest size; then he holsters the baton. He steps quickly toward the door. Pounding and shouting continues from the other side of the door.

Knowing there might be more than one person standing on the other side of the door, he pulls his Beretta. He wants their attention on the gun or running from the gun, not looking at his face.

Rig pulls his ball-cap bill downward to cover more of his face. He twists the doorknob and the lock disengages. He opens the door slightly, then he pushes the locking button.

The knocking and shouting on the other side of the door stops.

Rig opens the door quickly and forcibly.

A medium height man in denim clothes, leather cowboy hat, and cowboy drooping mustache stands in the doorway. The barrel of Rig's Berretta points at the cowboy's forehead. Rig closes the bathroom door behind him; the lock engages.

A mix of men and women in the corridor see the gun, turn, and run away. Women are shrieking.

Rig knows he would never shoot any of these people. He might fire the gun at the ceiling to scare them but never shoot any of them. He is willing to be captured other than harm an innocent person. He is bluffing and no one is calling.

He runs to the end of the corridor; then he slows his pace. Just before turning to enter the dance floor, he pockets the gun. He makes a right turn, and bumps into a tall, solidly built man who wears black shirt, black pants, black cowboy hat, and drooping thick and bushy cowboy mustache. Rig recognizes him as one of the dancehall bouncers.

"What's going on in there?!" the bouncer asks in a demanding tone.

With a fearful tone and manner, Rig looks up toward the bouncers face and responds, "Someone said there's a guy with a gun in the bathroom."

The bouncer starts toward the doorway to the corridor. Then he stops, turns his head toward Rig and orders in a gruff voice, "Don't leave. I might have some questions later!"

Rig nods acknowledgement, "I'll be at the bar."

As Rig walks quickly toward the nearest exit at the other end of the bar, no one appears to recognize him as the gunman. Out of the corner of his eye, he observes Max Robertson staring curiously toward the corridor doorway that leads to the bathrooms.

Not wanting to appear that he is running away from anything, he maneuvers himself behind three other patrons on their way to the exit and walks at their pace.

Rig walks across the parking lot toward his car. The dozen people in the parking lot pay no attention to him.

As he drives off, he is frustrated that his chance to inflict justice on Max Robertson must be delayed. Rig knows that Max Robertson will be constantly on his guard from this time forward.

Chapter 42

Rig sits in the parked Cougar XR-7 in an industrial area of Long Beach. Only the intersections have streetlights; however, he can see the CLWUA Southern California Headquarters building one-block away. He looks at his watch—10:45 PM. On this Saturday night in this section of Long Beach, people find little reason to drive through this area and find no reason to be walking through it. The Cougar is one of only three vehicles parked within visible range. His conspicuous presence motivates him to accomplish his mission quickly.

As a result of his previous surveillance and intelligence gathering on the building four months ago, he knows that security cameras will capture his presence. He also knows that no security guards protect the two-story brick building. Protection against intruders includes thick iron bars on all windows and heavy metal access doors with industrial locks. Floodlights cast illumination down from the roof toward the sidewalk and toward the streets surrounding the building.

He exits the Cougar and begins the one-block trek. His footsteps sound loudly on the vacant street. In his right hand, he holds an explosive device used to blow down doors.

Just before coming into the range of the security cameras, he tugs the bill of his CAT ball cap down to cover his face. He still wears the same clothes that he wore earlier in the Wagon Wheel Dancehall. Although he does not want his face revealed, he wants CLWUA security personnel to connect the mysterious saboteur as the attacker against Villanueva at the Wagon Wheel Dancehall.

He approaches the front door of the CLWUA building. He calculates the security cameras will capture thirty seconds of his activity. His head is bowed. He walks up three steps to the main door. Then he presses the explosive device against the steel framed door. The device's magnet holds the device to the door. He flips the switch that arms the device.

Rig turns, then jumps from the steps to the sidewalk. He jogs along the street toward his vehicle on the next street.

Thirty seconds later, he enters the Cougar and starts the engine. He engages the transmission and drives about twenty feet. He turns right toward an alley entrance. He brakes the car to a stop before entering the alley. He picks up the remote detonator from the passenger seat. Before pointing the antenna of the detonator toward the CLWUA building, he quickly verifies no people walk about. He presses the button.

The explosion blasts the door inward. The blast shockwave is mild and hardly felt where Rig sits. He releases the footbrake and the Cougar moves forward.

Five minutes later, he is ten blocks away from the CLWUA building. He hears sirens in the distance. Rig speculates that in the future, the CLWUA will have security guards at that building day and night.

Chapter 43

Every part of the *Long Beach Times* front lobby is brightly illuminated and can be easily viewed from one-block away through its ceiling-to-floor, wrap-around glass panel windows. The *Long Beach Times* building occupies one-quarter of a large city-block near the city's business center. Six people walk about in the lobby. A security guard sits behind a horseshoe-shaped counter. Every few minutes, employees enter or exit side doorways. Obviously, the employees are busy publishing the Sunday morning edition.

Rig sighs deeply as he looks through the binoculars. He had not previously investigated the reporter, Weston Pyth, and he had not previously reconnoitered the newspaper building. Rig glances at the luminescent dial of his wristwatch—1:53 AM.

Rig's sister, Kate, mailed him several articles written by Weston Pyth that glorified the CLWUA as caring and benevolent and reported the actions of the Page family as rightwing extremists with no compassion for the common man. In his articles, Pyth completely misrepresented the conflict between the Page family and members of the CLWUA. Pyth published Lombardi's story of being knocked unconscious outside a bar and transported by James Page and Rigney Page to the Pages' home backyard. Pyth described Rig's beating of Lombardi as a battle between good and evil and evil won. None of Pyth's articles reference police report evidence that proved the truth told by the Page family. Articles included quotes from CLWUA members but no quotes from the Page family, no quotes from the police, and no quotes from James Page's employees. Pyth called the Page family a clear and present danger to the working class. He misrepresented James Page and his brother Dave Page as profit-seeking, privileged-class capitalists who crusade to oppress the working class with long and brutal hours and low pay.

Dave Page, Rig's uncle, owns a prospering roofing business in Los Angeles County. Pyth accused the Page Family of firing low-wage family men without cause. At the end of each article, Pyth warned citizens to boycott the Pages' businesses; because in a civilized world, association with evil will eventually result in punishment. The message was clear to those who are friends and business associates of the Page family: Associate with the Pages and you risk being intimidated or harmed by unions, and you risk your own home or own business being torched.

Rig lowers the binoculars and glances at his watch—2:10 AM. He decides not to bomb the building because of the risk of harming innocent people. He does not know where Pyth lives or where else the reporter might be at this time early Sunday morning. He resigns himself to the fact that he must go back to Washington without attacking Pyth and the *Long Beach Times*.

He decides to observe the building from a different location. He is about to start the car when he sees three people exit a side entrance. He brings the binoculars to his eyes. He immediately identifies Weston Pyth from photos in the articles that Kate sent him. Pyth's appearance and arrogant strutting manner reminds Rig of hippies who threw garbage at military men returning from Vietnam.

Pyth chats with his coworkers for a few moments. Then he crosses the street and enters the newspaper's employee parking lot.

Rig drives closer to the parking lot. One minute later, Pyth drives his 1970 dark-blue MG Midget convertible out of the lot and turns north. Rig follows.

Twenty minutes later, Pyth parks on a residential street in front of an apartment complex located in the Belmont Shore area of Long Beach.

Rig passes the MG and parks on the next block, close to the occan.

Pyth exits his MG; then he locks the MG's driver side door with a key. He enters the apartment complex.

Rig waits twenty minutes. Then he exits the Cougar and walks to Pyth's MG. There are no street lights; only the front door lights of homes and apartment buildings cast illumination. In the event that he is seen, he will be described as a man in denim clothing, long hair, beard and wearing a ball cap.

The MG is tightly parked between two sedans. Rig knows those two sedans will be damaged in the explosion. He stoops behind the MG and feels for the gas tank. He finds it; then he attaches an explosive device similar to the one he used on the CLWUA building, although this device is one-eighth the yield.

Several minutes later, Rig stands next to the Cougar. Using the night vision binoculars, he makes a final security and safety check of the area around Pyth's MG. Then he extends the remote detonator antenna to its full length; he presses the button. The MG explodes in a fire ball. Windows of nearby vehicles are blown inward. The fire spreads to three other vehicles and to the trunk of a palm tree.

Rig becomes concerned that the fire might spread farther than he calculated it would. The MG is engulfed in fire, and three other vehicles have fire on their roofs, trunks, and hoods. Those fires illuminate half the block.

He waits for sixty seconds and notes that the fires on the surface of other cars are diminishing. He becomes confident that the gas tanks on the other three vehicles will not explode. However, the fire on the palm tree continues to spread up the trunk. Knowing that residents will soon come to the street to investigate, he must now flee the scene. He also knows that if he does not depart now, the Cougar could be blocked by fire trucks and police cars.

He drives the Cougar one-and-a-half blocks; then he turns right onto Ocean Boulevard. Although Rig cannot see it, he knows the Pacific Ocean lies across the road to his left. After several blocks he turns right onto Corona Avenue and drives north toward 2nd Street. When he stops at the intersection of Corona Avenue and 2nd Street; fire trucks, ambulances and police cars speed east on 2nd Street with sirens blaring.

Rig makes a quick decision to depart Long Beach, now, and drive to San Diego. He calculates the fastest path to the San Diego Freeway.

After all the emergency vehicles pass through the intersection, he turns right and drives east on 2nd Street, which is Belmont Shore's shopping and business center. The emergency vehicles are speeding ahead of him. After a few moments, all emergency vehicles turn right, toward the fire. Rig continues east on 2nd street.

Thirty minutes later, Rig exits the interstate at the Huntington Beach exit. He stops at a gas station. In the men's bathroom he changes into his black leisure suit and Panama hat disguise. At the gas station phone booth, he calls the toll free number for Andrews Air Force Base and arranges a flight from Naval Station North Island, San Diego to Washington D.C. Then he calls the San Diego contact and arranges return of the Cougar and weapons bag.

During the drive to San Diego, Rig reflects on the justice he dealt tonight. His only concern is the possibility that innocent people might have been hurt as a result of the fire on Weston Pyth's street. His actions were quickly planned and, therefore, increased chances of unintentional results. He knows he will not rest well until he confirms no one was hurt by the fire.

Chapter 44

Rig arrives at Andrews Air Force Base at 4:03 PM. Two hours after that, he is back in his third-floor apartment in Arlington, Virginia. His telephone is ringing as he enters.

"Hello,"

"Well, Rig, so you are in Washington and not in Long Beach. Where ya been all day? I've been calling since noon."

Rig recognizes his father's voice. He responds, "Hello, Dad. What are you talking about?"

James Page explains: "About noon time, all the television and radio news broadcasts started reporting that a rightwing mad bomber is at war with the CLWUA. Last night, Villanueva, one of those union bullies who came after you and me, was nearly beat to death in a Long Beach dancehall by a man carrying a gun. Then, early this morning, the same man who nearly killed Villanueva bombed the CLWUA headquarters in Long Beach. And someone blew up that reporter's car. Ya, know, Weston Pyth, that reporter who takes the union side. Then, this afternoon, your sister Kate called, and she told me that she talked to you a few days ago and told you about my warehouse being burned."

Rig asks in a lighthearted, curious tone, "Why would you think this rightwing mad bomber was me?"

"Because I think you are capable of such things." James Page pauses for a moment; then asks, "So where were you all day."

"At the Smithsonian, then I went to the Chiefs Club for dinner and a few drinks."

"Well, yes, of course. Not possible that it was you. Nevertheless, I am glad someone finally took action against those thugs and against that lying liberal nut-job reporter."

Rig asks, "What's the prognosis on Villanueva?"

"Differing reports on that from various television stations. Some say he was nearly beat to death, and some say he was just maimed, that the attacker purposely concentrated on maiming Villanueva. One reporter speculated that the attacker was a rightwing antiunion terrorist who wanted to ensure that Villanueva could never again work in construction; thereby, depriving Villanueva of his livelihood."

"He will live, then?"

"He is listed in fair condition. I guess he will live."

Sounding curious, Rig queries, "What about the explosions at the CLWUA and the reporter's car—anyone hurt?"

"No reports of anyone hurt."

Rig exhales a deep, relieving sigh.

After a short pause, Rig asks, "Why do they call him a rightwing mad bomber?"

"Just some television and radio reporters are calling him that. Other reporters are just calling him the attacker or the perpetrator."

"Do they have any clues as to who he is?"

"A police captain on the news said there have been a number of cases of CLWUA union violence against Southern California small businesses. He said they were investigating the business owners."

Rig's anger flares briefly. Then he asks with irritation edging his tone, "Are any sane people stepping forward and demanding that the CLWUA should be investigated for its criminal activity?!"

"That would be futile, Rig. The U.S. Supreme Court ruled several years ago that union violence is legal if the violence is in pursuit of legitimate union objectives."

"What?!"

"That's right. They did a piece about it on the news tonight."

"Dad, that's unbelievable. Are you sure you heard it right?"

"No doubt about it, Rig."

With an insistent tone, Rig asserts, "Those news reporters must have misinterpreted the Supreme Court ruling."

"I know what I heard, Rig."

Rig makes a mental note to go to the library and research that information.

Rig asks, "Do the police have a description of this so-called rightwing mad bomber?"

"Yeah, tall, long brown hair and beard. Witnesses say he looks like a lumberjack, wearing denim clothing and ball cap."

Rig chuckles into the phone and asks, "So how did you think that was me?"

"Come on, Son, I know what you do. You know how to do things. But obviously you're in D.C. and not in Southern California."

After a short pause, Rig asks in a concerned and sincere tone, "What about the family of that security guard who was killed in your warehouse fire? What is their fate?"

"Well, he worked for a security company that has excellent benefits. The wife and kids will have health care benefits under the company plan for five years. The guard also had a large life insurance policy. So they will be okay financially. I cannot possibly understand their grief, though."

After a few moments of thought, Rig inquires, "How has the loss of your warehouse affected your business?"

"Insurance will cover the cost of the inventory. I have already located another warehouse and have ordered stock. Money will be extremely tight for about six months. The loss of business transactions will eat into my savings. I have lost twenty-percent of my repeat customers because those articles written by that fuckin' reporter scares my customers. My customers fear union reprisal against their own businesses."

"Dammit, dad, these unions are domestic terrorists. They are enemies of the American way of life. I am just totally bewildered that they cannot be prosecuted for their violent acts."

"They definitely have the advantage. But it looks like small businessmen have an avenger. Whoever that guy is, I hope he keeps it up. It's satisfying to see someone attacking the CLWUA and their supporters in the press—getting a dose of their own medicine."

"Dad, have you thought of suing the *Long Beach Times* for slander?"

"Yeah. I talked with a lawyer last week, and I showed him the articles written by Pyth. The lawyer said that I had no case because of the way the articles are formulated around political opinion. He said that claiming loss of income would be too hard to prove. The Lawyer said that we would need to prove that the *Long Beach Times* was specifically inciting the public against me, and there is no hard evidence that is fact."

After a short pause, Rig says, "Dad, please let me know if there is anything I can do. Don't hide anything from me."

"Will do, Son. Goodbye, now."

"Goodbye, Dad."

Rig ponders the phone call from his father several hours ago. He knows he must attack the CLWUA again—more aggressively and causing extra damage. During his next trip to Southern California, he will also go after Max Robertson. Rig knows that Robertson will be on guard. He formulates a mental list of equipment and weapons that he will need during his next secret trip to Southern California. And, he needs a new disguise. Rig also commits to going after CLWUA leadership. *It's time for that union to feel the same fear that they cause others to feel.*

After taking a shower and slipping into fresh t-shirt and shorts, he goes to the kitchen and pours several shots of his favorite brandy into a snifter. He sits in an overstuffed chair and turns on the T.V. to watch the 11:00 PM newscast. At the top of the news is an update on the train explosion in Elias, Idaho. Two more people have died in the hospital, bringing the death total to eighty-three. More than sixty buildings burned to the ground. Dozens of civil lawsuits have been initiated against the railroad and against the oil company that owned the gasoline in the rail tanker cars. Members of congress who demanded nationalization of oil companies after the Gulf oilrig explosions have re-emphasized their demands for nationalization. After the transportation board reported that rotted rail ties and rusted and broken rail spikes were found at the scene, those same members of congress are also calling for nationalization of America's railroad companies because, obviously, railroad companies place profit ahead to maintenance, safety, and American lives.

Rig shakes his head and chuckles at the chaos that would occur with the federal government owning and operating major industries.

The newscaster then provides an update on the Gulf of Mexico oilrig explosions that took place last spring. All three oilrigs are still out of operation. All the American oil companies involved have created a victims' fund. The media continues to vilify oil companies for the profit motive above safety and security. The salaries and benefits of oil company CEOs and directors are repeatedly broadcasted by the media. Rig shakes his head and expresses disgust at a media that no longer mentions that the oilrig explosions were the result of sabotage.

"In other news, last night in Long Beach, California, several explosions rocked the Pacific coast city. Local Police and local media outlets have labeled the perpetrator as the rightwing mad bomber. According to our T.V. affiliate in Long Beach, the rightwing mad bomber attacked and permanently maimed a member of the Construction and Labor Workers Union at a popular nightclub. One hour later, the Southern California Headquarters of the CLWUA was bombed. During a news conference, Long Beach Police say they have identified the perpetrator of both crimes to be the same person. Then, during the early morning hours, the car owned by a local newspaper reporter was blown up outside his apartment building. The newspaper reporter often writes articles in support or worker unions. Surveillance camera videos from all three crime scenes show that the same person committed all three crimes. Police are searching for a man who is six feet and six inches tall with long reddish hair and long reddish beard, wearing denim clothing and madman piercing eyes."

A drawing, sketched by a police portrait artist, appears on the T.V. screen.

As Rig stares at the sketch of a giant-sized person with a wild-man face, he exhibits amusement. He feels confident that no one can logically point a finger at him and claim that he is the same man as in the drawing.

Chapter 45

Four days have passed since the metal front door to the Southern California CLWUA District Headquarters building was blown to pieces and flying door fragments destroyed the interior of the front door hallway. All damage has been repaired, and a stronger door was installed.

The Southern California CLWUA District Director, Harold Oatman, sits behind his desk and listens carefully to the report from the district Sargent-at-Arms, Melvin Spartan. Oatman shifts a lit stub of a cigar to the corner of his mouth.

The Sargent-at-Arms advises, "The Simms National Detective Agency has not yet discovered the identity of the rightwing mad bomber. I had them specifically investigate Rigney Page, but Simms reports that Page is in Washington D.C. and has been there for months, although they cannot confirm his locations for last weekend. Simms checked all the national airlines, and there is no record of Rigney Page on any flight for last weekend."

Oatman nods acceptance of the information. He asks, "Does Simms have someone following Max Robertson? If Page is the rightwing mad bomber, he will probably go after Robertson next."

"Yes, Simms operatives are following Robertson."

"And does Simms now have operatives following Rigney Page? If he boards a flight to Southern California, we need to know about it."

"Yes, Simms operatives are following Page."

Again, Oatman nods acceptance of the information. He directs, "Contact Simms. I want complete background checks done on James Page, Dave Page, and Rigney Page. I want all their biographies going back to when they were children.

"I want the same background investigations done on that Bollinger and his son—who own that non-union cable manufacturing plant in Torrance. They have been fighting back. When we sent our toughs over there to rough them up, they beat our members with baseball bats.

"We currently have thirty-plus non-union small businesses targeted for unionization. The owners of those businesses are fighting back, and they have the support of the National Chamber of Commerce and a few newspapers. We must teach those antiunion assholes that they cannot win a fight with us." Oatman pushes a slip of paper across the table to Spartan and directs, "Increase the intimidation of business owners on this list and increase theft and vandalism of their property."

Spartan reads the list of eight businesses, he asks, "There is an asterisk next to Page Office Supply. What does that mean?"

"I want you to increase the intimidation on James Page's daughters. If Rigney Page is the rightwing mad bomber, aggression against his sisters should bring him back to Southern California. We will set a trap for him when he goes after Robertson."

The Sergeant at Arms advises, "This is going to cost, Harold. I do not have a budget for all these investigations and all these intimidation missions."

"No problem," Oatman advises. "National headquarters is funding our actions to intimidate these antiunion businesses and fight off these acts of terror against us. There is no limit on what you can spend on this."

Chapter 46

Rig sits in the sprawling multi-floor Arlington County Library. He spent the last four hours researching the United States Supreme Court decision in the case of *United States v. Enmons*, 1973 and its effect on the *Hobbs Anti-Racketeering Act of 1946*. Although the Supreme Court decision protects unions and their members from prosecution for perpetrating violence and vandalism in some cases, Rig concludes that the Supreme Court decision does not protect the CLWUA from prosecution in its acts against his family and his father's business.

He reaches into his inside coat pocket and retrieves the snipped article from the *Long Beach Times* that his father sent him. He reads it for the third time. The article, actually from the editor's opinion page written by Weston Pyth, cited the Supreme Court case as justification for the CLWUA to conduct acts of aggression against profiteering rightwing capitalists who victimize their employees. In Rig's mind, Pyth misrepresents who and what is protected against prosecution by the Supreme Court decision.

The note from his father that accompanied the article states that the article is typical of the leftwing lies and deceit written in most of the Southern California newspapers. Rig contemplates the numerous events of union violence reported in news magazines during the past year. As he ponders the note from his father and all the media reports of union violence nationwide, he considers a possible conspiracy. *Could all this union violence and support by the media be a conspiracy—all managed and directed from a central power?*

Rig goes to one of the phone booths in the library lobby. He dials John Smith's work phone number from memory.

John reports, "Extension 4289."

"Can we meet today?" Rig asks.

John recognizes Rig's voice. He responds, "How about same place as last time—6:00 PM?"

"See ya there," Rig responds.

215

Rig arrives at Danny's Irish Pub at 5:55 PM.

John Smith sits at the bar.

Rig quickly scans the interior of the pub. The décor epitomizes the rich dark wood paneling of the real thing in Ireland. Irish symbols and icons hang on the walls. All the pub's employees wear green colored bib aprons and green bowties. The pub is half-full of patrons this early on a Thursday evening.

Before Rig seats himself, John asks, "Do you want to eat dinner? I have reserved us a booth in the far corner."

Rig nods and says, "Yes. Let's do that."

Five minutes later, they are seated comfortably in the booth with pewter mugs of beer in front of them. They have already given the waiter their order.

John advises, "The hostess is a friend of mine, and I asked her not to seat anyone near us. She said she can do that for an hour, but they start filling up around 7:00 PM. So we have an hour to talk."

Rig casts an appreciative grin and says, "I want to thank you again for helping me with obtaining the equipment I needed on such short notice."

John chuckles and responds, "No problem, Rig. I hope you found the weapons and explosives useful. Oh, my associate in San Diego reports that you did not return two of the shaped explosive charges. That's will cost you three-hundred dollars—cash. My associate cleaned the blood off the steel baton and one of the daggers— no charge for that."

"Oh! Sorry about the blood. I forgot. I'll clean everything next time."

John arches his eyebrows and expresses curiosity as he questions, "Next time?"

"Well, that's why I asked for this meeting. I need you to supply me again—not right away—a couple of weeks from now."

John looks upward and expresses thoughtfulness. After a few moments he comments, "I have read an intelligence report about a rightwing antiunion domestic terrorist running rampant in Long Beach while you were there two weekends ago. I read that he exploded a few things and beat the shit out of a man who is being investigated for attacking you and your father some months back."

Rig displays discomfort and shifts in his seat. "I heard about that from my father. How did you hear about it?"

"My company contracts with a lot of government agencies in addition to CIA and ONI. We have operatives all over and any act of terrorism is reported to our operations center. I read all the reports."

Fearful astonishment crosses Rig's face. He questions, "So you and your company and a number of government agencies know about the CLWUA attack against my father and his business?"

"Yeah, but not just you and your father. The Southern California CLWUA has been harassing some thirty non-union companies. So you are not in the spotlight. Last night, an optic cable manufacturing warehouse in Torrance, California was set afire, causing a million dollars in damage."

"Anyone hurt," Rig asks in a sincere, compassionate tone.

"Yeah, several firefighters are in the hospital. They'll recover and return to work. The manufacturing plant has closed down for two months. They had to lay off all their workers.

"Now, we have operatives swarming all over Southern California gathering intel on all CLWUA activities and attempting to identify that so-called terrorist that the press and police are calling the rightwing mad bomber."

Rig sits back and sighs deeply. In a resigned tone, he asks John, "Are you going to report me?"

John flinches and expresses that he is offended. "Of course not, Rig. How could you think such a thing?" John pauses and appears thoughtful. Then he says, "But I might not supply you again. Tell me the history of this conflict you have with that union . . . to help me make up my mind."

Rig tells John everything, including the details of his avenger mission two weekends ago.

John comments, "You called the CLWUA a domestic enemy. I'm unsure as to what you mean by that."

"John, the CLWUA is an organization that acts to deny business owners their constitutional rights. The CLWUA's goal is to force unionization through intimidation, violence, and vandalism. It's the CLWUA that are domestic terrorists—domestic enemies against the freedom and liberty guaranteed by the Constitution. Business owners must fight back using the same methods the CLWUA uses. I hope to motivate those business owners with my actions."

John nods and expresses both understanding and approval. He informs, "Okay, Rig. I will supply you; but like before, you must pay for what you use. I must replace what you use so that annual inventory checks do not reveal missing weapons and equipment."

"No problem. I'll pay." Rig hands John a sheet of paper.

John reads the list. Then he flinches and expresses disbelief. He stares at Rig with an astonished expression. He challenges, "Five LAW Rocket Launchers?!"

Rig chuckles; then he comments, "I thought that would raise your eyebrows."

John glances at Rig, shakes his head, then he continues reading the list.

Rig waits patiently.

"Look, Rig, this is ten-thousand-dollars' worth of weapons and equipment, including the old dented pickup truck. I must cover my ass on this. You could be arrested or killed on your next mission and I am out ten-thousand, and subsequent investigations will inform my superiors that I provided you with weapons and equipment. I must ask for all ten-thousand up front. Then I will give back your money on what you return."

"No problem," Rig advises. "Give me a couple of days, and I will have the money."

John expresses doubt as he responds in a challenging tone, "You have that kind of money?" A conspiratorial grin appears on John's face as he suggests, "You been paddin' that expense account?"

"No, John. I need to convert some stocks, gold, and oil future certificates to cash. That will take a few days."

John slumps back. He grins and expresses respect. He states, "You never cease to amaze me, Rig. I sure wish you had accepted my job offer last year instead of reenlisting."

"I am what I want to be," Rig declares.

John responds, "Of that, I have no doubt."

Chapter 47

Diane Love and Congressman Billy Thayer enter Diane's opulent Georgetown townhouse. Earlier in the evening, they attended a cocktail party with members of congress and members of the Carter Administration. Bill Thayer was Diane's escort, and he transported them to the party in his own car.

Diane invites Billy in for a nightcap. Once they are settled in comfortable stuffed chairs with brandy snifters in hand, he informs Diane, "I have a private detective following Rig."

Diane stares curiously at Billy, wondering what prompted him to have Rig followed.

Billy pulls folded papers from his pocket; he unfolds two stapled sheets. "My operative who spent thirty years in the military considers that Rig's routine out of the ordinary."

"Like what?" Diane demands in a protesting tone. Thayer's unrelenting challenge to her relationship with Rig irritates the hell out of her.

"He is assigned to Commander Naval Telecommunications Command, located on the compound of the Naval Security Station on Massachusetts Avenue Northwest. However, he spends days at a time at the Naval Communications Unit in Cheltenham, Maryland."

"What does that tell you?" Diane challenges.

Billy holds out his hand, palm toward Diane, and declares, "I'm not finished. During the past month, your chief had lunch and dinner on seven occasions with a female naval officer at the Sheraton Hotel near the Suitland Maryland military complex. On several occasions after dinner, they went to her apartment in Clinton, Maryland and he spent the night." Billy pauses and stares into Diane's face, attempting to evaluate her feelings.

Diane knows that Rig sees other women. She is more curious than jealous. She asks, "Who is she?"

"Lieutenant Commander Sally Macfurson. She lives in Clinton, Maryland."

"Where does she work?"

Billy glances down at the paper and reports, "She splits her work days between that Naval Communications Unit in Cheltenham where Chief Page spends so much time and the Office of Naval Intelligence located at the Suitland Federal Complex."

"What does she do?"

"My investigator does not know for sure, but all evidence points to her being a naval communications officer."

"What does she look like?"

"Petite attractive redhead—walks proud and erect."

Diane comments, "That's against military rules, isn't it—for an officer and an enlisted man to have a relationship?"

Billy responds, "Yes, I believe it is against the rules. The military calls it fraternization. And something else unusual, he was renting a little car for transportation. Then one day he drives up to his home in Arlington in a rusted and dented Jeep Cherokee."

"Yes, I have ridden in that Jeep. It's in better shape than what it looks like from the outside."

"My private detective investigated that Jeep's license number and discovered that Jeep belongs to the Department of the Navy."

"Is that unusual?" Diane casts an inquisitive expression.

"According to the detective following your chief, it is unusual for an enlisted man to be assigned a military owned vehicle for private use."

Diane expresses thoughtfulness while staring at the floor and wondering what it means.

Billy glances at his notes, "Rig and Commander Macfurson spend many days on that Cheltenham base at the same time." He looks up and stares into Diane's face to gauge her reaction.

"What do they do there?"

"My detective doesn't know. For some reason, civilians who don't work on that base are not allowed unescorted access, even if the civilian has a DOD car sticker and DOD credentials."

"Your detective has DOD credentials?"

"Yes. He is ex-army Criminal Investigation Division who currently works as a DOD contractor and does undercover work for me sometimes."

"Undercover work for The Longjumeau Alliance?" Diane queries.

Billy nods and states, "Yes, but he does not know about The Alliance. He does not know why I employ him to follow Rigney Page."

"Why are you investigating Rig?"

"Because he is too close to us. It is unusual for someone like him to be in a circle of friends like us. We must ensure he is not a threat."

"I have known Rig since junior high school. He was my high school boyfriend. He is close to us because he is my lifelong friend."

"Yes, Diane, your point is valid, but his manner and intelligence is superior to his position in life. He hides his true self. I'm sure of it."

Diane rolls her eyes and expresses frustrated doubt. "What else can he be?"

"I don't know, but The Alliance must be protected at all costs. We cannot take any chances."

At first, Diane wants to object to an investigation into Rig's life, but she is also curious. She too suspects there is more to Rig than what he reveals to her. She sometimes considers that he is more than an ex-surfer from Seal Beach, California and suspects that he is more than a navy radioman involved in classified work. She often considers the physical ability that earned him the *Hero of Thurso* title must be more than that of the typical navy radio operator.

Diane asks Billy, "Will you keep me informed as to what you discover about him?"

"Yes, off course, as I will keep informed all directors of The Longjumeau Alliance."

Chapter 48

Rig enters the small conference room located next to Room number four in the ONI Building on the Cheltenham navy base. ONI Intelligence Analyst Lieutenant Commander Sally Macfurson and Senior ONI Intelligence Analyst Bob Mater sit at the round table. A tape recorder sits in the center of the table. Rig takes a seat.

Since being assigned to the Washington D.C. area and whenever Rig needs to meet with his associates from naval intelligence headquarters, they meet at the ONI building on the Cheltenham, Maryland Naval Communications Unit. Rig must avoid being seen entering the Suitland Naval Intelligence Headquarters building.

Rig nods hello and asks, "Have you played the tape, yet?"

Bob Mater advises, "Not yet—waiting for you."

Rig sits next to Sally Macfurson.

Sally advises, "This is the tape of some of the conversations that took place in Diane Love's residence during the past few weeks. I need you to identify the voices as the tape plays."

Over the next few hours, the tape is played a number of times as Sally and Bob take notes on what they hear and notes on Rig's comments.

After they have listened to all the tapes, Commander Macfurson glances at her notes and in a quizzical tone says, "We need more intel on this Longjumeau Alliance."

Rig comments, "That's an odd word—Longjumeau. I wonder what it means."

Sally offers, "Diane and her friends mispronounce it."

Bob Mater and Rigney Page focus their attention on Sally.

"Longjumeau is a small village outside Paris. Its only notoriety being that during the years 1911 through 1914, a school promoting communism existed there. Vladimir Lenin taught at the school."

Rig queries, "If this alliance that Diane and her friends refer to is a communist organization, wouldn't naming it Longjumeau be an obvious giveaway?"

Sally expresses amusement as she responds, "Rig, you must

come to understand the leftist educated elite. They see the rest of the world as ignorant sheep, the great unwashed, who need the leftist educated elite to advise them, to guide them, to rule over them." Sally pauses and evaluates Rig's response.

Rig expresses interest.

She continues, "Their arrogance named their organization The Longjumeau Alliance. Only those who have studied, thoroughly, the Bolshevik Revolution might stumble across this little-known piece of information in the few books that refer to it. Diane and her educated elitist friends probably view it as an arrogant tease."

Rig expresses amusement as he comments, "Well, I guess they never considered someone like you with a doctorate in European History would cross their path."

Sally exhibits humility.

Bob Mater inquires, "Commander, you're sure about this Longjumeau reference?"

"I am sure about the association with Lenin and the Bolsheviks, and confident that arrogant, American communist elitists would come up with such a name for their organization."

Rig shakes his head, expressing doubt as he comments, "Over the years, Diane has become a radical leftist. But a communist, I just can't make that connection. She and her friends are leftwing radicals. They advocate socialism, but they don't preach communism."

Sally informs, "Rig, American leftists seldom consider themselves communists. Yet, everything they advocate is communal, classless society, share the wealth ideology. In Diane's case, we already know that she reports to a Soviet KGB agent. Marxist doctrine specifies that a socialist state is just a stepping stone to a communist state."

Rig evaluates Sally's words; then he says, "I don't understand her connection to the KGB. Diane and her friends consider Soviet leaders to be uneducated, unenlightened, Bolshevik thugs. Diane and her friends say that the Soviets give socialism a bad name. She and her educated elitist friends believe that socialism can be a utopia when administered by compassionate and enlightened leaders."

Sally comments, "That shows you how out of touch with reality they are. Their philosophy denies the basic human right to be rewarded to the level of your achievements—the right to pursue happiness for yourself and not for the collective welfare."

Rig asks, "That would make them a clear and present danger to the safety and security of the United States because their crusade's objective is to subvert the U.S. constitution . . . right?"

Bob Mater comments, "Depends on their agenda and the extent to which they force their agenda on others. Their Longjumeau Alliance might just be a think tank or discussion group."

Sally, assuming her mission controller role, directs Rig, "You must get more information on The Longjumeau Alliance."

Rig nods; then he advises, "Next week, I am house-sitting for Diane while she is out of town."

"Does she have filing cabinets and a safe or safes?"

"I've seen filing cabinets but no safes."

"Do the filing cabinets have locks?"

Rig nods.

Sally informs, "I will arrange for the technical department to assist you in opening those file cabinets and any safes you find."

"New Subject," Bob Mater interjects. "We can use this tail that Congressman Thayer has on you to our advantage."

"How?"

"You can attend some leftist events." Bob exhibits a cynical smile and advises, "I was reading this morning that the American Socialist Party is sponsoring military unionization rallies here in D.C. during the next two weeks."

"I read about that," Rig advises. "If I attend those rallies, The Longjumeau Alliance might interpret that I am there as a military undercover operative and not a participant."

"Tell Diane Love in advance that you are attending those rallies because you are curiously interested."

Rig nods agreement and understanding.

Bob Mater offers, "Senator Ted Kennedy is speaking to the

American Progressive Union next week. I can get you a membership card and a ticket."

"C'mon, Bob, Diane and her lefty friends will never buy that I advocate leftwing causes."

"Maybe, but attending those events could put doubts in their minds that you are a committed rightwing ideologue. They might consider that you are open to other ideologies."

Chapter 49

Rig sits at his desk at COMNAVTELCOM and reviews a draft technical manual for the Common User Digital Information Exchange Subsystem, CUDIXS.

His desk phone rings. He answers the phone with the required and recently-modified phone answering disclosure: "Commander Naval Telecommunications Command, Chief Page speaking, this is a non-secure line, how may I help you sir or ma'am."

John Smith chuckles; then comments, "Rig, that military hello gets longer each time I hear it."

Rig responds, "Well, yes, every week or so a memo is issued—revising it and expanding it."

"We need to meet." John's tone becomes serious. "Are you available tomorrow afternoon?"

"Yes."

"Watergate Hotel—room 718—2:00 PM—wear one of your civilian disguises and use surveillance evasion tactics on your way to the Watergate."

"I'll be there."

Rig walks into the lobby of the Watergate wearing black-rim glasses, black mustache, long black curly wig that covers the top of his ears and touches his collar, and wearing a blue pinstripe business suit. He does not attract attention because most of the men in the lobby are dressed in business suits and nearly half of them wear glasses. Rig proceeds to the elevators, confident that his deception works.

On the seventh floor, Rig exits the elevator and walks to room 718. John Smith answers the door and invites Rig to enter the suite. The suite includes a sitting area and small conference table near the window.

A man wearing a gray business suit and sporting sandy colored hair and a sandy colored, short, well-trimmed beard sits at the conference table. Rig recognizes the man but cannot place him. The man rises from his chair to greet Rig.

John performs the introductions. "Rigney Page, please meet Denton Phillips."

While Rig shakes Phillips's hand, Philips says, "Rigney, we have met before. Do you remember?"

"Please call me Rig. Yes, you look familiar, but I can't remember exactly. You wore a military uniform, no beard, but I—"

"Six years ago at a post mission debriefing in Frankfurt, Germany. My task at that debriefing was to extract from you every detail of that mission. You had escorted a defecting East German official from Hamburg to Paris. I remember that you killed two Stasi agents on that mission."

"Yes," Rig confirms. "But not until after those Stasi agents gave me the beating of my life."

"I remember," Phillips affirms. "You and the defector were abducted by those Stasi agents when you made a stop in Stuttgart. Their mistake was not killing you immediately. They took you and the defector to a house in the German countryside where the defector was to be picked up several days later by other Stasi agents and returned to East Germany."

Rig adds, "Yes, I was too confident. I dropped my guard for a few minutes in the Stuttgart train station. But those Stasi agents violated the first rule of survival. Instead of killing me right away, they wanted to beat me to death. Then deliver my body to a U.S. military base—in an attempt to send a brutal message to U.S. intelligence not to fuck with the Stasi."

"You killed them with your bare hands, if I remember correctly."

"They underestimated my stamina to withstand their beating, and they underestimated my strength to break my bonds. They had their backs turned when I busted out of that heavy oak chair that I was tied to. I beat them to death with the busted chair legs, not with my bare hands."

Phillips nods; then comments, "Then you and the defector made it back to the Stuttgart train station and boarded a train for Paris."

Rig remembers the kind, older gentleman that he escorted to Paris. "Yes, we had a private compartment to ourselves. He nursed my wounds and brought me meals. In Paris, two American agents took charge of him." Rig pauses and expresses thoughtfulness; then he says, "I often wonder what happened to him."

After a short pause, John Smith blurts, "Wait a second, Rig. You don't get off that easy. How in the hell did you kill two armed Stasi agents with broken chair legs?!"

"When I broke out of that chair I was tied to, their guns were holstered. Instead of them immediately attacking me physically, which is what they should have done, they spent valuable seconds drawing their guns, which had the leather hammer loop engaged. Before they could draw their guns, I busted their heads open with full-force blows from those solid oak chair legs."

John declares, "Another amazing and secret event in the life of Rigney Page."

"We should get down to business," Denton Phillips suggests as he waves his hand toward the small conference table.

John and Rig nod and express agreement. All three men sit down at the table.

Rig appraises Denton Phillips's appearance, then states, "I assume you are no longer in the military."

"When I debriefed you in Frankfurt, I was serving in the air force and was assigned to NATO intelligence. I am a civilian now, and I represent a group of private patriotic Americans who appreciate your vengeful attacks against unions who blatantly and shamelessly terrorize citizens engaged in free enterprise. We want to fund your missions against those unions."

Rig casts a suspicious stare at Phillips and challenges, "In exchange for what?"

"Submit to debriefings after each of your missions. We collect intelligence on anti-American activities. We have been building a database on the CLWUA and on other unions that engage in violence and property destruction."

"And what else?" Rig asks in a less challenging tone.

"We want all the information on your friend, Diane Love, and reports of all her activities. We also want reports on all her acquaintances. We believe that she and her friends are involved in an anti-American conspiracy, but we have no details."

Rig expresses surprise; then he comments, "But ONI and the other intelligence agencies already have me doing that."

John Smith advises, "Rig, Denton and I are not representing any government agencies or defense contracting companies, today. This is a private organization—free from the oversight of Congress and free to act secretly to protect those individual liberties guaranteed by the Constitution."

Rig asks, "But that's illegal, right?" Rig glances back and forth between Phillips and John Smith.

Denton responds, "No more illegal than maiming union thugs and bombing union buildings and journalist's automobiles. We hide our existence so that America's domestic enemies cannot find us. Occasionally we engage in illegal activity to further the cause of protecting the American Republic and preserving individual liberties guaranteed by the *Bill of Rights*."

Rig becomes wary. He concludes aloud, "You tell me these things because you can hold my illegal activities over my head as a threat not to expose you."

With deep conviction and honesty, John tells Rig, "That's not the way we operate. We only want volunteers. If you don't want to be part of this, no problem."

Rig feels more at ease after John's words. In the past, Rig had entrusted his life to John. Rig has always considered the two of them to be comrades in arms and trusted friends.

Rig puts his trust in John to the test. "How long have you been part of Denton's secret organization and what have you done for them?"

John looks at Denton Phillips. Denton nods approval to answer Rig's questions.

"Three years," John answers. "Mostly, I have gone on missions they assigned me."

Rig expresses curiosity as he questions, "And the company you work for and the CIA do not know about this?"

"That's correct. They don't know."

Rig inquires, "How long has your organization existed?"

Denton replies, "We are called The Guardians. The name complies with our charter to defend constitutional freedoms and support limited, constitutional government. We are a secret organization known only to the membership. We operate on a cell structure to maximize our anonymity and security. We were originally formed in the 1870s to fight against the powerful Democratic Party in The South who refused to comply with federal civil rights laws. Then a new threat against the constitution emerged in the late Nineteenth Century. Socialist, communist, and other type collectivist politicians were on the rise and began infiltrating local, state, and federal government. Woodrow Wilson paved the way to entrench those collectivist politicians in federal government. Woodrow Wilson was the new breed of collectivist Democrats who thought it his birthright to rule over an American people who he thought were too dumb to govern themselves. With the aid of a Democrat controlled congress, Wilson implemented stranglehold laws on commerce and individual liberties, including the income tax. During those years when Wilson was president, The Guardians tripled its membership. The Democratic Party was the Party of Jim Crow and Segregation. When Wilson became president, the Democratic Party also became the party of socialists and communists. During the years of Franklin Roosevelt and Lyndon Johnson, our membership again tripled. We are well funded and have operatives in all states."

Rig asks, "So you are a Republican organization, then?"

"No, Rig. We are not defined by political party. Many powerful Republican politicians have aligned with collectivists and other anti-constitutional organizations. During the last century, we have become enlightened to the reality that a politician's registered party does not necessarily define that politician's beliefs and agenda." Denton pauses as he considers what to say next.

Rig waits patiently.

Denton continues, "By modern definition, we are a rightwing organization because of our mission to protect American liberties that are guaranteed by the U.S. Constitution. We actively funded and supported rightwing politicians and rightwing organizations that opposed Teddy Roosevelt and Richard Nixon."

"So you don't accept Democrats or other left-wingers into your organization."

"Actually we have recruited some Democrats," Denton informs. "But only after detailed investigation of their backgrounds and past actions, which we conduct on all potential members. Most often, we find that those Democrats we accepted into our organization are Democrats in name only. For example, they are Democrats because that is the party of their parents, but their actual beliefs are rightwing. But we will not even consider those who are registered in Communist Parties or Socialist Parties."

Rig asks, "What about those who belong to unions?"

Denton responds, "Hundreds of Guardians belong to unions. We are not antiunion. We are pro liberty. We believe that people should have the choice to belong to unions or not belong to unions. We do not support state laws that require individuals to join a union in order to be employed."

Rig expresses understanding; then he asks, "If I accept your offer, what else besides providing information on Diane Love's circle of friends will I be requested to do?"

Denton responds, "Difficult to say right now. However, you should understand you are making a lifetime commitment. Joining The Guardians is not a temporary obligation. We have long-term goals to destroy America's domestic enemies. No matter where you go or what you achieve from this day forward, you could be requested to help us. Years might pass before we ask you to perform an action, although we currently have some tasks that we want to discuss with you. From this date forward, we will provide you with money and resources beyond your current ability to obtain, assuming we agree with your self-assigned mission."

"Like what?"

"Private airplane travel to your mission locations—endless disguises and identities—detailed intel on your targets."

"Must I always do what you ask?"

"No. We only accept volunteers and there is no paycheck. We only pay expenses and pay for equipment and weapons and intel assets. You will do it because you want to protect your country. And we might not always fund what you want to do. Nevertheless, your current activities are in line with our long-term goals."

Rig smiles appreciatively. "Had you told me that I would be paid, I would have turned you down flat. I'm in."

John pushes an envelope across the table toward Rig.

Rig recognizes the envelope as the one containing the advanced ten-thousand dollars he gave to John.

Denton advises, "We're picking up the tab for your next attack against the CLWUA. We have a schedule of such actions elsewhere in the country. We would like to discuss it with you."

Rig protests, "I am not at war with all unions, just the CLWUA. My sisters belong to other unions that act civilly. I am not out to destroy unions."

Denton states, "Neither are we, Rig. We embrace the freedom of workers to collectively bargain. One of our missions is to stop union violence against freedom loving Americans who have risked all to start a business and achieve The American Dream. This year, union violence is rampant throughout the country. Acts of union violence are not random and spontaneous by a few union members. Union violence is well planned and well executed at the orders of union leaders. We want union leaders to feel the same fear that their victims feel. When union officials come to understand that they are targets of unknown avengers, they will halt their violent actions."

Rig says, "Yes, that all makes sense."

Denton queries, "Will you agree to another meeting so that we can brief you and discuss missions that we recommend? We also want to exchange with you information on the secret activities of Diane Love and her friends."

Rig nods and expresses sincerity. He says, "Yes. I agree to that."

During Rig's second meeting with John Smith and Denton Phillips, Denton offers office space where Rig can conduct reconnaissance of the CLWUA national headquarters in Chevy Chase, Maryland.

During that second meeting, Denton Phillips assures, "We will provide you with the necessary weapons, equipment, and intel that you will need to drive fear into the hearts of the CLWUA leadership."

Chapter 50

Rig sits at a window in a vacant office on the top floor of a four-story office building located in Chevy Chase, Maryland. The window faces the CLWUA national headquarters complex across a three-acre, grassy city park. He uses high power binoculars to scan the complex. His position provides an unobstructed view of the west side of the CLWUA building that includes the main entrance, employee entrance, and visitor's lobby and provides an unobstructed view of the south side of the building where the executive's entrance is located mid-building. This excellent observation location was provided by The Guardians.

A twelve-foot-high chain-link fence surrounds the entire CLWUA complex, which is situated at the northern city limits of Chevy Chase, Maryland. Five strands of barbed wire sit atop the fence and angle outward. All shrubbery is cut back 20 feet around the outside of the fence. The sprawling complex includes the four-story headquarters building, one large rectangle shaped single-story building, several utility buildings, and a five-hundred-spaces employee parking lot. The parking lot is half-full. Two black stretch limousines are parked in reserved parking spaces near the executive's entrance.

All walking traffic and vehicle traffic must pass through a guarded gate. Individual security passes and authorized vehicle passes are required for entry. Rig observed earlier that the guard at the gate glanced at a green sticker on the windshield of each car. He shifts his attention to the parking lot and focuses the binoculars on windshields. Each car that he views has the same green sticker located low on the windshield on the driver's side. As he scans each vehicle, he becomes aware that the reserved spaces close to the executive's entrance are filled with Cadillacs, Lincolns, BMWs, and Mercedes automobiles. Proletariat parking spaces are filled with cheap Fords and Chevrolets. Rig concludes that the CLWUA reigning Bourgeoisie live an opulent lifestyle without need and without want. He wonders how much money the nine-million rank-

and-file CLWUA members pay in union dues to support the lifestyles of the union's top officials.

Rig wears his businessman disguise that allows him to move around the nation's capital without notice. He always draws stares when he is in uniform. The businessman disguise consists of a curly black hair wig that covers his short reddish-brown hairs and covers half his ears and touches his collar, a thick dark mustache, deep-blue colored contact lenses that hide his green colored eyes, expensive suit, expensive gold watch, and expensive gold with diamond stud cufflinks. Rig exchanged the glasses for deep-blue colored contact lenses on a recommendation from Denton Phillips.

Rig raises the binoculars to his eyes. He surveys the countryside surrounding the CLWUA Headquarters, looking for hiding places from where he can launch rockets. He also checks for weak points in the fence and checks the angles of surveillance cameras.

A black stretch limousine with green sticker on the window approaches the CLWUA complex; then stops at the guard house. Rig focuses the binoculars on the limousine. The passenger windows are darkly tinted; he cannot see the occupants.

The guard makes an entry in his logbook and waves the limousine into the complex.

The limousine stops at the curb near the executive's entrance. The limo driver opens the rear door on the curbside.

Rig jumps to his feet as he sees Peter Mandrake exit the limo, followed by Diane Love and Congressman Billy Thayer. He sets aside the binoculars; he grabs the Cannon camera with a telescopic lens. He focuses the lens; then he pushes the automatic button. The sound of the camera shutter repeatedly opening and closing echoes loudly throughout the empty room.

Through the camera lens, Rig observes two more men in business suits exit the limousine. He recognizes them as Congressmen who were attendees at several cocktail parties where he and Diane also attended.

Rig notices that the limousine passengers gather on the sidewalk near the executive's entrance. Diane looks at her watch. Several in the group look toward the front gate.

Rig lowers the camera; then he looks toward the front gate. Another stretch limousine passes through the gate. Rig raises the camera; he watches the limousine through the telescopic lens. This arriving limousine also has a green sticker on the window.

At the curb near the executive's entrance, four men dressed in business suits exit the limousine. They are greeted by the others with smiles and handshakes.

Rig snaps more pictures.

All the arrivals enter the executive's entrance.

From his briefcase, Rig retrieves sheets of paper that contain room diagrams of each floor of the CLWUA building. The office of the CLWUA national president is located on the fourth floor above the front entrance.

Rig brings the binoculars to his eyes. The windows of the president's office are heavily tinted, which prevents any viewing of what will take place in that office.

The national president of the CLWUA, Gaylord Tarkingson, sits at the head of the conference table. The fifty-year-old Tarkingson, a fat and balding man in a seven-hundred-dollar light wool suit, would not be revered or noticed in an environment away from his union and away from Washington elite. Behind his back, he is often referred to as the *Al Capone* of unions. His gnarled, calloused hands and several scars on his face tell of his dockworker origins.

Also seated at the table are members of the White House staff and members of the United States Congress. Everyone in the room is a member of The Longjumeau Alliance.

Federal law prohibits unions from making contributions to political campaigns. Nevertheless, all members of Congress in the room receive generous campaign contributions by indirect, secret and illegal means from the CLWUA and The Longjumeau Alliance.

Gaylord Tarkingson asks U.S. Senator Clay Porter, "Senator, how is the *Employee Fairness Act* progressing in the Senate?"

Tarkingson refers to legislation that if it becomes law would require all companies with ten or more permanent employees to hire union labor. The legislation establishes a Federal Business License Agency and that agency would verify employee union membership before issuing the Federal Business License. The legislation would make it illegal for any business with ten or more employees to operate without a Federal Business License.

The tall, athletic, and graying five-term senator explains, "I have thirty-six cosponsors, all Democrats, supporting the legislation as the CLWUA wrote it. Five additional Democrats will cosponsor the bill with some minor changes. That's enough votes to pass it through committee and bring it to a vote on the senate floor."

Tarkingson advises, "Have any Republicans committed to voting for the bill?"

The senator responds, "No, not even with amendments."

"What are their reasons for not supporting?"

"They say it's unconstitutional to require every employer in America with more than ten employees to be unionized, and specifically targeting fast-food franchises and family-owned businesses. And they are against establishment of a federal agency to ensure compliance and issuing federal business licenses."

Tarkingson shakes his head and states, "Unconstitutional?! Since when does that make a difference to members of the U.S. Congress?!"

Senator Porter frowns as he advises, "This legislation is not a slam-dunk in the senate."

"Why not?" Tarkingson challenges, "The Democrats have a filibuster proof majority."

Senator Porter informs, "Nine Democrat senators will not support this bill, and they will not vote to close a filibuster by Republicans."

For a few moments, Tarkingson stares at the table while in thought. Then he looks up and says to Senator Porter, "Who are the Democrat senator holdouts?"

Porter slides a written list of those dissenting Democratic Party senators to Tarkingson.

Tarkingson ask Porter, "Did you also bring a list of Republican senators who might be persuaded?"

Senator Porter slides another slip of paper across the table.

Tarkingson glances at the list of names. Then he focuses on Representative Billy Thayer. "How about the House? Are there enough votes to pass the legislation?"

"Not yet," Thayer announces. "We have a powerful Democrat majority. House leadership has promised hundreds of millions of dollars in pork programs for those districts of every Democrat who votes *Yea*. Only a few House Democrats have expressed negativity."

Tarkingson then focuses on Diane Love and asks, "Can we count on President Carter supporting this legislation?"

Diane responds, "Depends on public opinion at the time the bill reaches Jimmy's desk. If the mood of the country is anti-corporation and pro-union at the time, Jimmy will sign it."

Again, Tarkingson sits back, deep in thought for a full minute. Then he advises, "I will talk to the skeptics on these lists."

Chapter 51

Diane Love asked Rig to house-sit her townhouse and care for her cat while she is away for a week. Diane's absence provides Rig with the opportunity to search every inch of the three-floor townhouse for information on the mysterious Longjumeau Alliance mentioned in the taped conversation between Diane and her friends.

The first day, he spent eight hours searching the basement and the first floor. Then, three hours into the second day, he found a safe under a camouflaged, carpeted floorboard in the guest bedroom closet on the second floor. He called his mission controller, Lieutenant Commander Sally Macfurson, to request assistance from ONI Technical Branch.

Two hours later, a geeky technician arrives with a large equipment case that is disguised as a suitcase. The technician wears a black sweatshirt and jeans. On the front of the sweatshirt is a picture of the Starship Enterprise with words underneath, "Everything I need to know about life I learned on Star Trek."

"My name is Colin," The tech advises.

Rig escorts Colin to Diane's den and identifies the two file cabinets with key locks.

Colin queries, "Has this residence been swept for hidden microphones and hidden cameras?"

"Yes," Rig answers. "The only hidden microphones are the ones planted by naval intelligence. The only surveillance camera was installed by naval intelligence and is located on the roof of the building across the street—pointed at the front door of this townhouse."

Colin uses a set of master keys to unlock all filing cabinets in less than five minutes. He advises, "Just press in the locks to relock."

Rig guides Colin to the location of the combination safe in the guest bedroom. He lifts the floorboard and exposes the well in which the safe is installed.

Colin performs a quick inspection of the digital keypad and

digital display combination lock on the safe's door. Then he removes a device from his equipment case that has a square panel with protruding mechanical fingers on one end of a thick cable and a miniature programmable console connected to the opposite end of the cable. Colin explains the operation. "I position the mechanical fingers assembly over the digital keypad. Magnets hold it in place. Then, at the console, I run programs that automatically push the buttons in a sequence of the most commonly used combination lock sequences."

"How fast does it work?" Rig inquires.

"Depends on the model of safe, which determines how long it takes for safe electronics and mechanics to respond to entered combination sequences. This model will allow one sequence every two seconds."

Rig expresses thoughtfulness. After a few moments his eyes go wide, expressing revelation. He comments, "That could take forever."

"Maybe," Colin states. "We will start with the most common combination sources that people use."

"Okay. What's first?"

Colin asks, "What is the birthdate of the person who owns the safe?"

"July tenth, nineteen forty-seven."

Colin enters the numerical equivalents for Diane's birthdate and presses the enter key. The device calculates all the possible number sequences for Diane's birthdate, starting with the most common day, month, and year sequence to be performed first.

Rig and Colin stare at the safe's digital display as the console sends varying sequences to the mechanical fingers. Every two seconds, the word "ERROR" appears on the safe's digital display. Several minutes later, Colin's console sounds a soft beep— signaling all combination sequences complete.

"How about a zip code of owner's home town?"

"Nine zero seven four zero," Rig advises.

Five minutes later, Colin's console reports failure.

Colin asks, "Does the owner have any children?"

Rig shakes his head.

Rig and Colin catch a movement at the bedroom doorway. Then Diane's calico cat walks across the bedroom floor.

"What's the cat's name?" Colin asks.

"Striper."

Colin enters "Striper" into the console.

Rig asks, "It takes alphabet characters also?"

"Yes. The program converts letters to number combinations."

For three minutes, the safe's digital display reports "ERROR" every two seconds. Then the word "OPEN" appears in the display. Colin stops the program; then he grins and declares, "That was too easy."

Rig turns the handle on the safe door and opens it.

Rig and Colin look into the safe. Documents and file folders are piled two feet deep.

Colin records the combination in a notebook. Then he writes the combination on a slip of paper and hands it to Rig. He stands and packs his gear.

Rig pulls out the contents of the safe and lays the contents on the floor.

Colin lifts his equipment case by the handle and walks toward the bedroom door. "I'll see myself out. Good hunting."

"Okay, Colin. Thanks!"

Rig carries the documents and folders to Diane's den and places the stack on the desktop. He spends thirty minutes glancing through the pages of documents. Then he opens both filing cabinets and scans the labels on the hanging folders.

Rig concludes that he has possession of a thirty-year plan for restructuring the American government and American society. He craves to scrutinize the pages, but his orders from Sally Macfurson are to deliver the contents of the safe and file cabinets immediately to her Cheltenham office for reproduction.

Rig dials Sally's Cheltenham office telephone number.

"Commander Macfurson—this is a non-secure line."

"I have the documents," Rig advises. "I want a couple of days to read them before I bring them in."

"No. You must deliver all documents immediately to my office." Sally Macfurson sets aside their private relationship and now acts in the best interest of national security.

Rig says, "What is the best way for me to comply with your order and also give me the opportunity to read these documents?"

"Have you read any of those documents?"

"I have scanned them."

Sally orders, "Bring them in. After they are copied, I will make copies available to you."

"Okay, see you in two hours."

Chapter 52

Rig enters the conference room at the ONI building on the Cheltenham, Maryland navy base. He wears his Service Dress Blue uniform as do all the navy personnel in the conference room. The meeting has not yet started, and no one sits at the conference table. Three weeks have passed since Rig delivered to Commander Macfurson the documents found in Diane Love's safe and file cabinets. Although he has read those documents, he is anxious to hear what the analysts have to say.

Rig quickly identifies some in the room: Admiral Willcroft, Director of Naval Intelligence; Captain Bradley Watson, Assistant Director Naval Intelligence for Counterespionage; Mr. Robert Mater, Senior Naval Intelligence Analyst; Lieutenant Commander Sally Macfurson, Naval Intelligence Analyst and mission controller. Mr. John Smith, contractor intelligence analyst for CIA stands near the U.S. Flag with four men and one woman who wear civilian suits and who Rig does not recognize.

When Captain Watson observes Rig entering the conference room, he orders, "Everyone is here. Let's get started."

Rig maneuvers to sit next to John Smith. John introduces the four men and one woman as contract intelligence analysts from his company who are recently assigned to augment the naval intelligence investigation of The Longjumeau Alliance.

Commander Sally Macfurson stands at the head of the conference table. A white screen stands behind her. She opens a three-ring binder that sits on the tabletop before her; then she reads aloud, "The content of this briefing is classified U.S. Top Secret Sensitive Compartmented Information. Those file folders before you are classified the same. You cannot take those file folders with you. All that I cover today and all the information in those file folders are available for checkout from central files. *Operation Shark* is the ONI and CIA codename for any and all of our actions regarding The Longjumeau Alliance, hereafter referred to as TLA. Everyone in this room is cleared to checkout Operation Shark files.

Operation Shark information is only available to those with the *need to know* within ONI and CIA. Before we discuss a plan going forward, I will provide an overview of what we know."

Everyone at the table focuses on the slender, petite, and attractive female commander. To comply with navy uniform regulations, Commander Macfurson wears her shoulder-length red hair pinned up.

"Among the files discovered in Diane Love's home are descriptions of TLA organization, membership, charter, and financial statements. The membership includes thirty-five members of the U.S. House of Representatives and ten members of the U.S. Senate. Also among TLA members are White House staffers, university professors, lawyers, executives of large corporations, union leaders, and state and local politicians. File folders in front of you contain a list of their names. I'll pause while you take a quick look at the names."

All at the conference table open the file folders before them. Some gasp as they recognize names. Several conversations start up. Some are surprised that the list contains names of prominent Democrats, Republicans, and Independents.

Commander Macfurson continues, "TLA's Charter commits to transforming the American Republic into a single communist political party by the year 2004. A supplement to the charter provides a schedule of milestones leading up to the 2004 elections. A copy of the charter and the milestone schedule supplement are also in your folders."

Some around the table exhibit astonishment and incredulity as they study the milestone schedule. Again, several conversations start. The words "impossible" and "unbelievable" rise above the din.

Commander Macfurson turns a page in her briefing binder. "All the financial accounts are coded. The general ledger lists inflow and outflow of cash to coded accounts. We cannot go any further with research and analysis in that area without the code key.

"We uncovered Diane Love's connection to TLA while following her movements after we discovered she was having clandestine meetings with a known Soviet KGB agent. We don't know if her connection with TLA and her connection with the KGB are related."

She orders, "First slide."

Chief Randson powers up the slide projector that sits in the middle of the conference table. Then he pushes a button on the handheld controller. A picture of Diane Love from shoulders up appears on the screen.

"Diane Love works as a political analyst on President Carter's White House staff. At least once every two months for the past six months, she has visited the Edwin Kendley Estate in Connecticut . . . slide 2, Chief."

An aerial view of the sprawling Kendley Estate in a thickly wooded area appears on the screen.

"Each time she visits, so do some or all the directors of TLA. We conclude that the Kendley Estate is the headquarters of TLA . . . slide 3."

A photo of Edwin Kendley appears on the screen. Kendley's black colored hair, brown eyes, and confident smile convey charm.

"Edwin Kendley and Diane Love first made national news during violent protests that they organized at the 1968 Democratic Convention in Chicago. They were leaders in the Students for a Democratic Society. From our research so far, we conclude that Edwin Kendley formed TLA when the SDS dissolved itself in 1969 . . . slide 4."

A photograph of Edwin Kendley wearing a Panama hat and sunglasses and a man with Hispanic features who wears tropical apparel display on the screen. The two men sit at a table in an airport restaurant.

"One of TLA's objectives is to nationalize American industry—to include oil, steel, utilities, automotive, railroads, airlines, pharmaceutical, nuclear power, and others. One of their strategies is to drive the American public into believing these industries place profits over public safety and profits over employment security. Our analyses of events convince us that TLA was responsible for funding and contracting the oilrig explosions in the Gulf of Mexico last summer, the derailing of the gasoline tanker train in Elias Idaho several months ago, and poisoning of flu medicines distributed throughout the United States two years ago. The man with Kendley is Enrico Mendoza who was the leading operative that led those murderous missions resulting in the death of over 300 people.

"The American press was brutal in its criticisms of companies targeted by TLA and Mendoza—accusing those companies of inadequate security measures and inherent disregard for public safety to provide greater profits to stockholders. Members of Congress are calling for nationalization of those companies . . . next slide."

A picture of five textbooks appears on the screen.

Commander Macfurson explains, "TLA conspires to rewrite American history textbooks to paint America's past as evil, imperialistic, and pirating the resources of other countries.

"We know from history, that the Democratic Party has been the party of racism and Jim Crow. We know from history that the Republican Party was created to fight the Democratic Party's racism and pro Jim Crow agenda. We know that for one-hundred years following the Civil War, Republicans sponsored all Civil Rights legislation, and the Democratic Party fought Civil Rights legislation. During the late 1950s and early 1960s, The Democratic Party leadership came to understand that the racism, discrimination, and Jim Crow of the past were over. President Eisenhower's actions of sending in federal troops to force school segregation and to support black voter registration were the turning events to give blacks the vote and better educations. Minority leaders like Martin Luther King were registered Republicans for valid reasons.

"The Democratic Party saw the light. Starting with the Johnson Administration, there has been a concerted effort by the Democratic Party and the American media to paint the Democratic Party as the party of compassion for minorities and paint the Republican Party as the historically racist party. The TLA attempts to revise one-hundred-and-fifty years of history when the Democratic Party openly and violently oppressed blacks and other minorities. We have identified eight Senators and fourteen Representatives in the House who are openly professing and proclaiming this revisionist history. Through dummy subsidiaries and fake organizations, TLA is the major campaign fund contributor to those members of Congress who are also members of TLA.

"TLA is a major funder of the effort to revise and rewrite that history. Five years ago, TLA formed a holding company that is purchasing America's largest and most influential textbook publishing companies. Textbooks with revisionist history are already in America's primary schools. College textbooks are in early stages of distribution. An example of their revisionism is to vilify America's founding fathers and to pronounce dead the Declaration of Independence and the U.S. Constitution. Some text books already advocate setting aside the U.S. Constitution as an out-of-date governing document and replacing it with a set of goals instead.

"You might remember that special election last year in Texas to fill the seat of that senator who died in a car crash. The Republican candidate was twenty points ahead in the polls until the Ku Klux Clan showed up in hoods and robes at one of his speeches and announced their support for him. Two weeks later, he lost the election to the Democrat. Documents found in Diane Love's condo reveal that the TLA organized and funded the whole fake KKK incident. Diane Love planned the whole thing. Oh, and they were not real members of the KKK. It was all deceit and fraud to place a socialist in the House of Representatives.

"Diane Love also planned the lap dancer scandal that recently caused the seated Republican Governor of Nevada to lose reelection. There was no truth in those claims of those dancers. The entire scandal was manufactured by TLA. In all, Diane Love manufactured incidents and scandals that resulted in more than twenty Republicans not being elected or not winning reelection."

Commander Macfurson pauses for questions.

One of the new analysts, a studious appearing woman with thick owl glasses and short, pageboy style black hair raises her hand.

Commander Macfurson focuses on the new contract analyst, Kathy Benning, who was one of her students at Brown University several years back when Sally was still in the navy reserve—before Sally went permanent active duty. Kathy recently earned her Master's degree in International Relations. "Yes, Kathy, do you have a comment or question?"

"Professor Mac—excuse me—Commander, your briefing so far focuses on TLA enacting change through the Democratic Party. Yet, there are many Republicans on the TLA membership list. What is your analysis of that?"

"We have completed background checks on most of those Republican TLA members. All of them were Marxist activists in college. They represent districts where Democrats never win. So they had to join the Republican Party in order to be elected to Congress. Their voting records reveal their leftist agenda."

Kathy Benning expresses disbelief that people can be so despicably dishonest.

Commander Macfurson casts a knowing smile and comments, "Kathy, as you gain more experience, you will come to understand that those who seek to destroy the American Republic have no moral or ethical standards. For them, no lie is too big, no deceit is too deep, and no misrepresentation is too outrageous."

Another new analyst, Terry Coldenberg, who recently earned his Master's Degree in Political Science with a minor in history, shakes his head, expressing doubt.

Commander Macfurson eyes the slight of build, medium height gentlemen with drooping mustache and brown hair that hangs over his ears. She queries, "Do you have something to add, Terry?"

"Uh, well, yes," Terry responds. "I follow politics closely. Most Democrats in Congress vote leftwing and so do many Republicans in Congress. My question is why do we focus on Democrats for this operation?"

The commander smiles, nods, and exhibits understanding; she responds, "It's not that ONI focuses on Democrats; it's TLA that focuses on recruiting Democrats." Macfurson pauses for effect; then she opines, "My personal view is that both political parties legislate outside the bounds of the U.S. Constitution. That is why the American Conservative Party and the American Libertarian Party were formed—to provide opposition to anti-constitutional elected politicians, both Democrat and Republican."

Terry Coldenberg nods his head and expresses agreement; then comments, "But there is nothing illegal about modifying textbooks, fraudulent political tactics, and politicians deceiving their constituency. And there is nothing illegal regarding private groups funding and crusading to fundamentally transform America from a multiple party republic into a democratically elected communist state. I mean, there are several American Socialist and Communist Parties that operate openly."

Captain Brad Watson explains, "What you say is correct, Mr. Coldenberg. However, the murderous actions of The Longjumeau Alliance are illegal and can be classified as treasonous acts for the purpose of overthrowing the constitutionally formed government of the United States."

Kathy Benning inserts, "But TLA is only *suspected* of those terrorist acts—no proof, right?"

"All evidence points to TLA," Commander Macfurson affirms. "We need to build the case against the TLA. That's why we have expanded our resources by bringing on five additional analysts—to build that case."

Chief Page asks, "What happens when the case is built?"

Captain Watson advises, "The case is turned over to the Justice Department."

After the briefing, Commander Sally Macfurson, Chief Page, John Smith, and Senior Analyst Bob Mater stand in a circle and discuss known details regarding The Longjumeau Alliance.

Rig says, "I can't see such criminals coming to power. Opposition to their communist revolution will stop them."

Bob Mater explains, "Ya, see, Rig. They are so brainwashed and so arrogantly confident that their leftwing philosophy is the best way to 'rule' America they will tell any lie and will break any law to eliminate the opposition. It's *the ends justify the means* mentality. When TLA makes their move to take over America, there will not be any opposition because TLA will have eliminated opposition through lies, deceit, and unlawful actions."

Rig shakes his head and expresses doubt that the American people will accept such lies, deceit, and unlawful actions. He looks around the circle and challenges, "But we're going to stop TLA, right? I mean we, the government, will stop them, right?"

Commander Macfurson advises, "All we can do is build the case, then turn it over to the Justice Department."

"What will the Justice Department do?" Rig asks.

Bob Mater answers, "Depends which political party controls the Executive Branch and how deeply TLA has infiltrated the Executive Branch."

Chief Page casts a curious stare toward John Smith. John returns a conspiratorial smile. Both Rig and John are thinking about their meeting tomorrow with The Guardians' representative Denton Phillips. At that meeting, John and Rig will provide Denton with a copy of The Longjumeau Alliance's membership list.

Commander Macfurson observed the glances between Page and Smith. She wonders: *What the hell was that all about?!*

Chapter 53

Roger Walker, private investigator, sits in his nondescript sedan one-quarter block from Rigney Page's apartment building. Walker is a heavyset balding man, who is three years retired from the Army where he last served as a chief warrant officer in the Criminal Investigation Division.

Because of inadequate street lighting, Walker has an unclear view of the stairs leading to the front door landing of Page's third floor residence. When he needs a better view, he looks through the lens of his telescopic camera.

In the dark of his vehicle, he glances at the luminesce dial of his wristwatch—9:38 PM. He anticipates that Page will go to bed at 10:00 PM.

From the beginning of this investigation, frustrating obstacles have blocked him from gathering some details. The first obstacle was being denied access to the Naval Communications Unit at Cheltenham, Maryland where he had followed Page. Page drove through the gate without problems. When Walker attempted to follow Page into the base by flashing his retired military I.D. card and pointing to the Andrews Air Force Base decal on his windshield, the gate sentries denied him access. Only those vehicles with Naval Communications Unit Cheltenham base decals and Naval Communications Unit I.D. passes are allowed unescorted access. Walker currently searches for a subcontractor private investigator who has unescorted access to the Cheltenham base.

The second obstacle is similar to the first. He easily accesses the navy installation on Massachusetts Avenue N.W., but he cannot obtain unescorted access into the Commander Naval Telecommunications Command building where Page works.

The third and most frustrating of all obstacles is that he cannot enter Page's residence to plant listening devices. One evening after Page had departed his residence, Walker climbed the stairs to the third-floor landing front door of Page's apartment. Walker immediately identified security devices that would sound alarms should anyone attempt entry through the door or windows. Only two of the four windows of Page's apartment are accessible from the landing. All windows have mesh screen security sensors.

Several nights later, Walker set up sound sensing equipment in his van. The small parabolic antenna could not detect any sounds coming from Page's apartment, although the antenna easily detected sounds from residences at a farther distance. Walker concluded that the apartment must have sound dampening or sound grounding devices. He concluded the wire mesh on the inside of the apartment windows might double as part of a sound grounding network. Walker went in search of the apartment building owner. Records at the county courthouse, listed a company with an overseas address.

Two weeks ago, Walker concluded that Chief Petty Officer Rigney Page is not the normal, run-of-the-mill sailor. He called his contact at the Naval Personnel Department who, for fifty dollars, will provide detailed information on any sailor. The report from his Naval Personnel Department contact contained information regarding *The Hero of Thurso* and high awards for valor during classified operations. Walker remembers his astonishment when he read Page's navy personnel file. He remembers his feelings a year ago when he first read about the terrorist attacks at that U.S. Navy base in Scotland. Walker remembers feeling pride that two enlisted men led the counter attack and neutralized those terrorists. Walker was an enlisted man for twenty of the thirty years he spent in the army.

A passing car brings Walker back to the present. The car stops in front of Page's building. Walker lifts the camera with telescopic lens to his eye. The driver of the car opens the car door and steps onto the street. Through the telescopic lens camera, Walker sees a man with reddish-brown shoulder length hair, full beard of the same color, and who wears a black leisure suit. The man also wears a wide-brimmed, black Panama hat with white band. The man has his head bowed and turned away from Walker, as if he is watching where he steps in the dark. The wide brim of the Panama hat hides the man's face above the beard. The man ascends the steps toward

Page's apartment. Walker notes the man holds a paper bag.

Walker snaps a dozen photographs, which are automatically date and time stamped. But none of the photographs capture the man's full face. Walker's critical sense of observation tells him something unusual just happened, but he cannot pinpoint what it is.

When the man reaches the third-floor landing, he knocks on the door. Several moments later, the door opens.

Through the telescopic lens, walker easily views Rigney Page in the doorway wearing pajamas. Page motions for the man to enter. The man in the Panama hat enters the apartment. Page closes the door.

Walker focuses the telescopic lens on the only window of the apartment that faces him. A thick curtain allows only a few slivers of light to exit the window. The window provides no view into the interior of the apartment.

Walker speculates on what would have a civilian delivering something in a paper bag to Page at this time of night. Then, again, the nagging sense that something was unusual about the sequence of events from the time the civilian arrived in the car and the time the civilian entered Page's apartment. He takes several photographs of the car's license plate.

John Smith places the paper bag on the small dining table. Then he removes the Panama hat and lays it on the small dining table. He lays the keys to his car on the table. John advises, "Your tail is about one-quarter of a block away southward."

Rig nods. He asks, "What's in the bag?"

"Some empty cans."

Rig begins to unbutton his pajamas.

John Smith removes the leisure-suit jacket and unbuttons his shirt.

As they both undress, John briefs Rig. "Denton has arranged the private jet. You will board in a private hangar at National Airport." John places a slip of paper on the table. "This provides directions to that private hangar. A pass that will get you in the gate is in the glove compartment of my car. That private jet will fly you to the Orange County Airport in Southern California. The plane and pilots will wait for you. There is a telephone number on those directions that you must call at least four hours before you want to fly back to Washington."

As Rig slips into the trousers of the black leisure suit, he expresses appreciation as he comments, "With all this support from The Guardians, I feel as if I am sharing my revenge on those union killers."

John Smith reminds, "You are now a Guardian . . . for life."

Rig spends a few moments staring into space while he considers the seriousness of being a Guardian.

As John slips into Rig's pajamas, he continues his brief. "The Guardians hired a private detective to keep tabs on Max Robertson. Robertson now has two armed bodyguards twenty-four seven, provided by the CLWUA."

Rig stands motionless. His eyes go wide and he exhibits concern over the bodyguard information.

John says in a jesting tone, "C'mon, Rig. You once killed two armed Stasi Agents with your bare hands. You can't possibly fear two armed bodyguards."

"Bodyguards increase the difficulty of completing my task."

"Whatever you do, Rig. The Guardians are behind you. They want justice done for that security guard killed in that fire at your father's warehouse."

"That's not the total reason why I am going after Robertson. He threatened my parents and my sisters."

John nods and expresses understanding; he advises, "There is a full report on Robertson's movements over the past two weeks waiting for you on the plane. The report will tell you that he is repeating his routine every two days. He is frequenting the same places over and over again, and those bodyguards stay out-of-site and hidden. You know what that means, right?"

Rig responds, "Yes, I understand. They are laying a trap for me."

"Rig, your task would be much easier with a suppressor equipped sniper rifle, which was not on the list of weapons you requested. But I added one anyway before giving your list to Denton Phillips."

"I do not want to kill Max Robertson. I want to maim him so that he cannot work and cannot walk unassisted. I want him to be a living reminder to all union members of what can happen to union thugs and union killers. I want unions to fear using violence to get their way because they will know defenders of freedom will fight back."

John Smith offers, "Rig, The Guardians have men who specialize in what you want to do. They will maim Robertson per your specific instructions. That way you get what you want, and you remain safe and un-accused."

"No. I must do this myself. No matter who does it, I will be suspected and accused, anyway."

"You can maim with a sniper rifle. You're an expert shot."

"Only as a last resort," Rig specifies.

"Okay. Good. Now, there will be a four-wheel drive Chevy Blazer waiting for you in the Orange County Airport hangar. All the weapons, equipment, and disguises that you requested will be in the Blazer. That Blazer is customized with a high performance engine and is bullet proof and blast resistant. It is also equipped with a homing device. The Guardians will know your location at all times."

Rig enters the bathroom so that he can don the long hair wig and beard while looking into the mirror. When he is satisfied with his disguise, he goes back to the dining table. He puts the Panama hat on his head and angles it down over the left side of his face, which is the side that would be exposed to his tail down the street. He picks up John's car keys and starts for the door.

With a concerned and compassionate tone, John says, "Rig, remember not to become impatient while tracking Robertson. If you don't have an opportunity this trip, you can always try again at a later date. You are needed more as an undercover operative for your country than you are needed as an avenging crusader fighting against union brutality."

Before he opens the door, Rig assures, "I know, John. I will not act irrationally."

Through the telescopic lens of his camera, Walker sees the front door to Page's apartment open. The man with the wide brimmed hat exits the apartment. The man does not carry the paper bag. Walker snaps a dozen photographs, but again the man never provides a full view of his face. The man enters his car and drives off.

Walker looks toward the apartment. The few slivers of light that come from the window extinguish. He assumes that Page is going to bed, which is normal at this time of night.

After he is relieved at midnight, Walker drives home.

Three hours later, Walker still cannot fall asleep. He continually runs the sequence of events regarding Page's visitor through his mind. The sense that something unusual occurred nags at his thoughts.

Suddenly, revelation comes to his mind. His eyes go wide with astonishment as he chastises himself for missing it. *When the man with the Panama hat opened the door to his car, arriving and departing, the car's interior lights did not come on. And when the man knocked on Page's door, Page did not turn on the front door light before opening the door. And when the visitor departed the apartment, the front door light remained off.*

Realizing there is nothing he can do about it now; he closes his eyes and rapidly falls asleep.

Chapter 54

Eight hours later while eating a leisurely late breakfast at home, still in his bathrobe, Walker pulls his notebook and opens to a paper-clipped page. He reads the telephone number on the notebook page as he dials.

The phone is answered on the other end and a voice states, "Commander Naval Telecommunications Command, Systems Testing and Certification Department, this is a non-secure line, RM1 Rose speaking, how can I help you, sir or ma'am?"

Walker says, "I would like to speak to Chief Page, please."

"Chief Page is not here, sir. May I take a message?"

"Uh, no. When would be the best time to call to catch the chief in the office?"

"Chief Page is out sick with the flu. He could be out three-to-four days."

Walker responds, "I'll call back next week." He hangs up the phone.

He turns to another page in his notebook. Before dialing the next number, he takes two sips of coffee.

"Construction and Labor Workers Union of America, Southern California District, this is Julie how may I help you?"

"This is Roger Walker of Simms Investigations. I need to talk with Melvin Spartan."

Julie checks Spartan's list of those who Spartan allows immediate and direct access. She finds Walker's name on the list. "I'll put you through immediately, Mr. Walker."

"This is Melvin Spartan. What's happened?"

"Chief Page has left town. He told his office he will be out three-to-four days with the flu."

Spartan inquires, "What are the chances of you discovering where he went?"

Walker advises. "He is traveling disguised and undercover and probably using classified military transportation."

Spartan demands, more than asks, "You will check manifests

with all the major transportation centers, correct?"

"Yes, of course."

Spartan hangs up the phone.

Walker immediately dials the next telephone number.

A voice on the other end announces, "Congressman Thayer's office, this is Mark, how can I help you."

"This is Roger Walker of Simms Investigations. I need to speak with the Congressman."

"Just a moment, Mr. Walker."

Nearly one minute later Billy Thayer speaks into the phone, "Good morning, Mr. Walker. What do you have for me?"

"Chief Page has left town. He told his office he will be out three-to-four days with the flu."

"Any idea where he is going?"

"No, but he departed wearing a disguise—means he is probably traveling undercover."

"Undercover?!" the Congressman responds with a startled tone. "Undercover usually translates to military operations, correct?"

Walker explains, "Undercover is my interpretation. Although I have no proof yet, Page's actions and behavior are similar to many military undercover operatives that I encountered during thirty years in the Army CID."

Congressman Thayer responds, "Interesting interpretation. Keep me informed and call me when Rigney Page is back in Washington."

Walker takes a bite of toast, takes a sip of coffee, and then he dials the pager number of the operative who tails Chief Page during the morning.

Fifteen minutes later, Walker's phone rings.

"Walker."

"This is Drake. You called me."

"Where are you?" Walker asks.

"At a pay phone a couple of blocks from Page's apartment. Doesn't look like he is going to work today, or he is going in late. Just before you paged me, he came out on his landing and picked up the paper. He was still in his pajamas."

"Are you sure it was Page?"

"Yes."

"Did you look through binoculars when he came out onto the landing?"

"No need. I saw him clearly without the binoculars."

Walker advises, "You can leave. I won't need you for about four days. I'll call you."

"Okay, Mr. Walker. See ya later."

Walker pours another cup of coffee. He sits back in his chair and assesses why union officials in Southern California and why a U.S. Congressman from California are both interested in the same person. The CLWUA and Congressman Thayer have separate contracts with Simms Investigations. Each do not know that the other initiated investigations into the activities of the same person. Walker's boss at Simms ordered Walker not to reveal either client to the other.

Walker decides to go to the Library of Congress this afternoon and research recent articles on the CLWUA in the Southern California newspapers.

Chapter 55

Rig exits the private jet in a private hangar at the Orange County Airport wearing his businessman disguise—long black curly hair wig that covers half his ears and touches the collar of his dark-blue pinstripe suit, a black mustache, and deep-blue colored contact lenses.

The Chevy Blazer is parked inside the hanger near the open hangar door. He opens the Blazer's tailgate and finds two large canvas bags that contain all the gear, weapons, and disguises that he ordered from Denton Phillips. Included with the weapons is a Chinese sniper rifle with scope and foot-long suppressor—not ordered by Rig but added to the weapons list by John Smith.

He drives directly to the Long Beach Hyatt on Shoreline drive and registers as Mr. Jonathan Segal of Pensacola, Florida. After checking-in, he visits the Hertz Rental Car booth in the hotel lobby and orders four different cars for the next four days. He does not want Max Robertson's professional bodyguards noticing the same vehicle always in the vicinity.

After shaving and showering, Rig stands before the bathroom mirror and dons the curly black colored wig that covers his short reddish-brown hair. Then he applies the thick black mustache. He places contact lenses over the iris of each eye that changes his eye color from green to deep-blue. Then he dresses in a summer-weight gray suit and red tie.

He drives a rented brown-colored sedan to the construction site described in The Guardians' report on Max Robertson. Rig sits in the sedan one block from the construction site. Through binoculars, he easily finds Max Robertson's pickup truck. Five minutes later, he locates the tall, blond haired and bearded, physically fit Max Robertson.

Thirty minutes later, two men in casual clothes exit a dark blue sports utility vehicle, SUV, directly across the street from the construction site. They stop to talk with Max Robertson; then they return to their SUV. Rig notices the two-way radio antenna centered on the SUV's roof.

Several moments later, Robertson departs the construction site. A dozen construction workers stare after Robertson as he drives his red pickup truck off the site at 3:33 in the afternoon.

Rig concludes the two men from the sports utility vehicle are Robertson's bodyguards. Rig also concludes that those bodyguards informed Robertson that Rigney Page had departed Washington, and it was time to trap Page at one of Robertson's usual haunts.

During early evening, Rig goes to the country and western themed Wagon Wheel Dancehall—the same dancehall where he attacked and maimed Allen Villanueva in the men's bathroom. This evening, Rig wears his businessman wig, mustache, and deep-blue colored contact lenses. But tonight, instead of a business suit he wears a tan-colored western-style jacket, steer-head bolo tie, and a felt tan-colored cowboy hat. He carries a holstered automatic pistol on his belt that is hidden by his jacket. A six-inch blade dagger in its sheath is strapped to his left forearm.

Rig sits at a table in the crowded middle area of the floor. His location in the dancehall provides a clear view of the bar and front door. With his head slightly bowed, the brim of his hat hides the top half of his face. He buys three mugs of beer and explains to the waitress he is waiting for two friends. The two additional beers at empty seats at his table convey that the customer is not alone. Rig feels secure in the sea of cowboy hats that surround him.

Max Robertson enters the dancehall; Robertson's bodyguards enter thirty-seconds later. Robertson sits at one end of the bar and his bodyguards sit at the other end. All three continually scan the male patrons looking for Rigney Page or someone of Rigney Page's build wearing a disguise—probably a construction worker disguise similar to that night when the rightwing mad bomber attacked Allen Villanueva and set off explosives at the CLWUA building.

Forty minutes later, Robertson slips off his barstool and walks toward the bathroom.

Several seconds later, both bodyguards slip off their barstools; they walk to the hallway entrance that leads to the bathrooms and station themselves on the right side of the hall entrance.

Rig notices that both bodyguards scrutinize every male that enters the hallway. He chuckles because he has no intention of attacking Robertson in this place. He came to the Wagon Wheel only to evaluate Robertson's behavior and to observe the tactics of the bodyguards.

Rig hears the man at the next table announce that it is time to leave. The man and two women stand. Rig seizes this opportunity to depart the dancehall. He stands; then walks behind the second woman as they make for the front door. A casual observer would conclude that Rig is with the woman who walks ahead of him.

At approximately 9:00 PM, Rig parks his nondescript rental car one-full block away from Robertson's apartment building. Through night-vision binoculars, he has a full and clear view of the apartment building's main entrance. When a car approaches from either direction, he slides down in the car seat to avoid being caught in the vehicles headlights.

One hour later, the bodyguards' SUV passes Rig; then parks along the curb near the apartment building. Several minutes later, Robertson drives his pickup truck past Rig's position. Robertson parks his truck behind the bodyguards' SUV but does not exit.

Rig becomes cautious. He pulls the nine-millimeter Beretta automatic pistol from the holster on his belt. *Why haven't they exited their vehicles?! Have they spotted me?!* He rapidly scans the areas around his car.

An identical SUV arrives and parks across the street from the other SUV. The first SUV drives off.

Rig expels a deep sigh of relief. *They were waiting for the graveyard shift!*

Robertson exits his pickup truck and walks toward the apartment building. A graveyard-shift bodyguard exits the recently arrived SUV and follows Robertson into the apartment building.

After an hour, the bodyguard who followed Robertson into the building has not returned to the SUV. Rig shakes his head and expresses futility. He gives up surveillance for this night.

Chapter 56

Rig sits in a midsized, blue Chevy Bel Air sedan that is parked at the curb pointed southwest on Main Street in Seal Beach, California. Through the windshield and using high power binoculars he easily finds the solidly built, blond-haired, blond-bearded Max Robertson fishing off the Seal Beach Pier. He also identifies Robertson's two bodyguards fishing fifty feet away from Robertson's position.

Rig wears his businessman's disguise of black curly wig, black mustache, deep-blue colored contact lenses, and dark-blue pinstripe suit with red tie. He draws curious stares from some women pedestrians as they pass his car. During the hour he has sat at this location, he has not recognized anyone from his hometown.

As Rig reconnoiters the area, memories of his youth flood his thoughts. As he watches the ocean swells, he vividly remembers his days surfing near the pier. Back then, living life undercover and fighting evil men never entered his mind. Back then, he thought his future would be designing state-of-the-art radio equipment for large telecommunications equipment manufacturers.

He sighs deeply, expressing his frustration that no opportunity has occurred during the past three days for him to attack Robertson free from the threat of dangerous bodyguards. This is the second consecutive workday morning that Robertson spent on the Seal Beach Pier at the same location on the pier, as if Robertson and his bodyguards are openly challenging Rigney Page to come near. Rig is close to yielding to the reality that if he wants to deal justice to Max Robertson during this trip without risk of being captured by the bodyguards, he will need to use the sniper rifle. He formulates a plan.

Rig starts the car and drives southwest on Main Street toward the pier. Then he turns left onto Ocean Drive. He drives one block and turns right onto 10th Street. He drives one short block; then he turns onto Seal Way, actually an alley more than a street. The beach is just beyond the row of houses to his right. He searches for an advantageous sniper location.

His parents' home is on Seal Way but several short blocks away. He does not worry about bumping into his mother or father because they are working during this time of day.

After passing seven houses, he parks behind the garage of the old Wyman house. He remembers that his father told him that the Wymans moved away eight years ago. Now a family from Nevada owns the house, but they only occupy it during the summer months.

Rig exits the vehicle. He walks along the narrow sandy path between the Wyman garage and the house next door where Mrs. Noonan lives. The sandy path leads to the backyard of the old Wyman house. He notes that the doors and windows of the old Wyman house are the same as when he was a teenager. He concludes that the doors and windows have not been replaced since the house was originally constructed in the 1920s.

As he nears the front of the house, the view of the beach widens. When he reaches the front of the house, he steps onto a cement sidewalk that borders the sand of the beach. He glances at the partly cloudy sky. Then he scans the beach. The beach is mostly unoccupied on this weekday morning. He remains stationary as he evaluates window and door locations on the front of the old Wyman house that faces the beach. He hears a screen door open and shut behind him. He turns and sees Mrs. Noonan walking toward him.

He fondly remembers the wispy, deeply tanned, and gray haired Mrs. Noonan who was always kind to the teenage surfers who gathered daily at the Wyman house during the summer. She never complained about the noise and often engaged in conversation with all the teenagers. He remembers the many times Mrs. Noonan helped Mrs. Wyman make lunch for Judy Wyman's surfer friends. Rig also remembers that Mrs. Noonan's husband was a World War II navy pilot who was killed during the Battle of Midway. She never remarried. He figures she must be in her mid-sixties now.

"May I help you, sir?" Mrs. Noonan asks as she stops five feet away from Rig.

Rig smiles and expresses remembrance as the breeze from the sea tosses her graying hair and flaps her loose fitting cotton dress.

He calculates that she stood at that same spot dozens of times during his teenage years and talked with him as if he were an adult. In an enthusiastic manner, he greets her. "Hello, Mrs. Noonan, nice to see you again."

Mrs. Noonan stares suspiciously at Rig. The man with long black curly hair and mustache and deep-blue eyes looks familiar to her, but she cannot place him. While scrutinizing his face, she takes a few extra seconds staring at the jagged one-inch long scar on his forehead. "Who are you?" she asks, unsuccessfully suppressing a demanding tone.

"I am Jonathan Segal. I dated Judy Wyman in high school. I spent most days during the summer hanging out here and surfing with Judy and our friends. I live in Florida now. I am visiting my parents and thought I would drop by and see if Judy was here."

Mrs. Noonan looks up into the face of the ruggedly handsome man before her and scrutinizes his features again. Then she observes his expensive suit, silk tie, gold watch and gold cufflinks, and highly shined leather shoes. Her mind reaches back to the early 1960s when all those teenagers hung out at the Wyman's. She enjoyed those young adults. She thought that if her husband had come back from the war, they would have had children like those teenagers. She does not remember the name Jonathan Segal, but she certainly remembers his face and physique. She responds, "Yes, I do remember you."

Rig exhibits appreciation of her memory.

"But the Wymans no longer live here. They moved to San Diego eight years ago, and I haven't seen Judy since she graduated from college. I think she lives in San Diego also. The Becks own that house now, and its closed up for the winter. They live in Las Vegas most of the year, and only occupy the house during the summer."

Rig sighs and exhibits disappointment. He asks, "Do you have a telephone number for the Wymans?"

"Yes, in the house. I'll get it for you."

While Mrs. Noonan is in her house, Rig again evaluates the locations and construction of doors and windows. He concludes that the third floor bay window will provide the best view of the Seal Beach Pier.

Several minutes later, Mrs. Noonan returns with the Wymans' telephone number on a slip of paper.

Rig says goodbye to Mrs. Noonan and again tells her what a pleasure it is to see her again.

On his way back to the hotel, he drives past the CLWUA building. Rig observes four unmarked security vehicles parked at the four corners of the building, and each vehicle is occupied with two civilian clothed security agents. The building's front door has been replaced. Rig speculates the new door is stronger than the last one.

Chapter 57

Later, during early afternoon in his hotel room, Rig dials his father's business number.

"Page Office Supply, James Page speaking."

"Hi, Dad."

"Hey, Rig. What's up?"

"I am home with the flu. I've been thinking about the family. So I thought I would give you a call."

"Are you on the getting worse side or on the getting better side of the flu?"

"Getting better—finally got out of bed for more than an hour."

"Glad to hear it." James pauses; then he says. "I've been watching on the news that your Commander-in-Chief is about to give away the Panama Canal."

Rig responds, "Yeah, it's another one of those events where temporary office holders cause permanent damage."

"Well put, Son."

"So how's the business going? Getting better?"

"Yes, it is—back to making a profit. I move into the new warehouse next month. But those articles written by Weston Pyth is keeping some of my longtime customers from doing business with me."

Rig asks the question for which he called his father: "Is the CLWUA still harassing the family?"

"Interesting that you asked. They stopped all that harassment more than a month ago. Then, just a few days ago, they started following us again—your mother and I and your sisters. But no intimidation this time, just following. Actually, they are trying to hide they are following us, but we know how to spot them now."

Rig asks, "So they are not scaring Kate and Teri anymore?"

"No, just following, according to Kate and Teri. I don't know what they expect to gain by that."

James Page just confirmed what Rig assumed. The CLWUA suspects that Rig is in the area, and they are setting traps. Rig also concludes that the deceptive and disguised effort with John Smith several nights ago did not fool that Simms detective."

"Dad, please let me know if you need help. I can be out there within twenty-four hours."

"Thanks son. We are okay."

"Okay, Dad, I'll call again soon. Love ya."

"Love you too, Son."

After Rig hangs up, he goes to the desk and lays out the twelve-inch by twelve-inch aerial photograph of the four-block area surrounding the Long Beach CLWUA building. Then he unfolds the internal diagram of the Long Beach CLWUA building. Both the aerial photograph and internal building diagram were on his list to The Guardians. Rig spends twenty minutes studying both items and plans his attack.

He picks up the desk phone and dials The Guardians' contact number.

"Hello."

Rig informs, "This is Segal. Be ready for takeoff at ten-hundred hours tomorrow."

"We'll be ready," the voice on the other end of the phone promises.

Then Rig calls his Arlington, Virginia apartment. His answering machine answers the phone. He says, "John, it's Rig, pick up the phone."

"Hey Rig, how's it going?"

"I'm getting ready to make my move. I should be back by tomorrow evening."

"Good, I need to get back to work. Next time we need to come up with another ruse. I can't be gone from work this long."

Rig responds, "I don't think our ruse worked. CLWUA suspects that I am here."

"Okay, we'll discuss it for your next trip."

Rig inquiries, "Do I have any messages?"

"Yes. Several people left messages on your answering machine. Mostly, wanting to know how you are doing with the flu—Diane

Love, Sally Macfurson, Brad Watson, Captain Blakely, and that lieutenant who is your boss at COMNAVTELCOM."

"Okay. If they left a number, give it to me."

Rig spends the next hour calling people back. He apologizes for not returning their calls sooner; he blames being sick and in bed. He did not return calls to ONI Headquarters telephone numbers because he knows that caller telephone number identification is installed at the ONI headquarters. Instead, he left a message on Commander Sally Macfurson's home answering machine and asked her to inform others of his still highly infectious condition.

Rig hangs up the phone. Then he slips out of his clothes. He lies on the bed and closes his eyes. He needs rest to prepare for the long night ahead.

Chapter 58

At 2:00 AM, Rig checks out of the Long Beach Hyatt. He walks to the hotel parking area. When he is twenty feet away from the armored and bullet proof Chevy Blazer, he pulls the remote from his pocket and enters the four-number combination. The driver's side door unlocks and the motor roars to life. When he opens the door, the inside light does not operate, which is an intentionally designed feature for this super security and surveillance vehicle. After driving out of the Hyatt parking lot, he turns right and drives toward the CLWUA building. Traffic is practically nonexistent at this time of morning in the Long Beach business district.

Ten minutes later, he enters the Long Beach industrial area. He drives into an alley two blocks from the CLWUA building and parks the Blazer between two large dumpsters—hiding the Blazer from anyone who looks into the alley from either entrance.

Inside the Blazer, he dons a black-colored, light-weight coverall. Then he slips on a black colored ski mask, followed by slipping into black running shoes with rubber soles.

He exits the Blazer; then opens the tailgate. From one of the canvas bags, he retrieves a one-hundred-fifty-foot coiled rope with grappling hook attached.

He steps to the middle of the alley; then he looks toward the top of the three-floor building that he will climb. He knows that on the roof on this side of the building there is a matrix of pipes. He holds the rope four feet from the hook and twirls the hook twice and then release the rope. The grappling hook clears the top of the building and lands among the matrix of pipes. He pulls two feet of rope before it becomes taut; then he yanks hard. He moves to the side of the building, then climbs three feet up the rope. He hangs for a few moments to ensure the grappling hook grip on the pipes will hold his weight.

Rig returns to the open tailgate. From one of the canvas bags he pulls out one of the LAW Rocket Launchers. He slips his right arm between the sling and LAW tube; then he pulls the sling over his head; the weapon now hangs bandoleer style on his body.

Back at the rope, Rig grabs hold with both hands and hangs for a few moments to again test the reliability of the grappling hook hold. He effortlessly climbs the rope hand-over-hand. He feels some weakness as the result of muscle damage caused by the bullet wounds that Ensign Ryan inflicted on him in Sardinia last summer, but the weakness is hardly noticeable—thanks to the daily exercises prescribed by his physical therapist. He stops at a third floor window and places his feet on the windowsill for a short rest. Then he springs outward and quickly climbs the remaining twenty feet. At the top, he pulls himself over the roof's edge and rolls onto the flat rooftop. He pulls all the rope up to the rooftop and coils it loosely near the roof's edge.

Rig moves quickly across the flat roof to the building's northeast corner. From this position, he has a clear shot to the six-foot-high windows of Harold Oatman's office on the top floor.

He slips the LAW Rocket Launcher over his head, then holds it in both hands. The rocket warhead is filled with fire accelerant and a small explosive charge that will ignite the accelerant upon solid impact. The rocket has no guidance assembly. Rig must rely on accurate dead reckoning to deliver the rocket through the six-foot-high window that is two blocks away.

Rig has not used this weapon since a sabotage mission in 1973, when he was assigned to a NATO counterespionage unit. His target then was at a greater distance than tonight's target. That night in West Germany, he had successfully delivered the rocket to the intended target. Tonight, Rig feels confident because there is only a light breeze and the target is within the specified effective range of the weapon.

Rig reasons that this obvious act of sabotage will confirm in the minds of CLWUA leadership that the rightwing mad bomber has returned to his vengeful crusade. The CLWUA leadership, believing that Rigney Page is the rightwing mad bomber, will ensure that Max Robertson is on the Seal Beach Pier at 7:00 AM with more than two bodyguards.

Rig removes the launcher's pull pin and lowers the rear cover. He extends the launcher tube until the two tube segments are locked in place. He places the launching tube on his right shoulder, then looks behind him to verify that the back-blast area is clear. He pushes the trigger safety handle forward. He rests the forward tube in the palm of his left hand and places the fingers of his right hand on the trigger spring boot. When he has the target aligned in the front and rear sights, he presses the trigger. The rocket propels itself toward the targeted window at 500 feet per second.

Two seconds later, the rocket crashes through the window and travels across the office and explodes against a metal filing cabinet. Three seconds later, the entire office is afire. Fire alarms sound all over the building.

Rig stands fast for thirty seconds and waits for flames to shoot from the window. When the flames appear, he slings the empty LAW tube over his head—bandoleer style.

He steps quickly to the side of the roof next to the alley. He picks up the grappling hook and tosses it over a pipe two feet above his head; the grappling hook end of the rope loops over the pipe. Then he pulls the grappling hook to roof's edge and drapes it over. He picks up the coil of rope, and throws the coil over the roof's edge. Rig has constructed a rudimentary, hand-pull elevator.

He places his feet on the grappling hook flukes; then lowers himself with his own muscle power.

When he arrives on the alley surface, he pulls the rope hand-over-hand until all the rope his fallen to the alley surface. He pitches the rope and empty rocket launcher into the back of the Blazer.

Thirty seconds later, Rig drives out of the alley. He removes the ski mask.

Two minutes later he turns left onto Pacific Coast Highway and drives toward Seal Beach.

Chapter 59

Rig drives across the San Gabriel Bridge and enters Seal Beach. At the Main Street intersection, he turns right. Main Street is deserted during the dark of early morning. He drives the entire length of Main Street; then he turns left onto Ocean Avenue. He finds a parking place on a residential street that is a three minute walk to the old Wyman house. He does not want to park the Blazer on Seal Way close to the Wyman house for fear that residents might report to the police an unfamiliar car parked at a house that is closed up for the winter.

From the rear cargo area of the Blazer, he retrieves a pre-packed large beach bag. When he is ten feet from the Blazer, he pulls the remote locking device from his pocket and pushes the lock button.

Several minutes later he walks along Seal Way. Two and three-story houses on both sides of Seal Way block illumination from the half-moon. Although he still wears the black coveralls, he does not wear the ski mask, which would draw mission-ending attention should anyone see him. He still wears his businessman wig, mustache, and contact lenses that change his eye color from green to deep blue.

Rig stops behind the detached garage of the old Wyman house. He surveys the area to verify no one moves about. He trusts to luck that no insomniacs are watching him through windows in the darkened houses of Seal Way.

He darts to the area between the garage and Mrs. Noonan's house next door. Then he enters the backyard. The ground in the backyard is a mixture of sand and grass patches. He walks to the back of the house, stoops and searches for loose fitting lattice woodwork that cosmetically blocks the view of the crawlspace under the house. He removes a section of lattice work and enters the four-foot high crawlspace; he drags the beach bag with him.

He searches for the trapdoor that leads into a storage closet under the staircase that goes from the first floor to the second floor of the house. Judy Wyman showed him the trap door during their sophomore year in high school. Judy had told Rig that she discovered the trapdoor while playing hide-and-seek as a little girl. Judy had informed Rig that she was the only one of the Wyman family who knows about the trapdoor. The origin and purpose of the trapdoor was unknown to Judy. To the best of their knowledge, no other house along the beach had such a trapdoor. The last time he was in that closet, the closet stored beach chairs, beach umbrellas, beach toys, and beach blankets.

From the closet side of the trapdoor, the trapdoor is not easily identified. The edges of the trapdoor follow the edges of the wood planks. He speculates that the current owners do not know about it.

The crawlspace is dark. He cannot risk using a flashlight. He crawls to the area where he believes the trapdoor to be located. He lies on his back and presses his feet against the underside of the house's floor. After several seconds, a section of the floor gives way. The sound of something falling to the floor above tells that something was stored over the trapdoor.

Rig gets to his knees. He slips on lightweight, black colored cotton gloves. Using his gloved hands, he pushes up on the trapdoor and lays it to the side of the closet. Then he pushes his beach bag through the opening, followed by him lifting himself up and into the storage closet.

He pulls a small, low-powered flashlight from his coverall pocket. The illumination of the flashlight reveals that stacks of boxes block the path to the closet door. He relocates the stacks of boxes and clears a path to the door. Then he grabs the beach bag and opens the closet door.

Using the low-powered flashlight to lead the way, Rig steps up the stairs to the second floor, moves quickly through the second floor hallway, then walks up the steps to the third floor attic.

When he arrives in the attic, he goes immediately to the bay window. Through the angled side of the bay window, Rig sees the area of the pier that is over the water. The location on the pier where Max Robertson fished the previous two days is within his view. He unlatches the upper window and lowers it.

Knowing that he will need to make a quick and anonymous getaway, he quickly changes into what most beach goers would call khaki fishing clothes.

He reaches into the beach bag and retrieves the three sections of the Chinese sniper rifle that need to be assembled. First, he attaches the barrel to the stock. Then he screws on the eighteen-inch suppressor.

He moves a five-foot high chest of drawers to a position just back a few feet from the open window. Then he raises the rifle and rests the barrel bipod on the top of the chest of drawers. Through the sniper scope, Rig easily finds the location on the pier where he expects Robertson to be several hours from now.

He pulls a chair close to the window and sits. His mind wanders to the days of his youth that were spent mostly on the beach near the pier. He remembers the décor of this room when it was Judy's bedroom. Back then, there was one double bed, now there are two sets of bunk beds. Back then, the walls were adorned with teen idols of the early 1960s, mostly posters of The Beatles. Now, childlike images hang from the walls. The pastel colored laced curtains have been replaced with bamboo blinds.

Rig attempts to recall the details of that afternoon during their high school junior year when Judy lost her virginity to him in this bedroom. All his high school sexual experiences mix together into one blur. The only sexual event that he remembers vividly is when he lost his virginity one night when he was fourteen behind some rocks on the beach before him.

As he remembers those carefree days of high school and of living on the beach and surfing, scuba diving, girls and sex; he also remembers how unaware he was of the evil in the world. The worst evil he encountered back then was when he fought bullies.

Rig remembers that Saturday when he was ten years old that his father sat him down and explained freedom. *"Son, Americans enjoy a freedom unknown throughout the rest of the world. And the basis of freedom is self-reliance. No man is free who depends on the charity of others to live. Freedom breeds self-reliance. No person can be free unless he is financially free, and becoming financially free requires hard work. When you hear people say 'freedom is not free' they do not mean just the cost in human life in war to preserve American freedom. It also means that a person must earn his freedom, financially, so that he is not a burden on his fellow citizens. A person who cannot pursue his own version of happiness because he is dependent on the charity of others will never be free. So from this day forward you will no longer be the recipient of charity. From this day forward, the chores you perform will be the rent you pay for living under my roof.*

"Today is the day I set you free to earn your own way. Saturday has always been allowance day, but no more. If you want spending money, you must earn it yourself. And to that end, I have found you a job—a newspaper route. According to the route boss, who I spoke to on the phone earlier, you should earn forty dollars a month, which is four times the allowance I currently give you in a month."

Rig remembers he was astonished at the thought of earning so much money at the age of ten. He thought that he could begin to buy those radio Heath Kits he had been dreaming about. But on that day, he was also concerned about being broke; he objected, *"But dad, I have no money now. I need that allowance today. What do I do until I start getting money from the paper route?"*

His father pulled five dollars from his wallet and handed it to Rig and said, *"This is a loan. This should get you to the end of the month. You will pay me back at the end of the month."*

That same evening the man from the newspaper came to the house and explained Rig's duties and responsibilities and advised that Rig would start delivering papers two days hence. During those next two days, Rig constructed an open-top wooden box to sit on the handlebars of his bicycle that would hold the newspapers. His job was to accept newspapers from the distributer every morning at 4:00 AM and deliver those newspapers to the list of subscribers.

Because Rig was earning his own way, his parents gave him the freedom to follow his own choices and to come and go as he pleased with the one restriction that he must be home every evening by dark.

His parents would counsel Rig on the wisdom or lack of wisdom in his choices. As Rig entered his teenage years, the time restriction moved to later in the evening. By the time he was sixteen, there were no restrictions on the time that he must be home.

He kept that newspaper route for four years. Then he moved on to part-time and temporary jobs in warehouses and stocking shelves. He came to understand the value of self-reliance and the freedom it brought.

When was the best time of my youth? Rig asks himself. Then he answers himself: *My high school junior and senior years and the summer between—when I had that 1951 Ford pickup to drive around. Yeah, that was a happy and carefree time.*

Then, one week after graduating high school, he entered the navy. After several years of the normal routine of navy life, the Office of Naval Intelligence offered him a mission to hunt down an American traitor. During that first mission he discovered those evil foreign forces that would deny their fellow humans the right to life, liberty, and the pursuit of happiness. For ten years as an undercover counterespionage agent for naval intelligence, he fought that evil in Europe and in the islands of the Western Pacific. Now, he has discovered enemies he never knew existed—domestic enemies— American citizens who plot violent acts to deny their fellow citizens of the right to life, liberty, and the pursuit of happiness. He is astonished that domestic enemies reside in labor unions, the U.S. Congress, university faculties, the president's administration, business, and state legislatures. More astonishing and more shocking was when he discovered that one of his high school girlfriends, Diane Love, is a leader in that evil domestic crusade.

"Damn them!" He curses aloud at those evil people who conspire and act to destroy freedom and tranquility.

He recalls his teenage acts of vengeance against bullies. Back then he battled those bullies who quested to control a small patch of ground. Now, he battles bullies who quest to control an entire country.

Rig looks at his watch—6:33 AM. He retrieves binoculars from the beach bag and scans the pier. He flinches with surprise when he finds Max Robertson already settled in his beach chair on the far side of the pier—facing away from Rig—and with fishing line in the water. He scans the lightly occupied pier; few people are fishing on this weekday morning. Rig finds two teams of two bodyguards, each team fifty feet on both sides of Robertson. Rig assumes the increased security might be the result of the rightwing mad bomber's actions earlier this morning. Rig also concludes, correctly, that there are teams of bodyguards at the entrance to the pier.

Rig stands up and lays the binoculars on the chair; then he moves to his firing position behind the stacked nightstands.

He lifts the stock of the sniper rifle and rests it against his right shoulder. The barrel rests on the bipod. Rig closes his left eyelid as he looks through the scope with his right eye. The blond-haired, blond-bearded Max Robertson comes into focus. Robertson's back is toward Rig.

Rig makes a few adjustments to scope optics controls. He brings the crosshairs of the scope optics to Robertson's right leg. The loose fitting workpants that Robertson wears requires Rig to estimate the location of Robertson's knee.

Robertson sits in a beach chair and he rests his right foot on the bottom metal rail. His fishing pole rests against the top rail while he waits for a bite on the baited hook.

Rig has a partial view on Robertson's right leg from knee to ankle. Robertson's body blocks most of his right leg from Rig's view through the scope. Rig wants to destroy Robertson's right leg and right arm, but he wants the best chance of the bullet not hitting Robertson's head or torso. His goal is to maim Robertson for life, not kill him.

Rig decides to wait for a better shot. He knows he has plenty of time because he knows that Robertson and those bodyguards expect a face-to-face attack from the rightwing mad bomber.

Ten minutes later, Robertson shifts his position, which presents a clear shot to the right side of his right knee.

Rig shifts his position by a degree and places the scope's

crosshairs on where he believes Robertson's knee to be. He squeezes the trigger. The rifle stock kicks Rig's shoulder. The sound of the shot is suppressed to no louder than a light slap. The expended round casing ejects from the rifle's chamber.

Through the scope, Rig sees a hole appear in Robertson's pants at knee level, blood appears immediately.

Feeling the searing pain in his leg, Robertson cries out. He falls to the pier's surface. He grabs his leg with both hands.

Rig realizes that he has only a few moments for his second shot before those bodyguards reach Robertson's side. He becomes frustrated waiting for a clear shot on one of Robertson's arms—a shot that would not pass through an arm and enter the torso. Noticing that Robertson has his hands wrapped around his right knee, Rig places the crosshairs over Robertson's right hand and pulls the trigger. Through the scope, he sees a large bloody hole open up in Robertson's right hand. Rig knows the high caliber round passed through Robertson's hand and, then passed through the leg, tearing away more bone and flesh.

Rig lowers the stock of the rifle to the surface of the stacked nightstands. He picks up the binoculars and watches activity on the pier. Four bodyguards huddle around Robertson. One bodyguard kneels on one leg and applies his belt as a tourniquet around Robertson's right thigh. Then another bodyguard hands the kneeling bodyguard a belt and the kneeling bodyguard quickly applies the belt as a tourniquet around Robertson's right forearm.

One of the bodyguards talks on a handheld radio. Rig assumes the radio conversation is about calling an ambulance.

Two more bodyguards arrive on the scene.

All bodyguards are quickly scanning in all directions looking for the shooter. Several of them express concern that they might be the next victim.

Rig disassembles the sniper rifle and places it into the beach bag along with the two ejected bullet casings. He quickly returns all furniture to original locations. His last action is to close the window.

Several minutes later, he crawls from under the house. He pulls three segments of a ten-foot-long fishing pole from the beach bag. Then, while holding the segments of the fishing pole in his left hand and the beach bag in his right hand, he steps quickly across the backyard, moves past the garage, and walks onto Seal Way. Anyone watching would believe he was surf fishing on the beach, which is best just after sunrise.

When he walks onto Ocean Avenue, sirens sound in the distance.

Two minutes later, he is driving south on Ocean Avenue and sirens are still sounding in the distance.

Five minutes after that, he is driving south on Pacific Coast Highway.

During his drive to the Orange County Airport, Rig considers that an individual can drastically change his or her fate in a moment of impulsive decision. He concedes that there are uncontrollable, adverse forces that we cannot master and that there are invalid beliefs instilled in us that we do not challenge. Nevertheless, making careful, thoughtful decisions in our lives will minimize the effect of those uncontrollable forces and will minimize the effect of those invalid beliefs. Occasionally, there are those instant, split-second decisions that we make to ensure our safety and survivability, like jumping away from an oncoming vehicle. Sometimes, that split-second decision damages us for life.

So goes the saga of CLWUA members Horace Lombardi, Allen Villanueva, and Max Robertson who six months ago made an impulsive choice to use intimidation and threats of violence to impose their values and beliefs upon two people they thought to be employees of Page Office Supply. Those three union thugs chose to enter the building where Rig and his father were assembling office furniture, and those thugs attempted to scare Rig and his father off the worksite. Rig and his father fought back. Later attacks on the Page Family and the death of the night watchman at the Page Office Supply warehouse sealed the fate of those three union bullies. Horace Lombardi, Allen Villanueva, and Max Robertson chose their path, and as a result they will go through life physically disabled. Those three union thugs had been emboldened by their unions to use violence to force others to comply. They made their decision, not even considering that they would face a relentless uncontrollable force that would drastically change their lives—that relentless uncontrollable force being U.S. Navy Chief Petty Officer Rigney Michael Page.

Chapter 60

Seven hours later, Rig arrives at his apartment building in John Smith's car. He had changed into the leisure suit, reddish-brown long hair and beard, and Panama hat disguise on the plane.

John Smith, wearing bathrobe and four day beard growth, greets Rig with a conspiratorial grin. "You made the national news broadcasts tonight."

"What?"

"All three networks reporting that rightwing extremists are at war with unions in Southern California. The news reported a union headquarters building was bombed for the second time in several months, and over the last several months, two members of the same union were attacked and maimed, the second being shot this morning."

In a questioning tone, Rig asks, "Those news reports did not specify it was only the CLWUA and not all unions?"

"No. They made it appear that all unions are under attack."

Rig snorts disgust. "Typical media bias!" He pauses, then speculates, "I bet news reports did not include that those maimed union punks instigated the whole thing by threatening the owners of businesses and their families?"

John says, "Correct, the news did not include that. The news said that when the attacks first began police thought it was only one person. But now, because of the expensive weapons used, they believe it's a conspiracy with rich rightwing financiers funding the war against unions."

Rig chuckles; then comments, "The media acts unethically. They ignore the truth that my actions are a quest for justice and revenge."

Expressing disgust, John states sarcastically, "Yes, and their ignorance of the truth gets worse as each year passes."

Rig nods and conveys agreement.

John asks, "Did you see that national news reporter admitting that he made up stories of Panamanian protest violence over the

Panama Canal treaty—to spice up his televised reports?"

Rig states, "Yes, I saw it. I guess he'll never work as a reporter again."

"Humph!" John spurts in a disgusted manner. "Don't be so quick to banish him. This is the era of affirmative action and he is a minority."

Rig appears thoughtful as he considers John's comments.

John advises, "Oh, by the way, speaking of reporters, your father left you a message on your answering machine a couple of hours ago. He said that *Long Beach Times* reporter, Weston Pyth, was on television tonight. The news anchor introduced Pyth as an expert on rightwing violence against unions. Your father said Pyth is accusing the police of not investigating you and your father in the Rightwing Extremist Mad Bomber Case."

Rig expresses astonishment; then with a concerned tone, "Was that on the national news?!"

"Yes."

"That means I will be answering questions at work from my superiors—both at ONI and at COMNAVTELCOM. They will be suspicious of me out with the flu when reporters from Southern California are accusing me of being the mad bomber."

"Let me know how that goes," John requests. "It could affect your assignment to future joint ONI CIA missions."

"Will do," Rig promises.

John says, "Get out of that disguise, so I can put it on. I want to go home."

"You think our watchdogs could still be outside, then?"

"I haven't seen them, but we should not take chances."

Rig strips down to his t-shirt and boxer shorts.

Chapter 61

After John departs, Rig calls his father.

"Thanks for calling, Rig. How are you feeling?"

"Much better, I think I can go back to work."

"I thought you would want to know that Max Robertson was shot on Seal Beach Pier this morning."

"Is he dead?"

"No. He is in the hospital undergoing surgery."

"Shot by whom?" Rig inquires.

"According to the news broadcasts, he was shot by the rightwing mad bomber. According to Weston Pyth of the *Long Beach Times* who was interviewed by national television news, you and I should be investigated for the attacks on the Long Beach CLWUA building and attacks on union members and the firebombing of his car. Pyth declared he would not be scared off by firebombing rightwing terrorists. He declared he exists to protect the American people from the oppression imposed by profit motivated criminals."

"Did Pyth specifically say my name?"

"Yes, he said, and I quote, "James Page's son, Rigney Page, who is a chief petty officer in the navy."

"Did Pyth provide any evidence that we are in involved in those attacks?"

James Page replies, "No. He told the television interviewer that he is still gathering facts on the guilty and will publish those facts later. On national T.V. news, Pyth threatened law enforcement with exposing their bias toward members in the military."

Rig yawns; then glances at his watch. He asks, "Anything else I should know?"

"Yes, the Orange County Sheriff's Office, Lieutenant Mitchell, came by a few hours ago and asked a lot of questions."

"Like what?" Concern edges Rig's tone.

"He wanted to know if I owned a foreign-made high-power rifle and wanted to know where I was between 6:30 AM and 7:00 AM this morning. I told him that I did not own any rifles and during the specified time I was having breakfast with your mother."

"Did your answers satisfy him?"

"I don't know. Then he started asking questions about you. He wanted to know where you are and if you own any high-power rifles. I told him that you are in Washington D.C. and that I do not know what firearms you own, if any. I think he will contact you."

"I have nothing to tell him."

After Rig hangs up the phone, he considers staying up to watch the 11:00 PM Washington D.C. newscasts. He decides he must watch the local news to see if the Seal Beach rightwing mad bomber incidents are repeated or updated on local Washington D.C. news stations.

During the thirty minutes of local television news, Rig changes channels every 40 seconds to cover the six local channels on his television cable system. He finds no reports regarding Seal Beach. However, a story regarding Congressional schedules grabs his attention. According to the news report, a Senate Armed Services Subcommittee will investigate the shooting death of a naval officer in Sardinia last July.

The newscast also reports that the House of Representatives will debate the *Employee Fairness Act.* The legislation, should it become law, requires all companies to allow union organizers unrestricted access to company employees and company property during working hours. Under the legislation, employers are prohibited from taking actions against any employee joining a union. And any company with a mix of union and non-union workers must collect union dues through payroll deduction from all employees, including non-union employees. The legislation specifically targets fast-food franchises and family-owned businesses. The Act, should it become law, will establish a federal agency to ensure compliance by requiring all businesses in America to obtain a Federal Business License."

Rig shakes head and holds in contempt those character-flawed politicians who have sworn to protect and defend the U.S. Constitution but design socialist and redistributionist laws.

He is wide awake now. He moves off the couch and turns off the television. Then he pours several jiggers of peach brandy.

After returning to the couch, he turns off the lamp. As he sits in the dark and sips brandy, he contemplates how the Senate investigation into Ensign Ryan's death will involve him. He remembers someone telling him that Ryan's uncle was a U.S. senator. He wonders about the purpose of a Congressional investigation.

After gulping down the second helping of brandy, Rig leans his head back against the couch and closes his eyes. Events of the past few days race through his mind.

Chapter 62

"Hey, Chief, can I talk to ya for a minute?"

Chief Page looks up from the technical manual he is reading at his office in the COMNAVTELCOM building.

A heavyset sailor with sandy colored hair and fleshy face wearing Winter Blue uniform with second class radioman crow and who looks familiar stands in the doorway. The sailor holds a cup of coffee in each hand.

"RM2 Archer—we met at the Hail and Farewell last Friday. You said I could come and talk with you."

Chief Page nods recognition. Then he offers, "Come in and sit."

Archer enters the ten-foot by ten-foot office. He places a cup of coffee in front of the chief and comments, "I was told you take your coffee with just a dash of cream."

Chief Page expresses appreciation and confirms, "Yes. That's it."

Archer selects one of the two straight-back chairs in front of the chief's desk and sits.

"What's on your mind, Petty Officer Archer?"

"I wanted to talk ta ya about a decision I must make."

Chief Page knows what's coming. Several times every year, young sailors come to him in search of valid reasons to reenlist.

"I am on the advancement list for first class. I have only four months left on my enlistment, and the personnel office says I must reenlist for at least three years to put on the first class crow."

"How much time do you have in?"

"Approaching four years."

Chief Page exhibits surprise and comments, "First class in less than four years is unusual. How did you do that?"

"Oh, because I had an associate's degree when I joined. I came out of boot camp as an E-3. Then I was granted six-month waivers for advancement to third class and second class."

"Associate's degree in what?"

"Liberal Arts."

"Okay, so what are you going to do?"

"My division chief said the admiral would frock me to RM1 now, if I reenlist."

"Are you considering reenlisting?"

"Yes,"

"And how does that involve me?"

"I am searching for pros and cons from those first class and chiefs that I respect." Archer pauses, indicating he formulates a question. He asks, "What do you consider the pros and cons of a navy career?"

"I don't weigh the positive and negatives. The navy is a lifestyle that I enjoy. My work in the navy fulfills me and is of value to my country. No other line of work interests me."

"I understand, Chief, but I need reasons that will satisfy my parents."

Chief Page casts a curious stare at Archer.

"What Chief?"

"Why did you enlist in the navy in the first place?"

"I was going to college and ran out of money. I came into the navy to take advantage of the G.I. Bill education benefits—so that I can earn a Master's in Finance."

"And, now, you are considering reenlisting instead of returning to academia."

"That's right."

Chief Page advises, "A career in the navy is a life of serving and sacrificing, meaning that you would be expected to give more than you receive. You must decide that you are willing to do that, or you will be miserable in the navy."

Archer appears thoughtful; then he says "If I reenlist, I will be issued transfer orders to sea duty because I spent the last three years on shore duty. Going to sea is not something I want to do."

Chief Page states as a matter of fact, "Then your decision is easy. Leave the navy and earn your degree in finance."

Archer exhibits slight frustration as he states, "The last four years have been a lot of fun—an easy life."

Chief Page explains, "You have been living in Washington D.C. with the navy taking care of all your needs. Of course, it has been easy." Chief Page becomes more serious and states, "Serving at sea for three years is tough—tougher than college life—tougher than a career in business."

Archer expresses doubt as he challenges, "Have you gone to college, Chief? Have you worked in business?"

"I earned two associate's degrees while in the navy, and, no, I have not worked in business, other than summer jobs stocking shelves when I was a teenager."

"Two associate's degrees? In what?"

"One in Electronics Engineering and the other in General Studies."

Archer nods and for a moment shows he is impressed; then he challenges, "So what experience proves to you that a life in business is so easy?"

"I didn't say business is easy. I said that life at sea is tougher."

"How do you know?"

"Some I know who served at sea and now work in business have told me."

Archer shrugs his shoulders and sighs deeply. His face reflects dilemma.

Chief Page inquires, "I think you have already made the decision to reenlist, but you are worried about what your parents will think. Is that it?"

"My parents were very angry at me when I quit school and joined the navy. I started college with the intention of earning a Bachelor's Degree in Sociology. My parents were paying for my college. Then, deep into my second year, I changed my major to Finance. My parents were so angry they stopped paying my college costs. They said that if I wanted to be a greedy capitalist working in finance, then I must pay for my own college. I had to quit school because I had no money. I enlisted in the navy to earn G.I. Bill education benefits.

"My parents said I could have obtained student loans or worked my way through. I don't even go home on leave anymore, for fear of my family and friends dumping their anti-capitalist rants on me."

"Where is your hometown?"

"Berkley, California."

Chief Page nods and speculates, "And you were attending University of California at Berkeley, right?"

Archer's eyes widen and he exhibits astonishment. "How did ya know?"

"I've had this conversation several times before. You are searching for an honorable reason to make the navy a career—a reason that your parents and friends back home will accept."

"Well, yes, I guess that's it."

Chief Page advises, "Here is a dose of reality. Your parents and friends will never accept it. I recommend you not even attempt to rationalize your actions to anyone. Are you so unconfident that you believe you must justify your actions to others?"

Archer flushes red with embarrassment. He knows the chief nailed it.

Chief Page counsels, "The only way to be happy in this world is to do what you want without guilt or remorse, which means you must not be concerned about how others judge you. You guarantee yourself a miserable life if you torture yourself over what others might think of you."

"I worry about how my parents and friends will react to me reenlisting. They believe a military career is for losers."

"What's relevant is how you feel about yourself. Like I said, do not be concerned about how others judge you."

"You make sense, Chief, but I still have no strategy for satisfying my parents."

Chief Page casts a befuddled expression at Archer. "You're not understanding me. You cannot be concerned about satisfying your parents. You must be only concerned about satisfying yourself."

"I'll write them a letter."

"No." Chief Page dictates. "You must be face-to-face with them when you tell them. Do not delay that."

"They'll disown me."

"You must own yourself."

"Yeah, you're right, Chief. I must do it."

Chief Page advises, "Never answer 'why' questions about your decisions. People who ask you 'why' are just searching for ammunition to attack your decisions."

"Whoa, Chief! I can't dishonor my parents if they ask me why I am making the navy a career."

Chief Page advises, "It is not wise to provide challengers with ammunition to engage you in argument. There is no act more futile than arguing with those whose mind will not change."

"I think I can get my parents on my side if I give them a good enough reason."

"Good enough for whom?"

"Well, Chief, why did you reenlist the first time."

Chief Page shakes his head in dismissal and expresses disappointment. "You're dismissed, Petty Officer Archer. Come back when you have gained confidence to stand by your decisions."

Archer exhibits frustration. Then he asks, "Please, Chief, I must tell my parents something that sounds reasonable to them. How would you respond if someone asked you why you reenlisted?"

"I would tell them that I could not stay in the navy without reenlisting."

Archer responds in a sarcastic tone, "Very funny, Chief!" Then, in a serious tone, he asks, "If you respected and honored someone who asked you why you made the navy a career, how would you answer?"

"I would tell them that serving my country in the navy fulfills my needs and wants."

"They will ask me how serving in the navy fulfills me."

"Of course they will. You should already know the answer to that question. What are you going to tell them?"

"Actually, Chief, my motives are selfish. Living and working in the navy pleases me. I enjoy the work and comradery. I prefer to live and work in the navy instead of pursuing a career in finance.

The navy appreciates my contribution. Look how fast I have advanced. I'm thinking about applying for Limited Duty Officer when I become eligible."

Chief Page states, "Nothing wrong with that response; it's honest. That's what you should tell your parents."

"My parents abhor selfishness. They are committed to improving the welfare of their fellow human beings, and they criticize anyone who is not so committed."

Chief Page responds, "If protecting your country by serving in the United States Navy does not improve the welfare of fellow human beings, then I don't know what does."

"My parents and friends don't think that way. They believe in direct contact with those who need assistance."

What do your parents do to provide direct assistance to their fellow human beings?"

"My father is a director in the California Department of Social Services. My mom is fund raiser."

"Fund raiser for what?"

"Some political organization."

Chief Page asks, "What political organization?"

"Oh, it's called Move America Forward something-something. I really never paid much attention to my parents' political activities. They talk and breathe politics. I find it boring."

Chief Page inquires, "How does fund raising for political organizations provide direct assistance to those in need?"

Archer responds, "I dunno, Chief. My mother tried to explain it to me once. Something about getting compassionate politicians elected to public office."

Chief Page asks, "Do you accept money or other things of value from your parents?"

"No, not since I joined the navy."

"So for the last four years you have been independent from them. Your life is yours, now. Your life does not belong to your parents and friends back home. Do what you want and do not be discouraged by the judgments of others."

Archer nods, then queries, "So it is okay to stay in the navy because of self-serving reasons and not for patriotic self-sacrificing reasons?"

"Yes."

"Okay Chief, thanks. Now, how do I avoid sea duty? Will the navy let me reenlist for another tour of shore duty?"

"Probably," the chief responds. "But do not expect to be selected for chief or LDO without any sea duty. If you want to advance to chief or LDO in minimum time, you should reenlist for Radioman 'C' school and your choice of ship type after school."

"Why Radioman 'C' school?"

"Because you'll go to sea as a first class radioman. Your shipmates will expect you to know more about your rate than what you learned during four years in a message center. Radioman 'C' school will provide you with the skills you'll need."

"But I passed the RM1 test the first time and will be advanced with less than four years in service."

"I recommend that you not boast about that to your shipmates but be truthful if they ask."

Archer stands and says, "Thanks, Chief. You've given me a lot to think about."

"You're welcome."

Archer turns and exits the office.

After Archer is out of sight, Chief Page chuckles and comments under his breath, "I bet his anti-capitalism parents have a mortgage on their house, loans on their cars, and mutual funds in their retirement accounts."

Chapter 63

During this early afternoon in Seal Beach, the comfortable climate and temperate sea breeze energizes Orange County Sheriff Detective Lieutenant Mitchell and Deputy Sergeant Davis. They go from house-to-house along the beachfront and interview every resident—searching for anyone who noticed anything unusual during the days and morning leading up to the shooting of Max Robertson on the Seal Beach Pier.

No one answers the door at the Beck House. Both detectives raise their eyes to the third floor and evaluate the angle of the bay window to the pier. They perform this evaluation task with every house they visit. Both Lieutenant Mitchell and Deputy Davis agree that the third floor window of the Beck house provides an excellent view of that area of the pier that Robertson sat when he was shot.

They also comment to each other that the Beck house and the Noonan house next door are among the few houses along the beach that have not undergone remodeling or rebuilding on the lot. The two 1920s style homes reflect the early days of Seal Beach's shady past that included land speculation corruption, gambling houses, and a cheap pier-side amusement park. Many landowners along the beachfront have torn down the old single-family homes and replaced them with three-floor buildings with vacation rentals on each floor.

Both deputies move toward the front door of the Noonan home. Before they knock, Mrs. Noonan opens her front door.

"Come in, officers," invites the wispy white-haired Mrs. Noonan.

After the two officers enter the house and the door is closed, Mrs. Noonan comments, "I was wondering when you would get to me. Your house-to-house investigation is the talk of the hair salons, markets, and drug stores."

Mitchell queries, "You're Mrs. Noonan, then?"

"Yes, that's right."

"Mrs. Noonan, I am Detective Mitchell with the Orange County

Sheriff's office." Mitchell nods toward Davis and says, "This is Deputy Davis."

With an enthusiastic expression on her face, Mrs. Noonan states, "It's a pleasure to meet you both."

Mitchell asks, "Is Mr. Noonan home?"

"My husband was killed in World War Two."

Deputy Davis states sincerely, "Americans appreciate your sacrifice and that of your husband's."

"Thank you, Deputy. You're so kind. It was a long time ago."

Mitchell asks, "Mrs. Noonan, do you mind if Deputy Davis walks through your house? He won't create any mess."

"Sure. No problem, Detective."

Davis walks toward the dining room.

Mitchell quickly scans the interior. The living room is immaculately clean with no clutter. He guesses the interior furnishings to be 1940s style. Area rugs cover most of the hardwood floors.

"Mrs. Noonan, may I ask you about your livelihood?"

"My father left me a trust fund. The trust fund owns thousands of acres of land in Southern California that oil companies lease. The trust fund also owns this house."

"Are you the sole trustee of the fund?"

"Yes."

Mitchell pauses and nods acceptance of the trust fund information. Then he pulls a notebook and pen from his pocket. He asks, "You are aware of the man who was shot on the pier several days ago."

"Yes."

"Do you know him?"

"No."

"What do you know about the shooting, if anything?"

Mrs. Noonan responds, "The papers say that man was shot by a sniper who is rightwing terrorist and probably the mad bomber."

"Is that what you believe, Mrs. Noonan—that the shooter is a rightwing terrorist?"

Her eyes and expression reveal the depth of her clear thinking mind, "No, Detective, I do not believe the shooter was a terrorist, rightwing or otherwise. I mean, he could be a Republican, but that's not the reason he shot the man."

"How do you reason that, Mrs. Noonan?"

"Because the sniper only shot one person—twice! If the shooter was a terrorist, he would have shot more people." She pauses for a few minutes; then reveals, "All my neighbors say the same thing. We've all been following this so-called labor union war. We all think he was shot by someone the labor union harmed. That reporter from the *Times* said as much. And the bombings of that labor union building were done early in the morning when the building was empty. Terrorists would have bombed to kill the maximum number of people."

Detective Mitchell smiles. Mrs. Noonan answered the question the same as most he has interviewed. He considers that the newspapers and television news have painted these attacks on the CLWUA as rightwing terrorism, but the public isn't buying it.

"Did you observe anything unusual during the days leading up to the shooting or on the morning of the shooting?"

Mrs. Noonan stares at the floor as she recalls the time periods specified by the detective. She attempts to remember if she saw any sinister looking men stalking the neighborhood. Twenty seconds later she looks into Mitchells eyes and says, "No."

Mitchell pulls two photographs and one laminated newspaper photograph from his breast pocket. He hands the items to Mrs. Noonan and asks, "Do you recognize any of these men?"

She slips on her reading glasses that are needed for close up viewing. She stares intently at the pictures of the three men. None of the pictures specify the name of the man. She spends extra time studying the black and white newspaper clipping picture of Rigney Page in his navy chief's coat and tie uniform. She remembers the picture from the newspaper articles last year reporting that he was a hero who stopped a terrorist attack somewhere in Europe. She holds up the picture of Rigney Page and says, "I don't recognize the other

297

two. This is the Page boy . . . uh, Robert . . . no, Rodney . . . or is it Richard? Oh, I can't remember his first name. His parents live a couple of blocks from here—across from the fence of the navy base. He was our neighborhood paperboy for years. When he was a teenager, he was one of Judy Wyman's boyfriends—the girl of the family that lived next door back then.

"I see James and Margaret Page from time-to-time at the market and on Main Street. The last time I saw the Page boy was about ten years ago when he was home on leave. He was jogging around the beach. We chatted for a few minutes. Haven't seen him since then."

Mrs. Noonan pauses for a moment as she remembers an event. "Oh, I see, you think the Page boy might be involved in this shooting because of that ruckus at the Page house awhile back. I remember the papers saying he crippled the man that tried to burn down the Pages' house. I remember that labor union was involved in that somehow."

"Rigney Page?" Mitchell questions for clarification.

"Yes! That's it!"

Mitchell had jotted down notes during her statement. Now, he reviews his notes. He asks, "Which house is the Wyman house?"

She points northward and says, "The Becks own it now. The house is closed up for the winter. They live in Las Vegas. I look after the house for them, and I—" Mrs. Noonan stops suddenly as she remembers the man who came by three or four days ago looking for Judy Wyman.

"What is it, Mrs. Noonan? What are you remembering?"

She brings Rigney Page's picture close to her face and studies his image through her glasses, concentrating on Rig's facial features. She expresses bewilderment. After a few moments, she shakes her head while expressing dismissal.

With his tone insistent and official, Mitchell demands, "What do you remember?!"

While expressing puzzlement, she explains, "Three or four days ago, one of Judy's old high school friends came looking for her. He was one of the many boys who gathered at the Wyman house for several summers, like the Page boy did. I told him that the Wymans have not lived there for many years. I gave him the Wyman's telephone number in San Diego."

"What day was that exactly, before or after the shooting?"

"The day before the shooting."

"Did he mention his name?"

"Not that I remember."

"Give me his description."

"A tall man with a trim broad-shouldered build, curly black hair down over his ears, thick mustache, expensive gray suit and leather shoes, and he wore expensive jewelry."

After completing his note writing, Mitchell asks "Was there anything unusual about his appearance?"

"Oh, yes. He had the deepest blue eyes I have ever seen."

Mitchell writes down *deep-blue eyes*; then asks, "Anything else?"

She looks up and to the right while recalling details of the man; then she remembers, "He had a grainy red complexion, like a Viking. I never saw a person before with a Viking like complexion and black hair and blue eyes. At the time, I was wondering about what linage would produce such a combination of features . . . oh, and a jagged scar in the center of his forehead."

At the mention of the forehead scar, Mitchell nearly drops his pen. He suppresses excitement. "That's quite a detailed description. You must have been impressed for some reason."

"He was an extraordinarily handsome man, in a rugged sort of way. Women notice those things."

"Why didn't you tell me about him when I first asked about anything unusual happening?"

"Many of those kids have come looking for the Wymans over the years. I didn't think about mentioning him until—" Her mind searches for what keyed her mind to that man. She raises the picture of Rigney Page and holds it ten inches from her eyes. She shakes her head slightly and casts a doubtful stare at the picture.

With a knowing tone, Mitchell states, "Setting aside hair color, mustache, and blue eyes; Rigney Page and that man looking for the Wymans have the same face, don't they, Mrs. Noonan?"

She turns Rig's picture toward Mitchell's face and says, "Well, maybe, but see, no scar on his forehead."

Mitchell expels a deep satisfying sigh. The picture of Rigney Page in uniform was taken over a year ago. When Mitchell first met Rigney Page six months ago, the first two facial features he noticed was Page's reddish complexion and that jagged scar exactly where Mrs. Noonan described.

Chapter 64

U.S. Senator Clay Porter sits in his Capitol Hill office.

Congressman Billy Thayer sits across the desk.

Porter queries, "How is support for the *Employee Fairness Act* shaping up in the House?"

"One-hundred and eighty-eight Democrats and sixteen Republicans will vote for it, but we're a dozen votes short."

"What will it take to get those dozen votes?"

"Nothing short of bribery or blackmail."

For a few moments, Senator Porter considers Thayer's words; then he queries, "What are the major objections?"

"The number one objection is the requirement for every employer in America with more than ten employees to be unionized, and specifically targeting fast-food franchises and family-owned businesses.

"Second objection is they are against establishment of a federal agency to ensure compliance with the law by issuing federal business licenses.

"Number three is objection to the provision in the bill that holds union officials legally guiltless, blameless, harmless, and inculpable, of any intimidation, vandalism, violence, or crime committed by rank and file union members."

Senator Porter responds, "Those are the same objections that I am getting from my colleagues in the Senate."

Congressman Thayer offers, "We need some event that emphasizes the oppression of the working class by the rightwing. We need some event that will close down dissent against this legislation, make it too embarrassing to not support the legislation."

The senator nods agreement and expresses that he has an idea, "What about those mad bomber attacks on union members in your district? Maybe we can use it some way. Do the police have any suspects?"

"Not that I am aware. The *Long Beach Times* is pointing a finger at an acquaintance of mine."

Senator Porter flinches and exhibits astonishment. "Who?"

"A navy chief petty officer named Rigney Page."

"Rigney Page?! You mean *Hero of Thurso* Rigney Page?!"

"Yes," Thayer answers.

Senator Porter advises, "He was involved in the shooting death of my grandnephew in Sardinia last summer. A Senate Armed Services subcommittee that I chair will soon hold hearings on that shooting."

Congressman Thayer stares downward and contemplates the political concerns of what he just learned.

Porter asks in a curious tone, "What is your connection with Chief Page?"

"Rigney Page is a friend of Diane Love. They were boyfriend and girlfriend in high school. Page is stationed here in D.C., and he and Diane have resumed their romantic relationship. Diane is a friend of mine from UCLA days. I have attended several parties at Diane's home when Chief Page was present."

Senator Porter shakes his head and expresses distress. He states, "This situation is not good. If he is the mad bomber, we must find a way to distance Page from you and Diane and your friends.

Thayer states, "Too late for that, Senator. The press already knows that the *Hero of Thurso* is an integral member of our circle of friends."

Senator Porter responds, "Then we must find a way to publicly destroy his character but keep you and your friends pure. We must make it known to the American people that the *Hero of Thurso* is an undercover operative for a vast rightwing conspiracy—that he is on a conspiratorial mission to damage the image of Congress and the White House—that his plan includes using Diane and her friends as a path to infiltrate Congress and the Carter Administration—that you and Diane and your other friends are unknowing victims of a diabolical vast rightwing conspiracy to destroy unions and the Democratic Party."

Congressman Thayer nods and offers, "Maybe *The Alliance* can create an event for us—something that includes Page in a nationwide rightwing conspiracy against unions and also gets us the votes necessary to pass the *Employees Fairness Act*."

The Senator advises, "Edwin Kendley is in town—staying at the Watergate. I will make an appointment for this afternoon."

Congressman Thayer opines confidently, "I'm sure Ed will come up with something effective."

Senator Porter states, "It's to our advantage that a lone avenger remains unidentified as the perpetrator of these anti-union violent actions. The American public must believe that a huge rightwing conspiracy exists to destroy the working class through violence— paving the way for the common man to accept federal government protection with legislation like the *Employee Fairness Act*."

Billy Thayer expresses admiration. He learns political strategy from the master.

The senator shuffles some papers on his desk, then queries, "What about this other bill, the *Fair Profits Tax Act*? What's the support?"

"We still do not have a majority of support in the House. The provision that the federal government confiscates all profits over ten percent does not have a lot of support. The *Fair Profits Tax Act* would get more support if the profits confiscation provision were changed to list specific industries like oil, insurance, banks, pharmaceutical, investment companies.

"Also gaining momentum in the House is a draft amendment to the bill, should it come to the floor, to nationalize any industry that posts net profits of more than ten percent for three consecutive years. Another amendment to the bill is for government to confiscate amounts equal to the corporate tax on profits made overseas and deposited in foreign bank accounts."

Senator Porter nods his head and expresses that he approves of both amendments. "Who sponsors those amendments?"

"Three representatives from Connecticut and five representatives from California."

"Oil is big business in California, isn't it?" Porter questions.

"Yes, but not in the districts of the five sponsors, but that is moot because the amendment to nationalize would also include a provision that no blue collar jobs would be eliminated by nationalization, which would bring on more support for the bill."

Senator Porter comments, "Yes, similar thoughts are circulating in the Democrat Caucus."

"Good to hear that," Congressman Thayer responds in a joyful tone.

Porter displays deep thought. Then he asks, "Have you received results of the public opinion polls that you commissioned on both these bills?"

"Yes, but I hesitate to publish the results. For the *Employee Fairness Act*, 62 percent of the American Public are *against*, 32 percent are *for*, and 6 percent have no opinion. For the *Fair Profits Tax Act*, we have 73 percent of Americans *against*, 17 percent *for*, and 10 percent have no opinion."

Senator Porter expresses astonishment as he comments, "How can the American public be so clueless? They obviously do not know what benefits them individually and the country as a whole."

Thayer suggests, "I think it's this new Individual Retirement Accounts craze. Americans are enrolling by the millions, and most of those accounts invest in stock mutual funds. More and more Americans are watching corporate profits and want to see those profits grow. Therefore, the public does not see the benefit to laws that restrict corporate profits. More of the public would support the bill if it lowers gas prices, but the public sees only more taxpayer money dumped into the federal program waste bucket."

Senator Porter casts an expression of bemused bewilderment toward Billy Thayer. "Billy, both these bills will raise prices on everything, especially, oil, gas, medical care, food, and other needs. After a couple years of soaring prices, the public will be demanding we nationalize those industries. That's the purpose and design of these bills. The public never connects rising prices to federal legislation that contains the words *fair, equal,* or *affordable*."

Congressman Thayer argues, "But some will make the connection, and they will alert the public."

Senator Porter retorts, "Those who do make the connection are few, and they have no pulpit. After a few years, the public will be demanding Congress do something about raising prices. That's when our colleagues will stand on the floor of the House and the floor of the Senate and point fingers at greedy capitalists who oppress the working class. Few will oppose nationalization. The people will come to understand that capitalism is the enemy of fairness and equality."

Billy Thayer admires the senator's knowledge and experience. *The senator shares his brilliance with me, and I am grateful.*

Porter explains, "However, we must first get the legislation into law. With current public opinion heavily against these two bills, we must perform all negotiations behind closed doors, and we must find a way to keep the media from reporting what we are doing."

Congressman Thayer comments, "Not sure the media is a problem, Senator. During the past few weeks, I have attended cocktail parties with some other House members where editors and publishers of three national newspapers were in attendance. The subject of these two bills became topics of conversations, and all those editors and publishers support those bills."

In a doubtful tone, the senator challenges, "Those bills are still being amended in committee and we have the press on our side already?"

"On the side of the oppressed," Thayer clarifies.

"Uh, yes, of course."

Chapter 65

Diane Love enters the office of Ben Oswald, a mid-level administrator working in the FBI bureaucracy. As she walks across the office toward the fiftyish, tall and flabby administrator who wears white shirt and red tie, she attempts to immediately judge his manner. She notes that he combs long strands of his light brown hair from just above his left ear over the large bald spot on the top of his head. *Vain*, she judges. She also judges that twenty years ago he was a strong and handsome man.

Ben Oswald is stunned by Diane Love's sexuality. He was told she was an attractive woman, but he never anticipated a shapely redhead with bright-green eyes wearing a tight, expensive black pants suit and exhibiting a seductive manner. For several seconds, sexual fantasies dance in his head.

Two days ago when his admin assistant informed him that he had another security clearance issue on the phone, Oswald was about to tell his assistant to initiate the usual stalling tactics. Thousands of new security clearance applications flooded his office when a new Administration and new Congress was elected, and he did not want to hear another sob story about how lack of security clearance limited job accomplishment. But then his assistant said that the complainer was from the White House. Oswald decided to take the call.

After introduction pleasantries, Oswald sits at his desk; Diane sits in a wooden, straight-back, uncomfortable chair. Diane knows that the uncomfortable chair is to motivate people not to stay in the office longer than necessary.

Oswald tells Diane, "First I need to explain the process. For a government employee to be allowed access to secret level and below classified information, that employee must pass a National Agency Check, NAC, performed by the FBI. Plus, that employee must by authorized access to secret and below material by competent authority.

"For a government employee to be allowed access to the next

highest level above secret, top secret, that employee must pass both a NAC and a Background Investigation, BI, performed by the FBI. Then access to top secret material must be authorized by competent authority. The NAC is done first; if the employee fails the NAC, the BI is not initiated. A fail on a NAC is an automatic fail on a BI.

"When the Carter Administration took office sixteen months ago, my office was flooded with NAC applications, which is the norm when a new administration comes into power. After our telephone conversation the other day, I pulled your file and the files of the other four people in your office that you inquired about. The first thing I noticed was that you and your four coworkers failed NACs because all of you had arrests for anti-American activities while members of the Students for a Democrat Society. By law, those who fail NACs are not allowed access to classified material.

"Four months ago, my office received BI applications for many on the White House Staff, including you and your four coworkers. Access to top secret information requires, by law, completion of a satisfactory BI. Because you and your four coworkers failed NACs, my office automatically assigned failed BIs. A failed NAC is an automatic failed BI. And your case has additional negatives. Your residence and activities for 1970 and 1971 cannot be verified. Your security clearance application lists addresses in Germany and Italy, but no one you referenced on the application can verify your residence and activities for those two years."

Diane responds, "Mr. Oswald, am I correct that our Background Investigations are not yet complete?"

"That's correct, Ms. Love. We must give the BI at least six months. But like I said before, the failed NAC will result in a failed BI."

Diane purses her lips as she gathers her thoughts; then she asks, "Am I correct that assigning pass or fail to NACs and BIs is your job and sometimes a judgment call on your part?"

"Yes, but in your case and the case of your coworkers the law is clear. I need not make any judgment."

Diane explains, "My section at the White House provides

political analysis to the president and also writes his speeches. Without access to top secret material, we cannot do our job. The president has become extremely frustrated by this impossible situation."

"Let me be clear, Ms. Love. All I do is assign *pass* or *fail* on the NAC and BI paperwork. Your superiors at the White House are the ones who allow you access or deny you access to classified information."

Diane expresses thoughtfulness. Several times she nods her head, indicating that she has made a decision.

Oswald checks his watch and expresses that in his opinion this meeting is over. He stands to emphasize that it is time for Diane to leave.

Diane stares up into Oswald's impatient face. She asks, "Mr. Oswald, does your wife and four children and your FBI superiors know about Marie Lewis?"

Oswald flinches; his eyes blink rapidly. He expresses astonishment and falls back into his chair.

Diane continues, "Do they know you pay Miss Lewis's rent and utilities, and you have been doing so for five years?"

Nearly a minute passes before Oswald regains his composure. He attempts to cover. "Ms. Love, my relationship with Miss Lewis is not—"

Diane interrupts, "I have motion pictures of you and Miss Lewis entering motel rooms. I have pictures of you two cuddling and kissing in North Carolina restaurants and at North Carolina beaches."

Endeavoring to establish that he is in charge, he challenges in an angry tone, "Are you attempting to blackmail me into assigning satisfactory on your BI paperwork and the BI paperwork of your White House coworkers?"

Diane casts a condescending expression toward Oswald and answers, "Obviously."

"Well, it won't work! I would rather expose myself and my family to scandal and risk my job before I would falsify BI paperwork!"

Still with a condescending expression on her face, Diane asks, "Mr. Oswald, you were once the Special Agent in Charge of the San Francisco Field Office, correct?"

Oswald exhibits trepidation.

"During 1968, agents assigned to your field office arrested a gang of gun smugglers and captured crates of guns and several suitcases containing a total of five-hundred-and-fifty-two-thousand dollars. Several days later when your agents were transporting the guns and cash to your field office's evidence warehouse, your agents were robbed of the cash. One of your agents was wounded during a gunfight with the robbers. One week later, three known criminals were found shot to death in a Sausalito beach house. Forty-thousand dollars of the gun smuggler money was found in that same beach house. Although, you were not held accountable for the incompetence of your field agents, you were subsequently relieved as the Field Agent in Charge and were transferred to Washington D.C. and assigned to your current position." Diane pauses while expanding the smile on her face; then she asks, "Do I have those details correct?"

"Those details are a matter of record." Oswald is red-faced, sweating, and breathing rapidly in fear of what Diane will reveal next.

Diane reaches into the breast pocket of her pantsuit jacket. She pulls out a small slip of paper and hands it to Oswald.

Oswald reads the series of numbers on the slip of paper. He chokes up. His heart beats fast and thunderous. He believes he will pass out.

Diane states, "That is the number of your Caribbean offshore bank account. You opened that account ten years ago with an initial deposit of five-hundred-thousand dollars. The current balance is four-hundred-seventy-two-thousand dollars."

The room is silent while Oswald regains his composure and gets his breathing under control. Finally he asks, "What are you going to do with all the information you have about me?"

"All that information is safe with me, if you are cooperative."

In an exhausted, defeated manner; Oswald states, "You have my cooperation."

"Quickly, I hope."

"Yes, I will sign the BI paperwork today."

Diane stands, then walks toward the door. She abruptly and dramatically turns and faces Oswald. She warns, "If anything should happen to me, I have merciless associates who will gain ownership of the information I have." She turns and exits the office.

Oswald is emotionally fatigued. He sits in silence for ten minutes as he runs all the details of Diane Love's visit through his mind. No doubt in his mind that he is now enslaved to the will of Diane Love and her merciless associates.

He opens the bottom right-hand drawer of his desk. For several moments he stares at the turning tape reels of the tape recorder. Then he flips the switch to stop. He considers what he should do with the tape. All previous tapes are stored in safe deposit boxes.

After thirty minutes of thought, Oswald rewinds the tape to the beginning; then he turns the operating switch to the erase position; then depresses the start button.

Chapter 66

Three days have passed since Detective Lieutenant Mitchell interviewed Mrs. Noonan. He believes that her statement places Rigney Page in proximity of the Seal Beach Pier the day before Max Robertson was shot, and he believes her testimony will stand up in court.

Mitchell sits in the sheriff's office and faces the sheriff and the Orange County ADA—assistant district attorney.

The sheriff, a tall and fit balding man in his mid-forties, wears his police blue coat and tie uniform. Four gold stripes wrap around the bottom of both coat sleeves. He sits behind his desk and casts a penetrating impatience.

The ADA, a youthful looking mid-sized man, sits in a leather chair against a far wall. He has removed the coat of his light blue suit.

The sheriff says "I am under increasing political pressure to solve this case. Are we ready to make an arrest?"

"I believe so," Mitchell responds. "I suspect a navy chief petty officer named Rigney Page was the shooter at the Seal Beach Pier."

"What's your evidence?"

Lieutenant Mitchell explains, "Several months ago, statements from Max Robertson, Horace Lombardi, and Allen Villanueva claimed that Rigney Page attacked them at a Seal Beach intersection and shot up Robertson's pickup truck.

"I questioned Rigney Page the next morning. He was home on leave at the time. He denied that he was involved in that intersection shooting incident. Page also told me that a red pickup truck followed him home the previous evening. He also reported that the occupants of that red pickup had attacked him and his father at Harris Shipping several days earlier. I watched the security videos at Harris Shipping and those videos confirm Page's version of what happened. Robertson, Villanueva, and Lombardi are being prosecuted by the Los Angeles County District Attorney for that attack."

The ADA questions, "Why did those three attack the Pages?"

Mitchell answers, "Robertson, Villanueva, and Lombardi are members of the Construction and Labor Workers Union of America and were working on a building at Harris Shipping. They were attempting to force the Pages, who are non-union, off the Harris Shipping complex. The Pages fought back."

"What were the Pages doing at Harris Shipping?"

"They were installing office furniture. Rigney Page also stated that men in a red pickup truck were stalking his sisters and parents, and that same pickup truck was driving around the Page Office Supply warehouse late at night. I viewed the security tapes at the Page warehouse and the tapes confirm Page's report, and I traced the license number on the pickup in the security tapes and it belongs to Robertson.

"Several days later, James Page called nine-one-one and reported a man lying unconscious in his backyard. That man was Horace Lombardi. Rigney Page said Lombardi was carrying a gas can. When Page confronted Lombardi, Lombardi pulled a gun. Rigney Page beat the man into unconsciousness. A full gas can with Lombardi's name etched in the metal was found close to where Lombardi laid in the Pages' backyard. Two guns were found at the scene—a revolver on the ground near Lombardi and an automatic with silencer in Lombardi's coat pockets. The revolver is registered to Lombardi, but the serial numbers were filed off the automatic. The automatic is the same caliber as the shell casings found at the intersection where Robertson's pickup was shot up."

The ADA questions, "What do you mean by *where Lombardi laid*?"

"Lombardi was still unconscious in the backyard when our officers arrived. The beating that Lombardi took from Rigney Page has resulted in him being disabled for life.

"Some months later, James Page's warehouse was torched, and the night guard was killed. There are no leads on that incident. I questioned Max Robertson regarding that fire. He admitted to driving around the warehouse from time to time but not on the night of the fire. The fire destroyed all security tapes.

"Several nights after the Page Office Supply warehouse fire, Allen Villanueva was beat up at the Wagon Wheel Dancehall. Villanueva is also disabled for life. Later that same night a male, matching the same description as the person who beat up Villanueva, bombed the Long Beach CLWUA building. Several hours after that, the car of *Long Beach Times* reporter, Weston Pyth, was bombed outside the reporter's residence."

The ADA queries, "What is Pyth's connection to the war between the Pages and the union?"

"Pyth wrote a series of articles in the *Times* that takes the union's side. Pyth describes the Pages and other small family businesses as rightwing extremists and capitalist oppressors because of their resistance to unionization."

Sheriff Bernard adds, "Pyth has been demanding prosecution of the Page family for the attacks against Lombardi, Villanueva, Robertson, the CLWUA bombings and the bombing of Pyth's car."

Mitchell continues, "Last week, Max Robertson was shot by a sniper. He is still in the hospital. Half his right hand needed amputated, and doctors are saying they might need to amputate Robertson's right leg above the knee.

"Investigations led us to question Mrs. Agatha Noonan. She is the one who places Page in Seal Beach on the day before the Robertson shooting. She encountered Page, who was disguised, walking around the outside of the house next door, which is a summer home for the Becks who live in Las Vegas."

"What do you mean, disguised?" asks the A.D.A.

"Mrs. Noonan recognized the man as one of the many teenagers who hung around the house during the early 1960s when the house was owned by the Wymans. She didn't recognize the man as Rigney Page because of the disguise that she described as long black hair, blue eyes, and thick mustache. Page has reddish hair, green eyes, and no mustache. I showed her a picture of Rigney Page in uniform that was taken more than a year ago. She said she had not seen Rigney Page for more than ten years, but there is no doubt in my mind that she connected Page's face to the man who was looking for Judy Wyman the day before Robertson was shot.

"The Beck house is on the beach near the pier. The house was closed up for the winter. I called the Becks, and they drove down from Las Vegas and opened the house for us.

"The Becks and I and Deputy Davis entered the house through the front door. Immediately, we all saw footprints in the dust on the floor leading to and from a closet under the staircase that leads to the second floor. We later discovered a trapdoor in that closet with access to the crawl space under the house. We followed the footsteps in the dust up to the third floor attic bedroom. Mrs. Beck said the furniture in that attic bedroom had been moved around, marks in the dust on the floor confirmed that.

"I called in the crime scene investigation team. They found evidence of burnt ammo powder residue. They verified that a firearm had been discharged in that room recently.

"Mrs. Noonan's statement places Rigney Page, in disguise, at the Beck's house near Seal Beach Pier the day before the shooting."

The ADA queries, "Did Mrs. Noonan agree to a lineup to identify the man looking for Judy Wyman?"

"I did not ask her about that. I didn't think a lineup would be a good idea because we cannot have anyone wearing a disguise in a lineup."

"Have you contacted the Wymans?" The assistant D.A. asks.

"Not yet?"

The assistant D.A. says, "Find the Wymans and ask them if Rigney Page knows about that trapdoor. If you get an affirmative on that, then convince Mrs. Noonan to witness a lineup. If you get those two things done, I will get a judge to issue a warrant for the arrest of Rigney Page."

Chapter 67

Several days later, Orange County Sheriff Glendon Bernard sits at his desk and opens his alphabet-tabbed pocket notebook to the appropriate page; he finds the telephone number, then dials it.

The voice on the other end answers, "Construction and Labor Workers Union of America, Southern California District, how may I direct your call?"

The sheriff responds, "Harold Oatman, please—access code harmony."

The access code provides the sheriff with immediate access to the CLWUA Southern California Director.

Harold Oatman sits at his temporary office and reads the latest surveillance reports on Rigney Page. Several weeks ago, Oatman's permanent office was destroyed by the rightwing mad bomber, and he moved into the Assistant Director's office. Instead of creating chaos by everyone in the pecking order moving down one step, office-wise, the Assistant Director went on a two week vacation.

Oatman notices his private line indicator blinking. He picks up the handset and says, "Harold Oatman."

"Hello Harold, Glendon Bernard here. I have some information regarding Rigney Page."

"Hello, Glendon. I hope your news is that Rigney Page is under arrest."

"Not yet," the sheriff advises. "But the arrest warrant has been issued. We need to extradite him from his current state of residence, which is Virginia."

Oatman asks, "What evidence did you gather that resulted with the arrest warrant?"

"Page knows about the hidden trapdoor in the house where the sniper fired the shots at Robertson. Page's high school girlfriend, who lived in that house, provided a statement that she showed Page the trapdoor during the summer of 1964. And, we have a witness who has agreed to a lineup to identify Rigney Page as the person she talked with face-to-face the day before the shooting in front of that same house."

Oatman comments, "I detect a lack of confidence in your tone. What are the problems with that witness?"

"When we showed the witness a photograph of Rigney Page, she did not absolutely identify him as the person she talked with the day before the shooting. Page was wearing a disguise."

Oatman considers options; then he asks, "You are not allowed to put people in disguises in a lineup, right?"

"That's right."

In a conspiratorial tone, Oatman asks, "So how do we guarantee the witness will identify Rigney Page?"

"We choose lineup participants significantly different in appearance to Page but similar enough in appearance to be in conformance with lineup laws."

Oatman is silent while he considers other actions; then he asks, "What about James Page? When will he be arrested?"

In a surprised tone, Sheriff Bernard states, "We have no evidence that James Page has broken any laws."

With a demanding tone, the CLWUA District Director states, "We need the headlines to read father and son arrested for rightwing conspiracy attacks against the union. Without the father, all we have is a lone-wolf avenger and not a rightwing conspiracy against the workingman. The CLWUA has its own investigators and they have uncovered a nationwide, vast rightwing conspiracy against union labor."

"But we have no evidence against James Page. I would need to convince the D.A. that we have evidence we really don't have. I don't see arresting James Page as a possibility. The best we could do is arrest James Page on suspicion. We would be required to release him forty-eight hours later."

Oatman insists again in a demanding tone, "Glendon, I want James Page and Rigney Page in handcuffs, surrounded by cops being taking into the police headquarters and plenty of reporters there to take the pictures. Once we have the photos and the headlines, you can quietly and without fanfare release James Page.

Damage to the Pages will be done and a rightwing conspiracy will be validated. Being arrested is enough for most to believe James Page is guilty."

Sheriff Bernard informs, "Harold, I must advise you that our evidence is fragile. Rigney Page could walk."

Oatman responds, "Glendon, it doesn't matter. What we need is pictures of the Pages in handcuffs in front of the sheriff's station with headlines reading *arrested for rightwing conspiracy against union labor*. If you quietly release them later for lack of evidence, it doesn't matter because we will have the headlines."

Sheriff Bernard knows that at risk are tens of thousands of dollars in campaign contributions from union members and thousands of votes from union members during the next election. He responds, "Okay, Harold, I will get it done."

Chapter 68

Since the beginning of spring, Diane Love and Rigney Page have met several times on the National Mall for a picnic lunch. As happened during all previous lunches on the National Mall, Diane prepared the food and brought it with her. Today, they sit on their usual bench near the *Declaration of Independence Memorial*. They munch on whole-wheat BLT sandwiches. Perrier water is their beverage of choice.

Rig wears his coat and tie Service Dress Blue uniform. While sitting, his combination cap lies behind him on the bench. As usual, Rig draws long appraising stares from passing females.

Diane wears a black pantsuit with white blouse. Stands of her long red hair flap in the light breeze. As usual, Diane draws long appraising stares from passing males.

After swallowing his first bite of sandwich, he mentions to Diane, "When I got off the bus, I saw an unusual number of policemen around the intersection of Constitution Avenue and 17th Street."

Diane responds, "Yes, I saw them. They must be there for crowd control during the protest march."

"Do you know who's protesting?"

"Yes, some two-thousand environmentalists are protesting the Trans-Alaska oil pipeline."

Rig exhibits concern as he comments, "I hope they don't mess up the bus schedule. I must be back to work by two o'clock."

"Probably not," Diane opines. "They are marching south on 17th Street, crossing Constitution Avenue to enter The Mall, and then marching to the Lincoln Memorial where there will be speakers all afternoon. Speakers start at one o'clock. So it should not affect your bus schedule." Diane glances around; then states, "They will probably pass close by us."

The expression of concern drops from Rig's face. Then he asks, "What is it about the pipeline they don't like?"

"Its existence," Diane responds in a disapproving, sarcastic tone.

318

Rig appears thoughtful as he remembers reading that the Trans-Alaska pipeline went into operation some months back.

"What are you thinking?" Diane asks in a slightly challenging tone.

"I'm thinking that there must be a lot of people who favor the pipeline's existence. Otherwise, it wouldn't exist. Must be providing a lot of jobs."

"It exists because of greedy, rich, special-interest groups who want to destroy the environment."

Rig furrows his brow as he asks, "How does the pipeline's existence destroy the environment and why would anyone want to destroy the environment?"

Diane responds, "Flaws in the pipeline design and construction by rich people cutting corners resulting in eventual massive oil spills along the pipeline."

Rig challenges, "But aren't there inspectors, shutoff valves, and continuous monitoring to reduce the chance of that happening?"

With a protesting tone, Diane states, "The slightest chance that it can happen is enough reason not to have built it in the first place."

"But it was built to decrease oil delivery time and decrease transportation cost. Isn't that a good reason to have built it?"

"Only the rich will benefit and profit from decreased delivery time."

Rig challenges, "Won't lower transportation costs result in lower gasoline prices, which will be good for everyone?"

"Oil pollutes the earth. We must restrict the use of oil products. We must find a clean alternative."

"Who would restrict it?" Rig asks.

"The U.S. Government, of course."

With incredulity edging his tone, Rig responds, "So you would have the U.S. Government restrict the flow of oil so that it becomes so expensive that Americans will stop using it."

"Yes, that's the only way. Democrats in Congress are working on a plan to restrict production of domestic oil. Republicans in Congress are fighting it."

"Diane, the whole country operates on oil—cars, airplanes, railroads, tanks, warships, heating, cooling, and government. You're talking about crashing America's economy."

"No, Rig, you don't understand. The higher that gasoline prices go, the more motivated people become to find an alternative."

Rig counters, "What alternative? There is no fuel more abundant than and cheaper than oil. The more the supply of oil, the less it will cost, and the more the economy will prosper."

Diane argues, "But oil pollutes. It is the responsibility of government to eliminate its use. And because America is the largest polluter in the world, America must lead the way to a pollution free earth."

Rig responds, "Some magazine articles that I have read disagree with you. They say Soviet Bloc countries are the largest polluters because of a single totalitarian political party and no clean air regulations and a cell in a gulag for anyone who protests."

"Regardless, Rig, America must abandon its oil-driven economy."

"What about your Cadillac with a 400-cubic-inch engine and your townhouse that is heated by an oil furnace and the oil-driven machines that built your condo? Skyrocketing oil prices will drain your trust fund."

Diane expresses revelation as she realizes the hypocrisy of her lifestyle as a rich, leftwing elitist. She never considered that what she promotes would adversely affect her. She just assumed that because she is a member of the government privileged class, she would be exempt from what she would have government impose on the unwashed masses.

Rig adds, "And I guess you and your lefty friends must give up arriving at those Washington elite events and those highbrow concerts in Lincoln Town Cars and stretch limousines."

With frustration in her tone, she retorts, "Not if those cars are powered with nonpolluting fuels."

"What nonpolluting fuel exists that is more abundant and less costly than oil?"

"I don't know, but several Congressional Caucuses are drafting legislation to fund research into alternative fuels."

Rig shakes his head slightly and expresses futility, "I don't think the average American taxpayer would approve."

Diane chuckles, then she informs, "Taxpayers will not pay for the research. The research will be funded by an excessive-profits tax on oil and energy corporations."

Appearing baffled by Diane's declaration, Rig asks for clarification, "Are you saying that a tax on corporations is not a tax on individual taxpayers?"

"That's right," Diane responds haughtily as she casts a quizzical stare at Rig as to why he would think otherwise. "Besides, the average American does not understand the transformation needed to achieve a safe and fair America. Government must do what's right, even when what's right conflicts with the will of the people."

Rig advises, "As you know, I am heavily invested in gold and oil. My broker told me the other day that average profit margins of American oil companies have been historically under twelve percent. He said that profit margin is low when compared to other American industries."

Diane blurts, "But that twelve percent profit is billions of dollars per year!"

Diane's naive and illogical reasoning stuns and baffles Rig. Logic, fact, and reality are lost on Diane. He is bewildered as to how a person with a degree in economics can reason so illogically. All those arguments he has had with leftists in the past flash through his mind—fact, logic, and reality were lost on them too. He comes to understand that Diane's leftist ideology trumps what she learned while earning a degree in economics. *That must be true for all educated leftists*, he concludes.

Diane stares intently at Rig. She knows he thinks deeply for a comeback. *I have stumped him this time.*

He attempts to understand the scope and depth of economic damage that would be caused by the Legislative Branch, Executive Branch, and Judicial Branch if all three branches had a majority of leftists. He concludes that the American Republic would not survive such a government. Once again, he concludes that there is no greater futile act than attempting to enlighten leftists.

Diane queries, "What are you thinking, Rig?"

"I am thinking that in a free country, enterprising individuals should be allowed to produce as much of a product as other citizens want to buy. A government that opposes and fights against economic freedom aligns with the definition of fascism."

Diane rolls her eyes and expresses amusement. She is about to respond when the sound of chanting voices catches their attention.

They watch protesters march toward the Lincoln Memorial. The banners they carry claim:

"OIL IS EVIL"

"OIL FILLS THE POCKETS OF CORRUPT RICH"

"STOP THE PIPELINE NOW!"

"STOP PRODUCTION OF POLLUTING OIL."

"GREEN PEACE AGAINST THE PIPELINE"

The lead chanter yells into a battery-powered megaphone, "What do we want?!"

"Shutdown the pipeline!" the protesters yell in unison,

"When do we want it?!"

"Now!"

Rig turns toward Diane and comments, "There are only a couple hundred protesters."

Diane appears perplexed as she responds, "The paper said there would be thousands."

Rig declares, "Looks like the opposition to the pipeline is not as strong as the media reports."

Chapter 69

Later that evening, Rig sits in his Arlington apartment and sips from a snifter of his favorite brandy. He purposely dimmed the lights, which allows him to think without distractions. He worries over his relationship with Diane Love. They have grown far apart over the years; once, high school sweethearts, now each using the other. Rig uses Diane to gain information about her involvement in The Longjumeau Alliance and her involvement with a Soviet KGB agent, but Diane does not know that. Diane uses Rig to obtain classified information to pass to her KGB controller, and Rig knows that. Their conversation at the National Mall earlier in the day about industrial energy sources and about oil companies finally brought him to the conclusion that Diane has lost all sense of reason and reality. He knows, now, that fact and logic will never turn her towards reality; so he will never try again.

The phone rings. He decides not to answer and let the answering machine record a message.

After the machine's outgoing message is sent, the excited voice on the other end orders, "Rig, This is Denton! Turnoff your answering machine and pick up the phone!"

Rig turns off the answering machine: then he picks up the telephone handset. "Hello, Denton, what's up?"

"The Orange County, California District Attorney has issued a warrant for your arrest. You will be arrested within a few minutes and transported to Orange County. I have arranged for a lawyer to meet you in Southern California. Please assure me that there is nothing in your apartment to connect you to me."

Rig asserts, "There is nothing here."

"What about your disguises?"

"In a secret compartment in my bedroom, behind the closet. They won't find it."

"Guardian operatives in Southern California will be watching out for you and providing any assistance they can. They will contact you and—"

The doorbell sounds.

"Was that your doorbell?"

"Yes."

"Good luck, Rig. We will be in contact." Denton hangs up.

Rig walks the few steps to the door and opens it. He is not surprised to see Orange County Detective Lieutenant George Mitchell and Orange County Deputy Ogden Davis, both wearing civilian clothes. A mixture of uniformed and civilian-clothed officers stands behind the two Orange County deputies.

Mitchell holds his badge toward Rig and advises, "Rigney Page you are under arrest for conspiracy to commit murder, attempted murder, conspiracy to assault and battery, assault and battery, conspiracy to exercise violence against a union, violence against a union member, illegal discharge of a firearm." Mitchell pauses for a few moments; then continues, "We have a warrant to search your residence."

Rig opens the door wider, stands aside, and says is a calm voice, "Please enter."

A total of eight officers enter the apartment. Mitchell and Davis stand on either side of Rig, and two other civilian-clothed officers stand behind Rig—filling the small dining area. The other four officers spread throughout the apartment in search of evidence.

Mitchell says to Rig, "Deputy Davis must handcuff you. Please do not resist."

"I will not resist," Rig responds in a mild, cooperative tone.

Mitchell nods toward the two civilian-clothed officers standing behind them and explains to Rig, "Those two are local police detectives who hold the paperwork that allows us to extradite you to California. Those searching your apartment are Orange County forensic investigators."

Several minutes later, one of the uniformed officers comes from the bedroom with an automatic handgun. The officer had tied an identification tag to the trigger guard and wrote on the tag where the gun was found.

"Do you have a permit for this?" the officer asks Rig.

"Yes—in the top drawer of the desk."

Mitchell orders, "Let me see that weapon."

The uniformed officer hands the weapon to Mitchell.

Mitchell inspects the weapon; then asks Rig, "This is foreign made. Where did you get it?"

"In Italy—last year."

Mitchell hands the weapon back to the uniformed officer.

The uniformed officer finds the gun permit; then places the gun and the permit in a plastic bag.

Several minutes later, a short, thin civilian-clothed forensic investigator who wears black horn-rimmed glasses and sprouts a sparsely haired mustache approaches Mitchell and says, "Let's talk—out on the porch."

When Mitchell and the forensic investigator are on the porch and out of hearing range of others, the forensic investigator says to Mitchell, "Strangely constructed apartment building here. I have not seen a building like this since I worked in army intelligence. This building is sound-proofed with industrial strength sound dampening tiles and electromagnetic filters that prevent any voice or radio frequency from exiting the building or penetrating the building from the outside."

Mitchell queries, "What does that mean to you?"

"Well, it could mean several things. This apartment building might be a safe house for government intelligence agents. Or, it could be an operation center for government clandestine operations by the U.S. Government or maybe foreign government."

Mitchell offers, "Rigney Page is a U.S. Navy Chief Petty Officer."

"Does he belong to any of the military intelligent services?"

Mitchell shrugs and does not answer, but he understands that a lot of questions are answered if Page was some kind of spy."

The forensic investigator advises, "I will write a detailed report on the unusual construction of the building." Then the forensic investigator turns and enters the apartment.

Roger Walker, contract private investigator to Simms Investigations, sits at the console in his surveillance equipment van that is parked one-quarter block from Page's apartment. Through the one-way tinted windows on the side of the van, he has a clear view of the stairs leading to Page's apartment and a clear view of the landing where Page's front door is located.

Ninety minutes ago, he was surprised by the silent approach of three police vehicles; emergency lights were not flashing. After parking in front of Page's apartment building, eight men exited their vehicles and climbed the stairs to Page's apartment.

Through his sensitive sound equipment, Roger easily heard and recorded the police officer's statement that Page was under arrest. Thirty minutes ago, two officers stepped onto the landing and held a conversation that Roger also recorded. He was not surprised regarding the construction of the building. Nor was he surprised when one of the men suggested that Page might be a spy. Roger has suspected for months that Page is some kind of undercover operative—a suspicion that he has not shared with his clients for lack of proof.

Activity on the apartment landing causes Roger to pick up his binoculars. Two civilian-clothed officers aid the handcuffed Rigney Page down the stairs. One of the officers carries a navy-blue colored gym bag. Roger accurately reasons that if Page were being taken to a local jail, a gym bag of personal items would not be necessary; therefore, they must be extraditing him to California.

Roger quickly shuts down his equipment. Then he moves to the driver's seat and starts the engine.

Page and two officers get into the back seat of a police car; the car pulls away from the curb.

Roger follows one-half block behind. When the police car turns onto the National Airport's access road, Roger does not follow. He heads for home where he will telephone his clients.

Chapter 70

At 9:15 the next morning, Detective Mitchell and Deputy Davis lead Rigney Page, still in handcuffs, through the Orange County Airport. They walk through the baggage claim area; then through the exit. Two Orange County Sheriff's cars idle at the curb with emergency lights flashing.

Deputy Davis guides Rig into the back seat of the rear sheriff's car. Then Davis climbs into the front passenger seat of the rear vehicle. Detective Mitchell enters the back seat of the front vehicle.

Rig expresses surprise at his father sitting next to him. Tears well up in the eyes of the tough and callous Rigney Page. He thought he had taken care not to have the finger of suspicion pointed at his father. "When were you arrested?"

"No talking!" Deputy Davis demands loudly.

Up till now, Rig had been polite and courteous but seeing his father handcuffed angers the usually unemotional chief petty officer. He snaps back, "What are you gonna do, Deputy?! Beat me into silence?!"

James Page says, "I was arrested an hour ago on the charges of conspiracy for all sorts of crimes."

"You must be quiet!" Davis demands again.

Rig responds, "Deputy, if you didn't want us to talk, why did you put us together? What's going on here?"

Davis turns in his seat so he can look Rig in the eye; he advises with a slight edge of apology in his tone, "You'll find out in a few minutes."

Five minutes later, the two sheriff's cars drive up to the front entrance of the Orange County Sheriff's Headquarters building, instead of the side entrance that is usually used for delivering arrestees. A crowd of about forty reporters and photographers stand behind two rows of officers that provide an unobstructed ten-foot-wide path from the curb to the building's main entrance.

Detective Mitchell exits the front vehicle and walks to the rear vehicle and opens the left rear door. He reaches into the vehicle, wraps his hand around Rig's elbow, and guides Rig out of the vehicle and onto the sidewalk.

Deputy Davis opens the opposite rear door and guides James Page out of the vehicle. Davis guides James to the sidewalk to stand next to Rig.

James and Rig stand between Mitchell and Davis. Two uniformed officers stand behind James and Rig. They do not immediately move toward the main entrance. For nearly a minute the six men stand at the sidewalk curb while reporters yell questions, take photographs, and television cameramen record the event on film.

As Rig and James are led toward the main entrance, reporters continue to yell accusatory questions; including, "Mr. Page did you torch your own warehouse—that killed the night watchman—for insurance money?!"

James Page, who wears a blue suit and tie, keeps his head high and does not respond to reporters' accusatory questions.

Rig remains emotionless; he wears tight jeans and a tight fitting sweater. His tall, broad-shouldered frame and rugged features project the image of a man tough enough to battle equally tough union thugs.

Then a reporter yells out, "Chief Petty Officer Rigney Page, why did you blow up my car?!"

Rig glances in the direction of the voice and catches a glance of Weston Pyth.

After entering the building, James and Rig are taken to separate, adjoining holding cells to await booking. But they sit there for hours. Rig nearly comes to tears as he watches his father become despondent.

James Page sits on the bunk and stares at the floor. The once tough teenage street fighter who escaped the gangs to become a decorated World War II hero, and then became a self-made successful businessman comes to tears as he envisions all the work in his life being for naught. He now worries that this war with the unions will ruin him. He believes his life has become valueless, and all he accumulated through diligence and hard work will disappear. *Thank God all the kids are grown and on their own.* Then he thinks of the woman who has been his wife for thirty-two years. He worries about her and how she will endure this travesty of justice.

Rig watches his father cry. His father's misery rips Rig's heart. Tears come to his eyes as he sees the first hero in his life break down emotionally. Rig regrets the harm he has caused his parents. Rare feelings of guilt wash over him.

After four hours pass, Rig contemplates what happens next. He knows more about military law than he does California state law, but he knows that not being *booked* yet is a good sign.

Two policemen arrive at Rig's cell. They unlock the cell door. Then they lead him upstairs to an interrogation room.

In the interrogation room, the handcuffs are removed, and Rig sits at a wooden table with four chairs. The room contains six other wooden chairs that stand against the walls. A video camera mounted in a corner monitors his actions. A one-way window faces him across the room. His side of the window is a mirror.

The door to the interrogation room opens. A tall, physically fit man with salt-and-pepper colored hair wearing a black pinstripe suit and red tie and carrying a briefcase enters. He places his briefcase on the tabletop. Then he extends his right hand toward Rig and introduces himself. "Rig, I am Brian Sanderhill. I am your lawyer. You were told about me, correct?"

Rig stands, then shakes Brian's hand; he responds, "Nice to meet you Mr. Sanderhill. Yes, I was told about you."

"We only have a few minutes to talk," Sanderhill advises.

"What about my father? Do you know where he is?"

"He is currently in a cell. I am his lawyer also. The police will not interrogate him without me being present."

"I'm worried about him," Rigney informs. "He does not deserve this, and he is not taking it well."

"The police have nothing against your father unless they can pin you to the Robertson shooting and the bombing of the CLWUA building in Long Beach."

Rig glances around the room; then asks, "Can we talk in here? They must have sound recording equipment."

"It's turned off—against the law for them to listen to our conversation."

"You're sure?" Rig challenges.

"Yes, I am sure. The police will not violate that law. They will not risk losing a conviction based on a technicality."

Rig nods understanding.

"Sheriff's detectives will interrogate you, starting in a few minutes. I need to know two things before they arrive. One, do you know about the trapdoor under the stairs of the house from which the shooting took place?"

Rig appears surprised, "How do you know about that?"

"The Guardians have local operatives who have contacts in the sheriff's office. I know most of the case against you."

Rig grins and states, "Trapdoor? You must be talking about Judy Wyman's old house."

Attorney Sanderhill explains, "They didn't say which house. They just said that knowledge of that trapdoor is evidence against you. The police will ask you about it. Don't lie to them. They have a witness that states you know about it."

"Judy Wyman?"

"I don't know who it is."

Rig tells Brian Sanderhill, "I am not the only one who knows about that trapdoor. A bunch of her friends know about it."

Brian expresses surprise; then advises, "How many would you say know about it?"

"All of her friends, only her parents didn't know. At least, that is what Judy told me."

"That is valuable information. It diminishes the district attorney's case. Can you name others who know about it?"

"Sure—probably twenty or more."

"Excellent!" Brian declares in a raised tone.

Rig casts a bewildering look at Brian and states, "Is that all they have? That cannot possibly be enough to connect me to shooting Robertson."

"The D.A. has more. They have a witness that places you at the crime scene house the day before the shooting."

Rig nods acceptance of that information. He concludes that witness must be Mrs. Noonan.

"They will ask you where you were the day before the shooting and where you were the day of the shooting. How will you answer that question?"

Rig appears thoughtful, then he inquires, "What were those dates?"

Expressing a conspiratorial smile, Attorney Sanderhill states, "That is exactly how you should respond. Then they will provide you with the dates of the 7th and 8th of last month. How will you respond?"

"I was in Washington D.C."

"Can you prove it? They will ask."

Rig contemplates how he will respond.

"You will ask for a calendar, so that you can refresh your memory about where you were on those dates. You must convey those dates are not significant to you. Analyze the calendar. Then tell them how you can prove you were in D.C."

Rig nods understanding.

"What will you tell them about those dates?"

"I will tell them I was home with the flu—at my apartment in Arlington."

"Can you prove that?"

"Sure. My friend, John Smith, visited me several times."

"They will contact John Smith."

"No problem," Rig states confidently.

"Detectives will ask you questions, and those questions will be accusatory. They will attempt to trap you. I will sit alongside you. Wait a few seconds before answering because I might tell you not to answer. Do not provide any details that you are not asked to provide. Do not expand on anything. Above all else, remain cool, collected, and confident."

Rig responds, "I can do that. No problem."

"Okay, then. We are ready. Oh, after the interrogation, you will participate in a lineup."

"A lineup—why?"

"I suspect that their eyewitness to you being at the crime scene did not provide a positive I.D."

Rig expresses concern. He wonders if Mrs. Noonan will identify him as the person that she talked with outside the old Wyman house. He wonders if his disguise worked. "What happens if the witness identifies me?"

"We will cross that bridge when we come to it." Sanderhill motions a come in gesture toward the one-way window. Then he moves his chair to Rig's side and sits.

Seconds later, Detective Mitchell, Sheriff Bernard, and Assistant District Attorney, Samuel Levin enter the room. Mitchell takes a chair directly across the table from Rig. Sheriff Bernard and A.D.A. Levin sit down in chairs that stand against the wall immediately under the one-way window.

Mitchell states, "Rigney, our conversation will be recorded."

"No problem," Rig declares in a friendly tone.

"Why did you shoot Max Robertson?"

Brian Sanderhill orders, "Don't answer that question."

Rig is silent and waits for the next question.

"Do you know Max Robertson?"

Rig waits several seconds for an objection for his lawyer, but none comes. He answers, "I know who he is."

"Do you own, or have you ever been in possession of weapons known as sniper rifles?"

"No."

"Do you own, or have you ever been in possession of handheld rocket launching weapons?"

"No."

"Have you ever owned or been in possession of any weapons."

"Yes."

"Describe the weapons."

"Hand guns."

"Automatics or revolvers?"

"Both."

"Have you ever shot anyone?"

"Yes."

"When, where, and why?"

"Eighteen months ago in Scotland while fighting off terrorists who invaded the base where I was stationed."

"Are you an expert in hand-to-hand combat?"

"I don't know."

Mitchell challenges, "How can you not know?"

"I have never been tested. So I don't know."

"But you have been trained in hand-to-hand combat, correct?"

"Yes."

"When and where did you receive hand-to-hand combat training?"

"Over the years, I have taken courses in several martial arts disciplines. Not all the communities where I have lived had martial arts schools."

"Rigney, are you saying that you never received hand-to-hand combat training by the military?"

"That's correct," Rig lies.

"Where were you on the 7th and 8th of last month?"

"Washington D.C."

"What were you doing on those two days?"

Rig expresses thoughtfulness for several moments; then he informs, "I need to look at a calendar."

"I'll get one," the sheriff states. Then he exits the room.

No one speaks while the sheriff is away.

The sheriff returns several minutes later and places a calendar in front of Rig."

Rig studies the calendar; then he advises, "I was home with the flu . . . at my apartment in Arlington."

"Can anyone verify that?"

"Yes."

"Who? What's his or her name?"

"John Smith."

"What is your relationship with John Smith?"

"A friend for more than ten years."

"How can we contact him?"

Rig glances at his watch, then states, "He should be at work. I have his telephone number in my wallet."

"Give it to me."

Rig pulls his wallet from his back pocket; he searches through it and several seconds later hands a slip of paper to Detective Mitchell."

"I'll take that," Sheriff Bernard demands as he stands. Then he walks to the table and takes the slip of paper from Mitchell. The sheriff exits the room.

Mitchell continues the questioning. "Where do you work?"

"At the headquarters of Commander Naval Telecommunications Command."

"Where is that exactly?"

"It's in northwest Washington D.C. on Massachusetts Avenue."

"What do you do there?"

"My work in the navy is classified. I cannot talk about it."

"Rigney, this is an investigation into serious criminal activities. You have the right not to answer questions that will incriminate you. But all information is relevant. Unless what you do in the navy incriminates you, you must answer."

Calm and even tempered, Rig responds, "I cannot reveal classified information without the written authority of my navy superiors."

"Okay. We will pass over that for now."

"My superiors will want to know where I am. May I call them?"

"You have no right to make a phone call."

"But I must—"

Attorney Sanderhill tugs at Rig's sleeve and advises, "Don't worry about that, Rig. I talked with Captain Blakely. She said she would inform your immediate chain-of-command."

Sheriff Bernard returns to the room and retakes his seat.

Detective Mitchell orders, "Back on subject. Why is your apartment building in Arlington constructed to obstruct electronic surveillance?"

Rig shakes his head and states, "If I told you, I would reveal classified information."

Detective Mitchell expels a deep sigh and expresses frustration. Then he jumps to his feet, points his finger at Rig's face and accuses, "You and your father conspired to maim or kill Allen Villanueva, Max Robertson, and Horace Lombardi! Admit it, and admit it now or the punishment for your crimes will be worse!"

"Do not respond to that," Attorney Sanderhill directs.

With an angry expression and raised voice and still pointing his finger, Mitchell states, "We have surveillance videos of you placing explosive charges at the Long Beach CLWUA District Headquarters! Admit that you and your father conspired to blow up that building! Admit to it now and the D.A. will request lighter sentences for you and your father!"

Rig remains silent.

While still expressing anger and in a loud and intimidating manner, Mitchell declares, "We have a witness that places you at the Wyman house on the day of the shooting. If you admit to the shooting now, avoiding a long trial, the district attorney will request a shorter sentence than when a jury finds you guilty!"

"Do not respond to that," Brian Sanderhill directs.

Mitchell continues to cast an angry stare at Rig. Then he realizes that intimidation will not work on Rigney Page.

The sheriff and A.D.A. Levin stand and start for the door.

Mitchell turns and starts for the door.

After the sheriff and A.D.A. have exited, Mitchell turns around and says, "Rigney, this is your last chance for a lighter sentence. I cannot help you if you are not willing to admit to these crimes now."

Rig remains silent.

335

Detective Mitchell turns and exits the room.

Rig exhibits wonderment and shrugs. He turns toward his attorney. "What now?"

"Line-up should be next."

Rig questions, "Do you think that—"

Sanderhill swiftly places his index finger to his lips, conveying that Rig should stop talking.

Several minutes later, two uniformed officers enter the room. One of the officers motions for Rig to stand; then they guide Rig out of the room.

"Where are you taking him?" Sanderhill asks.

"Line-up."

Chapter 71

Attorney Brian Sanderhill walks to the lobby and finds a payphone. He calls his office. After his receptionist answers, he asks, "Megan, do I have any messages?"

"Yes, several, from—"

"Is there a message from John Smith?"

"Yes,"

"Read it to me."

"John Smith says he got a call from the Orange County Sheriff's Office asking if he could verify the presence of Rigney Page in Washington D.C. on the 7th and 8th of this month. John Smith said he could verify that, and he agreed to mail a notarized affidavit to the Orange County Sheriff."

Brian Sanderhill hangs up the phone. Then he quickly climbs the steps to the second floor. He enters the ten-foot-wide by eight-foot-deep viewing room. A one-way viewing window stretches along the top half of the ten-foot-long wall. Standing in the room, staring through the one-way glass, are Detective Mitchell, Sheriff Bernard, A.D.A. Levin, and an elderly woman wearing a dark sweater over a flowered print dress. He assumes the woman is the witness who will identify Rig as the man she talked with in front of the old Wyman house the day before the shooting.

Sanderhill stands behind the other occupants in the viewing room.

Everyone in the viewing room is silent as six men file into the lineup room on the other side of the window.

Each man in the lineup stands against the far wall. The far wall has measurements marked in feet and inches. Rig is number five. All men are of the same height and of similar build as Rig. Facial features and style and color of hair vary sharply among them.

Lieutenant Mitchell says to the woman, "Mrs. Noonan, do you recognize any of the men in that line-up as the man you talked with the day before the shooting?"

Mrs. Noonan says, "The man I talked to that day had black hair that came down over his ears and wore a blue suit and tie. None of these men have that."

Mitchell advises, "Mrs. Noonan, we believe that the man you talked with wore a disguise. The law does not allow us to dress up those in a line-up to match a description."

"They're too far away," Mrs. Noonan advises. "They must come closer."

Mitchell flips a spring-operated switch on the wall and says, "Number one, come closer to the mirror." Then he releases the switch.

Number one walks the eight feet to the mirror.

Mrs. Noonan shakes her head and states, "No. That is not him."

Mrs. Noonan reports the same for the following three men.

Then Rig comes close to the one-way window.

Mrs. Noonan steps closer to the window. Rig's face and Mrs. Noonan's face are three feet apart. Rig sees his own image in the mirror.

Mrs. Noonan smiles.

"What is it, Mrs. Noonan?" Mitchell asks in an anxious tone.

"That man is Rigney Page. I have known him since he was a boy."

Attorney Sanderhill expresses relief at Mrs. Noonan's comment. Now, even if she identifies Rig as the man she talked with that day at the old Wyman house, her testimony in court can be challenged. She has known Rig most of his life, but she did not immediately recognize him as Rigney Page that day before the shooting in front of the old Wyman house.

A.D.A. Levin urges, "Mrs. Noonan, is he the man you talked with the day before the shooting?"

Mrs. Noonan stares through the window and studies Rig's face.

All others in the room hold their breath while waiting anxiously.

"No," Mrs. Noonan announces. "That's not him."

Disappointment appears on the faces of Mitchell, the sheriff, and the A.D.A.

Sanderhill casts a smile of relief.

Mitchell challenges in a pleading tone, "Are you sure, Mrs. Noonan?"

Sanderhill could legally object to Mitchell's question, but he waits because Mitchell digs the grave for the state's case.

Mrs. Noonan shows curiosity as she says, "Detective, you did not ask me that about the other four."

With frustration in his tone, Mitchell attempts to coax Mrs. Noonan. At this point, he does not worry about the veteran defense attorney in the room. "What about the scar, Mrs. Noonan? You said the man had a scar on his forehead. Number five has a jagged scar similar to what you described in your verbal and written statements."

Sanderhill could legally object, but the grave is getting deeper. He remains silent.

Mrs. Noonan responds, "The scar is similar. This morning when I saw the news reports of James and Rigney being escorted by police into this building, there were several close-ups of Rigney's face and I saw the scar, which confused me because the picture you showed me of Rigney last week did not show a scar."

Sanderhill cannot suppress his chuckle. The witness has known Rig all her life, and last week she was shown a picture of Rig by the police, and she saw his face on television news this morning. Even if she had identified Rig as the man, her testimony would not be allowed in any court in America.

Mitchel flips the microphone switch and says, "Number five, return to your spot. Number six, come forward to the mirror."

"Not necessary," Mrs. Noonan declares. "I can tell from here that number six is not him."

Silence falls over the viewing room. Everyone, except Mrs. Noonan, knows that the next step is for defense counsel to demand his clients be released due to lack of evidence. But protocol requires that Mrs. Noonan depart first.

Mitchell says, "Mrs. Noonan, thank you for your cooperation. You can go now. The officer outside the door will escort you to the lobby."

After Mrs. Noonan departs, Brian Sanderhill announces, "You have no evidence to substantiate the charges against James Page and Rigney Page. Please release them now."

A.D.A. Levin states, "We have circumstantial evidence, enough to take them both to trial. I suggest you advise your clients to sign confessions now. If they do, we can make a deal for lesser sentences."

"You have nothing. Release my clients now or I will get a court order to have them released."

The A.D.A. counters, "We have a witness that will verify in court that Rigney Page knows of the secret access to the Wyman house that the shooter used to enter that house."

Sanderhill counters, "If you mean the trapdoor in the closet under the stairs, I will bring into court dozens of people who know about that trapdoor, and those dozens will name others who know. The list of those who know could easily reach one-hundred. Knowledge of that trapdoor is not valid evidence against Rigney Page, and you cannot place him at the crime scene. You must release both Rigney Page and James Page."

The A.D.A. casts a questioning glance at Sheriff Bernard; then at Detective Mitchell.

Mitchell nods verification of Sanderhill's evaluation of the evidence.

A.D.A. Levin stares at the floor while he considers what to do next. Then he looks up and focuses on Sanderhill and informs, "We can hold the Pages twenty-four more hours without arraigning them. They could confess during that time."

Sanderhill casts an amusing smile as he offers, "Release them now and drop the charges and the Pages will not sue for false arrest."

A.D.A. Levin counters, "Add to that a promise that your clients will not speak negatively about the Orange County Sheriff's Department and the District Attorney's office and they will be released within the hour."

"Deal," Sanderhill affirms. "Do you want that in writing?"

Levin states, "Not necessary, Brian. You have never violated a verbal agreement."

Thirty minutes later, James and Rig and attorney Brian Sanderhill stand in the lobby of the Orange County Sheriff's building.

Attorney Sanderhill explains, "Most of the media have gone back to their offices and to their studios to write and broadcast their lies, deceit, and misrepresentations of your involvement in the Rightwing Mad Bomber Case. Some of the media are still outside the door—the bottom feeders hoping to catch a headline morsel that their colleagues missed.

"In order to get you released, now, I had to promise the A.D.A. that you two would not sue for false arrest and will never say anything negative about the sheriff's department and the district attorney's office. So, when the reporters outside circle us like feeding frenzy sharks, I will do all the talking. Also, for the next few weeks, the media will stalk you. The best you can do is to always answer *no comment*. The media will also go after your family in attempts to get them to say something controversial. Convince your family members to always answer *no comment*.

"After I provide a short statement to the press, I will drive you home."

A dozen reporters and cameramen circle around Brian, James, and Rig. Reporters chaotically shout questions at James and Rig.

James and his son remain silent.

Brian holds up his hands as a motion to quiet the reporters. "I have a short statement. We will not answer any questions."

The bloodsucking, bottom feeders become quiet.

"My clients have been released due to lack of evidence and all charges have been dropped. While they were under arrest, my clients were treated with dignity and courtesy. That's all."

James Page sees Weston Pyth standing six feet away.

Pyth expresses mocking amusement at the rookie reporters surrounding the Pages.

James Page walks the distance to Pyth. With venom in his tone, James tells Pyth, "You are responsible for this injustice. You are a lying, deceiving commie bastard with no scruples and no honor. Your existence is nothing more than a turd in a toilet bowl."

Pyth is silent and exhibits amused condescension toward James.

"And I am in control of the flush valve." James finishes in a threatening tone.

Pyth faces turns ashen gray. James Page's threat slices through Pyth's confident arrogance.

Rig says, "Dad, come on."

James, Rig, and Brian break from the circle of reporters and walk in the direction of the parking lot. Several reporters and cameramen follow and shout questions.

As they enter the parking lot, a reporter and a cameraman jump in front of Rig, causing Rig to stop abruptly so that his forward motion does not knock them over.

The reporter accuses, "Chief Page, will you continue your attempts to murder union members?!" The reporter shoves the microphone toward Rig's face, hitting him in the chin.

Rig jerks his head backward. Rage flows through is body. He looks down into the face of the short, flabby, and sneering reporter. Rig notices that the reporter is stiff and leans forward, as if he expects to be hit. Rig glances around and notes that three cameramen are filming this event. Rig wants to lift up the deceitful low-life asshole creep reporter and throw him into the windshield of the closest car. But he quickly realizes that is exactly what these weasels want. He suppresses his rage and walks around the reporter; then he follows Brian to the car.

Chapter 72

During early evening at the Page residence in Seal Beach, Rig and his parents sit in the living room and watch the local television evening news. They sip brandy and nibble hors d'oeuvres.

After the report on James's and Rig's arrests that focused on the accusatory questions thrown at them on the way into the sheriff's building, Margaret Page comments, "They spent ten minutes on that story but never mentioned that you were released hours later due to lack of evidence."

Rig comments, "Those reporters are not in search of the truth."

James comments, "I worry how all this will affect our lives and will affect my business."

The phone rings for the seventh time during the past hour. James disconnects it.

Several minutes later, the doorbell rings. James Page walks toward the front door. The reporters who were gathered in front of the house and in back of the house on Seal Way and careful not to set foot on Page's property, departed about an hour ago. He does not expect the person at the door to be a reporter. Several moments later, James escorts Agatha Noonan into the living room.

Rig exhibits surprise and jumps to his feet.

James leads Agatha to an overstuffed chair; then he offers, "Agatha, may I get you anything?"

Mrs. Noonan nods toward the bottle of brandy on the coffee table and says, "I'll have some of that."

James pours several ounces into a brandy glass and hands it to Agatha Noonan.

Margaret Page says, "Agatha, nice to see you again. It's been a while."

Agatha takes a sip of brandy; then nods her head in approval of the quality drink. She explains, "I watched the news reports this morning when James and Rigney were arrested. Then, about thirty minutes ago, I heard on the radio that they were released. That got me thinking that it had been years since we visited, so I thought I would come over and chat."

James states, "You are welcome in our home anytime."

"And you in mine," Agatha responds. She shifts her gaze to Rig and says, "All of Seal Beach is proud of Rigney's brave acts in Europe. I am sorry about your recent problems with the unions and the police. Is that all over now?"

Rig responds, "I hope so."

Agatha reminisces, "I enjoyed all those years when Rigney and his friends gathered at the Wyman house. I never had children of my own and those teenagers always treated me like their second mom—seeking my advice and talking with me about their problems. I miss those days. I have always appreciated those errands you ran for me, like to the grocery store and drug store."

Rig responds, "Those years were precious to me also. I remember the many talks we had."

James and Peggy cast proud expressions toward Rig, indicating approval of his respect and compassion toward Agatha Noonan.

After taking another sip of brandy, Agatha sighs deeply and exhibits commitment to task—conveying that she is about to say what she came to the Page house to say. She glances quickly at their faces; then queries, "Did I ever tell you about my brother, Craig?"

The Pages shake their heads. They did not know Mrs. Noonan had a brother.

Agatha explains, "When I was a little girl, Craig always took care of me. He protected me from bullies and ensured I avoided danger. We were so close.

"I think you know that my father earned his wealth in oil. He had his own company, and many of the wells in Orange County still belong to his estate. He was very busy with building his business. Craig was like my second father.

"After Craig graduated from college, he went to work in my father's company. During the late 1930s, the oil workers union went on strike. My father and Craig would not accept union demands. One night, some men from the union blew up one of my father's oilrigs near Huntington Beach. My brother, Craig, was caught in the blast. They never found all his body parts.

"My parents never recovered from Craig's death. It destroyed them emotionally and physically and put them both into an early grave. When my husband was killed during World War Two, 1942, I had no family to console me. My husband and I had no children. That is why I enjoyed those years with Rigney and Judy and all their friends." Agatha pauses as emotion chokes her words, and tears well in her eyes.

Rig moves to Agatha's chair and sits on one of the padded arms. He puts his arm around her. Her head falls against his chest as she completely lets go with a burst of moaning and crying. His shirt becomes wet with her tears.

Emotion overcomes all the Pages. They all share Mrs. Noonan's sorrow. They choke back sobs. Their eyes fill with tears.

Ten minutes later, Agatha recovers and so have the Pages. Agatha's eyes are red and so is her face. She downs the last of the brandy in her glass; then apologizes. "Please excuse me. When I focus on those times, I break down." She pauses; then inhales deeply. "Labor union violence took a toll on my family and on my life." She looks lovingly into Rig's face and declares, "And when it is in my power to do so, I will not allow unions to damage the lives of those who have the courage to fight back."

Rig's eyes mist over. He exhibits appreciation.

Agatha stands; then comments, "Well, I do not want to intrude on your time. Thank you for the brandy. I wanted to thank all of you for your courage to fight the devil." She starts for the door.

With concern in his tone, Rig queries, "Mrs. Noonan, will you be okay?"

A grateful smile appears on Agatha's face; she responds, "Rigney, you do not need to worry about me. I have my church and my charities and all my neighbors and the support of my old ladies club." She pauses for a moment, then says, "Visit me once in a while, and drop me a postcard from time to time."

"I will do that," Rig promises.

After Agatha Noonan departs, Margaret Page expresses

bewilderment as she stares at Rig. "What was that all about?"

Rig responds, "I think she was the line-up witness who did not identify me as the sniper who shot Max Robertson from a window in the old Wyman house. Her house is next door."

James Page casts a suspicious stare at his son as he inquires, "Should she have identified you as the shooter?"

Margaret Page utters a gasp as revelation strikes her.

Rig responds, "The Orange County Police have no evidence that I am the so-called rightwing mad bomber as some call it. The CLWUA pushed the police into arresting us, and now they are embarrassed. They will lie low for a while. Then they will be back."

"How will you hand them when they come back?" James Page asks

With a cold and calculating expression on his face, Rig states, "The same as before. Anyone who comes after me or my family will regret the day they crossed my path."

Margaret becomes apprehensive. She worries about her son's safety. She warns, "They are dangerous, Rig."

"Mom, they don't know dangerous. But they will come to know dangerous if they come after me or my family."

Margaret Page gasps.

Rig glances at his watch. He leans forward and stands up from the chair.

James and Margaret stand, knowing it is time for Rig to leave.

Rig gives his mother a loving hug.

"Time we get going, Dad. Missing that midnight flight will anger my bosses in Washington."

Chapter 73

Three Weeks Later

Rig drives his Jeep Cherokee on I-70 East toward Washington D.C. Lieutenant Commander Sally Macfurson sits in the passenger seat. Rig wears his coat and tie Service Dress Blue uniform. Sally wears a semi-formal style dress. They are returning from a Saturday wedding and reception of a mutual navy friend in the small town of Hagerstown, Maryland. Yesterday evening, Sally drove her car to Rig's apartment and spent the night. This morning they drove to Hagerstown for the 1:00 PM wedding, followed by a reception.

The sun is setting. Rig turns on the headlights.

While driving, his mind wanders to the telephone conversation he had with his father yesterday morning. His father reports that there have been no actions by the CLWUA since Rig was released from jail and departed Seal Beach three weeks ago.

Rig glances at gauges on the dashboard. "I need to get some gas. I'll get off at the next exit."

As Rig pumps gas, Sally studies the sign on the restaurant across the country road. *Homemade apple pie - Best coffee in Maryland!*

After Rig gets behind the wheel and starts the Jeep, Sally asks, "I noticed you only ate a few bites of food at the reception."

"Yeah, too rich in fatty sauces."

Sally comments, "I didn't eat for the same reason." She points to the restaurant across the road and asks, "I haven't eaten since breakfast—how about some apple pie and coffee?"

Rig reads the sign; then responds, "Sounds good to me."

He parks the Jeep in front of the restaurant within the illumination of the outside lights mounted on the roof of the building. As he exits the Jeep, he tracks the direction of a tan-colored panel van that enters the parking lot—the same tan-colored panel van that was parked outside the wedding reception hall in Hagerstown. He sees two men in the van.

As soon as Rig enters the diner, he immediately looks for a rear exit. He doesn't see one and assumes the path to the rear exit is through the kitchen. He notes the location of the kitchen door.

The waitress escorts Rig and Sally to a table.

"Looks like we are the only customers," Rig comments to the waitress.

The waitress responds, "We mostly get tourist traffic going to and from D.C. Saturday nights are the slowest."

Rig comments back, "Must be just you and the cook, huh?"

"That's right. Uh, what would you like?"

"Apple pie and coffee for both of us."

The waitress walks away.

Sally asks, "What was that all about?"

"We are being followed. I expect two men to come through the door, shortly. If there is a confrontation, I need to know how many people are in the building."

Sally begins to look over her shoulder.

"Don't look," Rig directs. "I have an excellent view of the front door."

"Do you have a gun?" Sally asks with a slight edge of fear in her voice.

"I never leave home without one."

The two men in the tan-colored panel van are ex-marines in their late twenties who served in Vietnam but were dishonorably discharged because of their black market activities. They have combat experience; they have extensive hand-to-hand combat training, and both are experts with firearms. They are in top physical shape.

The leader of the two sits in the passenger seat. He says, "Remember, we are not to kill them. We are just to take them to a remote wooded area and beat the crap out of them. My instructions were clear that we must rape the woman. Then let them go on the side of a country road."

The man in the driver seat says in an amused tone, "Okay, you handle the beatings, I'll do the woman."

"We're both supposed to do the woman. My instructions were clear."

The ex-marine in the driver seat comments with a chuckle. "Okay, we we'll both do her. You're the senior, so you can soften her up and go first."

"Don't take any chances," the leader cautions. "I was informed that this guy is tough and knows how to handle himself."

"He's a squid!" says the driver in a sarcastic tone. "Since when can't two marines handle a squid?!"

As the two mercenary lowlife scumbags enter the diner, they pretend not to notice Rig and Sally.

Rig watches the two men enter the diner and take seats at the counter. They order coffee and hamburgers.

Sally watches Rig's face; she whispers, "Did they come in?"

"Yes," Rig whispers back. "When I jump up from my seat, I want you diving for the floor in the opposite direction."

Sally nods.

Rig slowly reaches for the snub nose nine-millimeter automatic in his ankle holster. He holds the gun in his lap and waits for the two goons to act.

The two men cannot see Rig's actions under the table.

Acting casual and preoccupied as if looking for the bathroom, the two lower life-forms slip off their stools and walk in the general direction of Rig and Sally.

When the two men are ten feet away, Rig jumps to his feet and aims his pistol at them.

Sally dives to the floor in the opposite direction.

The two ex-marines stop, stunned, but not appearing fearful.

Every few seconds, Rig alternates his aim between the chests of the two men. He orders, "Hands over your head!"

The two men hesitate; then they move their arms slowly upward and step sideways to put distance between each other.

Rig immediately recognizes the tactic the two scumbags are using. He knows that his two targets believe the scenario will unfold as follows: Two targets move slowly apart. While Rig has aim on *target one*, *target two* jumps farther away and goes for his weapon. That should cause Rig to shift his aim and attention to *target two*. Then *target one* goes for his weapon. The tactic normally results in *target one* getting off a shot to kill or disable Rig and both targets survive.

But the two targets underestimate the combat skills of the *unconquerable* Rigney Page.

While Rig has aim on *target one*, *target two* jumps sideways and reaches for his weapon at the same time.

Rig does not shift his aim. He fires a bullet into the heart of *target one*; *target one* falls. Then Rig stoops, swivels on his feet, and shifts his aim to *target two*.

Target two has his weapon in his right hand and attempts to regain his balance from the jump sideways.

Rig fires a bullet at *target two*, aiming at his heart but hitting him in the left shoulder just above the lung.

Target two drops his gun and falls to the floor

Rig's intention was to fire a bullet into *target two's* heart, which would comply with his number one rule of survival: Never give an attacker a chance to recover and attack you in the future.

Rig rises from his stooped position. He walks over to *target two* and picks up *target two's* automatic handgun; then he aims his pistol at *target two's* head.

Target two exhibits a mixture of pain and horror as he realizes Page's intentions. "No! Please don't kill me!" he pleads.

Sally gasps as she reads Rig's intention.

The gasp from Sally causes Rig to pause. He glances at *target one*, who lies dead on the floor with blood spreading outward from his body. Movement by the counter causes Rig to look in that direction. He sees the waitress. Fear spreads across her face. The short order cook is visible through the window into the kitchen. The cook also exhibits fear.

While he still has his weapon aimed at *target two's* head, Rig alternates glances between the faces of the waitress and the cook; then he says, "I will not harm you. Call the police. Tell them what happened. Tell them I will not resist arrest, and I will give up my weapon to them when they arrive."

Rig's sincere tone and his military uniform calm the waitress and the cook. The waitress picks up the phone next to the register.

Usually, in a situation like this, Rig would search the two targets for additional weapons and remove them. This time, however, he concludes it would be best for the police to discover weapons on these two lower than whale shit lower life forms.

After a night of interrogation by the Maryland State Police, Rig and Sally Macfurson were released. Rig had displayed his federal concealed weapons permit to the police, of which the police made a copy. The police had verified Sally's and Rig's positions in the U.S. Navy with the ONI Duty officer for Sally and the COMNAVTELCOM duty officer for Rig.

The police found concealed weapons on each of the dishonorably discharged lowlife scumbags. Each had an automatic pistol in a holster on their belts; each had a snub-nosed automatic in ankle holsters; each had six-inch switchblades. Neither thug had weapons permits. The waitress and cook at the restaurant confirmed Rig's and Sally's statement that Rig acted in self-defense, although a loose end exists in that the thug killed by Rig had not pulled any weapon. Neither target has traceable identification. The lowlife scumbag asshole creep that survived is in the hospital and under arrest.

The police advised Rig and Sally that the investigation will continue. The police told them to expect frequent visits and phone calls.

Rig and Sally drive directly to Rig's residence. As usual, Rig's tail is parked across the street and Rig waves to him. Rig no longer pretends he does notice his tail and started waving several days ago.

When Rig and Sally departed yesterday morning in Rig's Jeep, Roger Walker followed them to Hagerstown. When Roger discovered they were attending a wedding, he reported their location to The Simms Agency office. After making his report, he was kept on hold for thirty minutes; then The Simms Agency office ordered Roger to return to Page's residence and report all activities there.

Chapter 74

Rig and Denton Phillips sit at the small table in a hotel room in the Watergate. Again, Rig had entered the Watergate cloaked in his businessman disguise. Denton, who is a retired U.S. Air Force officer and now a representative of The Guardians, also wears a business suit. They both sip brandy that Denton poured from a decanter on the bar top.

"Okay, Rig, you called this meeting. What's on your mind?"

"I fear for the safety of my mother and father and my sisters. I received a call yesterday from my sister, Kate. She tells me that the entire family is being followed again, and they are being threatened face-to-face and getting threatening phone calls. Those union punks are now threating rape against my sisters. Several times, some of those fuckin' goons groped my sisters."

Denton responds, "Yes, I know. The Guardians have been keeping an eye on your family. The CLWUA has hired professionals that showed up about a week ago and began harassing your family."

Rig expresses surprise; then he asks, "How long have—"

"Since you shot Max Robertson. We reasoned that the CLWUA would not surrender. These professionals are a different breed than those local union punks and local bodyguards who were harassing your family before. These guys are mercenaries—the ones who advertise in the back of adventure magazines, like *Soldier of Fortune*."

Concern for his family's safety overwhelms Rig's thoughts. He considers the odds of his success against such professionals.

Denton asks, "Did you call this meeting to ask for resources for another trip to Southern California?"

Rig nods affirmative.

"You, alone, cannot beat these professionals. They are well financed, abundantly equipped, organized, and will not hesitate to harm or kill on orders from their financiers. For your family alone, there are about twenty mercenaries being controlled out of an operations center in a hotel meeting room in Long Beach."

Rig shakes his head; he comments, "I find it unbelievable that a union would go to so much effort and so much expense just to force my father's small business to go union."

"It's not just your father's business. Several other business owners and their families are under the same pressure with an equal number of mercenaries harassing each family. Several organizations have come together to force small businesses in Orange County to go union, and they have orders to destroy your reputation and credibility."

Rig shakes his head and expresses incredulity. "How do you know all this?"

"All the intelligence you have provided on The Longjumeau Alliance and the CLWUA has allowed us to strategically position our own operatives. We know for sure that The Longjumeau Alliance, the national headquarters of the CLWUA, and the office of Congressman Billy Thayer have joined forces. The Longjumeau Alliance is funding the whole operation against your family and the families of other small business owners. The mercenary operation center in Southern California receives orders from Congressman Thayer. We also know that Thayer is fronting for a secret caucus of Congress led by Senator Porter."

Rig shakes his head and expresses bewilderment. He asks, "Why are they determined to unionize small family-owned businesses? These unions have millions of members already."

Denton answers, "Union membership is declining because large industrial corporations are moving their manufacturing operations overseas to escape the high cost of union labor, to escape stranglehold regulation, and escape higher taxes imposed by federal and state governments."

Rig's eyes go wide and he expresses astonishment. He comments, "So my family is a victim of incompetent and economics-illiterate politicians."

Denton continues, "The Guardians have also discovered that Congressman Thayer appears to have something against you personally. According to our operatives, he is pushing for you to be harmed and disabled."

Rig chuckles; then he comments, "Billy is jealous. He has been enamored with Diane Love since college. He feels cheated that Diane prefers a navy enlisted man over a congressman."

Denton expresses understanding. Then he cautions, "Rig, you cannot go to Seal Beach and fight these mercenaries. You must let The Guardians do it for you."

"What will you do?" Rig inquires in a cautious tone.

"We will make an offer to the leaders and financiers of this unlawful conspiracy that they cannot refuse."

"What are you planning?"

"We are planning an operation that will change the minds of those who lead these enemies of the American Republic, and we will use sniper rifles against those mercenaries, like you did against Max Robertson. We will show the CLWUA and The Longjumeau Alliance what happens to those who crusade to deny Americans those freedoms guaranteed by the U.S. Constitution."

Rig expresses a combination of apprehension and disapproval.

"Rig, these tactics work. We have been using such tactics for a century."

"Then why are the enemies of liberty and freedom still operating?"

Denton responds, "We are winning battles, but the war goes on. And that war will continue until American citizens finally wake up and understand the destructive power of Totalitarianism and Marxism and accept the fact that Totalitarians and Marxists are infiltrating government. This war will only be won in the voting booth."

Rig sighs deeply and nods understanding.

"Rig, The Guardians are organizing an operation to go after the CLWUA and The Longjumeau Alliance at the same time, including those members of Congress who are members of The Longjumeau Alliance. We would like you to be part of it but not in Southern California."

"What do you want me to do?"

"It's too early to provide details."

"Denton, I cannot wait to take charge of the safety of my family. I must do something soon to get rid of those mercenaries."

"We have our own operatives watching after your family. If an attack against your family is imminent, we'll shoot those bastards. Believe me, your family is safe."

Rig nods and expresses appreciation. Then he requests, "Please tell me more about what you want me to do."

"We will conduct briefings prior to the operation. You will be told everything then."

Rig evaluates all that Denton has told him. He shakes his head while expressing disbelief.

"What is it, Rig?"

"I have known Diane Love for most of my life, and we have been intimate since high school. I find it unbelievable that she has aligned with communists and murderers. I don't understand it."

Denton counsels, "Don't beat yourself up about it. There is no understanding the Marxist mind. There is no sanity in their reasoning. Fact and logic will not move them off their invalid ideology."

Rig nods and expresses his agreement. Then his thoughts turn to Diane's fate.

Chapter 75

As Rig walks into the Senate hearing room, dozens of flashing camera bulbs brighten the already well-illuminated room. His Navy assigned lawyer, Captain Michael Maston, walks beside him. Both navy men wear their Summer Dress White uniform.

Above Rig's right breast pocket, three rows of military award ribbons broadcast his bravery and achievements. Captain Brad Watson, Assistant Director of Naval Intelligence for Counterespionage, ordered Rig not to wear any ribbons that he was awarded as a result of working undercover as a naval intelligence field agent; those awards are listed in Rig's classified personnel file but not in Rig's official unclassified personnel file. Brad Watson also allows Rig to wear the enlisted submarine warfare insignia above his ribbons that signify Rig has qualified in submarine operations, and to wear his enlisted surface warfare insignia below his ribbons that signify he has qualified in surface operations. Both warfare insignias are listed as achievements in Rig's official unclassified personnel file.

JAG Captain Michael Maston's broad-shouldered slender build, graying temples and confident stride convey his legal competence. Michael Maston and Rig are not strangers. Maston was Rig's lawyer ten years ago at U.S. Naval Communications Station Nea Makri, Greece when Rig was a second class petty officer. Maston, a lieutenant at the time, defended Rig against assault and battery charges upon an officer. After Maston had investigated Rig's background, Maston concluded that Rig was an undercover field operative for naval intelligence. Maston's knowledge of that fact is the reason why he was selected to provide counsel to Rig during this Senate hearing. Otherwise, another JAG officer would need to be briefed into Rig's affiliation with naval intelligence.

The large wood-paneled hearing room has over one-hundred spectator seats, but only a dozen spectators are seated. Reporters and photographers outnumber spectators.

Rig and Captain Maston sit down at the witness table. They face an ornate curved multilevel dais that seats a total of twenty-four. Photographers stoop against the dais and snap pictures and record videos of Chief Petty Officer Rigney Page and his navy lawyer.

Several minutes later, five senators come through a door behind the dais, followed by staffers for each senator. The subcommittee numbers three Democrats and two Republicans. Rig identifies all three Democrat senators from the membership list of The Longjumeau Alliance, which includes the chairman of the subcommittee, Democrat Senator Clay Porter.

As the Armed Services Subcommittee members and their advising staffers find their seats, Rig recollects events leading up to his appearing as a witness at this subcommittee. He received a witness summons two weeks ago. He immediately notified his superiors at COMNAVTELCOM Headquarters on Massachusetts Avenue Northwest and his superiors at the Office of Naval Intelligence located on the federal complex at Suitland, Maryland. Rig suggested that Captain Michael Maston be his lawyer because Maston is the only navy lawyer who knows Rig is a navy intelligence undercover operative. All field operatives are required to report instances when unauthorized persons become aware of an operative's undercover identity, and such reports are made a permanent part of the undercover operative's classified file. The official request for Captain Michael Maston to be Rig's counselor at the hearing came from Captain Mary Blakely at COMNAVTELCOM. The navy JAG, a rear admiral, initially denied the request for Michael Maston and assigned an inexperienced navy lieutenant. Two days later, the Vice Chief of Naval Operations, a four-star admiral, called the navy JAG and ordered JAG to assign Captain Michael Maston as Chief Page's counsel.

During a closed-door meeting at the naval intelligence building on the Cheltenham navy station between Captain Watson of ONI, Captain Maston of JAG, and Chief Page; Captain Watson ordered Rig not to answer any question that reveals classified information and not to answer any question that reveals Rig's affiliation with naval intelligence.

"Have you read the unclassified Naval Investigative Service report on the shooting of Ensign Ryan?" Captain Watson had asked Rig at that meeting.

"Yes, several times," Rig had responded. "To the best of my knowledge, that NIS report contains no classified information. NIS did not name Barbara. They referred to her only as Subject Two."

Captain Maston advised Rig, "That senate subcommittee will have a copy of the unclassified NIS report, which states that you and Subject Two shared an apartment. They will order you to reveal her identity. How will you respond?"

Rig had expressed bewilderment and asked, "Did the subcommittee not receive a copy of the classified NIS report that includes names and identifies everyone and explains some of the classified events leading up to the shooting?"

Captain Watson had responded, "No, none of those senators are cleared for that category of top secret information. Some of them do not have top secret clearances at all."

Rig had nodded understanding; then stated, "So all I do is provide information that is already in the unclassified report."

"That's right," Captain Watson had responded.

JAG Captain Michael Maston had advised, "You will be sworn in before the subcommittee and told that you are a witness and can be prosecuted for giving false testimony. On the other hand, subcommittee members are not required to conform to facts and truth and can ask accusatory questions in political grandstanding maneuvers that would never be allowed in a court of law. So, you must assume that providing any information outside of what is in the unclassified report would reveal classified information, and, therefore, you cannot provide the information. You must state that answering the question would reveal classified information. You might be asked questions that would be best answered by stating 'I do not recall, Senator.' If I want you to respond with 'I do not recall, Senator,' I will tap my index finger twice."

The tapping of a gavel by Senator Porter draws Rigney's

attention to actions within the hearing room. The chatter in the room ends and most people in the room focus on Senator Porter as he speaks. "The Armed Services Subcommittee is now in session. The scope of this subcommittee is to investigate the substance and sequence of events in the Maddalena Archipelago and aboard the USS *Randal* that led to the death of Ensign Franklyn Ryan. The purpose of this subcommittee is to develop applicable legislation as necessary to modify military policy and military regulations.

"The time limit of each member has been set and will be strictly enforced. Several rounds of questioning are permitted. I will now swear in the witness."

Rig stands and raises his right hand. Senator Porter administers the witness oath whereby Rig promises to tell the truth to be best of his ability and whereby Rig acknowledges false testimony might result in fines and imprisonment. Then Rig sits.

Senator Porter queries, "Chief Page, you were ordered by this subcommittee to file a prehearing statement regarding the relevant events leading up to the shooting of Ensign Ryan. You failed to comply. What is your justification for not filing a statement?"

Rig stares directly into the eyes of Senator Porter as he speaks into the microphone, "I submitted a letter to the subcommittee stating that I had been interviewed by the NIS, uh Naval Investigative Service, and that everything I told the NIS is in their report. I have nothing to add to the report."

Porter responds in a challenging tone, "Are you testifying that you are not knowledgeable of any facts regarding Ensign Ryan's death other than what is in the NIS report?"

"Senator, my testimony is that the NIS report contains all the unclassified details, and I have nothing of an unclassified nature to add."

Porter advises, "Chief, the NIS report has been read into the record and so has your verbal statement regarding the cover letter. Should later testimony reveal you have not been truthful, you could be charged with Contempt of Congress or Providing False Statements to Congress. Do you understand that?"

Rig hesitates to answer, considering the possibilities that he could be caught in a lie.

Captain Maston whispers into Rig's ear, "State that you understand and appear confident as you say it."

"I understand, Senator."

Senator Porter informs the subcommittee, "Chief Page's cover letter has been entered into the record. Before the questioning begins, we will hear the Chief's opening statement."

Captain Maston whispers into Chief Page's ear, "You have no opening statement."

Rig says into the microphone, "I have no opening statement."

Senator Porter's amused grin conveys that he acknowledges Chief Page has expert counsel by his side. Then Porter asks, "Chief Page, why was there animosity between you and Ensign Ryan?"

Rig responds, "I felt no animosity toward Ensign Ryan. I cannot speak for Ensign Ryan's feelings toward me."

Senator Porter counters, "Chief Page, statements from a dozen USS *Randal* crew members that are included in the NIS report say otherwise. Those crew members report a number of instances when you and Ensign Ryan argued and yelled at each other. Would you like to amend your testimony regarding no animosity between you and Ensign Ryan?"

"I never yelled or exhibited anger toward Ensign Ryan."

Senator Porter, confident that he has trapped Chief Page, challenges, "Are you claiming that those dozen *Randal* sailors are lying?"

"No, Senator."

Porter and other senators express bewilderment.

Senator Porter questions, "Then what is your testimony regarding those statements that animosity existed between you and Ensign Ryan? Are those statements true or not true?"

Rig responds, "Senator, I am confused by your question. I read all those statements attached to the NIS report and not one of my shipmates said that animosity existed between me and Ensign Ryan."

Several gasps rise from the spectators.

Senator Porter turns red-faced. He knows that he has been caught in a misrepresentation of the NIS report.

In an effort to recover, Senator Porter claims, "Chief, animosity is a collective description of what all those statements convey. Now, what is your proof that animosity did not exist between you and Ensign Ryan." Porter believes he has maneuvered Chief Page into the impossible situation of proving something did not exist.

Rig responds, "My testimony is that those statements do not specify that animosity existed between me and Ensign Ryan, and to conclude otherwise is a misinterpretation of the facts."

Senator Porter stares, dumbfounded, at Chief Page. Porter thought he was leading Chief Page toward reversing his testimony. Instead, Porter was publicly exposed as a distorter of facts.

The amused expressions on the other senators' faces convey that they acknowledge Senator Porter was exposed as a liar by the witness, and that exposure is obvious to the reporters and spectators in the hearing room.

Senator Porter glances quickly around the room; he observes colleagues, reporters, and spectators chuckling. Porter's face flushes red with embarrassment. He suppresses the urge to lash out at this impudent navy enlisted man who dares embarrass a U.S. Senator. He decides to continue his strategy to discredit the witness.

Captain Maston whispers into Rig's ear, "Be careful, Chief, you do not want to anger U.S. Senators."

Rig whispers back, "I just speak the truth—was not my intention to offend anyone."

Maston whispers his response. "Okay, Chief, just be careful not to offend U.S. Senators. Remember, you are sitting in the chambers of those who seldom honor truth and are never humbled by it either."

In a sharp, irritated tone, Senator Porter questions, "Captain, Chief, are you done conspiring? Are you ready to continue?"

Chief Page is about to object to the senator's *conspiracy* accusation when Captain Maston reads Rig's intention. Maston grabs Rig's elbow. Rig turns his head to face the officer. Maston shakes his head slightly and utters a soft, "Don't."

"Aye, sir," Rig acknowledges. Then he turns his head and faces Senator Porter.

Senator Porter, whose face has returned to normal color, takes on an arrogant chastising manner as challenges, "In your statement to NIS, you describe an incident in the *Randal* radio room when Ensign Ryan yelled at you and he hit you in the chest with his fists and knocked you backwards against a patch panel. That incident was witnessed by three of your subordinates which they describe in each of their corroborating statements. My question is this: Why would you report that situation to NIS if you did not believe that animosity existed between you and Ensign Ryan?"

Rig cocks his head to the side and casts a quizzical stare at Senator Porter. Rig wonders why the senator would ask that question. First, the question makes no sense; second, the NIS report is crystal clear that Rig's description of the episode was a result of a direct question from NIS investigators, and not Rig volunteering the information. Rig would not have told NIS what he considered an insignificant action by an officer who could not handle stress. Rig shifts his stare to Captain Maston, indicating he does not know how to answer.

Captain Maston whispers, "The senator is playing to the cameras. It's not a question; it's an accusation. Remember, most of these senators are not here to gain relevant information to construct legislation. They are here to discredit you and exonerate Ensign Ryan of any wrong doing. Senator Porter is attempting to place the fault of Ensign Ryan's death at your feet."

Rig exhibits surprise and asks, "Why?"

"Senator Porter was Ensign Ryan's granduncle. That's the only motivation I see."

Rig nods understanding; but he also considers that Senator Porter, who has a leadership position in the CLWUA's war against the Page family, might be continuing that war in this hearing room. He asks Captain Maston, "How do I answer? His question is based on the false premise that I volunteered my description of that incident to NIS. I did not. NIS demanded I provide a statement regarding that incident."

Captain Maston advises, "Just tell the truth but be careful of what you say. Senator Porter is attempting to destroy your character."

Rig faces Senator Porter and states, "I did not volunteer a description of that incident to NIS investigators. The NIS investigator demanded that I provide a description of that incident. I never considered that incident important enough to report it to anyone."

Porter questions, "Why was Ensign Ryan yelling at you and why did he hit you?"

"I don't know," Rig answers in a mild tone.

In a challenging tone, Porter accuses, "Then your testimony is that you did nothing to provoke Ensign Ryan's behavior."

Rig responds, "Ensign Ryan was an officer in the United States Navy. He was responsible for his behavior—not me and not anyone else."

Again, Senator Porter reveals he is accusing and not investigating. Chuckling arises from the spectators and the media.

Porter slams the gavel to the desktop and warns, "The media and spectators will remain silent or I will clear the hearing room!"

After the hearing room becomes quiet, Porter lifts a piece of paper from his desktop so that all in the room can see it. He explains, "I have a copy of a letter from Ensign Ryan to his father. The letter was written the night of the incident in the USS *Randal* radio room when Ensign Ryan hit Chief Page. I will read the relevant paragraph:

"I placed the Chief Radioman on report today. I charged him with insubordination and incompetence. Later in the radio room he confronted me in an intimidating, physically aggressive manner. I thought he was going to hit me. In self-defense, I struck him first, knocking him back a few feet. The Chief Radioman is a mean street-tough aggressor. On the ship, the crew calls him 'The Tiger' because he moves about the ship like a tiger prowling-for-prey. I

quickly departed the radio room to avoid him attacking me. I retrieved the report chit from the operations officer and added assault to the charges against him."

Porter hands the letter to the clerk and instructs, "Copy this letter and include it in the subcommittee record and give a copy to the witness." Then Porter stares arrogantly at Rig and in a challenging tone inquires, "What is your response to Ensign Ryan's description of that incident in the radio room?"

Rig responds, "I did not act aggressively in any way toward Ensign Ryan, and the three witnesses to that event do not state that I acted aggressively. And—"

Porter interrupts, "Chief Page, before you go down the path of calling a navy officer a liar, you should talk with your counsel. I will give you a few moments to do that."

Rig and Captain Maston engage in whispering conversation for nearly a minute. Then Rig, faces Senator Porter and advises, "I am ready to continue."

"Go ahead, Chief."

"I did not act aggressively in any way toward Ensign Ryan, and the three witnesses to that event do not state that I acted aggressively. And—"

Senator Porter interrupts, "Let us be clear, Chief. Are you accusing your division officer of lying?"

"My testimony is that Ensign Ryan's letter did not accurately describe all the details of that incident."

Senator Porter casts an exaggerated doubt-filled stare at Rig. The exaggeration is for the cameras in an effort to convey that this honorable, experienced, and ethical senator is not fooled by the lying and deceiving Chief Page. After several moments, Porter asks, "What else do you claim Ensign Ryan lied about in the letter?"

Rig reveals, "The report chit was initiated after the incident in the radio room, not before."

Senator Porter utters a sarcastic filled chuckle and casts a disbelieving expression. Then he makes the classic mistake of those who engage in false accusations towards others. He publicly asks a question of which he does not already know the answer. "Chief, are we supposed to take your word over what a naval officer wrote to his father?"

Rig replies, "Sir, Lieutenant Tarpon, the USS *Randal* Operations Officer can verify that the report chit was initiated after the incident, not before. Lieutenant Tarpon is scheduled to appear before this subcommittee two days from now."

To hide his embarrassment, Porter holds the schedule of witnesses in front of his face. He notes Lieutenant Tarpon is scheduled to appear and he immediately connives ways to stop Tarpon from testifying.

A buzzer sounds, signaling that Senator Porter's time for this round of questioning is over.

Senator Richard Todd, a Republican from a western state, is next to ask questions. But first, he greets Rig. "Chief Page, it is an honor to have one of America's decorated heroes appear before this subcommittee. I welcome the *Hero of Thurso* into our chambers. America is grateful for your bravery in saving the lives of your shipmates and their wives during that terrorist attack in Scotland last year." Todd pauses and expresses respect for the chief; then he asks, "Have you healed completely from the three bullets that Ensign Ryan shot into you?"

Rig replies, "Senator, thank you for your kind words. I am only one of several that the international press labeled as *Heroes of Thurso*. One of my fellow chiefs is permanently disabled from gunshot wounds that he took during a shootout in the antenna field between himself and two of the terrorists." Rig pauses to inhale; then he advises, "Yes, I have recovered from the gunshot wounds inflicted on me by Ensign Ryan."

"Chief, describe your relationship with Ensign Ryan."

"He was my division officer. I reported directly to him. After he was declared a deserter, I assumed all his duties."

Several senators, including Todd blink and express befuddlement. Then Todd asks, "Yes, Chief, we all know that. What I want to know is how well you and Ensign Ryan get along onboard the USS *Randal*. Did you always obey his orders?"

"I obeyed his orders to the best of my ability and within the realm of reality."

Chuckles come from the spectators and several senators, including Todd.

Senator Todd asks, "What do you mean by *within the realm of realty*."

"Ensign Ryan often ordered me to fix communications problems that did not exist."

"Provide some examples, Chief."

"On several occasions when we could not communicate with other units within line-of-sight, Ensign Ryan would order me to fix *Randal* communications systems when the problem was not with *Randal* communications systems, and I told him so."

"How did Ensign Ryan react to your reports of the problems not being aboard *Randal*?" Senator Todd asks.

Rig responds, "He would become angry and sometimes yelled at me."

Senator Todd spends a few moments studying some papers before him; then he asks, "I have before me a NAVPERS Form 1626, Report and Disposition of Offenses that Ensign Ryan used to report you for incompetence, insubordination, and assault. The form does not list any actions taken against you. Have you been subjected to Uniform Code of Military Justice investigations or punishment as a result of this report?"

"No, Senator, I have not."

"We must be clear for the record, Chief. Your testimony is that no official investigation of these accusations was conducted?"

"That's correct, Senator."

"You are stating that you were never awarded Non-Judicial Punishment or found guilty at court-martial as a result of these accusations, is that correct?"

"That's correct, Senator."

Senator Todd raises his eyebrows as he quickly glances at the room; then he asks. "So your chain-of-command found no credibility in Ensign Ryan's accusations?"

As he answers, Rig chooses his words carefully. "Senator, I do not know the judgments of my chain-of-command regarding those accusations. I can only report that I have no knowledge of a UCMJ investigation, and I never received Non-Judicial Punishment and I was not court-martialed."

"Chief, how much time elapsed from the time Ensign Ryan placed you on report and when he was removed from the ship and sent to the Naval Hospital in Naples, Italy for psychiatric evaluation and therapy."

"Several days—might have been five days. I can't remember for sure."

Chatter rises from the spectators.

The Chair, Senator Porter, slams the gavel several times. He casts a scolding stare at Senator Todd.

Spectators become quiet.

Senator Todd lifts a sheet of paper and performs a quick scan of the paper. He says, "Chief, on the day you were shot three times by Ensign Ryan, you were presented a Letter of Commendation for bravery and resourcefulness signed by the Chief of Naval Operations. What was the spread of time from when you were presented that letter and the time Ensign Ryan shot you?"

"Senator, I was not the only *Randal* crewmember who receive a Letter of Commendation that day. Several of my shipmates received the same award."

Senator Todd smiles, expressing appreciation; he comments, "Chief, your humility is refreshing. Please answer my question."

"Three hours."

The question timer sounds.

The Chair, Senator Porter, advises, "Senators must attend a roll call vote. This subcommittee is in recess until 1:30 PM." Porter slams the gavel once to the desktop.

Chief Page and Captain Maston eat small lunch salads and drink

Perrier mineral water at a small café several blocks from the Capitol Building. After they have consumed half of their salads, Captain Maston comments, "You did well this morning responding to Senator Porter's obvious attacks to discredit you. Porter wants to make it look like Ensign Ryan wanted to murder you because he was afraid of you. Porter's bias is obvious. I wonder if the press will report that Senator Porter is related to Ensign Ryan."

Rig pauses with fork in hand poised over his salad bowl. He exhibits deep thought. Then he says, "Captain, I don't think Senator Porter's only motive to discredit me is because he is related to Ensign Ryan."

"What then?"

"I told you about the problems my family is having with the CLWUA and how I had been arrested for questioning in the assault of a CLWUA member."

Maston nods his head up and down. "Yes."

"Members of the CLWUA are Senator Porter's number one campaign contributors—in the tens of thousands of dollars every year. And CLWUA members are the top contributors to every Democrat senator on the subcommittee."

Captain Maston stares curiously with one eyebrow raised at Rig while he inquires, ""How long have you been so paranoid?"

Rig chuckles as he responds. "Ever since I discovered the worldwide conspiracy against me."

The captain asks, "So how do you think those campaign contribution to those senators affect you and this hearing?"

"My father told me that the CLWUA will continue to harass our family until my father allows the CLWUA to unionize his business, and I think that this subcommittee hearing is designed to discredit and harass me."

"But, Chief, for that to be successful, Senator Porter and the other union slaves on that subcommittee would need to tie Ensign Ryan's death to your war on the union."

Rig takes another bite of his salad. As he chews, he reflects thoughtfulness. Then he suggests, "Senator Curtis is next to

369

question me. He is a Democrat from a New England state—can't remember which. His largest contributors are also members of the CLWUA. Maybe he will attempt to make the connection, publicly."

Captain Maston nods understanding. He states, "So far, you have done well with answering their questions. You made Senator Porter look foolish by exposing that he was misrepresenting the NIS report. Going forward, answer only the questions you are asked. Do not expand on your answers."

As they enter the hearing room, Chief Page and Captain Maston observe that every spectator seat is taken, and other spectators stand two deep at the back of the room. Reporters and photographers, who have doubled in numbers since the morning session, move about and converse in the area between the dais and the witness table.

After sitting down at the witness table, Rig comments to the captain, "Appears half the city was advised something big is going on in here."

Captain Maston expresses amusement as he offers, "Or the word has spread that Senator Porter looked foolish this morning while attempting to discredit a navy enlisted man and all these spectators are here for the entertainment."

Senator Porter slams the gavel and brings the hearing room to order. He glances at Senator Curtis and advises into his microphone, "Senator Curtis will now ask his first round of questions."

Rig turns his attention toward the slim, medium-height, impeccably dressed, graying, and aristocratic Senator Elvin Curtis. Elvin Curtis's arrogant and condescending manner instills hate in the hearts of most Congressional staffers and Congressional clerks. Senator Curtis's vile, vicious, and deceitful attacks against Republicans on the Senate floor are legend. Witnesses who have incurred his wrath are usually subjected to venomous accusations shouted down from the dais.

Curtis's great-grandfather created the Curtis fortune in the chemical industry during the late 1800s. When the Roosevelt

Administration was constructing New Deal legislation, Senator Curtis's grandfather switched his family from Republicans to Democrats; then Curtis's grandfather created holding companies in Panama and transferred the Curtis fortune to those Panamanian holding companies to avoid FDR New Deal tax hikes. Senator Elvin Curtis has never held a job in business or industry. His entire working life has been in the federal government; first in the U.S. House of Representatives and now in the U.S. Senate. Curtis has a reputation as a 'tax and spend' Democrat but always sponsors amendments to legislation that exempts certain types of trusts, like the type trusts that hold the entire Curtis fortune.

Rig has been thoroughly briefed by Sally Macfurson on Senator Curtis's biography, manner, and family history. Senator Curtis is a founding member of *The Longjumeau Alliance*. Rig is not intimidated; the truth causes him no fear. He is comfortable and relaxed.

Senator Curtis asks, "Chief Page, why did Ensign Ryan shoot you."

"I don't know, Senator."

Senator Curtis furrows his brow and purses his lips and stares down over the rims of his eyeglasses toward Chief Page. Curtis expresses that he does not believe Chief Page. Senator Curtis says, "The Naval Investigative Service report clearly conveys that you are a physically aggressive enlisted man who disrespects officers." Curtis sits back in his chair, folds his arms across his chest, and casts a knowing, smug expression toward the witness table.

Because no question was asked, Rig is silent.

Senator Curtis snips loudly, "Come on, Chief. You are wasting my allotted time with your silence."

Again, because no question was asked, Rig is silent.

"Respond, Chief!" Senator Curtis orders loudly.

Rig queries in a respectful tone, "Respond to what, Senator? You did not ask me a question."

Senator Curtis's face flushes red and he exhibits anger toward the brashness and the fearlessness of the enlisted man before him.

Chuckles and mild chatter rise from the spectator seats.

From The Chair, Senator Porter orders, "Silence in this hearing room. Only subcommittee members and witnesses are allowed to speak."

Then Senator Porter turns his attention toward Chief Page and cautions, "Chief, you must show respect for these proceedings and respect for the position of U.S. Senators."

Senator Porter announces, "Senator Curtis's time will be set back two minutes."

"Senator Curtis rephrases, "Chief Page, the Naval Investigative Service report clearly conveys that you are a physically aggressive enlisted man who disrespects officers. What is your response to that reality?"

"Senator, I do not consider your perception of my behavior to be reality."

A stunned silence falls over the hearing room. No one has ever seen a witness challenge Senator Curtis's words. Mouths are open and eyes are wide. Observers of Senator Curtis's behavior in the Senate expect the senator to comeback with a tongue lashing of innuendo and lies.

Senator Curtis is about to unleash a tongue lashing when he realizes the best way to discredit this witness is to catch him in a lie. Senator Curtis comments, "Well, let us substantiate the reality of your character." Curtis lifts several sheets of paper from the desktop. He gives those sheets a quick glance, then he asks, "Chief, were you awarded non-judicial punishment in 1968 aboard the USS *Barb* for disrespect toward an officer?"

"Point of order," Senator Todd declares into the microphone.

Curtis gives Todd an angry stare.

The clerk stops the clock on Senator Curtis.

"Explain," Porter asks while looking at Todd.

Todd explains, "Chief Page and Ensign Ryan met for the first time approximately one year ago. Any incident that occurred ten years ago must be irrelevant to the scope of this hearing."

Senator Porter turns toward Senator Curtis and orders,

"Response."

Curtis responds, "Chief Page states that he is not a physically aggressive person, although the NIS report conveys otherwise. Ensign Ryan's possible fear of that aggression might be the reason Ensign Ryan shot Chief Page in defense. The witness's denial of such behavior opens the door for me to provide evidence to the contrary."

The Chair, Senator Porter, looks toward Senator Todd and queries, "Rebuttal?"

"The NIS report contains no evidence that Ensign Ryan responded to an aggressive action by Chief Page. Dozens of statements by witnesses to the shooting in La Maddalena state that Chief Page was standing still about ten feet from Ensign Ryan when Ensign Ryan shot Chief Page."

Senator Porter rules, "We are here to gather all the facts regarding the shooting and all the facts about those involved. We cannot allow so-called points-of-order to interfere with gathering facts. The witness must answer."

Senator Todd rolls his eyes, which is caught by network news cameras.

The clerk restarts the clock on Senator Curtis.

Chief Page asks, "Can the question be repeated?"

Senator Curtis repeats his question. "Chief, were you awarded non-judicial punishment in 1968 aboard the USS *Barb* for disrespect toward an officer?"

"Yes," Rig answers.

Senator Curtis blinks his eyes, conveying befuddlement. He expected Chief Page to provide excuses.

Rig casts an amused expression at Senator Curtis.

Senator Cutis continues. "Then, later that year, 1968, while stationed at a U.S. Naval Communications Station in Greece; you were court-martialed for assault and battery on two enlisted men, on a naval officer, on two Greek nationals, and intimidation toward an officer for killing that officer's dog. Then, in 1976, you were court-martialed for assault and battery, dereliction of duty, and conduct unbecoming a chief petty officer when you engaged in a fist fight against Turkish sailors in a brothel in Subic City, Philippines." Curtis pauses while he casts a condescending stare at Chief Page; then questions, "Chief do you still claim that you are not physically aggressive towards others?"

Rig states calmly into the microphone, "I have never been court-martialed."

Gasps rise from the spectators. The witness just accused Senator Curtis of making a false statement.

Senator Curtis spends a few moments studying sheets of paper in front of him. Then he turns to an aid behind him and engages in a whispered exchange. Curtis hands the papers to the aid. The aid stands; then he exits the hearing room through a door behind the dais.

Curtis continues his questioning. "Chief Page, some months back, you nearly beat to death a member of the Construction and Labor Workers Union of America. That beating took place in the backyard of your father's home in Seal Beach, California. That union member is disabled for life. Last month, you were arrested at your apartment in Arlington and extradited to Orange County California and questioned regarding the shooting of another CLWUA member. Several weeks ago, you were arrested for shooting to death one man and for the shooting injury of the second man." Senator Curtis pauses. He glances at the timer. He stretches out his arms toward the spectators, palms up, and declares in a pontificating tone, "Chief Page, you are an openly violent person. Ensign Ryan probably knew that. I can understand why Ensign Ryan felt the need to stop you in La Maddalena before you injured or killed him."

The timer sounds.

Rig cannot suppress a laugh.

Spectators are disappointed that the witness will not have opportunity to respond.

The press salivates over the sound clips for the six-o'clock news.

Senator Porter speaks into his microphone, "Senator Landell has the floor."

Rig shifts his attention to the four-term Republican senator who is also a chief petty officer in the naval reserves.

The portly and balding fifty-two-year-old Senator Landell is well known for his outspoken blunt, finger-pointing rhetoric towards senators who connive to hide fact and truth. While casting an amused expression at Senator Curtis, Landell says into the microphone, "I was planning to pass on the first round of questioning, but I cannot allow Senator Curtis's false accusations toward the witness just before the timer expired to go unchallenged." Senator Landell turns his eyes toward Rig and states, "Chief Page, we will gain more detail on the events introduced by Senator Curtis. First, regarding that non-judicial punishment that you were awarded for disrespect toward an officer on the USS *Barb* during 1968, do you admit that you were disrespectful toward an officer?"

Rig answers, "Yes. It was an impulsive reaction to the officer hitting me."

"What did you do or say to the officer that was judged as disrespect?"

"I do not remember. I shouted something at him, but I cannot remember what it was."

"Chief, why did that officer hit you?"

"I do not know."

"Was that officer punished for hitting you?"

"I do not know."

Senator Landell nods, then moves to the next incident. "What is true about Senator Curtis's accusations regarding your actions while stationed at Naval Communications Station in Greece?"

"I was charged under the UCMJ, but I was never court-martialed."

"Why were you not court-martialed?"

"The charges were dropped due to lack of evidence after several of those who accused me admitted to lying and conspiring against me."

Senator Landell glances at this notes, then focuses on Chief Page and asks, "And what is the truth about these assault and battery and dereliction of duty charges as a result of a fight in a Subic City brothel?"

"I was driving from the Subic Bay Naval Base to the Naval Communications Station located at San Antonio, Philippines. The road passes through Subic City. I was stopped in traffic when several sailors approached me and asked that I help them save their shipmate from a beating by Turkish sailors. I went into the brothel's bar where I found three Turkish sailors beating on the U.S. sailor. Those Turkish sailors attacked me when I acted to remove the U.S. sailor from the premises. I fought off the Turks and got all the U.S. sailors out of there, and I took them to the USNAVCOMMSTA where I was stationed."

Nearly everyone in the room exhibits bewilderment as they attempt to understand why Chief Page would be charged with assault and battery for saving U.S. sailors from danger.

Senator Landell queries, "Who charged you with assault and battery and with dereliction of duty as a result of that incident?"

"My commanding officer."

"Didn't your commanding officer ask you to explain what happened before he charged you?"

"No, he did not."

Murmurs of astonishment rise from the spectators. They cannot comprehend why a commanding officer would do that. Some in the hearing room consider that Chief Page is not telling the truth.

"Chief, that does not make sense and does not sound fair. Why did your C.O. do that?"

"I don't know."

"You have no idea?"

"No."

"What happened after you were charged?"

"There was an investigation. Then the charges were dismissed."

"Dismissed by whom?"

"My commanding officer."

Whispers rise from the spectators as they comment to each other about the absurdity of such a situation.

Senator Landell glances at Senator Curtis and says, "Will Senator Curtis share his notes with us? Specifically those notes specifying that all those UCMJ charges were dropped against Chief Page."

Senator Curtis slams his fist on the table and charges loudly, "How dare you accuse me of hiding facts to which I have no knowledge!"

Senator Landell shakes his head and expresses disgust toward Senator Curtis. Then he focuses on Rig and asks, "Chief, where would one find proof you were never court-martialed?"

"I can answer that," Captain Maston states. "Regarding the accusations against Chief Page while in Greece ten years ago, I can verify that those charges were dismissed. I was Chief Page's defense counsel. He was a second class petty officer at the time. Regarding the charges against Chief Page while he was in the Philippines, I personally reviewed those records several days ago, and I confirm those records state all charges dismissed. I will have copies of those records delivered to your office within a few days."

Senator Landell responds, "That will not be necessary, Captain. I have the JAG records for those investigations and they clearly reveal that all charges were dropped in all cases specifically for the reasons that Chief Page explained." Senator Landell pauses and stares disapprovingly at Senator Curtis. Then he comments, "I know that Senator Curtis has the same copies of those JAG records that I have. I suggest that Senator Curtis read those records again with the assistance of someone who has reading comprehension skills above his own."

Chuckles ripple softly across the hearing room.

Senator Curtis exhibits no guilt for his lying. He considers that the end justifies the means.

Senator Landell asks, "Chief Page, what is your response to the suggestion by Senator Curtis that you are attacking CLWUA members?"

Rig reports, "The CLWUA has declared war on my father's business and many other small businesses in Southern California. The CLWUA is stalking my family and the family of others who own small businesses. One night I caught a CLWUA arsonist crossing my father's backyard toward the house. He had a full gas can in one hand and a pistol in the other hand. I was able to stop him before he could kill anyone.

"Regarding the shooting of the other CLWUA member on the Seal Beach Pier, The Orange County Sheriff's Office arrested me at my apartment in Arlington and transported me back to Orange County. After several hours of questioning and standing in a lineup, I was released. I was never booked."

Senator Landell queries, "And this incident in Maryland several weeks ago when you shot two men—killing one and seriously injuring another?"

"They were agents of the CLWUA, and they attempted to kidnap me and a friend. I pulled my gun and got the upper hand on them before they could abduct us."

"Outrageous lie!" Senator Curtis declares loudly from his seat at the dais.

Senator Porter casts a suspicious stare at Rig.

Spectators become noisy as they gasp and utter comments regarding the incredulous turn of events in this hearing room.

Senator Porter slams the gavel.

Senator Landell glances at the clock and notes he has less than two minutes remaining. He asks, "Chief, do you normally go about armed with a gun?"

"Yes."

"Do you have a permit to carry a gun?"

"Yes, I have a national concealed weapon permit."

"One last question, Chief. How do you know that those two men who attempted to abduct you and your friend were agents of the CLWUA?"

Rig answers, "Several days after the shooting, during questioning by the Maryland state police detective, he showed me a slip of paper he recovered from the dead man's wallet. The detective told me that he telephoned that number and it was the direct line to the Vice President for Security of the CLWUA. The detective wanted to know if I had any involvement with the CLWUA."

The timer sounds.

The Chair, Senator Porter, announces. "We have swayed too far from the purpose of this subcommittee. I urge my colleagues to return to our purpose, which is to establish the facts surrounding the death of Ensign Franklyn Ryan." Porter nods to U.S. Senator Reginald Ferndale and says, "Senator Ferndale has the floor."

Ferndale shifts some papers; then he asks Rig, "Chief Page, according to witness statements, you were walking along La Maddalena fleet landing. You stopped, stared at Ensign Ryan, and Ryan raised a pistol and shot you. You fell and landed on your back. Then Ensign Ryan walked closer to you and aimed his pistol at your head. Then Ensign Ryan was shot dead by a woman known only as Subject Two in the NIS reports. Is that your remembrance of the event?"

Rig answers, "Ensign Ryan had been declared a deserter several months before. So I was surprised when I saw him on fleet landing wearing rags for clothes and looking like a homeless vagrant. The last thing I remember seeing was Ryan lifting his pistol toward me. I awoke from a coma days later at the Naval Hospital in Naples."

"What was your relationship with the woman who shot Ensign Ryan?"

"Senator, that information is classified and is not within my authority to release."

"Statements from USS *Randal* crewmembers say that woman, Subject Two, and you shared an apartment. So you must have known her well, correct?"

"Senator, that information is classified and is not within my authority to release."

"Chief Page, did you and this woman of mystery conspire to kill Ensign Ryan."

"No."

"What did the two of you conspire to do?"

Captain Maston taps his index finger once, indicating that Rig is to get the answer from the captain.

Rig leans toward Captain Maston and receives instructions.

Rig responds to the senator, "The relationship between me and Subject Two is classified and not within my authority to release."

"This apartment you shared with Subject Two—who paid the rent?"

"I did."

"Not the CIA, then?"

Rig expresses befuddlement.

"Chief, you were on the island of La Maddalena when Oscar Reinhoffer was murdered, correct?"

Captain Maston taps his index finger twice.

Rig states, "Senator, I do not recall where I was on the day Oscar Reinhoffer was killed."

"Chief Page, I have evidence that you and the mystery woman, Subject Two, are undercover agents for the CIA and both of you were sent to La Maddalena to murder Oscar Reinhoffer. How do you respond to that?"

"Not true."

"Chief, is it true that Ensign Ryan, who was your immediate superior, discovered that you and Subject Two killed Oscar Reinhoffer, and you and Subject Two conspired to silence Ensign Ryan by murdering him. Correct?"

"No."

"Chief, do you know Weston Pyth?"

Rig shakes his head slightly as he attempts to remember; then he answers, "The name is familiar, but I can't . . ."

Senator Ferndale announces, "Weston Pyth, reporter for the *Long Beach Times*. Do you know him?"

"I know who he is but never met him?"

"Weston Pyth wrote scathing articles reporting violent actions that you and your father exercised against union members of the CLWUA. Have you read his articles?"

"I have read some. I don't know if I read all."

"Do you deny all that he wrote?"

"I say that Weston Pyth does not report. He opines and he misrepresents."

"Do not evade the answer!" Senator Ferndale demands in a loud voice."

Rig expresses amusement. Then he answers. "I do not know if I have read all that Weston Pyth wrote, and I do not remember all that I read. So I cannot answer yes or no. All that I can say for certain is that the Weston Pyth lied and misrepresented my actions and my father's actions."

Ferndale asks, "Chief, Do you know the current location of Weston Pyth?"

Rig shakes his head and answers, "No."

Senator Ferndale says loudly, "Weston Pyth disappeared last week, shortly after he had promised his readers a story that proves you are the rightwing mad bomber referred to in newspapers and police reports."

The timer sounds.

Senator Porter announces, "We are behind schedule in questioning Chief Page. High ranking naval officers are scheduled as witnesses for all day tomorrow. Chief Page is excused until such time he is summoned in writing to reappear. This subcommittee is recessed until 9:00 AM tomorrow."

Thirty minutes later, Chief Page and Captain Maston stand in the Capitol Building Visitor's Parking lot. Captain Maston tells Chief Page, "Senator Porter will ensure that you are not recalled."

Expressing amusement, Rig responds, "If I were in Porter's shoes, I would not recall me either."

Captain Matson asks, "Do you have any questions or concerns?"

Rig expresses concern. "Yes. My enemies list grows and now includes several U.S. Senators."

Chapter 76

Senator Porter's office in the Capitol Building is second only to the Senate Majority Leader's office in size and richly-appointed décor. The size of the office, the thick expensive carpet, and the wood-paneled walls speaks of his power and seniority in the Senate. The portraits of Presidents Woodrow Wilson, Franklin Roosevelt, Lyndon Johnson, and Jimmy Carter are the only president's portraits that adorn his walls. The presidential portraits along with numerous photographs of Senator Porter with President Johnson speak volumes regarding the senator's statist ideology.

Senator Porter sits behind his desk. Seated in a semicircle of six chairs facing Porter's desk are six members of the House of Representatives, all from California, including Representative Billy Thayer.

Senator Porter does what he does best—intimidating others. Porter expresses a friendly smile and says, "Representative Thayer is the sponsor in the House of the *Fair Profits Tax Act*. We need all of your votes to pass this legislation. It's time for the wealthy to pay their fair share. It's time for the affluent and elite to give back to those whom they victimize."

Each House member, except for Thayer, have expressed their vote is *NAY* on the *Fair Profits Tax Act*.

Senator Porter scans the faces of the five dissenting Congressmen. Then he focuses on the Representative from a district that lay just north of Los Angeles. "David, what are your objections?"

David responds, "The *Fair Profits Tax Act* will strangle economic growth. It will drive America into a depression. The larger corporations will move operations overseas. Millions of layoffs will result." Dave pauses for a moment; then he continues, "The *Fair Profits Tax Act* specifies corporate profits above a certain percentage to be confiscated by government and funneled into welfare and grant programs and infrastructure projects. Any member of Congress who votes for this Act will lose votes and will lose campaign funding from corporations and from corporate employees who are adversely affected by the Act."

"On the contrary," Senator Porter retorts. "All those profits will be redistributed to the common folks. Instead of profit sitting in bank accounts of the rich, those profits will be given to those who will spend it on products and services; which stimulates the economy. And you are wrong about the number of those in Congress supporting the Act. We only need five more votes in the House."

Another Representative advises, "When corporations move overseas, those profits will not be available for redistribution. The American economy will fall into a depression."

Senator Porter counters, "The Act calls for fines and imprisonment for directors and corporate officers who attempt to move their corporations overseas. The Act calls for nationalization of those corporations should those corporations attempt to move overseas."

The Representative states, "There are no government organizations whose purpose it is to manage commerce."

"You have, obviously, not read the Act in total," Senator Porter declares. "There are provisions to establish government agencies to manage commerce."

"The Act will destroy the economy, not make it prosper," declares another Representative.

The other Representatives nod their heads; indicating they agree that the Act will not work.

For a few moments, Senator Porter purses his lips and expresses contemplation of the Representatives' words. Porter knows that the legislation should it become law will collapse the economy. *That's the objective!*

Porter says, "All of you are sponsors of an addendum to the *Defense Appropriation Bill* for federal assistance to build a high-speed rail system from San Francisco to San Diego, passing through Los Angeles and Long Beach. The addendum also commits the federal government to subsidize rail operations up to a total of forty percent after the rail system is up and running. I understand that your rail bill is several votes short in both the House and Senate."

All six Representatives become attentive. They sense an offer is coming, but each considers they will not vote for the *Fair Profits Tax Act* in exchange for the senator's vote and support on their high-speed rail. In their minds, the *Fair Profits Tax Act* will destroy America's economy.

Senator Porter promises, "If all of you vote for the *Fair Profits Tax Act*, I can guarantee your high-speed rail addendum will pass both the House and the Senate."

One of the Representatives moans. Then he comments, "In the land of economic collapse that will result from the *Fair Profits Tax Act*, there will be no value and no purpose for building that high-speed rail system."

Three of the six Representatives nod and express agreement.

Senator Porter responds, "Gentlemen, fair distribution of the wealth does not cause a collapsed economy, it generates a growing economy. I find it disturbing that you do not understand that laissez faire capitalism creates masters and slaves; that is the reason FDR and his Democrat control Congress levied heavy regulation and taxes on commerce. As a result, America eventually prospered."

All Representatives know that FDR's actions did not recover the depression. They know that FDR's actions prolonged the depression, but the Representatives do not want to argue that point with such a powerful senator. Their expressions become blank.

"Gentleman, do I have your support for the *Fair Profits Tax Act*?"

All, except Representative Billy Thayer, provide either a verbal "no" or shake their heads.

Senator Porter says, "Billy, please wait in the outer office. I have something I want to discuss with these gentlemen."

Billy expresses surprised suspicion as he stands. Then he exits the room.

Porter advises, "When I first read your high-speed rail legislation, I noticed that provisions specify only companies whose employees are completely unionized and located in California and have experience with building railroads can bid for building tracks and facilities." Porter pauses for emphasis and glances at the faces of each Representative. Then he continues. "I hired an investigator to discover what companies would qualify. Turns out that only two California companies would qualify, and both those companies' corporate officers and union employees are large campaign contributors to each of you."

Each Representative exhibits nervousness. They fidget it their chairs.

Senator Porter continues. "Your legislation provides a recommended path for the railway line. My investigator discovered that during the year prior to your high-speed rail legislation being introduced options to purchase parcels of land along the proposed rail path were bought by *Continental Properties*, which is a real estate partnership with headquarters in the Bahamas. My investigator spent months breaking though the walls of a dozen dummy corporations and holding companies and had to spread around some money to Bahamian officials, but he finally discovered that *Continental Properties* is owned entirely by a partnership of you five gentleman."

All five Representatives are red-faced and express apprehensive embarrassment at being exposed as greedy, unethical political opportunists.

Senator Porter offers, "I can put that investigator's report in my safe and never allow it to be released to the press. Support the *Fair Profits Tax Act* in the House and that investigator's report will never see the light of day, and I will ensure that your high-speed rail legislation passes in the House and the Senate."

All five representatives express defeat.

Chapter 77

Five mercenaries are following and harassing Teri Page. Those five mercenaries are divided into three shifts: Two mercenaries on the day shift, two mercenaries on the swing shift, and one mercenary on the graveyard shift. Each shift reports to an operation center in a Long Beach hotel. Local Longjumeau Alliance cell members direct mercenaries from the operations center.

Harassment actions include delaying their targets from entering doorways, following them by a few feet in stores, threatening rape, groping the Page women in doorways and elevators, scratching and denting targets' cars, hanging dead dogs and dead cats in the doorways of targets' homes, calling targets several times each day with threatening phone calls.

Rick Kreske came on the graveyard shift at 2330—thirty minutes ago. For ten days now, he has sat in the radio-equipped vehicle one-quarter block away from Teri Page's Hollywood apartment building. Possession of the vehicle is passed along to the oncoming shift. Teri Page has never exited her apartment building during Rick's shift. His only activity being to respond to occasional communications checks with the operations center located in a Long Beach hotel meeting room.

Rick rests his head against the headrest. He relaxes his lean, hard-muscled, medium-height frame. He closes his eyes. He thinks back to the telephone call that he received in his trailer on the outskirts of Bakersfield, California. The caller stated he had read Rick's ad in an adventure magazine and wanted to know if Rick was available. The caller, who referred to himself as *Stanley*, made the offer: "Three-hundred dollars per day with night shift fifty-dollar bonus pay, plus expenses—to be paid weekly in cash. The job includes surveillance and face-to-face harassment of targeted individuals."

Following the caller's directions, Rick drove directly to the hotel in Long Beach. The man who had recruited Rick conducted a short interview, then assigned Rick to Teri Page.

While waiting in the operations center for issue of equipment and schedule, Rick crossed the paths of several mercenaries that he worked with in the past. All of them have military combat training. Some spent only a few years in the military, and some are retired from the military.

Two weeks after graduating from high school in 1968, Rick arrived at army boot camp. He anticipated six months of training, then a quick transport to Vietnam. Being a hardened athlete in high school, Rick easily passed army boot camp. After boot camp, he attended advanced infantryman school. After infantryman school, instead of being assigned to Vietnam, he was sent to an infantry battalion in Germany. Life was easy and safe. Several months after arriving in Germany, he met an attractive German woman who showed interest in him. She used sex to manipulate him into trading in American rationed items like American cigarettes, gasoline coupons, and American liquor available through the Army-Air Force Exchange stores. She trained him how to buy maximum rationed items from other soldiers. By the end of six months, Rick had accumulated over 100 soldier clients who would sell him their excess rations. Then he would sell his ill-gotten goods at his cost to his girlfriend. Eventually, he was caught, and the army punished him with a General Discharge.

After being released from the army, he applied to several national mercenary companies that provide security to overseas dignitaries and rich business men. The General Discharge discouraged employers from hiring him. He began advertising his skills in adventure magazines. Most of his contracts obligated him to watch and intimidate targets. He never knows the reason and seldom cares. He makes a living but not much more than that. He awaits the big contract that will bring him big bucks. Rick's story is common among those who advertise their services in adventure magazines.

A cracking noise causes Rick to open his eyes. He immediately sees the bullet hole in the windshield on the passenger side. Another bullet crashes through the windshield, closer to him, and slams into the passenger seat.

A two-man Guardians team comprised of one sniper and one spotter lie on the flat roof of a two-story apartment building two blocks from Rick's vehicle. Camouflaged in black clothing and black grease paint on their faces, they are confident that the target will not identify their position.

"He's jumping from the vehicle," the spotter announces. Then, a few moments later he announces, "Okay, he is clear of the vehicle."

The sniper picks up the radio detonator. He extends the antenna; then he uses his thumb to flip the lock-switch to the UNLOCK position.

"He's still clear," the spotter reports. "He's still running away."

The sniper presses the detonation button.

The mercenary's surveillance vehicle bursts into flame.

As he runs away, Rick glances over his shoulder and sees the vehicle on fire. He increases the pace of his running.

At three other locations in Los Angeles and Long Beach where the mercenary graveyard shift sits in a vehicle close to the homes of other families who own small businesses and refuse to unionize, the same events occur as did outside Teri Page's apartment building. During all three incidents, shots were fired into the windshield of the surveillance vehicle. The mercenary bolted from the vehicle. Then The Guardians sniper team destroyed the vehicle.

At the same time that Guardians operatives are blowing up cars in Southern California, a team of Guardian operatives penetrates the security perimeter on the grounds of the Potomac Maryland mansion of CLWUA National President, Gaylord Tarkingson. Guardians use two way radios to coordinate their attack. The radio is clipped to their belts, and a wire runs to an earphone and microphone sewn into the inside of their ski masks.

The Guardians operatives, clad in black colored clothes and wearing black ski masks, easily neutralize mansion security systems with a radio jamming device. Mansion security personnel are neutralized with knockout spray, followed by an injection that will keep them unconscious for at least three hours. Then the three Guardians who neutralized security personnel relocate to tactical locations inside the mansion and stand watch.

Four other Guardians move quickly and quietly toward Tarkingson's bedroom. As they enter the master bedroom, The Guardians operatives hear two people distinctly snoring. Then one operative moves to Mrs. Tarkingson's side of the large bed; another operative moves to Gaylord Tarkingson's side of the bed. Both operatives hold ends of a nine-inch strip of duct tape.

A third operative stands at the foot of the bed and points a large, suppressor-equipped automatic pistol at Mrs. Tarkingson.

The fourth operative stands at the light switch and verifies that all operatives are in place. Then he flips the light switch. The bedroom becomes brightly illuminated. The fourth operative steps to the foot of the bed and aims his suppressor-equipped automatic pistol at Gaylord Tarkingson.

Before the Tarkinsons can awake, operatives press the duct tape across the mouths of the Tarkinsons.

Gaylord is the first to awake.

The Guardian operative aiming his pistol at Gaylord warns, "Mr. Tarkingson, lie still and quiet."

Mrs. Tarkingson stirs awake.

The middle-aged, balding, and portly CLWUA national president lies still and quiet but does not express fear. Then he notices the gunman pointing a gun at his wife; now, he expresses fear.

Mrs. Tarkingson stirs awake. After taking in the scenario, her eyes go wide while expressing fear. The duct tape muffles her scream.

The operative who taped Gaylord's mouth orders, "Mr. Tarkingson, stand, put on your slippers, then put your hands behind your back."

Gaylord complies.

The operative clamps handcuffs on Gaylord's wrists.

Mrs. Tarkingson eyes follow her husband's movements. Several times, she glances fearfully at the gunman who points a gun at her husband.

The operative who taped Mrs. Tarkingson's mouth explains in a calm and courteous tone, "Mrs. Tarkingson, I will tape your hands behind your back, and I will tape your ankles together. You should be able to work yourself free within thirty minutes, or you can wait until your security men become conscious several hours from now."

Mrs. Tarkingson expresses relief as she understands these dangerous looking men will not harm her. Then she remembers her husband and casts a questioning expression toward Gaylord.

The operative explains as he tapes her wrists behind her. "We are taking your husband with us. He will not be harmed unless he resists."

After the four-man team and Tarkingson exit the bedroom, one of the Guardians operatives speaks into his radio, "Condition Bravo."

The roaring sound of an approaching helicopter fills the halls and rooms of the Tarkingson mansion.

Several hours later, U. S. Senator Clay Porter exits his colonial style house in an affluent neighborhood of Silver Spring, Maryland. As he walks along the paved walkway toward the driveway, he presses a button on a remote control device on his key ring that unlocks the doors on his 1977 black colored Cadillac Sedan Deville. He glances to the east and notes that the sun is only two-thirds above the horizon. The sound of a moving vehicle causes him to shift his attention to the street.

A dark-blue colored panel van slows to a stop, blocking the driveway.

Senator Porter stops walking toward his Cadillac. He stares

curiously at the van, wondering why the driver of the van chose that spot to stop.

Two darkly dressed figures, wearing ski masks and aiming large automatic pistols at Porter, appear from the side of the house and walk toward Porter.

Porter expresses fear and begins to raise his hands.

In a soft and calm voice, the taller gunman commands, "Do not raise your hands, Senator. Look at the van."

Porter, somewhat confused about the order not to raise his hands, quickly scans the driveway and the van. He looks over his shoulder and sees a neighbor walking her dog about half a block away.

The sound of the van's side-door sliding open causes Porter to look at the van. The interior of the windowless cargo area is exposed.

"Get in the van—quickly!" the tall gunman orders in a raised tone.

Senator Porter expresses fear of being killed. His knees begin to buckle. Before he falls, the two gunman run toward him and hold him up by the armpits. They drag Porter down the driveway; then toss him into the cargo area of the van.

The two gunmen enter the van through the side door. The tall one slides the door shut. Then the van moves slowly away.

Democrat Congressman Billy Thayer exits an exclusive, by application only with references apartment building in Suitland, Maryland where he shares an apartment with another congressman.

The short and fat doorman taps the rim of his uniform hat as he says, "Good morning, Congressman. Your car is already here."

Thayer glances at the curb and sees a black-colored stretch Lincoln Town Car. He expresses appreciation that his ride is on time.

The doorman opens the back door of the Town Car.

Thayer slides into the backseat on the passenger side.

The doorman closes the door.

The car moves away from the curb and enters traffic.

Thayer pays for the daily car service with money from the trust fund his grandfather passed down to him. When he was in negotiations with the car service company, he wanted the same driver every day at 8:00 AM. The car service, like all the car services he contacted, said they could not guarantee the same driver and same car every day but would do their best to cycle between the same four-to-five drivers and assigned cars. Occasionally a new driver might be assigned.

Congressman Thayer does not recognize the driver. He knows all the other drivers by their first names.

"Good Morning, Congressman," says the driver who wears black suit, black tie, and white shirt.

"Good morning, driver. What's your name?"

"Christopher."

"Well, Christopher, what is the traffic condition this morning?"

"There are a couple of accidents on Suitland Parkway. I will need to take an alternate route this morning . . . probably take an extra 20 minutes."

Congressman Thayer nods acceptance of the information. Then he unfolds a copy of the Washington Post newspaper and immediately becomes focused on an article regarding the *Fair Profits Tax Act* now being considered in Congress.

Chapter 78

Rig spent the night in Diane's townhouse. They were late in rising. Now, they sit at the kitchen table and sip coffee and eat toast. Diane wears her terrycloth robe. Rig wears t-shirt and jockey shorts. A portable television sits on the kitchen counter at low volume and tuned to one of those three-hour network morning shows.

Rig and Diane have their own section of the Washington Post newspaper, and each focuses on stories of interest. Rig reads the financial page and smiles at a report that gold reaches an all-time high of $200.00 per ounce. He expresses satisfaction that his broker knows what he is doing. The bad news is that gold is at an all-time high because the U.S. Dollar plunges to record low against many European currencies.

Diane reads the political page and tracks the progress of the *Fair Profits Tax Act* in the House of Representatives.

The mention of Senator Porter's name by the female newscaster on the television causes Rig to shift his attention from the newspaper to the television screen. He reaches the few feet to the television and increases the volume.

"... A woman walking her dog observed the abduction of United States Senator Clay Porter ..."

Diane shifts her attention from the newspaper page to the television screen.

"...around sunrise this morning. The witness states that two men with guns wearing black clothing and black ski masks forced the senator into a van. Then the van drove off slowly ..."

Rig and Diane's eyes shift from the television screen and lock on each other's eyes; they express astonishment. Then their eyes move back to the television screen.

"... what appears to be a related abduction, CLWUA President, Gaylord Tarkingson, was abducted from his bedroom about 3:30 AM this morning. Mrs. Tarkingson reported to police that a group of men wearing dark clothing and black colored ski masks and carrying automatic pistols broke into their home and bound and

gagged her husband; then they put him aboard a helicopter.

"Police have no leads as to the identity of those who adducted Senator Porter and CLWUA President Tarkingson, and no terrorist group has come forward and claimed responsibility for the abductions.

"In other news ..."

Rig lowers the volume on the television. "Wow!"

Diane shakes her head slightly and expresses bewilderment. "Who could do such a thing and for what purpose?"

Rig says, "I wonder if there is a connection between Tarkingson and Porter?"

Diane shrugs. Then she directs her eyes on the newspaper, pretending to read but thoughts race through her mind regarding the abduction of two key members of The Longjumeau Alliance.

Several minutes later, the phone rings. Diane says, "I will take it in the den."

Rig nods and exhibits disinterest while his eyes are staring at the newspaper.

"Hello," Diane says into the telephone handset.

"Have you heard about Senator Porter and Gaylord Tarkingson?"

Diane recognizes the voice of Edwin Kendley. "Yes," she responds in a low even tone.

"Are you alone?"

"In the den, yes."

Kendley is silent for a few moments while he considers who else would be in Diane's townhouse this time of the morning. A couple of different men come to mind, but he knows better than to ask her.

"Why did you call?" Diane inquires.

"I believe Billy Thayer has been abducted also."

Diane's heart skips a beat at the thought of her close friend being in danger. "What do you know?"

"The doorman at Billy's apartment building called the police and reported that ten minutes after Billy was picked up by his car service, another car arrived, and the driver explained to the doorman that he was late because of a fender bender at a stop light. The police called Billy's office and talked with Billy's chief of staff who told the police that Billy was late for a meeting. Billy's chief of staff called me as soon as he heard the news about Porter and Tarkingson."

Diane says, "I'll be on my guard. Plus, I have the best bodyguard in D.C. sitting in my kitchen."

"I want all The Alliance Directors in a safe location. My estate is well protected. We will stay there until we know it's safe to leave. I will send my plane for you. Be at my private hanger at National by 2:00 PM. You will not be the only passenger."

"How long should I anticipate staying at your estate?"

"I don't know—might be weeks. Will that be a problem?"

"No, I can go and come as I please at work. They just need to know how to contact me, and I need access to a fax machine."

"No problem, plenty of fax machines at my estate."

"Okay," Diane says in a soft and concerned tone. "Will you have a car waiting for me when I arrive at the airport in Connecticut?"

"Yes."

Diane returns to the kitchen and sits down across the table from Rig.

Rig does not lift his eyes off the newspaper.

Diane announces, "I must go away for a while."

Rig looks up from the paper and locks onto Diane's eyes. "How long?"

"I don't know. Will you look after Striper? Same routine for feeding and cleaning her litter box."

"Sure, where ya going?"

"California. My father is ill."

He knows Diane is lying. ONI has a tap on Diane's phone. When he checks in with his ONI superiors later today, he will be advised as to the content of the phone call that results in Diane leaving town.

In Diane's bedroom, Rig slips into blue jeans, light-weight summer shirt, and sneakers; Diane packs enough clothes for several weeks into a suitcase.

Rig asks, "Will I be able to contact you at your parents' house?"

"Uh . . . no. I will probably check into a hotel." Diane keeps her eyes on her packing, so her eyes do not reveal she is lying. "When I am settled, I will call you at your apartment. If you do not answer, I will leave a message on the answering machine."

Rig asks, "Can I take you to the airport?"

"No. I called a taxi."

Chapter 79

One hour later, Rig drives away from Diane's townhouse in his ONI issue Jeep Cherokee. He glances in the rearview mirror and sees his constant tail following. Recently, those private detectives that follow him drive a sedan with a shortwave radio antenna mounted on the rear bumper, just like the one he has mounted on the rear bumper of his Jeep. Rig reasons correctly that where he spent the night has already been reported to the private detective's client.

Three blocks from Diane's townhouse, Rig feels the pager on his belt vibrate. He drives into a corner gas station and stops next to the phone booth. From the glove box, Rig retrieves a paperback-book-size electronic device. As he exits his Jeep, he observes his tail parked at the curb fifty feet away. Rig waves at the tail; the tail nods and grins.

The tail places the audio surveillance device on the dashboard and points the parabolic antenna toward the phone booth.

Inside the phone booth, Rig places the audio surveillance jamming device on the metal shelf beneath the phone. He flips the switch to the on position. The device radiates a humming noise.

Rig glances at the number on the pager display. He recognizes Captain Watson's direct number at ONI headquarters. He dials the number.

"Captain Watson."

"You paged me."

"Where are you?"

"In a Georgetown phone booth."

Brad glances at his watch. "Georgetown, this time of day?"

Rig does not respond.

"Are you in uniform?" Brad inquires.

"No, but I have my Summer Khaki uniform in the Jeep."

"Is your tail following?"

"Yes. I have the jammer on."

"We need to meet right away," Brad states with urgency in his tone.

"Where?"

Brad cannot risk Rig's cover by having Rig come to Suitland ONI Headquarters, and the Cheltenham ONI building is too far away from Rig.

"Where were you going?"

"To work at COMNAVTELCOM."

A pause falls over the conversation. After thirty seconds of silence, Captain Watson asks, "Can your tail follow you into the COMNAVTELCOM compound?"

"Not any more. Base police banned them months ago."

Brad orders, "Go to the COMNAVTELCOM parking lot. Wait for Commander Macfurson. She will brief you and give you orders."

Thirty minutes later, Rig parks his Jeep in the farthest parking row away from the COMNAVTELCOM building. Rig glances at his watch. He calculates that the drive from Suitland this time of day will take one hour. He calculates Commander Sally Macfurson will not arrive at his location for thirty or forty minutes.

He reaches for his canvas gym bag on the floor behind the front passenger seat. He pulls a paperback copy of *YOUR ERRONEOUS ZONES*, by Dr. Wayne W. Dyer. Ten minutes later, he has finished chapter four—where Dr. Dyer, a renowned self-improvement guru, informs on the negatives of dwelling in the past.

Halfway through chapter six of *YOUR ERRONEOUS ZONES*, Commander Sally Macfurson knocks on the front passenger side window.

Rig operates the electric door-lock switch to the open position.

Sally wears civilian blouse and skirt. Her auburn hair hangs below her shoulders, which always enhances her attractive appeal.

In the past when they have met out-of-uniform, they always hugged and kissed. This time, however, Rig senses formality and he waits for Sally to make the first move.

"ONI has obtained proof that Diane Love is passing classified information regarding Panama Canal defenses to her Soviet contact."

Rig expresses surprise, "How did she get access to that information without a top secret security clearance?"

"I checked with the FBI. She has a satisfactory completed BI.

A look of concern crosses Rig's face. "How the hell did she get that?! With her having a top secret clearance, she has a better chance of discovering what I am!"

"That's moot, now," Sally informs. "She's about to find out exactly who you are, because you are ordered to deliver Diane Love to CIA. They want to turn her—make her a double agent." Sally retrieves a yellow colored envelope from her purse and hands it to Rig. "All the details on the route, contacts, code words, and delivery to CIA are in the envelope. Memorize it; then destroy it."

"Diane left town. She said she would be gone for several weeks."

"Yes, we know. She fled to the protection of Edwin Kendley's estate in Connecticut. We monitored the call she received from him this morning. She is not the only one. Kendley has ordered many other high-level members of The Longjumeau Alliance to his estate for protection, which is not surprising considering the events of the past twenty-four hours in Southern California and here in the D.C. area."

Rig expresses concerned curiosity and inquires, "What happened in Southern California?"

"We don't have all the details yet, but it appears that some armed mercenaries hired by The Longjumeau Alliance were following and harassing families who own small none-union businesses, your family included. Early this morning about midnight, Pacific Time, four of those mercenaries were parked at separate locations near the homes of some who own non-union businesses. Shots were fired at the mercenary's vehicles, chasing the mercenaries from their vehicles. Then their vehicles exploded. One was near your sister Teri's apartment in Hollywood. She is okay, not affected."

"Mercenaries!?" Rig responds in an astonished tone.

Sally explains, "Appears that the CLWUA realized that using their own union members was ineffective against the rightwing mad bomber. So the CLWUA asked The Longjumeau Alliance for help. Before the bombing of those vehicles this morning, CLWUA thought it was you stalking and attacking their members; but obviously there is more than one person fighting back against the CLWUA. They must know by now that you were in D.C. last night. CLWUA and national intelligence agencies are now dismissing the idea that you are that rightwing mad bomber."

Rig comments, "I know that the CLWUA is still stalking my family. They are following me, but they know better than to harass me."

"Are you still carrying weapons?"

"Yes."

Sally quickly scans Rig's clothing; she wonders where he hides his pistol and knives.

Rig notices Sally's scan but does not comment on it. He returns to the subject of their meeting. "Diane will not be back in D.C. for several weeks or maybe for longer than that. What do you want me to do?"

Sally orders with authority, "Go to Connecticut and get her."

"That might be difficult to do solo. I have read the report on that estate's security."

Sally nods and expresses understanding. "Go up there and evaluate what needs to done. We will provide additional resources, if need be."

"Okay, will do."

Sally questions, "You know about Senator Porter, Congressman Thayer, and CLWUA President Gaylord Tarkingson being abducted?"

"I knew about Tarkingson and Senator Porter—heard about them on the news this morning—didn't know about Billy Thayer?"

Sally inquires, "Do you have any idea on who is abducting them?"

"No."

Sally informs, "There is a journalist who writes socialist advocacy articles for the *Washington Post*. He has not been heard from for a week, same with that communist reporter for the *Long Beach Times*. Both of them are members of The Longjumeau Alliance. ONI, DIA, and CIA believe there is a large, well-funded organization behind these abductions of Longjumeau Alliance members. We are anticipating that more members of Congress who are Longjumeau Alliance members will be abducted."

Rig comments, "Appears that The Longjumeau Alliance might not be as secret as Diane and her friends think it is."

Sally expresses contemplation for a few moments; then she says, "Leave for Connecticut no later than this evening. Drive your Jeep. Use the radio in the Jeep to give us daily reports. You have the radio frequencies memorized, right?"

"Yes. I have them memorized."

Sally opens the door and exits the vehicle. She looks back into the vehicle with her eyes locked on Rig's eyes. She advocates, "Stay safe sailor. Maintaining your cover is your most important consideration. Only Diane Love is to know what you are."

Rig advises, "I will need cover with my COMNAVTELCOM superiors for being out of town for several days."

"I will contact Captain Blakely and ask her to cover for you."

He nods and exhibits understanding.

Sally shuts the door and walks toward her own vehicle.

Chapter 80

Five minutes later, Rig exits the Jeep. He opens the tailgate and retrieves the small suitcase that contains his Summer Khaki uniform. Then he enters the COMNAVTELCOM Headquarters building.

Fifteen minutes later, he exits the head where he changed into uniform. As he twists the doorknob on his office door, he hears someone call his name from behind. He turns and faces Lieutenant Angela Ramos, who was recently assigned as Testing Division Officer and is now his direct supervisor. His only contact with her prior to becoming his division officer was with the Inspector General Team where she serves as I.G. Team Administrative and Equal Opportunity inspector.

"We will talk in your office, Chief." The lieutenant's tone reflects impatience.

They stand three feet apart in front of Rig's desk.

"It's nearly noon, Chief. Where have you been?"

Rig answers calmly with a soft tone, "I was engaged in actions to save America from communism."

In a dismissive tone, Lieutenant Ramos responds, "We're all doing that, Chief."

Rig chuckles; then says, "Well, I was doing something extra special."

"What specifically have you been doing all morning?"

"Tracking an American who is a Soviet spy."

Ramos rolls her eyes; then says, "Uh huh. You missed the division meeting."

"Did I miss anything affecting me?"

"Yes, CNO is demanding to know why quality assurance testing on the CUDIXS upgrade is taking so long."

"Lieutenant, as I told you several days ago, it's not the testing that is taking so long; it's the program fixes."

Lieutenant Ramos appears confused; then she challenges, "But the test plan said testing would take thirty days. It's been two months."

He explains, "The test plan specifies thirty test-days, not thirty calendar days. QA testing was halted on test-day two because of a system lockup. Anytime that happens, QA testing is halted, and the firmware and software is sent back to the Engineering Division to be fixed. When Engineering Division delivers the firmware and software fixes to our division, we start all over again on test-day one."

"Well, we need to move it along!" Ramos says with determination.

"Move what along, ma'am?"

"QA testing on CUDIXS."

"Can't ma'am, not until Engineering Division delivers fixes."

"Chief, the admiral is becoming impatient. He has ordered all divisions to speed it up."

"Does the admiral believe his staff is purposely slowing down the process?"

"We must follow his orders to speed it up." Her tone lacks confidence.

"Ma'am, Engineering Division has the ball. Nothing can be done until they deliver the fixes."

"Come on, Chief. There must be something we can do."

Rig shakes his head and expresses a negative. "The admiral could only have been referring to the Engineering Division when he said *speed it up*. Testing Division is ready to continue as soon as the fixes are delivered from Engineering."

"I can't accept that, Chief. We must do something to move forward."

"Ma'am, last week's Project Manager Status Report on this CUDIXS upgrade stated that Engineer Division is still investigating, and they are still considering hiring a consultant to assist."

"That doesn't stop us from making some recommendations to the Engineering Division."

"That is not within the scope or qualification of our division, Ma'am. We have no programmers or firmware engineers in our division. We cited the function specification that failed during testing. It is up to engineering to design the program to perform the function properly."

"Chief, you are known for your naval communications technical expertise. Surely you must have some ideas how to fix programming errors."

"No, Ma'am. I do not."

Ramos counters, "I need to send a report to the chief of staff by tomorrow that specifies what Testing Division is doing to *move forward* with this CUDIXS upgrade."

"I have no recommendations, ma'am."

Ramos makes a judgment on Rig's behavior: "Chief, your personal life is interfering with your professional life. All these encounters with the police, family problems in California, and threats on your life are distracting you. The pressure of appearing before a Senate subcommittee put too much of a strain on you. That strain is interfering with your thinking processes. You need to find a way to remove all this stress on your life."

Rig cannot suppress an amusing grin.

Believing she is being mocked, Lieutenant Ramos orders in a demanding tone, "I want your recommendations on how to *move forward* on the CUDIXS testing on my desk before you depart today." She turns on her toes, and departs Rig's office.

Rig shakes his head. There is no doubt in his mind that this is one of those situations that for those who understand, no explanation is needed; for those who do not understand, no explanation is possible.

Several minutes pass before Rig clears Lieutenant Ramos's nonsensical reasoning from his brain. Knowing that there is no *move forward* until Engineering Division delivers fixes, he dismisses Ramos's order to deliver *move forward* recommendations by this afternoon.

His mind returns to his mission to abduct Diane Love from the Kendley Estate. He considers that The Guardians might have some intelligence on the Kendley Estate. Rig picks up the telephone handset and dials the number from memory.

"Hello," Denton Phillips says into the phone.

Rig states, "We must meet today."

"My time is committed until about 9:30 tonight. I will be near the Capitol Building then. How about we meet at 10:00 PM at that same park bench near the Capitol Building where we met before? Oh, and lose your tail."

"I'll be there," Rig states; then he hangs up the phone.

Chapter 81

As the crow flies, the Capitol Building is located six miles to the southeast of the COMNAVTELCOM building. During this time of evening, Rig estimates driving time to be forty minutes.

At 9:00 PM, Rig exits his office. As he passes the closed door of Lieutenant Ramos's Office, he recollects her demanding attitude and tone when she stormed into his office four hours earlier and asked for his recommendations on moving forward with CUDIXS testing. He handed her a short memo that stated his testing team will move forward with testing when he receives the fixed software and firmware from the Engineering Department. She crumpled the memo, turned, and stormed out of his office. He expects that sometime in the near future he will be called into a senior officer's office and be counseled on his inadequate and inappropriate handling of the situation.

Before starting his Jeep, he retrieves a holstered, nine-millimeter Beretta automatic pistol from the glove box. The ankle holster includes a pocket that holds a suppressor. He rolls up the cuffs of his khaki trousers and straps the ankle holster to the outside of his right ankle. Then he unrolls his trouser leg to cover the weapon.

After exiting the COMNAVTELCOM compound, he turns right and maneuvers the traffic circle that will lead him southwest on Nebraska Avenue toward Chain Bridge, which is the route he normally takes when going home to his apartment in Arlington. A glance into the rearview mirror reveals that Rig's tail is three cars back in the same center lane.

Although Rig departed work early, Rig's tail anticipates that Rig will make the normal lane shifts and turns to take him to the Chain Bridge.

Rig must lose his tail. He cannot risk his tail observing the meeting with Denton Phillips. Rig's normal route is to turn left at Arizona Avenue; so his tail will be expecting Rig to make a left turn, regardless of which lane he is currently in.

Rig's tail maneuvers to the left lane, assuming that Rig will do the same thing.

Rig quickly shifts into the right lane.

The tail is trapped to make the left turn because of the full lane of bumper-to-bumper cars on his right.

Rig moves rapidly along a residential street in a stream of a dozen other cars. When he is certain that he lost his tail, he pulls to the curb, exits the vehicle, steps to the rear of the Jeep, and opens the tailgate. He opens the false cargo area floor and retrieves a beacon transmitter detection device. He extends the handle; then runs the dish end of detector around the bumpers and underneath the Jeep. The detector radiates a sharp beeping tone underneath the Jeep just below the front passenger seat. He removes the beacon transmitter, disables it, and lays it on the curb. Then he scans the Jeep's underside and bumpers again. Confident that he has removed all beacon transmitters, he stows the detector. He climbs back into the Jeep and drives into an open spot in the traffic flow.

Forty minutes later, Rig brings the Jeep to a stop in the Senate Park parking lot which is several blocks away from the rendezvous location with Denton. No problem with parking spaces after working hours. He exits the Jeep and feels the warm, humid air of a typical D.C. summer evening.

Rig crosses Constitution Avenue NE; then enters the north side of the Capitol complex. The winding pathways are well-illuminated by overhead lights. The areas with grass and trees are not illuminated and looking toward the trees results in viewing only undefined shadowed images.

He walks eastward toward First Street NE. The rendezvous bench is located near the intersection of Constitution Avenue NE and First Street NE. The Capitol Building is now behind him and the Supreme Court building can be seen through the trees before him. He observes few people walking the pathways of the Capitol complex.

Several minutes later, he finds the concrete bench. He sits and faces the front of the Capitol Building. He glances at the illuminated face of his watch—9:55 PM.

While he waits for Denton, Rig surveys the surrounding area. Few people walk the path that leads to and from the Capitol Building. Floodlights illuminate the front of the Capitol Building. He contemplates how the American public would react if they knew seventy-two members of the House of Representatives and eleven members of the Senate belong to a secret organization that plots to transform America into a single-party, communist state.

Approaching footsteps cause Rig to look to his right. A tall man wearing a summer-weight gray colored suit walks toward the bench where Rig sits. Rig recognizes Denton Phillips.

Denton sits on the bench to Rig's right.

They shake hands.

Denton asks, "What's on your mind, Rig?"

"ONI has ordered me to abduct Diane Love and deliver her to a CIA safe house."

"For what purpose?"

"They plan to turn her—make her a double agent."

"I see," Denton responds. "And you require some resources to break into the Kendley Estate and whisk her away."

Rig flinches and exhibits surprise. "You're tracking her?!"

"We are tracking all senior members of The Longjumeau Alliance. Diane Love arrived at the Kendley Estate about 4:00 PM. We anticipate there will be more than twenty of them at the Kendley Estate by tomorrow evening."

Rig falls silent and considers all the events of the past twenty-four hours.

Denton casts a knowing smile as he watches Rig figure it out.

Rig's assessment takes less than a minute; then he concludes aloud, "The Guardians attacked those mercenaries following my sister and others, and The Guardians kidnapped Porter, Thayer, and Tarkingson, right?"

"Yes."

"Forcing senior members of The Longjumeau Alliance to demand or accept protection at the most protected location they know."

"Yes, Rig. You got it right."

Rig searches for a logical reason for The Guardians to force all the senior members of The Longjumeau Alliance into one location. He asks, "What's The Guardians' plan?"

Denton explains, "We are going to relocate all of them to a re-education center. They will spend two weeks learning about the slavery and tyranny of living in communist nations. We will educate them to the fact that tens of millions of people have been slaughtered by communist regimes in the name of bettering mankind through totalitarianism.

"They will be under constant threat of harm, like all citizens of communist countries. We will make them believe that they will be our hostages forever. Then, when they realize the brutal consequences of communism, we will release them to go back to their lives and undo the damage they have done."

Rig expresses doubt; he shakes his head slightly. After a few moments of thought, he stares into Denton's eyes and states, "I don't think that will work. The leftwing elite already know about the brutality of living under communist tyranny."

Denton casts a skeptical expression at Rig and says, "Rig, this is not your area of expertise. This plan has been devised by political experts."

Rig retorts, "But, obviously, not by anyone who spends a lot of time around leftwing elitists."

Suddenly, two men—each wearing dark hats and long-sleeved dark shirts—step into Rig's and Denton's threat zone and stop; one stops 100 feet to Rig's right and the other tops 100 feet to Rig's left. Rig makes a movement toward his weapon.

"Hold it, Rig." Denton places his hand on Rig's right forearm. "They're my security team and there is another one in the trees behind us."

Rig brings his right hand back to his lap; then he continues his explanation. "These lefty elitists are an educated group. They know history, although they often ignore it and misrepresent it."

Denton challenges, "Rig, what you say does not make sense. If they know the brutality of totalitarian communist countries, why would they want American to become one?"

Rig grins. "They believe that the members of the Soviet Communist Party are ignorant thugs that do not have a clue as how to establish a collective utopia. American lefty elitists believe they have the smarts and compassion to establish a kinder and gentler communist state with a benevolent totalitarian government that does only good for the people."

Denton comments, "That's neither logical nor realistic. No communist state in history was established with the cooperation and support of the people. The people are forced into compliance through intimidation, violence, and threats on their lives. Don't those lefty elites understand that?"

Rig answers, "Yes, they understand that. But they believe they are the educated, enlightened, and compassionate elite who know how to establish and maintain a communist utopia. They sincerely believe that because they are in charge and announce benevolent intentions Americans will flock to them for comfort and safety."

Denton shakes his head and concludes, "More illogical thinking. Communism is against human nature and that's why it has failed every time it was attempted."

Rig advises, "Diane Love and her crowd believe that their methods will succeed."

Denton spends a few moments contemplating Rig's words; then he inquires, "Where did you learn all this?"

"I often attend parties as Diane Love's companion, and Diane hosts dinners and parties at her townhouse. These are parties where university educators, members of Congress, and senior members of Jimmy Carter's Administration are in attendance. Most of them are members of The Longjumeau Alliance. I have been listening to these people for nine months. They continuously talk about these things."

"They are not cautious in your presence?"

"They do not see me as a political threat. To them, I am just an enlisted man with hero status. When they attempt to include me in their conversations, I tell them that I am not politically aware and that I am not permitted to talk politics."

Denton opines, "Recent events may have changed their minds. They must know that you are antiunion."

Rig responds, "I am not antiunion. I am anti CLWUA."

"I think you draw a line that escapes others. I bet in their minds you are antiunion."

Rig advises, "Leftwing elitists are also antiunion, they just lie about their support in order to get the union vote. American communists currently use union power to undermine capitalism. Unions, as they currently exist in America, would be adversaries to the communist state. Look around the world at communist states. Unions, if they exist, are powerless and serve only to enforce government labor policy."

Rig's explanation reverses Denton's opinion of Rig's political savvy.

One of Denton's security men talks into his hand.

Denton glances at his watch. Then, he says, "Rig, you have placed doubt in my mind that our reeducation plan will work. Do you have ideas on how to reform these members of The Longjumeau Alliance?"

"Yes."

"I will schedule another meeting, probably at the Watergate."

Rig advises, "Denton, I have been ordered to go to Connecticut and abduct Diane Love."

"That can wait a few days, can't it?"

Rig expresses doubt. "I don't know."

Denton informs, "The Guardians have plans to continue abducting Longjumeau Alliance members. So there will be no one leaving Kendley's safe haven anytime soon."

Rig nods; then advises, "Okay, but I will need to be on my way in a few days."

Denton stands. Then Rig stands.

Denton asks, "In what direction are you parked?"

Rig points to his left.

411

"Okay, I will depart in the opposite direction." Denton raises his right hand to his mouth and says, "Corner of Constitution and First."

Rig observes Denton's security men walking toward the corner of Constitution and First. He also hears someone moving around in the trees behind him.

Denton asks, "What is the best way to contact you?"

Rig pulls a card from his wallet and hands it to Denton. "My pager number is on this card."

"Tomorrow then," Denton declares. He turns and walks away.

Rig turns and scans the illuminated pathway that he will walk to exit the Capitol complex. The pathway is vacant of people for three-hundred feet; then the path curves to the right; view beyond that curve is blocked by trees.

Walking briskly, Rig quickly covers the first two-hundred feet. Then danger signals alert his senses. He does not see or hear a threat, but he feels fluttering changes in air pressure, and he sniffs a familiar odor that he cannot classify.

He jumps off the walkway and finds protection behind a tree. He pulls his Beretta automatic pistol; then he screws on the suppressor. The fluttering air pressure signals to Rig that large objects, most likely humans, are moving quickly around him. The odor that Rig detected still lingers but is now fading.

Rig steps from behind the tree but remains in the grassy area. He points his weapon toward the ground while he surveys the area. He sees no one.

For a few moments, Rig stares at the front of the Capitol Building. He concludes that the communists who were elected into powerful positions in that building are responsible for the dangerous situation in which he now finds himself. Then he curses the unaware, careless electorate who blindly vote collectivists into power.

A shadow shifts between some trees across the walkway from Rig's position. He raises his pistol, takes rapid aim on a tree trunk close to the shadow movement, and fires a round. The purposeful firing at the tree trunk was to let everyone know he is armed. He commits to not shooting any person who he cannot definitely identify as a threat.

Rig steps back inside the tree line and walks furtively westward. Suddenly, the odor is back. Rig does a slow 180 degree arc sweep with his pistol. He now faces eastward. The odor appears to come from the direction he now faces. He fires a round into a tree trunk, purposely hitting the edge of the trunk to create flying wood chips.

Rig reasons: *They are not here to kill me. They could have done that. They are here to capture me. But why don't they just shout out they have me covered and order me to toss my weapon. Might be that they are waiting to get a better position on me before shouting orders for me to halt.*

Rig about faces again and now faces the direction where his Jeep is parked. He jumps into a full-pace run. He hears at least three separate people running behind him. When he reaches Constitution Avenue NE, he slows his pace as he weaves between moving cars. The sound of screeching brakes and minor collisions does not cause him to stop. He still carries his weapon in his right hand.

When he is fifty feet from his Jeep, he reaches into his left trouser pocket and retrieves the car key. He no longer hears running footsteps behind him.

At the driver's door, Rig enters the security code into the keypad. After unlocking and opening the Jeep door, Rig rapidly scans the direction from which he came. No one follows. He speculates that his pursuers did not cross Constitution Avenue.

Several minutes later, Rig is driving south on the interstate highway with the ONI Building at Cheltenham as his destination. Rig analyzes the vehicle traffic around him and confirms that he is not being followed. He reasons, *I must have had two tails when I left COMNAVTELCOM. Who are they, and what was their objective at the Capitol, and why are they not following me now? And that odor, I know I have experienced it before—but where?*

A sign advertising a cheap hotel at the next exit presents his opportunity for remaining out of sight during the night. Rig changes his mind about spending the night at Cheltenham. He concludes that the forces against him probably have surveillance teams watching the front and back gates of the Cheltenham navy station.

Inside his Jeep in the motel parking lot, Rig changes into his civilian clothes. At the front desk of the Blair Motel, Rig asks for a room that faces away from the road. He tells the clerk a rear room for quiet, but it is really for hiding his Jeep from view of the road. He pays $22 in advance for one night. He also purchases a small travel kit from the desk clerk that includes small sized toothbrush, toothpaste, shaving cream, and razor.

In his motel room, Rig washes his socks in the bathroom sink; then he hangs the socks over a towel rack. He undresses down to his navy issue boxer shorts and climbs under the covers of the uncomfortable bed. He lies on his back in the dark with two pillows under his head. He considers his next course of action. Staying away from his Arlington apartment is a given. All the weapons and gear he needs to abduct Diane Love away from the Kendley Estate are in the Jeep, hidden under the floorboard of the cargo area.

He has disobeyed Sally Macfurson's order to depart for Connecticut today. He considers calling her and telling her that he is delayed for a few days. Then he decides against that because he cannot risk her speculating as to why he disobeyed her orders.

Sleep does not come easy to him this night. All that can go wrong with him penetrating the Kendley Estate stirs his mind. Wondering who followed him at the Capitol complex nags his thoughts, especially that odor that is familiar, but he cannot place.

After an hour of lying in bed, he finally drifts off to sleep.

Chapter 82

When he opens his eyes at 6:15 the next morning, Rig decides to get up, shave, shower, and dress; then wait for Denton's call. After taking a shower and with a towel still wrapped around his waist, Rig orders breakfast from the diner across the street. The advertisement card promised ten percent discount to Blair Motel residents.

Twenty minutes later, Rig is dressed, and he is watching the beginning of the local morning T.V. news when the diner delivery boy knocks at the door. He gives the delivery boy a tip equal to half the bill. Rig spreads out his breakfast on the small desktop. Then he eats while concentrating on the morning news.

A news report regarding Congressman Billy Thayer grabs Rig's attention. *"Congressman Thayer's abduction has been confirmed by the Capitol Police, the Washington D.C. Police, and by the Congressman's chief of staff.*

"What appears to be a related story, two nights ago in Congressman Thayer's Southern California district, three vehicles belonging to a security company hired by the CLWUA were fired upon and were exploded. Strong ties exist between Congressman Thayer and the CLWUA.

"Law enforcement agencies are investigating a possible connection between the abductions of Congressman Thayer, Senator Porter, and CLWUA President Gaylord Tarkingson. A strong affiliation between the three men is a matter of record.

"In other news, last night at approximately 10:30, four minor car crashes occurred on Constitution Avenue NE next to the Capitol Building. Motorists reported to the D.C. police that the crashes were caused by a navy chief petty officer carrying a silencer-equipped automatic pistol running across Constitution Avenue, dodging heavy traffic, from the direction of the Capitol Complex. Police continue to investigate.

"On the international front, Panama Canal Treaty negotiations continue to progress. State department officials report that—"

A series of beeps come from Rig's pager. He pulls the pager

from the snap-lock holder on his belt; then he stares at the number that he does not recognize. He turns his attention to the phone on the nightstand. After reading the instructions for making outside calls, he decides to return the call from the payphone in the motel lobby. He glances at his half-eaten egg sandwich and still nearly full cup of coffee and concludes both will be cold by the time he comes back. So he finishes his breakfast before departing the room for the lobby.

As Rig crosses the motel lobby, he nods toward the middle-aged woman behind the desk. The woman responds with a cheerful, "Good morning, sir!"

Rig enters the telephone booth, closes the door behind him, and dials the number on his pager screen.

"Hello," a voice answers that Rig does not recognize."

"You paged me."

"Hold on a minute."

A full minute passes before Denton Phillips's voice asks over the telephone, "Was that you they were talking about on the news— on Constitution Avenue last night?"

"Yes," Rig responds.

"Where are you?"

"At a motel in Southern Maryland."

Denton advises, "I want to meet with you this afternoon and bring that political strategist I told you about."

"Okay," Rig agrees. "But I think we should meet here. I can't risk going anywhere that I have been in the past."

"Give me directions to the motel."

Rig provides the directions; then he requests, "I need five-hundred dollars. I can't go back to my apartment to get it. Can you bring it with you?"

"Yes, I will bring it. We will be there at two o'clock."

Chapter 83

At 2:05 PM, Denton and a man introduced to Rig as Patrick sit in Rig's motel room. Since Denton didn't state Patrick's last name, Rig knows he should not ask. Patrick and Denton wear white shirts and ties. Denton appears trim and fit as normal. Patrick stands as tall as Rig but carries thirty pounds of fat around his middle.

Denton gives Rig an envelope containing five-hundred dollars and informs, "The expense money you requested."

"Thanks." Rig places the envelope on the bed.

"Denton and Patrick sit in the only two chairs in the room. Rig sits on the end of the bed. Denton starts the conversation. "Rig, I talked with Patrick about what you said last night regarding changing the minds of these leaders in the Longjumeau Alliance. Patrick has some questions for you."

Rig shifts his attention to Patrick.

Patrick asks, "Are you familiar with the Congressional legislation known as the *Fair Profits Tax Act*?"

Rig responds, "Yes, I have read the details in *The Washington Post*, and I have listened to Diane Love and her comrades in the Longjumeau Alliance praise the legislation."

"What is it that they like so much about that legislation?"

"Large redistribution of income."

"Don't they realize America's economy will be destroyed?"

"Yes, that's their goal. They will blame capitalism as the cause of economic destruction, which the American public will believe. Then, from the ashes, Diane and her comrades will build a communist country."

Patrick expresses bewilderment as he challenges, "They talk about that in front of you—a military man sworn to defend the country against all enemies, foreign and domestic?"

Rig nods. "Yes, but they do not talk in specifics. They talk philosophically about the coming capitalist collapse. They do not use terms like communism or socialism. They use words like *progress* and *forward* and *shared sacrifice* . . . words like *equality* and *fair* and *evil rich*. And they call themselves *progressives* and *liberals*."

"But the American public would never allow it," Patrick counters.

Rig shakes his head as he explains, "Diane and her comrades believe otherwise. They think that the American leftwing elite can successfully deceive the American public into believing the economic collapse was caused by capitalism and not caused by the *Fair Profits Tax Act*."

"They said that in front of you?" Denton questions and exhibits doubt.

"No. I read that in their thirty-year plan."

Patrick shakes his head and expresses doubt while stating, "That would take a lot of deep and lengthy deception. How would they spread their anti-capitalism deception?"

"Through the American news media—I mean, the news media is already doing that, right? All the T.V. network nightly news broadcasts and all major newspapers have a leftwing slant."

"Well, yes," Patrick admits, "But that's not enough to reach the majority of Americans. Most Americans do not watch the news or read newspapers."

Rig advises, "Cable television is how they could spread their deception."

Patrick objects, "That's only a few channels and most of them are just duplicates of the same networks."

Rig responds, "Yes, that is the way it is now. Growth of cable channels is unlimited. The Longjumeau Alliance can spread their deceptions over dozens of channels with programs disguised as entertainment and news."

Patrick shakes his head and expresses his disbelief while he opines, "That doesn't make sense. How could so many channels flow over a single wire?"

"Signal multiplexing," Rig informs.

Patrick is not a technical person. This is the first time he has heard the phrase *signal multiplexing*. He glances at Denton.

Denton nods back at Patrick and says, "Yes, the technology exists. It's just a matter of time before hundreds of channels broadcast over T.V. cable."

Patrick expresses thoughtfulness for a few moments with occasional expressions of doubt. While thinking, his eyes roam around the room. He sees Rig's Summer Khaki uniform hanging in the open closet. Patrick knows that Rig is a decorated navy chief. Then he turns his attention to the holstered pistol lying on the nightstand. Patrick refocuses on Rig's face and he asks, "Rig, I must be honest with you. What you say makes sense, but I look at your age and your profession and I wonder how a person of your position can hold an accurate assessment of the situation before us."

Rig expresses amusement as he redefines Patrick's comment. "You doubt that a thirty-year-old navy chief petty officer can accurately assess political situations."

"Yes."

"I have been a copious reader all my life. I have studied politics and history. But more than that, I have a brilliant mentor—Doctor Sally Macfurson, PhD in history and master of five languages. She provides me with a reading list, and she answers all my questions."

Patrick's eyes go wide and he expresses surprise; he comments, "I have read her books, and I met her once when she delivered a speech at Harvard." His expression changes to curiosity as he asks, "How long have you known her and what is the intensity of mentorship over you?"

"I have known her for ten years, and during the past eight months, I have met with her several times per week. She is in the navy now and works as a navy intelligence analyst."

Revelation overcomes Patrick's expression. He smiles appreciatively at Rig and says, "Okay, you know that The Guardians have abducted senior members of the Longjumeau Alliance. As you know, we planned on indoctrinating them on the horrors of communism, but you do not think that will have any effect on them, correct?"

"That's right," Rig affirms.

"Okay, then. What do you think The Guardians can do to change the behavior of America's most effective and most dangerous domestic enemies?"

"Actually, Sally Macfurson and I have had conversations about that because she leads the intel gathering on The Longjumeau Alliance. Elitists like Edwin Kendley, Senator Porter, and Diane Love will protect their wealth, even under a communist dictatorship. They see themselves as the enlightened elite who should rule over the unwashed masses because the unwashed masses are incapable of ruling themselves as a constitutional republic."

Denton asks, "But wouldn't people like Senator Porter, Diane Love, and Edwin Kendley lose their wealth with implementation of the *Fair Profits Tax Act*?"

"No. They will protect it in some way."

With slight frustration in his tone, Patrick asks, "So how do we neutralize their threat?"

Rig answers, "We get as dirty as they get. We threaten to remove them from power if they do not discontinue their communist crusade. If they persist in their crusade, we go after them with the same brutal and vile character assassinations as they use on others. We lie about them. We conspire to destroy their credibility. We threaten their hold on power. We create fake immoral and unethical situations in their past that they cannot disprove. If they do not comply, steal their wealth."

Patrick expresses contemplation as he stares at Rig; then he comments, "For that to work, we will need to destroy one of them in the manner you describe while we still hold them hostage . . . maybe two of them."

Rig does not respond. His expression conveys that he submits to the judgment of the more experienced.

Patrick closes the discussion with, "Okay, then. I have some planning to do."

Denton says, "Patrick, I need to talk with Rig privately. Please wait for me in the car."

Patrick stands and walks to Rig. He offers his hand as he says,

"Rig, again, it is a pleasure to meet an American hero."

Rig stands; then shakes hands with Patrick.

Patrick exits the motel room.

Rig sits down on the edge of the bed and faces Denton.

Denton advises, "You need to let us abduct Diane Love. She needs to go through our indoctrination like the other directors of The Longjumeau Alliance."

Rig casts a dubious stare at Denton.

Denton emphasizes, "If we don't take her with the rest of the directors, she will be suspect."

Rig asks, "When can I have her?"

"I don't know, Rig. We need to restructure our indoctrination program and execute a plan to destroy the careers of one or two of them before letting them go. Could be six weeks—maybe two months."

Rig opines, "That's a long time. Every federal investigative agency will spare no expense in finding all those high level people."

"They won't find them," Denton assures.

Rig adds, "Diane's KGB contact might—wait a second—the Russians! That's who was after me at the Capitol complex. That smell—a mixture of vodka and harsh tobacco cigarettes!"

"Are you sure?" Denton challenges.

"Yes," Rig responds. "I have been in a number of Russian buildings and around some Russian officials and a bunch of Russian sailors. They all reek of it. I'm surprised I did not recognize it right away."

"I don't think they are a physical threat to you. They know Diane left town and, probably, did not tell her KGB handler where she is going."

"I wonder what they thought about me shooting at them last night. If they have suspected I was a counterintelligence agent, shooting at them would confirm it."

"Not necessarily," Denton opines. "If they have been watching you, they know you carry a gun. Not only because you are a registered federal courier but also for protection against the

CLWUA."

Rig nods and expresses agreement. "That makes sense."

Denton brings them back on subject. "You need to go through the motions of following the orders of your ONI supervisors and go to Connecticut." Denton pauses as he constructs his thoughts; then he asks, "Do you have fake Connecticut license plates?"

"Yes, I have a complete set for all 50 states—hidden in security-locked storage space under the floorboard of my Jeep. All those fake plates will pass an initial database check but will lead to a dead end as a result of a detailed search like someone going to the address listed in the database."

Denton directs, "Put on those Connecticut license plates as soon as you cross the border into Connecticut. We don't want a local up there telling some investigator that a sinister looking man in a Jeep with D.C. plates was in the area during the abductions."

"Standard operating procedure," Rig announces.

"Good," Denton responds; then he asks, "What about undercover identification?"

"Also standard operating procedure."

Denton asks, "How will you make your reports to your naval intelligence supervisor?"

"I will use the secure voice crypto covered high-frequency radio equipment in the Jeep."

"What about beaconing devices?" Denton questions. "Is that Jeep transmitting any frequencies that are used for geographic positioning?"

"No. Too much of a chance that the enemy could use those frequencies to lock onto my position."

Denton orders, "Do not go within fifty miles of the Kendley Estate. Make your reports via radio. Your naval intelligence supervisors should not be able to tell your exact location while making radio reports, right?"

"That's right," Rig confirms.

"Then, when the local news up there reports the abduction of visitors at the Kendley Estate, you report to your naval intelligence

422

supervisor that Diane and other visitors at the Kendley Estate have been kidnapped."

"Okay. That's what I'll do."

Denton inquires, "I'm curious. How is all that equipment in your Jeep protected?"

"That Jeep has many safeguards. To sum it up, any unauthorized entry from any point around the vehicle will result in the vehicle exploding and burning."

Denton stands; then he walks toward the door.

Rig asks, "Uh, Denton, I am curious. What are your plans for Weston Pyth? To me, he is not on the same level as the others—no power or say in The Longjumeau Alliance."

"Who?" Denton questions, expressing curiosity.

"Weston Pyth—that leftwing reporter for the *Long Beach Times*."

Denton expresses recognition. "The Guardians have no interest in him."

"Didn't you abduct him?!" Rig inquires with surprise in his tone.

"No."

Rig explains, "Weston Pyth disappeared about two weeks ago. I just thought that—"

"Wasn't The Guardians." Denton places his hand on the doorknob. "Keep me up-to-date on what you are doing. Leave a message every couple of days." Denton exits the motel room.

Rig sits on the edge of the bed and contemplates what might have happened to Weston Pyth.

Chapter 84

Diane Love opens her eyes. Several soft nightlights cast insufficient illumination to clearly define unfamiliar furnishings. She spreads her arms, palms down on the surface of which lies. *I am in a bed, but the bed and covers are unfamiliar.* She senses that the bed is moving slightly beneath her.

She throws back the bedcovers; then she sits upright on the edge of the bed. When her feet land on the floor, she senses a swaying floor. She quickly scans the room and cannot identify it. The entire room is swaying. She reaches for the lamp on the nightstand and presses the switch. The low wattage bulb helps little to illuminate the room. Then she notices a light switch above the lamp. She must stand to reach the switch. The moving floor causing her to lose balance; she grabs the bed's headboard to steady herself. Then she flips the light switch.

The room becomes fully illuminated. *A ship's stateroom!* Her evaluation considers that the room is a lower priced stateroom; roughly fifteen feet by fifteen feet with modest but comfortable furniture and a well-padded dark-blue carpet. The stateroom's climate has a slight damp chill. A quick survey of the room reveals a private bath with toilet, sink, and shower. A small empty standalone wardrobe is positioned near the bathroom door. A twenty-four-hour clock on the bulkhead at the end of her bed advises the time to be 0545—5:45 AM. No porthole is visible. She searches all bulkheads for a calendar but does not find one. A glance at her wrist reveals that her watch that includes a date display is missing. She considers that Edwin Kendley is playing some sort of joke.

The telephone on the nightstand rings.

Diane picks up the handset. "Hello."

A voice that Diane does not recognize tells her, "Miss Love, breakfast will be served in forty-five minutes. The wardroom will be to your right after exiting your stateroom."

The phone goes dead.

Curiosity about her situation turns to a feeling of apprehension.

Then she notices that she wears her own nightgown, and her own robe lies across the back of the room's only chair. Her suitcase sits on the same chair as her robe. She first searches her suitcase for her .25 caliber automatic pistol that is usually stowed in a zipped pouch attached to the inside of the suitcase—not there, and the small travel radio she always packs is missing. Her watch is not to be found. Everything else she packed at her townhouse is in the suitcase. She retrieves items from her suitcase and enters the bathroom.

Fifty minutes later, Diane exits the bathroom wearing loose-fitting jeans and loose-fitting, light-blue colored turtleneck sweater. Her flaming red hair is pulled back in a ponytail. She glances at her purse and decides to not take it with her.

After exiting her stateroom, she turns right and walks slowly along the sea-green colored tiled passageway toward the door marked WARDROOM located at the end of the passageway. The pitch and roll of the deck has lessened and she walks easily. As she walks, she glances at doors of the thirty staterooms along the passageway—anticipating that someone might exit.

She opens the door to the wardroom and is astonished at what she sees. She knows everyone in the room. Edwin Kendley, Senator Porter, CLWUA President Gaylord Tarkingson, Congressman Billy Thayer, and Professor Bartholomew Goldman sit at an eight chair table nearest her. Edwin Kendley motions for her to sit at his table.

After sitting down next to Edwin Kendley, Diane asks in a demanding, raised tone, "What the hell is going on?!"

"I do not know," Kendley admits. "All I remember is that I went to sleep in my bed at my country estate. Then I woke up about an hour ago to a ringing telephone. The voice on the telephone told me to come in here." Kendley nods toward the end of the table; then he advises, "Clay, Billy, and Gaylord have been here for a few days. Billy was just about to tell us about this ship."

Congressmen Billy Thayer says, "I was kidnapped while riding in a limousine provided by my car service. I was on my way to Capitol Hill. We were stopped at a red light, when two men entered the back of the limousine—one from each side. They injected me with a drug. Then I woke up in my stateroom down the hall six days ago. When I came into the wardroom for the first time; Clay, Gaylord, and me were the only ones here. A few more people arrived over the next few days. Most of the people here arrived sometime last night. I could hear a lot of activity in the hallway around midnight last night. I attempted to investigate, but the door to my stateroom was locked.

"Our captors have remote control of the door locks. We only have access to our staterooms, the hallway, and this wardroom.

"Most of the time, they allow us to roam freely between staterooms and this wardroom." Billy points to a steam line that contains breakfast foods, coffee, tea, and milk. "Except for meal time, that steam line is hidden behind a locked wall that is lowered from the ceiling. I assume that is so we make no contact with the crew. You can hear the crew behind that sliding wall when they are laying out the meal.

"A couple of days ago, some of us refused to leave this room when they announced over the loudspeaker for us to return to our staterooms. When we would not leave, they announced that if we did not go back to our staterooms within five minutes the evening meal and the next morning's breakfast meal would not be served and that all water to all staterooms would be turned off for twenty-four hours. We waited seven minutes, two minutes past the warning, before we went back to our staterooms. They made good on their threat. Water was off for twenty-four hours and the wardroom door was locked until lunch the following day.

"Our captors announced why they denied us food and water for nearly twenty hours over the loud speakers in the hallway. They named me and my two coconspirators as responsible. The other captives gave me and my coconspirators hell and even threatened us with physical harm if we did it again. Then the next—"

"Billy, stop!" Diane demands adamantly. "What do they want with us?!"

Billy shrugs and casts a blank stare.

Professor Goldman states, "We don't know. They have not told us."

"We're being ransomed," The president of the CLWUA offers.

"I don't think so," Edwin Kendley counters. "Look around. Everyone here is a director or member of The Longjumeau Alliance. I believe we have been uncovered and we are here to satisfy some political motive."

Diane studies the interior of the wardroom. Then she turns her attention to Billy Thayer who is scooping a spoonful of scrambled eggs. Her stomach growls loud enough for all at the table to hear.

Professor Goldman advises, "Diane, you should get something to eat. The steam line is normally open until seven-thirty, but sometimes they lower the wall early without notice."

Diane stands; then makes her way to the steam line.

Twenty minutes later, Goldman and Thayer stand and go to the door. Goldman yanks on the doorknob a few times. Then Goldman and Thayer return to the table. Goldman announces, "The door is locked." He said it loud enough for those at other tables to relay the information. Some become apprehensive because the door has never before been locked while they were eating.

The sound of the steam line wall closing causes all in the room to glance in the direction of the closing wall. All anticipate something unusual is about to happen, and their apprehension heightens.

The loudspeaker crackles. A deep resonant voice fills the room. *"The Longjumeau Alliance was founded in 1969 by Edwin Kendley, who is the son of former six-term United States Senator and failed United States presidential candidate Robert Kendley and who is nephew of former Connecticut governor Jerald Kendley. As the communist directed Students for a Democratic Society fell apart, Edwin Kendley gathered leaders of the SDS to form a new, secret organization with the charter to transform the United States into a communist state. Kendley and the other original directors of The Longjumeau Alliance deliberated for more than a year as to what form of government their new communist utopia would have. They argued emotionally over parliamentary, republic, democracy, dictatorship, and oligarchy. They finally settled on oligarchy because they believed that oligarchy is the only government form that would sustain a single party led by a few educated elite with the purpose of ruling with compassion.*

"The original directors established a thirty-year Marxist plan to nationalize the major industries and to first establish a Socialist state before forcing the country to a Communist state. The plan calls for The Longjumeau Alliance to design and fund disasters with the goal to motivate federal legislators to nationalize industries, justifying such nationalization with accusations that industries pursue profit over safety. During the last year alone, Longjumeau Alliance actions to initiate nationalization have included destroying oilrigs in the Gulf of Mexico, poising aspirin bottles, and derailing trains carrying oil and gasoline."

Diane Love jumps to her feet and shouts, "Who the hell are you criminals who have the arrogance to kidnap people like us?!"

The speaker pauses during Diane's rant.

Diane sits down and waits for an answer.

The voice continues. *"These acts of terrorism resulted in the deaths of 203 Americans and the economic devastation for those whose livelihood depend on those industries. More than thirty-thousand Americans lost their jobs as a result. Reporters who work for national media outlets and who are here in this room acted as agents of The Longjumeau Alliance by focusing America's attention not on the terrorists who perpetrated these horrors but by demonizing and vilifying American corporations as greedy capitalists who placed profit over safety. As all of you in this room know, American citizen outrage toward those corporations resulted in some support for 'The American Nationalization Act' and the 'Fair Profits Tax Act.' Members of The Longjumeau Alliance in this room used their money, deceit, and political influence to gain votes in Congress.*

"The Alliance has also planned and funded political sabotage against rightwing opponents. The Alliance manufactured politically damaging situations against opponents and then ensured

nationwide media was on location when the manufactured plot was executed. For example, Texas U.S. Senate election when The Alliance planted fake Ku Klux Klan members at the Republican candidate rally, and the sexual misconduct situation manufactured by The Alliance against the Republican candidate in two governor elections."

Diane knows the political sabotage is true. She helped plan those manufactured scandals. She is a strong advocate for Saul Alinsky's *Rules for Radicals,* and she advocates deceit against the enemy using the rule that 'the ends justify the means.' No doubt exists in Diane's mind that every deceit possible must be initiated to propel America's advance toward its communist destiny.

"We brought all of you on this cruise with the goal of changing your ways."

Mocking chuckles sound throughout the wardroom.

Billy Thayer states courageously above the chuckles, "Yeah! Right! That's been tried before and the Marxists prevailed!"

"Before we allow your release, you will commit to actions that we discuss with you over the next few days."

Sighs of relief flow over the wardroom as members of The Longjumeau Alliance realize that this situation can end without physical harm.

"If you do not commit to the actions we specify, you will be here a long time. The sooner you commit the sooner that you will be released. The longer you take to commit the more uncomfortable your stay will become.

"We will talk privately with each of you to negotiate your release."

A few moans rise above the chatter. Most of the captives resolve not to surrender. One captive says softly, "My fight to bring social justice to victims of capitalism will not surrender to the lack of a few comforts."

Chapter 85

Some naval intelligence staff members meet in the ONI building located on the Cheltenham navy base. Sitting around the room are Captain Brad Watson, Lieutenant Commander Sally Macfurson, Chief Rigney Page, and Senior Analyst Bob Mater.

Rig states, "I do not know more than what the local news reported. I had the estate under surveillance for several days. Then one morning I woke up in my motel room, turned on the morning news and listened to the local news reports about the abductions of Edwin Kendley, Diane Love, Professor Goldman, those two Congress-women, and the others who we have identified as directors and officials of The Longjumeau Alliance.

"Initial reports included statements from Kendley Estate employees that sleeping gas was spread around the estate by an unknown source. When they all woke up, they discovered that Kendley and some of his visitors had disappeared. All the filing cabinets and all the safes had been forced open and the contents taken. Every file and every piece of paper in the house was gone. Some of the senior estate staff says that all the jewelry and all the money in the safes were stolen."

Captain Watson asks, "Is there any information on who conducted that raid? Are they the same people who abducted Senator Porter and those others from their homes?"

Rig shakes his head and shrugs.

Captain Watson glances back and forth between Sally Macfurson and Bob Mater.

Both Sally and Bob shake their heads.

Captain Watson states, "There is a meeting late this afternoon at the FBI headquarters. Representatives from all the investigative services and all the intelligence services will be there. The purpose of the meeting is to form a joint task force. I will be at the meeting and I will submit Commander Macfurson's name as the ONI member of the joint task force.

"After this meeting, I want Commander Macfurson and her team of analysts to perform a rigorous and detailed debrief of Chief Page."

Rig groans, knowing that such a debriefing will take half the day.

Captain Watson says, "I have another subject to discuss." Captain Watson looks toward Bob Mater and nods.

Bob Mater informs, "CIA has uncovered irrefutable evidence that Commander Pantero and Lieutenant Van Thorton at USNAVCOMMSTA Panama are engaged in espionage and black marketeering. They are connected with Central and South American smugglers and agents of communist countries.

"They first gained our attention when we investigated the involvement of Enrico Mendoza with Edwin Kendley of The Longjumeau Alliance. When we had Mendoza under surveillance at his hacienda in Panama, we noted the frequent visits by Commander Pantero and Lieutenant Van Thorton.

"We informed CIA, and CIA placed undercover agents in the USNAVCOMMSTA Panama administration office and in the communications center. ONI and CIA formed a joint team to scrutinize all documents flowing in-and-out of the admin office. The undercover agent in the communications center had the task of discovering unusual events in the communications center and closely observing the actions of Lieutenant Van Thorton.

"The first interesting piece of information came from the CIA undercover agent in the communications center. He heard some of the radiomen discussing the increasing volume of message traffic and the resulting increase in the number of burn bags. Those radiomen then calculated which officer generated the most burn bags. One of those radiomen commented that during the mid-watch when full burn bags were gathered, stapled, and stacked for the next burn run—the burn bag in Lieutenant Van Thorton's office was seldom full. Another radioman mentioned that was strange because the lieutenant was slotted a copy of every message processed by the message center and that numbered hundreds per day.

"Then our agents watching Mendoza's hacienda observed a truck with Canal Zone license plates arriving periodically and offload dozens of wooden boxes. The driver of the panel van, who was always dressed in civilian clothes, was followed back to the USNAVCOMMSTA supply warehouse in the Canal Zone. He was identified as Store Keeper First Class Jason Wendell. A few days later, some of Mendoza's men transported those wooden boxes to a warehouse near the Panama City commercial docks. Our agents snuck into the warehouse and discovered about fifty wooden boxes that had the navy markings painted over. Our agents opened some boxes and found large vacuum tubes and other electronic assemblies. They recorded the engraved serial numbers.

"We traced the serial numbers through the navy supply system to the U.S. Naval Communications Station Panama. Wondering why so many of the same parts were being ordered by USNAVCOMMSTA Panama, our joint team focused on 2-Kilo Maintenance Forms generated by USNAVCOMMSTA Panama.

"Well, anyway, to make a long investigative and analytical story short, we conclude that Commander Pantero, Lieutenant Van Thorton, and Store Keeper Wendell have stolen hundreds of thousands of dollars' worth of electronic equipment and sold it on the black market. Van Thorton is the command maintenance officer; he generates the fake equipment failure on a 2-Kilo form and creates fake technician names. The executive officer, Commander Pantero, signs the form for the commanding officer. Store Keeper Wendell writes up a DD1348 requisition form, includes the 2-killo serial number as justification, and pulls the item for delivery to the applicable work center. Their black market contact is Enrico Mendoza who gets a percentage of the profit. The financier of all this black market activity is Edwin Kendley. Van Thorton delivers classified material to Mendoza who is paid by Edwin Kendley for the classified material. Best we have concluded is that all profit goes to bank accounts of The Longjumeau Alliance."

Rig comments, "All that paperwork must be forwarded to NAVELEX and the Navy Supply System in order for replacement parts to be sent to USNAVCOMMSTA Panama supply department. All that paperwork is summarized in computer reports that would show excessive failures at USNAVCOMMSTA Panama as compared to similar type commands."

Commander Macfurson suggests, "Might be that they have not been doing it long enough for an abnormity to catch the eye of a NAVELEX analyst."

Rig shakes his head and expresses disgust. "Three career navy men—traitors to their country for money!"

Bob Mater comments, "Appears that Store Keeper Wendell is doing it for the money, but I think it's more than money for Commander Pantero and Lieutenant Van Thorton. Both of them were attending UCLA at the same time as Diane Love and Billy Thayer. We believe they all belonged to the Students for a Democratic Society cell led by Billy Thayer. During the time that Van Thorton, Pantero, and Diane Love were attending UCLA, Edwin Kendley rented a house close to the campus. Commander Pantero graduated from UCLA in 1966 and Lieutenant Van Thorton dropped out about the same time. Both joined the navy to avoid the military draft, but they continued their membership in the SDS, which they both hid from the navy. Their security clearance applications say nothing about the SDS. We conclude that when the SDS fell apart in 1969 Edwin Kendley contacted them and recruited them into The Longjumeau Alliance, although their names do not appear on the membership rolls."

Bob Mater passes a thick file folder to Sally Macfurson and advises, "This file contains all the information we have gathered on the Panama situation. Both you and Rig need to study it before Rig goes to Panama."

"I'm going back to Panama?" Rig responds with an inflected, questioning tone and with eyebrows arched.

"Yes," Captain Watson answers. "ONI, CIA, Naval Investigative Service, and Army CID are putting together a plan to arrest all those villains, including Mendoza."

"What will be my role?" Rig inquires.

Brad Watson answers, "As you know, USNAVCOMMSTA Panama failed the I.G. inspection that you were part of back in

February. You will go to Panama as a member of the COMNAVTELCOM I.G. re-inspection team, about three weeks from now. Your role in the arrest of those traitors and Mendoza has not been finalized. I expect you will get your briefing during the days just prior to your departure to Panama."

Rig responds in a fearless and cavalier tone and with one eyebrow raised, "Great! Nothing satisfies me more than getting the bad guys, blowing up their buildings, and making America safe from communism."

Sally shakes her head and rolls her eyes.

Bob Mater chuckles.

Captain Watson stares appraisingly at Chief Page and comments, "The Panama mission should be a walk on the beach for the *unconquerable* Rigney Page."

Chapter 86

"It's been forty-eight hours since they made their announcement to change our ways," Professor Goldman remarks to no one in particular at the breakfast table. He takes a sip of coffee; then he advises, "Our group has one less person this morning than we did yesterday."

All at the table stop eating. Some stare with a quizzical expression at Goldman, and some glance around the wardroom. The only sounds in the wardroom are sounds of silverware hitting plates the sounds of ventilation fan motors.

"Alice Bartner," Goldman advises.

Alice was one of those abducted at the Kendley Estate. She is a multi-millionaire who inherited her father's business, *Columbia Media International—CMI*. All of the manufactured scandals created by Diane Love against rightwing politicians first appeared in CMI's publications.

Edwin Kendley states, "She is a light eater. She has missed meals before."

"But not two in a row," Professor Goldman counters. "Whether I eat or not, I come in here for every meal, just for the conversation. Lying around in my stateroom and reading for hours drives me crazy."

"Well, they do provide us with lots of reading material," Billy Thayer comments while nodding toward a bulkhead lined with fully stocked bookshelves and magazine racks.

After taking a bite of Eggs Benedict, Diane lays down her fork and asks those at the table, "Have they talked to any of you?"

Each person at the table quickly glances at the others. No one admits they have.

The wardroom deck leans to starboard as the ship makes a sharp turn to port. Those in the wardroom use one hand to grab the edge of the table and one hand on their trays to keep them from sliding. All the chairs and tables are fixed to the deck. All tables have a one-inch high rail around the edge to prevent trays from sliding off the table.

After the ship is steady on its new course, all in the wardroom feel an increased pitch and roll of the ship—not a totally annoying pitch and roll but enough to cause most in the wardroom to finish their breakfasts quickly and return to the safety of their beds.

Gaylord Tarkingson, president of the CLWUA, lies on the bed in his stateroom. He fingers through a two-month-old issue of *TIME* Magazine. Actually, he just looks at the pictures and reads the captions. Most on his mind is what it will cost him to get back to his normal life.

The telephone on the nightstand rings.

"Hello," Tarkingson says into the handset.

A male voice tells him, "Exit your stateroom, turn right, and walk along the passageway. Stateroom fifteen will be on your left. Enter stateroom fifteen. Then sit at the table."

The interrogation center consists of two rooms: stateroom fifteen and a connecting control room. The stateroom furnishings consist only of a table with one chair, and that one chair faces a large one-way viewing window mounted on the bulkhead. The control room contains all climate, water, and locking controls for all the staterooms. The bulkheads, deck, and overhead of both rooms are covered with soundproofing tiles.

Inside the control room, a technician sits in front of a control panel. Denton Phillips and his strategist, Patrick, sit at a table facing the one-way viewing window. Both Denton and Patrick have a microphone in front of them. File folders are neatly stacked on the tabletop.

Denton hangs up the phone handset. Then he orders the controls technician, "Lock all doors except for Tarkingson's stateroom and stateroom fifteen."

The technician flips some switches; then reports, "Done."

Several minutes later, Denton and Patrick look through the one-way glass and watch Gaylord Tarkingson enter stateroom fifteen.

Denton orders the technician, "Lock stateroom fifteen and unlock all other doors."

The technician operates the locking panel; then reports, "All doors unlocked, except stateroom fifteen."

Gaylord stares suspiciously at the large mirror mounted on the far bulkhead. He immediately understands he is being watched through a one-way viewing window.

"Please sit, Mr. Tarkingson," orders a voice in a calm and polite tone.

Tarkingson shouts, "I demand you release me immediately!"

Denton says calmly into the microphone, "That is what this meeting is about, Mr. Tarkingson. We will discuss the conditions of your release."

In a fierce and angry tone, Tarkingson warns, "You do not understand the power I can use against you."

"If you do not wish to discuss the terms of your release, we will allow you to go back to your stateroom. Please understand that you will not be released until you agree to our terms. We are prepared to keep you here indefinitely. The longer you take to agree with the terms of release, the worse your living conditions will become."

"I am not intimidated by you!"

Denton says into the microphone, "I assure you, Mr. Tarkingson. You will eventually agree to our terms. Why put yourself through months of uncomfortable existence when in the end you will comply anyway?"

Tarkingson's fierce, stubborn expression turns sour. He never anticipated that he would be a captive indefinitely. He has believed since the moment he was abducted that no effort would be spared to rescue him. He knows that the FBI searches for him, and he knows the CLWUA security force searches for him. Nevertheless, he is the subject of intimidation, and he now realizes that he has no power here. He sits in the chair facing the one-way viewing glass. He expresses willingness to hear his captor's terms.

Denton explains, "If you agree to our terms, you will be returned to your life as you left it with a few exceptions. First, the CLWUA will never again use violence, intimidation, and vandalism against businesses, unionized or not. Second, the CLWUA will discontinue its threatening and violent actions against small businesses that by law are exempt from unionization. Third, you will resign your membership in The Longjumeau Alliance. Fourth, you sign a statement admitting that you were a member of the Longjumeau Alliance and admitting that you know that the Longjumeau Alliance has a charter and plan to transform America into a communist country. Fifth you forfeit one-third of your net worth to us. Sixth, you will sign undated quitclaim deeds on all your personal properties. Seventh, you will never discuss your visit with us. When asked about your abduction, you may only state that you were kidnapped, and you paid the ransom and were let go.

"If you do not agree to these terms within a timeframe unknown to you, we will forge all the financial documents necessary to steal all your wealth and you will remain our guest. When we abducted you from your mansion, we emptied all your safes and filing cabinets. We have all your personal account numbers, passwords, and access codes.

"If you agree to our terms and later violate those terms, all of your bank and investment accounts will be emptied, and we will date and record the quitclaim deeds. We will destroy your reputation with media releases reporting your sexual activities in Barbados with young adolescent boys. We will also provide the general public a detailed account of how you increased your net worth of one-hundred-and-twenty-thousand dollars five years ago when you were elected to president of the CLWUA to a net worth today of twenty-two-million dollars. And we will expose your membership in The Longjumeau Alliance."

"This is outrageous!" Gaylord shrieks. "There is no truth to that adolescent boys' story, and my net worth was legally accumulated."

Denton counters, "No truth, you say. Well, we have travel schedules and photographs of you with some of those boys while

438

engaged in sexual activity."

Gaylord declares, "Any photographs that you have are phony! I never did any of that."

"Nevertheless, we have such photographs."

A drawer slides out from the wall just below the one-way viewing window.

Gaylord stands; then walks over to the open drawer. He retrieves a stack of photographs and some stapled papers; then he returns to his chair. His jaw drops. With the viewing of each photograph, his eyes go wider, and his expression becomes more fearful. Photos of him lying naked with young boys are perfect fakes. The truth is that he never engaged in such acts.

After he views each photograph, he looks toward the one-way window. His cheeks tremble and his teeth repeatedly click together.

"You see, Mr. Tarkingson, we are an organization that can be just as deceitful as you and those with whom you affiliate. Now, take a look at the history of financial transactions."

The history of financial transactions shows dates of investment transactions using money from the CLWUA retirement fund. The last page of the transaction history shows that the highlighted investments were made in dummy corporations owned by one Gaylord Tarkingson. Of course, all those investments failed to the amount of twenty-million dollars."

Denton explains, "So you see, Mr. Tarkingson, even if you can eventually prove the photographs are fake, no one will care because by then you will have been convicted of securities fraud."

The drawer beneath the one-way window closes. Ten seconds later it opens.

"All the forms you must sign are in the drawer. Sign them now, and you will be home within forty-eight hours."

Tarkingson does not move from his seat. He decides to be defiant to see how far he can push the envelope. He questions, "Who are you people? You're obviously not organized crime because you have a political agenda. You cannot be government because what you are doing is criminal."

"Our identity will remain secret. Now is the time to sign the forms."

Tarkingson stands and expresses defiance. He steps to the door and attempts to open it.

Denton orders the technician, "Unlock the door to stateroom fifteen. Lock the door to the wardroom."

Tarkingson exits, letting the door slam shut behind him.

Denton watches the security T.V. screen that monitors the captive's passageway.

The security monitor displays Tarkingson attempts to enter the wardroom, but the door is locked. He turns and walks toward his stateroom.

The controls technician stares at Denton; his expression conveying that he anticipates an order.

"Turn off the water, toilet, and climate control in Mr. Tarkingson's stateroom. After he enters his stateroom, lock his door."

After entering his stateroom, Tarkingson goes directly to the bathroom to use the toilet. When he finishes, he depresses the flush button, but nothing happens. He shakes his head and expresses amusement. He attempts to wash his hands, but water does not flow. He decides to check with Billy Thayer in the adjacent stateroom to see if Billy is experiencing the same problems. When he finds his door locked, Gaylord frowns and groans as he comes to understand the discomforts that he will endure. Then he considers the fate of the missing Alice Bartner. He wonders if she agreed to terms and is gone from this place or is trapped in a stateroom from hell.

Chapter 87

Rig sits at the kitchen table in his small Arlington apartment and eats a light supper of skinless baked chicken breast and sliced raw tomatoes and raw cucumber. He sits comfortably in t-shirt and jockey shorts. He watches the local nightly news on a portable television sitting on the kitchen counter. The first report advises of rioting in the streets of Panama City over ongoing negations regarding the Panama Canal Treaty. The next news report covers the ongoing search for the twenty-three politicians and business tycoons kidnapped in mass abductions several weeks ago.

"A new development has surfaced in what has become to be known as the 'Nazi Raider Case'—Labeled 'Nazi' because of the police-state-style mass abduction of politicians and business leaders two weeks ago. A two-week long worldwide search and investigation by American authorities has produced no leads.

"Media Mogul, Alice Bartner, often nicked named 'bad little rich girl' by the press was found sedated last night in a motel room north of San Diego, just off Interstate 5. She was found after an anonymous phone call to the local FBI office. The FBI spent most of the night questioning, Ms. Bartner. The FBI responds 'no comment' to all questions from the press. A spokesman for Ms. Bartner's media empire, Columbia Media International, released this quote from Ms. Bartner: 'I can only say that I was kidnapped, and I paid the ransom. I cannot say more than that, and I have not told the FBI any more than that. The safety of my friends who are still held captive is at risk should I say anything more.'

"Among those kidnapped are Senator Clay Porter, Oil Tycoon and philanthropist Edwin Kendley, Congressman Billy Thayer, and Construction and Labor Workers Union President Gaylord Tarkingson.

"In other news . . ."

Rig tunes out the news as he considers the truth of Alice Bartner's comments. He wonders if she had the stamina to stand mute against FBI interrogators.

His mind turns to his Panama mission. He departs tomorrow morning from Andrews Air Force Base on a military chartered aircraft and then arrives at Howard Air Force Base Panama Canal Zone early tomorrow evening. He will be undercover as one of a four-person COMNAVTELCOM re-inspection team with the purpose of ensuring that USNAVCOMMSTA Panama has fixed several serious security violation problems discovered during the last COMNAVTELCOM Inspector General visit.

During the past two weeks, he attended training and briefing sessions regarding his ONI mission in Panama. When all briefings and training sessions were complete, he requested a meeting with Captain Bradley Watson, ONI Assistant Director for Counterespionage. They met in Room Four of the ONI building on the Cheltenham, Maryland navy base.

Rig had told Captain Watson, "I'm concerned about my cover being exposed during the Panama mission. My actions as directed by the mission plan will reveal who and what I really am to more than a dozen people; all of them being enemies of the United States."

Brad had explained, "This is a combined CIA, ONI operation. Our objective is to bring back to the U.S. all those criminals for prosecution by secret military tribunal. None of whom we set out to arrest can be killed. That means you must expose your role as a federal undercover agent to them."

Rig had declared in a resigned tone, "My days as a naval intelligence undercover agent will be over."

Captain Watson had responded, "You underestimate the government's ability to keep a secret. In the grand scheme, exposing your federal status to those criminals is negligible exposure. Those criminals will never again see the light of day and they will never again be in communications with anyone who can harm you. I do not see anything different in your future with naval intelligence."

Rig's mind returns to the present as he evaluates his future life in service to his country.

A knock on his front door breaks his thoughts. He steps to the door and looks through the peep hole and sees John Smith. Rig invites John to share some dinner.

"No thanks, Rig. I will be here only for a few minutes, and I have an appointment for dinner with Denton Phillips. I am here on Guardians business."

"How about a beer, then?" Rig offers.

"Sure—I'll sip one."

Rig pours a Heineken into a chilled mug and places it on the table before John.

Rig sits in his chair and expresses that he is ready to listen.

"You will be involved in the arrest of some criminals while you are in Panama. You will be part of a combined CIA, ONI team."

"That's what the plan directs," Rig confirms.

"Yes, I know," John states. "I was team leader on plan design."

Rig expresses curiosity.

"The Guardians want you to deviate from the designed plan."

Rig asks for clarification. "You want me to deviate from the plan you devised?"

"Yes."

"What do you want me to do?"

John explains Rig's task.

Rig leans back in his chair and considers John's words. He grabs John's chilled mug of Heineken and takes several long draws.

John glances at his watch; then he advises, "Rig, I must go soon. I must take your answer to Denton tonight."

"You're saying that I have but a few minutes to decide what might turn out to be my lifelong role with The Guardians?"

John nods; then glances at his watch.

Rig again considers his choice. He thinks about Diane Love who is still held by The Guardians. He worries about her. "What is Diane Love's fate?"

John smiles and expresses pleasure that he can provide Rig with good news. "She has agreed to The Guardians' terms for her release, and she will be released within the week."

Rig expresses relief.

"Well, Rig, will you do what The Guardians ask of you? Remember, you are under no obligation. Your refusal will not be held against you."

Rig declares, "I'll do it."

Chapter 88

Rig wears a short-sleeve Summer White uniform when he enters the Communications Center of NAVCOMMSTA Panama located at Fort Amador on the Pacific side of the Panama Canal. This time, there are no problems with unescorted access. He goes directly to Lieutenant Van Thorton's office. The re-inspection of Van Thorton's crypto account is scheduled to start five minutes from now.

Rig knocks on Van Thorton's office door.

No response.

Rig turns the door knob. The door is locked.

While Rig is looking at his watch, Van Thorton turns a corner and approaches his office.

When Van Thorton is within a few feet of his office door, he says to Rig, "No reason to go into my office. Let's go directly to the crypto vault in the technical control center."

Two minutes later, they arrive at the crypto vault door, and Van Thorton begins turning the combination dial.

While Van Thorton dials the combination, Rig surveys the immediate area. Two enlisted men wearing dungaree uniform stand watch in the technical control center. Since the nearest technical control equipment is thirty feet away, Rig concludes the two enlisted men will have no reason to come close to the crypto vault door.

They enter the ten-foot by ten-foot crypto vault. Lieutenant Van Thorton pulls on the solid metal vault door, nearly closing it except for a few inches. Then he sits in a chair behind a small desk. A microfiche reader and a phone sit on the desktop.

Since there are no other chairs in the vault, Rig remains standing.

Lieutenant Van Thorton advises, "I challenged the crypto account inspection done by that I.G. Team Lieutenant. I protested to my captain that the re-inspection should not be scheduled until my challenges to the inspection report were resolved. Research into my challenge would reveal that the discrepancies recorded during the inspection are invalid.

"I also challenged your assignment to re-inspect my account. I doubt that you have the credentials and experience to conduct a crypto account inspection. Did you read my challenges to the first inspection?"

"Yes, I did."

"And what was your conclusion after researching my challenge?"

Rig answers, "I didn't research your challenge. I was only ordered to conduct a crypto account inspection in accordance with COMNAVTELCOM instructions."

In a tone of demand and angry frustration, Van Thorton questions, "Did anyone in authority at COMNAVTELCOM research my challenges?!"

"I don't know," Rig responds.

Furious that no one at COMNAVTELCOM took his challenges seriously, Van Thorton confronts in an indignant tone, "What is your experience with crypto accounts?!"

Rig informs, "I was the crypto account manager at two commands, and several weeks ago I was certified as a crypto account inspector."

Van Thorton, now realizing that Chief Page has more experience, asks, "Okay, where do you want to start?"

"I will conduct an inventory. I need last month's computer inventory from the crypto issuing office."

Van Thorton searches a file drawer and retrieves the specified report.

Rig takes the computerized list to the shelves holding crypto key cards and begins the inventory.

Twenty minutes later, Van Thorton becomes impatient toward Chief Page's tedious inventory procedures. He stands and walks toward the door. When he is abreast of Rig, Van Thorton says, "Chief, I have other things to do. I do not need to be here."

Rig places the palm of his hand on Van Thorton's chest and pushes him slightly backward and states, "You are not leaving, Lieutenant."

Incredulous that the chief is getting physical, Van Thorton warns, "Chief, unless you want to be charged with assault on an officer, you will let me pass."

Rig glances at the vault door. Then he pushes Van Thorton into the chair.

Confusion overcomes Van Thorton. Chief Page's physical aggression makes no sense. He knows that he cannot overpower the chief. He glances at the telephone.

"Leave the phone alone," Rig orders in menacing manner.

Van Thorton lowers his hand to rest on the desktop.

Rig raises his left leg and brings his left foot to rest on the edge of his desk. He pulls a dagger with a six-inch blade from a sheath strapped to his ankle. He points the business end of the dagger toward Van Thorton.

Fear overcomes Van Thorton as he follows Chief Page's actions. "Have you gone crazy, Chief?! What the fuck are you doing?!"

Rig informs, "You have been found out, Lieutenant. You have been dipping into the public trough and have been passing classified information to the enemy."

Van Thorton refuses to accept that he is cornered. He gains some courage and declares, "You have no authority here. You're just a chief petty officer." He jumps to a standing position and attempts to use his position as an officer to overcome this situation. "I am walking out that door, going straight to the captain's office, and report your conduct."

With his left hand, Rig slams the officer back into the chair. Then he states, "Lieutenant, I have the authority to beat you and cut you, and then deliver you to the federal agents surrounding this building."

Fear overtakes Van Thorton. His skin color pales and his entire body sweats. He finally accepts that Chief Page is an authorized federal agent.

"Or, Lieutenant, you can cooperate with us and prosecutors will take your cooperation into consideration."

Several moments pass before Van Thorton accepts his fate.

"What do you want me to do?"

Rig glances at his watch, then he informs, "In about five minutes, we will walk out the main door and get into the back seat of a sedan that will take us to your residence. Tonight, you and I will attend the weekly poker game at Enrico Mendoza's hacienda. I am standing in for Commander Pantero at the poker game. Commander Pantero has already informed Mendoza that he cannot attend tonight's poker game, and that you will bring another officer to take his place."

Now realizing that he will not be beaten and stabbed if he cooperates, Van Thorton has regained composure. He asks, "What will happen at the poker game?"

Rig answers, "Just remain calm and do not attempt to leave the hacienda and you will not be harmed."

Five minutes later, Chief Page and Lieutenant Van Thorton exit the communications center building at the communications center's rear door. Just outside the door, a dark sedan with passenger-side backdoor open is parked with motor idling.

Chief Page guides Van Thorton into the backseat; then he slides into the backseat and closes the door. Several sailors near the scene stop and observe the unusual actions.

Van Thorton observes that the sedan's door and window handles for the rear doors are missing.

Five minutes later, the sedan stops in front Lieutenant Van Thorton's residence located on Fort Amador. The federal agent in the front passenger seat exits the vehicle. Then he opens the rear doors and he opens the trunk.

Chief Page retrieves a small suitcase from the trunk. He orders Van Thorton, "Give me your car keys. One of these agents will get your car and drive it here. This evening, you and I will go to the poker game in your car."

Van Thorton hands over his car keys.

Chapter 89

Van Thorton's small, one-bedroom Bachelor Officers' Quarters apartment has tropical, rattan furniture décor. High speed fan hum emanates from two small window-mounted air conditioners—one in the living room and one in the bedroom.

Rig stands in Van Thorton's living room.

One of the federal agents sits on the living room couch and fingers through a magazine.

The other federal agent stands guard over Van Thorton in the bedroom while Van Thorton dresses.

Rig is already dressed for the poker game, wearing casual tan-colored slacks and light-blue, short-sleeved guayabera. He lifts his left foot and rests it on the seat of a dining chair and adjusts the position of the dagger strapped to the outside of his left ankle. He reaches into his suitcase and pulls out his nine-millimeter Beretta in an ankle holster.

In the bedroom, Van Thorton inspects his image in the full-length mirror. He considers the cheap, white-colored, short-sleeve shirt, light-blue slacks, and soft leather slip-on shoes adequate for the jail cell that he knows he is soon to occupy. He assumes that sometime this evening he will be taken to a jail cell. He hopes for a jail in the Canal Zone and not one of those filthy, bug-infested jails in Panama City.

Van Thorton steps from the bedroom into the living room and utters a gasp when he sees Chief Page strapping on an ankle holster. In an apprehensive tone and manner, he asks, "Why do you need a gun, Chief? What are you planning?"

Rig casts a quizzical stare at Van Thorton.

Van Thorton has regained his arrogant manner.

Rig responds, "The only thing you need to know, Lieutenant, is that if I pull my weapon, you must hit the floor."

A look of fear crosses Van Thorton's face.

Rig says, "Don't be concerned, Lieutenant. Hit the deck like I said, and you will be okay. Now, what can I expect to happen from the time we get out of the car at Mendoza's hacienda and the start of the poker game?"

Van Thorton answers, "After entering through the front door, we walk to the end of the hallway where the game room is located. We will find some or all the players already gathered. All the players, except Mendoza, will be American military officers who have black-market dealings with Mendoza. We will drink cocktails and eat hors d'oeuvres for about an hour. During that cocktail hour, Mendoza will take each officer, individually, to the terrace just outside the game room. The poker game is a lure to get all his suppliers together at the same time. We all play because we enjoy the evening. The game is low stakes and low stress. While we play, we imbibe the finest liquors, consume quality food, and smoke the best Cuban cigars. It's sort of like a perk for doing business with him. But no business talk allowed while playing poker—Mendoza's strict rule. He does not want each of his suppliers knowing the products and prices of the others."

Rig asks, "How will Mendoza react to me, a stranger, being there?"

"No problem. We've had substitutes before—usually military officers that Mendoza might recruit into one of his many enterprises. He will ask you a lot of questions about your background and work in the navy. And a lot of times he invites Panamanian government officials to the game—another reason he does not want business discussed at the table. Oh, Mendoza is an acquaintance of Omar Torrijos. So Mendoza has influence with the Panamanian government." Van Thorton's tone becomes serious as he warns, "You need to be free with information about yourself. If you appear resistant, Mendoza will become suspicious."

Rig nods understanding and responds, "In that case, just introduce me as Chief Petty Officer Rigney Page. I will respond to any questions about me and what I do."

While Van Thorton navigates his car along the Pan-American

Highway through the city of Panama, Rig runs the CIA plan through his mind. The poker game should start at 7:30 PM. At 8:14 PM, Rig will pull his weapon, and order everyone to lie on the floor. At 8:15 PM, American Special Forces storm the hacienda, penetrate the building, killing or capturing Mendoza's guards and hacienda servants. At the same time that Special Forces enter the front door, an element of the Special Forces Team will go directly to the game room via the terrace, followed by federal agents who will relieve Rig and arrest Mendoza and the American officers. During the mission briefings, capturing Mendoza alive was emphasized as top priority. The government needs Mendoza's statements regarding his terrorist actions for The Longjumeau Alliance.

Rig has the ONI CIA mission plan down pat in his mind. Now, he runs through his mind The Guardians' modified plan—a small modification with significant results.

While driving, Lieutenant Van Thorton considers the promise made many times by Mendoza. *"If your business association with me is discovered, I will give you a new life with new identity. You will never want for anything."*

Van Thorton decides that when he and Mendoza are on the terrace discussing business, he will expose Chief Page; then he will ask Mendoza for a new life and new identity.

The armed guard at the gate to Mendoza's property stands under the security lights of the gatehouse; he motions for Van Thorton to stop.

Van Thorton dims his headlights.

The guard shines a flashlight into the car. He recognizes Van Thorton as a frequent visitor. He waves the car through.

Fifty yards later, Van Thorton brings his car to a stop in front of the sprawling Hacienda where five other cars are parked. Two guards with automatic rifles slung over their shoulders stand near the group of cars. Van Thorton gives Chief Page a glance that conveys danger awaits. He reaches for the keys to shutoff the engine.

"Wait!" Rig orders.

Van Thorton pulls his hand back from the keys.

Rig says, "I know what you are thinking, Lieutenant. You know that Mendoza has a total of six armed men standing guard inside and outside. Floodlights illuminate the outside of the hacienda for 150 feet toward the jungle. You doubt that I can do anything effective inside that hacienda and get away with it. Therefore, you consider betraying me to Mendoza." Rig pauses and judges Van Thorton's response.

Van Thorton expresses nothing.

Rig directs, "Look toward the jungle." Rig nods toward the jungle that is beyond the security floodlights and cannot be seen because of the dark of night.

Van Thorton looks toward the direction of the jungle that he cannot see.

Rig warns, "There are two dozen American Special Forces and federal agents out there. No one walks away free tonight. The forces against you are greater than you can imagine."

Van Thorton attempts to understand the strength of that force.

"You have nowhere to run, Lieutenant, not even The Longjumeau Alliance and Edwin Kendley who is already in custody."

Van Thorton flinches and his body goes stiff. He blinks his eyes, expressing astonishment that his affiliation with the Edwin Kendley and The Longjumeau Alliance has been discovered. His body goes limp as a result of knowing that his life no longer has any value."

Rig comments, "If you act depressed in that game room, Mendoza might become suspicious. Now, cheer up because if all goes as planned you will die only of old age."

Hoping to gain Rig's advocacy for special consideration after being arrested, Van Thorton advises, "Mendoza has some pistols and rifles in the game room, and they are always loaded."

Rig already knows that, but he asks, "Where?"

"The rifles are in gun racks mounted to the walls. Pistols are in the top drawer of a chest located under the painting of a leopard."

Rig commands, "Okay, let's go inside."

Chapter 90

The interior of the game room is mostly as Rig remembers it from the raid several months ago. The game room is the largest room in the hacienda. The walls are cream colored stucco and the floor is made from dark brown ceramic tile. Oil paintings of wildlife decorate the walls. A lion skin rug lies near a corner—outside of the normal walking path. Several settees with coffee tables stand against one wall. An official-size pool table stands in the middle of the room. An eight-seat, green felt covered poker table is located near the door to the terrace.

During that raid several months ago, all valuables were taken from the hacienda, including all the guns in the game room, to make the raid look like a robbery instead of an intelligence gathering raid. Mendoza wasted no time in replacing the guns.

Rig immediately recognizes Mendoza who stands near a sideboard full of hors d'oeuvres and bottles of liquor and wine. Mendoza sips from a brandy snifter.

 The other men in the room look like typical military men in civilian clothes—short hair, clothing that is too loose or too tight, and shoes that do not go with the style of clothes. The topic of conversation is sports, mostly baseball.

While Mendoza appears to be engaged in conversation with two of his American military business associates, he has one eye on the substitute player. Mendoza makes a quick evaluation of the navy chief that Commander Pantero suggested as a substitute for the poker game. Mendoza immediately evaluates Rigney Page as a person that can handle himself in adverse physical situations, as are several of the army officers currently in the game room.

Van Thorton guides Chief Page to the group where Mendoza converses with two American officers; Van Thorton performs the introductions. He presents the chief as *Rigney Page*. Mendoza and the two officers enthusiastically welcome Chief Page to the game.

"What is your job in the United States Navy?" Mendoza asks Rig.

Rig responds, "I work in test and certification of new communications systems and upgrades of current systems. I am also an inspector of telecommunications operations."

"That must be interesting work. How long have you been engaged in those activities?"

"Ten Months."

Mendoza spends a few moments contemplating Rig's words; then he comments, "I have read that the United States Navy relies more and more on satellites for communications, navigation, and intelligence gathering. Is that correct?"

Rig responds, "Yes. That is correct."

Mendoza asks, "How many satellites are used by your navy?"

"I don't know. Even if I did, that would be classified, and I could not reveal the number."

Mendoza casts an apologetic expression and responds, "Yes, of course, my regrets for asking." Mendoza turns his attention to Lieutenant Van Thorton and says, "Christian, I must have a few words with you. Please come with me to the terrace." Then Mendoza says to Rig, "Rigney, please enjoy the food and drink. We will start the game when Christian and I return from the terrace."

Having not eaten since breakfast this morning, the buffet draws Rig to it. He takes a small plate at the end of the table. Then he selects a filet of Chilean sea bass, one rolled tamale, and a scoop of cucumber and tomato salad. At the end of the table he selects a chilled bottle of *Panama Cerveza*. Then, he sits down at one of the settees next to one of the other guests.

Fifteen minutes later, Mendoza calls his guests to the poker table. Everyone has a traditional seat. Rig takes the open seat where Commander Pantero normally sits. Rig's seat puts the terrace door behind him and has him directly across the table from Mendoza.

Rig plays his poker hands as described in the books that he has read on the game. He loses every hand that he plays to the showdown. Occasionally, he glances at the ornate clock mounted on the far wall. While Van Thorton and Mendoza were on the terrace, Rig confirmed that the clock on the wall is in synch with his own watch. When he needs to check the time, he just stares across the room, disguising his actions as fixed on any object other than the clock. The joint plan calls for him to pull his weapon at 8:14 and order everyone in the game to lie on the floor facedown and side-by-side. At 8:15, Special Forces Teams and federal agents will attack the hacienda. The schedule calls for Special Forces and federal agents to come through the terrace door and into the game room sometime between 8:16 and 8:17. At maximum, Rig must keep his targets on the floor for three minutes, which could become extremely difficult if any of them illogically decide to become defiant. If any of his captives attack him, he is authorized to shoot them.

Van Thorton constantly has his eyes on Chief Page. He does not want to miss the signal to hit the deck.

Shouting and gunfire erupt outside the hacienda.

Rig glances at the clock—8:11.

The players look startled.

Mendoza jumps from his seat and dashes toward his weapons stash in the weapons chest against the wall under the leopard painting.

Rig jumps up from his seat with gun in hand. He shouts, "All of you on the floor—now! Face down—now! Do it now, or I start shooting!"

All the American officers hesitate a few seconds, attempting to understand and appraise the danger. Shouting in English and shouting in Spanish and gunfire from outside are still being heard by the poker players.

Rig fires a warning shot in the direction of the officers. Several of them begin their dive to the floor.

Rig shifts his attention to Mendoza who is away from the group of officers and who is opening the top draw of the weapons chest. Rig shouts, "Mendoza, down on the floor now, or I shoot!" Rig plans to shoot and kill Mendoza anyway because that is what he promised The Guardians via John Smith. Rig's loud warning to Mendoza was for witnesses to report later, "Yes, Page warned

Mendoza before shooting him to death."

During the span of a split second, Van Thorton decides he will side with Mendoza and he makes a dive toward Chief Page with the intention of disarming him.

Rig is in the act of pulling the trigger that will place a bullet in the back of Mendoza's head when he is knocked sideways by the charging Van Thorton. Rig's Beretta fires a fraction of a second after being knocked sideways. The nine-millimeter bullet shatters Mendoza's right elbow.

Mendoza falls to his knees, screaming in pain. He uses his left forearm against the top of weapons chest to keep himself from falling to the floor. He looks over his shoulder and sees Van Thorton wrestling with Rigney Page.

Page is on his back attempting to fight off Van Thorton. Van Thorton has both his hands wrapped around the gun in Chief Page's right hand. Chief Page balls his left fist; then slams his fist into Van Thorton's right kidney. Van Thorton yelps but does not lessen this grip on Page's gun.

Rig is surprised at Van Thorton's powerful two-handed death grip on the gun. Rig reasons quickly that Van Thorton made his choice and now will fight to the death to make his choice a success.

Using his left forearm, Mendoza pushes himself to a standing position. Then, with his left hand, he grabs an automatic pistol from the top drawer of the weapons chest. Excruciating pain shoots through Mendoza's right arm. Then, the futility of storing only automatic pistols in the weapons chest hits him. He has no strength in his right arm and hand to pull back the slide to chamber a round.

Sounds of men speaking English come from the terrace. Outside gunfire has ceased.

Mendoza again glances over his shoulder and sees five poker players lying face down on the floor and sees Van Thorton and Rigney Page struggling on the floor—Van Thorton on top of Page and Page on his back. Mendoza knows he has only a few seconds to escape. He decides to take the automatic with him, hoping he will discover a way to lock and load. He steps quickly to the side of the weapons chest and pulls back on the edge of a tapestry that hangs from ceiling to floor.

Rig has not yet overcome Van Thorton who still has a powerful two-handed death grip on Rig's gun. Rig's strength allows him to keep hold of his gun. He is about to smash his balled left fist into Van Thorton's kidney again, but he notices Mendoza's action of moving back the edge of the tapestry; Rig immediately concludes: *An escape passage!*

Rig hears multiple feet running on the terrace. He knows he does not have enough time to fight off Van Thorton and also stop Mendoza from disappearing behind that tapestry. Rig observes the automatic pistol in Mendoza's left hand. The unknown factor being how soon that U.S. Special Forces Team storms into the game room. Additional gunfire and shouting in Spanish coming from outside tells Rig that the Special Forces Team is delayed.

While still pinned down on his back by Van Thorton and his right hand occupied by Van Thorton's two-hand grip on the gun, Rig reaches to his left ankle with his left hand, pulls the dagger from its sheath, and throws the dagger at Mendoza.

The point of the dagger enters the right side of Mendoza's neck. The strong force behind Rig's throw drives the dagger blade through Mendoza's neck and slices Mendoza's windpipe. Blood flows into Mendoza's windpipe and down to his lungs. Mendoza topples and falls to the floor while choking on his own blood.

Rig returns to the task of overpowering Van Thorton.

Five seconds later, the Special Forces Team enters the game room, followed by federal agents from naval intelligence, Army CID, Navy NIS, and the CIA. One of the Special Forces soldiers smacks the back of Van Thorton's head with a rifle butt.

Van Thorton's body goes limp.

Rig pushes Van Thorton aside; then he stands. He glances at the clock on the wall. Less than ninety seconds have passed since the shouting and gunfire were first heard by the poker players.

All the Special Forces soldiers and all the civilian federal agents wear jungle cammies and boonie hats and have streaks of black and green grease paint on their hands and faces. They move around the room and frisk and handcuff the bad guys.

Two civilian agents wearing cammies stand over Mendoza and look down at him. Rig recognizes John Smith as one of the two men standing over Mendoza. Rig goes to John Smith's side. Rig notices that Mendoza jerks while still attempting to breathe.

John turns his head toward Rig and asks Rig, "Did you do this?"

"Yes," Rig responds. "He was going to escape. I had to stop him."

"Escape how?"

Rig pulls back on the tapestry and reveals a narrow passageway. He comments, "This passageway wasn't here during our previous raid on this place."

John comments amusingly, "Stopping him with a gun would have been easier; but no, you must be theatrical."

Rig responds, "Because you started shooting early, I had to improvise, adapt, and overcome."

John informs, "Oh, one of Mendoza's guards detected us. We had to move the battle plan up a little bit."

With a knowing grin on his face, Rig comments, "Well, that's the nature of battle plans, isn't it? When the shooting starts, battle plans become shit."

John responds, "That's been my experience."

Mendoza takes his last tortuous breath; then he lies still.

John states, "We were supposed to take Mendoza alive."

Rig informs, "That objective was overcome by events when the shooting started early."

"How unfortunate for Mendoza," John announces; his face casting a conspiratorial grin.

"Yeah," Rig responds.

Rig and John move away from Mendoza and walk to the middle of the room where Van Thorton lies handcuffed and unconscious.

John comments, "When I came into the room, that little guy there was giving you some trouble. A guy of your size and strength should have handled him easily."

Rig chuckles; then says, "Well, he was significantly motivated. He chose a side and could not about-face. He knew that surrendering to me would lead to an unhappy life ahead."

John comments back, "Appears that he will have an unhappy life ahead, anyway."

Rig sighs deeply; then says in a serious tone, "His choice."

Chapter 91

Senator Clay Porter, Professor Bartholomew Goldman, and CLWUA President Gaylord Tarkingson are the last three remaining captives. They believe their defiant courage will prevail and they will eventually be released without having to comply with their captors' demands.

They sit in the wardroom eating breakfast. They wear filthy, foul smelling clothes. Their hair is long and oily, and they all sprout beards of varying lengths. Water is available in their staterooms to sinks and toilets only for fifteen minutes per day. Those fifteen minutes are random; so they never know when they can take advantage of it.

The quality and quantity of the food drastically decreased over the last week. They no longer get fresh food. All their food comes from cans or frozen cartons. Gaylord Tarkingson describes the powdered eggs and spam as reminders of his four years in the U.S. Navy aboard an oiler.

They hear a noise coming from the bulkhead nearest them. They turn toward the noise just in time to see a panel door open and a stack of newspapers fall through the opening to the floor.

Professor Goldman gathers up the stack of *Washington Post* newspapers and lays them on the table. Each grab for their own copy. The two-inch high, bold, capitalized headline informs: PHILANTHROPIST EDWIN KENDLEY INDICTED!

All three captives are silent as they greedily read every word of the first current news since the beginning of their captivity. They read the charges against Kendley. Their first reaction is to think the evidence against Kendley was manufactured by their captors; but as the article reveals more details, the more convincing the charges become. Each of them inhales sharply and expresses fear and astonishment as the article quotes an FBI spokesman saying that investigations have been initiated into all who associate with Edwin Kendley, specifically those who were kidnapped at the Kendley Estate. The article also informs that Edwin Kendley his being held in a secret location by federal marshals.

Senator Clay Porter, Professor Bartholomew Goldman, and CLWUA President Gaylord Tarkingson know they need to be free to fight any evidence—manufactured or not—that might surface about them.

A crackling noise comes from the wardroom announcement speaker. A familiar electronic voice warns, "Your time is running out."

Chapter 92

Diane Love opens her eyes.

The room is mostly dark. Sunlight splashes around curtain edges.

She pushes back the sheets and blanket. She rises and turns to sit on the edge of the bed. She immediately sees a person sitting in a chair across the room. Her eyes adjust. She recognizes her lifelong friend, Rigney Page.

Rig reaches above his head and flips the light switch. The room becomes brightly illuminated.

Diane sighs deeply and expresses joy as she recognizes she is in a cheap hotel room and not the stateroom where she was held captive. She looks down at herself and sees that she wears the same pajamas she wore to bed in the stateroom. She scans the room. Her suitcase lies open on a bench at the foot of the bed. Rig wears casual jeans and a polo shirt. Then an expression of confusion crosses her face. "Where am I?"

"In a motel room along I-95 in Virginia."

Still expressing confusion, she questions, "I was kidnapped. Who brought me here?"

Rig lies. "I do not know who brought you here."

"Have those kidnappers been caught?"

"I don't know."

Diane furrows her eyebrows while attempting to understand what has happened. Then an expression of revelation crosses her face. She asks, "How did you know I was here, then?"

"An anonymous call to the CIA."

"The CIA!" Then she remembers her kidnappers told her that they knew she is an undercover agent for the KGB. "You're with the CIA?!"

Rig does not answer the question. He says, "I am here to prepare you for what happens next. One hour from now, three CIA agents will park a panel van just outside the door. You will exit this room with your suitcase and enter that van. They will strap you into a chair—a comfortable chair—in the back of the van. You will not have a view of the outside. They will take you to a CIA safe house where you will spend one week receiving training on how you will interact with your KGB controller in the future. You will also be taught how to convince the KGB that being kidnapped had nothing to do with your connection to the KGB. After CIA training, you will be sedated again and transferred to another motel. Then discovery of you being released from your kidnappers will unfold in the same manner as it did for those released before you. After a short questioning period with the FBI, you can go back to your life and your job at the White House."

Diane trembles. Tears flow from her eyes, and she weeps. Her life's goals are crumbling. "What if I refuse?" she challenges in a failed attempt at defiance.

"Then you will be tried and convicted of treason and espionage against the United States. You will go to federal prison for twenty years or more."

Diane knows that Rig tells the truth. During her meeting with her kidnappers, they showed her the evidence against her. They showed her pictures of her meeting with Jordan. Then they showed her a list of the classified documents to which she requested from the State Department and the Defense Department. They also had video and audio of two meetings between her and Jordan in which she handed Jordan copies of the plans for the new Ohio class Trident missile submarines and a list of military search radar upgrades to include new microchip technology.

Diane stops weeping as she accepts her fate. However, concern for her future safety places a constant frown on her face. "How long have you known about me and the KGB?"

"Since shortly after I returned from Sardinia last year."

"So you are more than a navy radioman, then?"

"That's right, but you will never tell anyone that."

Diane chokes back a few sobs as she concludes, "So you have not been my friend. You have been investigating me—using me."

"Diane, you're an enemy of the state. You are a traitor to your country. I have known that for the past year. My feelings toward you have not been friendly for a long time, especially after I uncovered your leadership role in The Longjumeau Alliance."

"Rig, America is an unjust country controlled by corporations. My cause is to change that—to make America a just and compassionate nation where all citizens are equal."

"And to do that you find it necessary to deceive the American people and to kill them in oilrig explosions, train explosions, and poisoning them with over-the-counter drugs. You crusade to enslave the American people in the name of justice and equality."

"Our vision of America is a social paradise where no one wants for anything. Income equality will produce happy and satisfied citizens."

Rig shakes his head and exhibits disagreement. "Diane, that's not true. You live in an unrealistic bubble. People are happiest when they are free to prosper by their own initiative. Government with an unconstitutional agenda destroys freedom and prosperity. Your cause—your agenda—is anti-constitution. Your social paradise would deny individual liberty to achieve reward in accordance with individual skills and productivity."

Diane explains, "Those who have superior ability will sacrifice reward for the good of the people."

Rig stares at Diane; he exhibits contempt. He asks, "And what happens to the wealth and property of individual Americans when you and your comrades establish this utopia?"

"All property will be confiscated by government and distributed fairly by government to those who need it."

"And once the lazy and unproductive have consumed all the property of producers and there is no more to redistribute, then what?"

"Then everyone will be equal, and everyone will work for the benefit of the collective good."

Rig shakes his head and exhibits contempt. He queries, "What about the millions in your trust fund and the trust funds of your friends? Will all of you give it up willingly?"

Diane expresses stunned revelation. She had always considered that she and her comrades who have the unique ability and insight to govern an American utopia would keep their wealth and property—as special privilege for their uniquely talented ability to transform America into a utopian society. Then reality hits her. She announces. "It doesn't matter anymore. As a condition of my release from those kidnappers I had to promise to resign from The Longjumeau Alliance, as did the others. The Alliance will fall apart, unless Edwin can rebuild it somehow."

"Not a chance," Rig declares. "Edwin Kendley is in jail. He has been indicted by a federal grand jury. He will stand trial for terrorism and for crimes against humanity and for securities fraud."

"What?!" Diane responds. "What rightwing conspiracy brought that on? Edwin Kendley is a kind and generous man. He is committed to the welfare of the American people." She is silent for a few moments while considering her next statement. "It's those kidnappers. They made us agree to discontinue what they called our 'Marxist pursuits' or they would expose our organization and our agenda. They said that if they caught me engaged in Marxist activities they would ruin me—personally, professionally, and financially. They took one-third of my wealth already. They must be an organized group of rightwing extremists—like the John Birch Society and that new Libertarian Party. Obviously, they have framed Edwin."

Rig shakes his head and expresses sadness for his high school girlfriend's warped sense of causality. He tells her, "The Longjumeau Alliance was the organizer and funder of terror. Your alliance created economic and environmental crises. Hundreds died. Your motive being that America's Marxist politicians could declare corporate greed at the cost of safety and call for nationalization of the oil, pharmaceutical, and railroad industries. And while The Longjumeau Alliance was controlling tragic events, Edwin Kendley positioned his stock portfolio to take advantage of those events before they happened. He made hundreds of millions of dollars. And you went along with it all."

Diane conveys defiance. She shows no shame.

"Diane, do you know what is meant by the term *useful idiots?*"

"Yes," Diane states still conveying defiance.

"Well, that's how Edwin Kendley used you and your friends. He capitalized on your Marxist zeal to contribute to his wealth."

Astonished and bewildered, Diane considers the waste her life has become.

"You better get dressed. The CIA will be here shortly."

With an embarrassed and dejected expression and with eyes cast down, she whimpers, "What you must think of me."

Rig shakes his head and expresses contempt. With resentment in his tone he tells her, "Diane, for the past ten years, I volunteered for dangerous missions in service to my country to protect the American Republic from the enslavement of communism. I was nearly killed a couple of times. I did it willingly to keep my country safe. I fought America's enemies in foreign lands so that my fellow countrymen need not face those enemies on American soil.

"Then I come back to the States and discover that you, rich Americans, media moguls, Congressmen, labor leaders, and reporters plot to transform America into a communist country. You and your kind use lies, intimidation, and murder as a means to progress your Marxist crusade. When honest, freedom loving politicians challenge your leftist crusade, you engage in venomous, unethical character assassination against those politicians. When you are on the attack against freedom loving Americans, no lie is too bold, no deceit is too deep, and no misrepresentation is too outrageous. You conspire to eliminate individual liberties and loot the earnings of common citizens. You demonize the quest for self-reliance, and you vilify the pursuit of financial independence, which is the path to the American dream. What is so sad about what you do is that millions of Americans believe what you say and have no idea as to the destructive nature of your collectivist ideology."

Rig shakes his head and expresses contempt as he adds, "What is it about leftists that you think you have the inherent right to control the lives of your fellow man and force your will on others?

What is it that makes leftists confident that their so-called altruistic cause justifies lying, deceiving, destroying, and killing to accumulate lemming followers? You lay down rules and laws that you exempt yourself from following. I'm disgusted by your arrogant, privileged governing class mentality."

Rig pauses. For a moment, he is subdued by Diane's apologetic and fearful expression. She cowers like prey that knows it is about to be eaten.

Rig explains, "Every four years when I reenlist, I pledge to support and defend the Constitution of the United States against all enemies, foreign and domestic. You and your Marxist friends are those domestic enemies that I pledge to fight. You are my enemy."

With the pleading eyes of one who is about to lose everything, she asks, "Will I ever see you again?"

"I don't know."

Tears flow from Diane's eyes. She states, "We were in love once. Does that mean nothing to you?"

Rig sighs deeply and expresses regret. "We believed in the same things back then. Those memories will always be in my heart."

Diane stands. She wobbles a bit. "What about Striper? Is she okay?"

"She's in a kitty kennel. Address and phone number are on your kitchen table."

"Thank you." Diane takes her suitcase and enters the bathroom.

Sadness overcomes Rig. Tears fill his eyes and flow down his cheeks.

Chapter 93

Four Months Later

Complying with regulations for travel on military transport, Rig wears his Service Dress Blue uniform. The rows of ribbons on his chest are topped with his Submarine Warfare Insignia. His Surface Warfare Insignia is positioned below those ribbons. The white colored star above his gold colored rank chevron signifies his new rank of senior chief petty officer.

Rig boarded the military charter flight at Andrews Air Force Base. The charter flight made one stop at Charleston, South Carolina to pick up the Blue Crew of the ballistic nuclear powered submarine USS *John Hancock* that is home-ported in Rota, Spain. The submarine tender USS *Antares*, also home-ported at Rota, is Rig's destination.

Several hours ago, Rig introduced himself to the Chief-of the-Boat of the Blue Crew and asked if he could hitch a ride with the Blue Crew on one of the charter buses that will transport them from the naval station air field to the submarine pier. The Chief-of-the-Boat—a master chief radioman—who was one of Rig's instructors in submarine radioman school more than a decade ago remembered Rig and readily granted his request for the ride.

Now, Rig stares out the airplane window at the choppy, white-capped North Atlantic Ocean below. He thinks about his transfer orders to the submarine tender, USS *Antares*, at Rota, Spain. ONI arranged the assignment three months ago   shortly after the Senior Chief Selection List was released navy wide.

His cover assignment will be that of USS *Antares* Communications Division Leading Chief. His naval intelligence missions will be assigned by the Officer-in-Charge Task Force 152 Detachment Rota, which is the cover name for the local naval intelligence office. Rig's chain-of-command aboard USS *Antares* is unaware of Rig's affiliation with naval intelligence.

Two weeks after his orders to USS *Antares* were issued. Rig received a welcome aboard package from the USS *Antares* Communications Officer, Lieutenant Christine Hawthorne. The welcome aboard letter was the standard typewritten and mimeographed style letter. At the bottom of the letter, Lieutenant Hawthorne handwrote a personal note: "Rig, I am thrilled you are coming to Rota. I'm looking forward to 'working' with you again." Rig chuckled when he read the *'working'* comment. He and Lieutenant Christine Hawthorne had a three-month romantic relationship two years ago when they were both stationed in Thurso, Scotland.

Then, to his surprise, Rig received a letter from Radioman First Class Sharon MacDill. He was surprise as he stared at the return address of USS *Antares*. During Rig's last four months at Thurso—months after Christine Hawthorne transferred—he and Sharon had a relationship. Sharon's letter was full of hopes that they would resume their love affair.

Rig is only moderately concerned that he will face two former lovers at the same location. He wonders if Lieutenant Christine Hawthorne and Radioman First Class Sharon MacDill know about the other's relationship with him.

He shifts his thoughts to his upcoming naval intelligence missions. Compared to his undercover work, romantic conflicts are minor.

His mind turns to events that occurred during the past four months. Stories about the Nazi Raiders Case saturated the Washington newspapers and T.V. news every day. Nazi Raiders is the name assigned by the media to those who made the daring raid on the Kendley Estate and abducted more than a dozen people, including members of Congress, union officials, and leaders of business.

All of those abducted had been released by the Nazi Raiders. None of those abducted revealed the terms of their release. However, over the months, the media quoted secret sources that all those who were kidnapped belonged to a secret cult and were engaged in cult rituals at the Kendley Estate. Other news outlets reported from secret sources that those abducted belonged to a secret communist organization plotting the overthrow of the U.S. Government. Of course, none of those reports were validated with solid facts.

When asked questions by reporters, those who had been abducted adhered to their stories that they were kidnapped by unknown people. None of those kidnapped knew the location of their captivity, and they would not reveal the details of their ransom for fear of reprisals from their kidnappers.

"We never saw our kidnappers," Congressman Billy Thayer told one reporter. "They talked to us through a speaker system and one-way windows."

"We were held on a ship," Professor Goldman told one reporter in a moment of forgetting the terms of his release.

"We were not held on a ship," replied CLWUA President Gaylord Tarkingson to a reporter's question on a Sunday morning talk show. "I was in the navy for four years. I know what the inside of a ship looks like, and I tell you that we were not held aboard a ship, although our kidnappers attempted to deceive us into believing we were on a ship."

Through classified CIA intelligence reports, Rig discovered that during FBI investigations of Edwin Kendley and the Nazi Raiders the FBI uncovered the existence of The Longjumeau Alliance. In America, people are free to belong to communist organizations, secret or not. The FBI judged the information about The Longjumeau Alliance as essential information for their ongoing investigation. Therefore, the FBI did not release information regarding The Longjumeau Alliance to the public.

Senator Clay Porter shocked many in Congress when he pulled his *Fair Profits Tax Act* bill and his *Employee Fairness Act* bill from committee consideration.

During an FBI press conference, the FBI announced that all abductees were persons of interest in the Edwin Kendley terrorism case. The FBI spokesman said, "We are interviewing everyone regarding terrorism and securities fraud charges against Mr.

Kendley."

The Ethics Committees in both the U.S. House of Representatives and the U.S. Senate advised through a press conference that they had received detailed reports from the FBI on the finances of some senators, including Senator Clay Porter and a dozen representatives in the House. The financial reports were accumulated as part of the Nazi Raiders Case. The Chairmen of the House Ethics Committee was quoted as saying, "How do those who had no measurable wealth a decade ago and with an annual salary of less than eighty-thousand dollars per year accumulate a net worth of tens of millions of dollars?" One area each committee declared they would investigate is Congressional insider trading of stocks and commodities. All those under investigation will be removed from committees until the Ethics Committees publish their findings.

The Armed Services Subcommittee, of which Clay Porter had been removed as Chairman, released its report on the shooting death of Ensign Franklyn Ryan. The conclusion of the committee was that Ensign Ryan was not mentally suitable to serve as an officer in the navy. Ensign Ryan suffered from paranoia and believed Chief Page led a conspiracy to discredit him. The subcommittee also concluded that when Ensign Ryan entered La Maddalena Fleet Landing where he shot Chief Page, he had entered an operation zone of undercover operatives. By chance, one of those operatives who was physically closest to Ensign Ryan properly read the situation and shot Ensign Ryan to prevent him from firing bullets into Chief Page's head. The Subcommittee's recommendation was that the U.S. Navy should tighten its mental stability requirements for new officers.

The surviving ex-marine who attempted to abduct Rig and Sally Macfurson in that Maryland café was found guilty of attempted kidnapping and found guilty of illegal possession of firearms. The CLWUA National Director of Security was found guilty of co-conspiracy to the kidnapping. According to a press release from CLWUA President Gaylord Tarkingson, *"The National Director of Security acted on his own and without the knowledge of the national president."* Tarkingson was quoted as calling the attempted kidnapping a *"despicable act that offends the sensibilities of the CLWUA rank and file."*

One Sunday evening around 10:00 PM, a caretaker at the Kendley Estate in Connecticut received a bomb threat over the telephone. The caretaker cleared the mansion of all servants. Thirty minutes later, the mansion exploded. The rubble has since been leveled and removed. Investigators later reported that the Nazi Raiders cleverly hid remote control explosives during the night they abducted Kendley and his guests.

On a Sunday morning at 2:00 AM, a team of terrorists launched four separate rockets at the CLWUA National Headquarters in Chevy Chase, Maryland. No one was injured. The rockets targeted the executive offices and caused over five-million dollars in damage. The FBI has no leads in that case, other than associating it with the attack on the CLWUA Southern California District Headquarters several months earlier.

In another development, The Washington Post published an opinion from the editor regarding a recent CLWUA strike against developers of a new casino in Las Vegas. The editor commented, *"During the two week workers strike, there were no occurrences of vandalism, intimidation, violence, or personal injuries that normally mark a CLWUA strike. The construction companies and the CLWUA came to an agreement peacefully."* The editor speculated, *"Appears that CLWUA President Gaylord Tarkingson may have been transformed during his recent kidnapping, and now the CLWUA is a 'kinder and gentler' labor union."*

Diane Love returned to her job on the White House staff. She spoke only once to the press. In responding to questions, she stated that she did not know the identity of the Nazi Raiders. She confirmed what others had said—that she and old college friends had gathered at the Kendley Estate for a reunion. Diane refused to discuss the terms of her release.

Rig has not seen Diane Love since that day he delivered her to the CIA. Several months ago, Diane left a message on Rig's apartment answering machine. She asked him to call her. He did not return her call.

The least significant event in Rig's life during the past four months was that the quality assurance testing of the software upgrade for the naval communication CUDIXS platform was finally completed and certified for release. The upgrade is currently being installed at naval communications stations around the world.

Rig's last contact with The Guardians occurred four nights after he returned from the Panama Mission. At the Watergate, Rig provided a detailed verbal report regarding the raid on Mendoza's hacienda. Denton Phillips advised Rig that The Guardians are appreciative of Rig's contributions. Rig committed to be cooperative in the future.

The most shocking event for Rig happened last week during his visit to the Page family home in Seal Beach, California. Rig and his father and his father's brother went on a weekend fishing trip to Catalina Island on his father's cabin cruiser.

While at anchor near Catalina Island on Saturday evening, Rig, James, and Dave sat in folding deckchairs on the boat's aft deck. They drank Mexican beer from brown-colored beer bottles and talked about events of the past year.

James Page commented, "It's been more than four months since those union thugs stopped harassing us. Those Nazi Raiders must have scared the hell out of that son-of-a-bitch Gaylord Tarkingson."

"Same with me," Dave Page stated. "They were gone soon after Tarkingson was released. Some of the papers say that Tarkingson was kidnapped by anti-union zealots who threatened to kill him if he did not stop his violence and intimidation against business owners."

Rig remembered that it was about four months ago when those tailing him discontinued.

"Customers that had abandoned me are coming back," James said.

"Same with me," Uncle Dave added.

Rig asked, "What about that reporter, Weston Pyth? Is he still missing?"

"Yep. Still missing," James Page responded.

With venom in his tone, Dave Page declared, "That lying commie son-of-a-bitch cost me lots of business because of his newspaper articles."

Rig asked, "How is business now—for both of you?"

James Page answered, "Been on the upswing for me since that Pyth went missing and his lies against me stopped."

"Same for me," Dave Page said. "My roofing business is growing rapidly now."

After a short pause in the conversation, Rig asked, "How are things going, generally, out here in Southern California?"

James answered, "County and state business regulations on the increase and so are business taxes. Chamber of Commerce reports that the cost of doing business in California has increased by twelve percent during the past four years. That is cutting into our margins and causing us to increase our prices. Most businesses in California have raised their prices due to the increased cost of doing business."

Rig asked, "Why are regulations increasing and why are taxes going up?"

"Goddamn mother-fuckin' Democrats," Dave Page spurted in an angry, bitter tone. "They need our tax money to buy votes from the fuckin' bottom feeders. And the no-balls Republicans not wanting to be called uncompassionate to the poor are going along with it." Dave paused for a second as he gathered his thoughts; then he stated, "California is becoming a goddamn welfare state, and people like me and your father are feeding the welfare beast."

"Can't anything be done about it?" Rig questioned.

"I don't know," James responded. "The Democrat voting base gets larger ever year. I fear that large corporations will flee California, forcing us small businessmen who remain behind to carry the welfare load."

Rig reached into the ice chest for another bottle of beer but could not find one. "We are out of beer," he announced.

James Page informed, "I've got about ten cases tied down in the forward void. You can get to it through a sliding panel in the forward sleeping compartment."

Rig stepped down into the cabin and walked forward. He easily found the sliding panel and opened it. He looked through the opening and observed that the void was dark. A small flashlight was mounted in straps next to the panel. He loosened the straps and removed the flashlight. He pointed the flashlight beam into the void and saw stacks of beer cases. Then he crawled through the opening. He stood bent over because of the low overhead. He pulled a small folding knife from his trouser pocket and cut several ropes; then he pulled a case of beer from the stack. He laid the knife on the deck to free his hands to tie together the cut ends of the rope.

After the ropes ends were securely tied, he pointed the flashlight beam toward the deck to locate his knife. The knife was gone. He notices that the deck slanted down toward the void's aft bulkhead. He knelt on the deck and bent down while shinning the flashlight where the deck and bulkhead come together. A crossbeam close to the deck formed a narrow cranny over the deck. He moved closer to the cranny, assuming his knife slid into it. With his face only inches from the cranny, he pointed the flashlight beam into the one-inch-high cranny and estimated the depth to be five inches—he saw his knife. He saw screws wedged between the deck and the crossbeam. Those screws served as snags for other items. He inserted the fingers of his left hand into the cranny and easily retrieved the knife. Then he used the knife blade to push away two wedged screws that trapped another item that he thought might be some kind of metal band.

Finally, the blade caught the item at the correct angle, and he pulled out a gold plated wristwatch with flexible gold plated band. The wristwatch was dirty and encrusted with grime. He used the bottom edge of his t-shirt to clean the face and back of the watch. He saw an engraving on the backside of the watch. He used some spit on his finger to clean away the last specks of dirt that covered the engraving. While the flashlight beam was directly pointed at the engraving, he brought the back of the watch close to his eyes and read the engraving. *To our son Weston upon your College*

Graduation : Your loving Parents.

"What the hell!" The full meaning of this find shocked him into trembling. "Damn, Dad, what have you done?!"

Several minutes later, Rig climbed the stairs up from the cabin to the deck, carrying a case of beer. Then he refilled the ice chest with beer bottles.

"I'll take one of those warm," Dave Page said.

"Me too," James Page said.

Several minutes later while James and Dave Page were talking business, Rig stood and walked to the portside rail. He reached into his trouser pocket and pulled out Weston Pyth's wristwatch and tossed it into the water.

After a few moments of thought, he returned to his deckchair. His mind focused on his find and its meaning.

Dave Page announced that he was going to bed and went below.

"What's on your mind, Son? James Page asked with a concerned tone. "You look like you have the troubles of the world on your shoulders."

Rig expressed anxiety as he explained. "My avenging justice has put targets on the backs of my family. I worry about these left-wing lunatics coming after you and mom and my sisters."

James Page responded, "Don't worry about us, Son. Dave and I fought the fascists during the war. We can handle ourselves."

"Dad, I am not talking about some thugs coming into your yard or business. I am talking about a well-funded, high-level conspiracy to destroy your lives. I am talking about powerful politicians and their cronies in law enforcement entrapping you and putting you in jail for a long time."

"They've backed off recently," James Page advised. "Like we said, we're no longer followed."

"They are dormant, now," Rig said. "The CLWUA and those political organizations that support it have been damaged and their power diminished. But they will rebuild, and they will be back. They receive funding from billionaires and foreign powers. So they have the resources to rebuild."

James Page stared into the night as he evaluated the reality of Rig's words.

"Dad, you must maintain frequent contact with Brian Sanderhill. Keep him informed of what's going on in our family. He will provide legal protection and physical protection when needed."

"Son, I cannot afford a lawyer like Brian Sanderhill."

"You will not be charged for his protection," Rig promised. "I have taken care of that."

"How did you come to know Brian and how can you pay for his services?"

Rig explained: "Recently, I became involved with a group of American patriots who secretly fight against those domestic enemies who conspire to destroy America's constitutional republic. I provide services to that group and in return they provide resources and protection."

"Is Brian a member of that group?"

"Yes," Rig disclosed, "but you cannot reveal to him or anyone else that you know about that group. Can I count on you to keep that secret?

"Yes, Son, of course."

After a few moments of silence, James Page asked, "What's next for you?"

"I return to the battle. My life is dedicated to fighting commies and fascists, both foreign and domestic. I just hope that I have both the courage and strength to defeat those I encounter."

James Page expressed pride for his son as he said, "You won't quit because you are a Page and because you know that the perpetual battle to preserve constitutional rights is worth the fight."

Spanish Nights
"The Secret of Sedo Mare"

Naval Intelligence assigns Senior Chief Rigney Page undercover to assist in the murder investigation of two navy officers near Rota, Spain.

Rig and Lieutenant Christine Hawthorne rekindle their romance that began several years ago in Scotland.

Rig battles a Spanish crime family engaged in espionage against NATO.

In the midst of the battle, Rig uncovers *The Secret of Sedo Mare.*

Spanish
Nights

"The Secret of Sedo Mare"

A Rigney Page Adventure
#6

Michael R. Ellis
USN Retired

Made in the USA
Middletown, DE
18 June 2020